Books by Nicole Keefer

STANDALONE

MY SAVIOR

Jimmy Yates Duology

His Victim's Torment (Book 1)

His Apprentice's Revenge (Book 2)

First edition

ISBN: 978-1-959881-18-6 (ebook), 978-1-959881-16-2 (Paperback), 978-1-959881-17-9 (Hardback)

Cover art by Booklytical Designs

Interior art by Nicole Nance

Editing by Sage Santiago

Formatting by Misti Flick

TO MY MOTHER, SUSAN.

You are the strongest woman I
know.

Success is not final,

failure is not fatal: it is

the courage to

continue that counts.

~WINSTON CHURCHILL

HIS APPRENTICE'S
REVENGE

NICOLE KEEFER

Chapter 1

Mary was going to die, and there was nothing Devon could do about it. After everything they've been through, he was going to lose her after all. Mary had defied the odds and survived the clutches of a serial killer, not once, but twice. Yet, this time, it would be what? An unforeseen medical tragedy that would take her? He wouldn't be able to save her.

Looking back at the previous thirty-six hours, he tried to pinpoint the moment when everything went wrong. Yesterday started out comparative to any other morning. Devon had woken up early and completed his four-mile run around the lake surrounding their property. He could still remember Mary's face months before when they pulled up with the real estate agent to view the property for the first time. One look at the lake behind the house and Mary was in love.

They didn't even look inside the house before she was determined this was going to be their forever home, the place where they would raise their family. As a surprise, before they even unpacked the moving boxes, Devon purchased a two-seater glider and placed it close to the water's edge. Mary spent most of her pregnancy down by the lake, staring out over the water; she said it calmed her.

Devon could sit there for hours and feel content watching the joy on Mary's face when she was at peace near the water. Her being at peace helped him be at peace, and after some of his more stressful days at work, it's exactly what he needed.

Yesterday morning, Mary had finished eating breakfast and was gathering her book and a drink to go sit by the lake when her water broke, and with every step, fluid gushed down her legs. She'd been feeling contractions for a few hours but refused to tell her husband because she knew he'd become hysterical and overcompensating.

Devon had walked in the door from his run, looking forward to jumping in the shower, when he caught Mary dragging out the mop and bucket. She stated, very matter of fact, "I am determined to clean up the mess before it ruins my beautiful, new, hardwood floors." The hardwood floors she drove Devon and Matthews crazy picking out. Mary had them bring in fifteen different sample wooden slats before she was positive she had the perfect color, only to change it twice more.

"There is absolutely no way this isn't going to be cleaned up before we go to the hospital. Our floors would be ruined by the time we get home, and that, mister, is unacceptable. No, this needs to be cleaned up now," she'd exclaimed firmly, with her hands on her hips, and a scowl on her face. He thought she looked absolutely adorable.

Shaking his head, he couldn't help but laugh as he pulled the mop from her hands. "Okay, love. I'll clean up this mess. Why don't you go change and then sit down and rest? The doctor said it could still be hours after your water broke for you to go into active labor. If you need help getting cleaned up, carefully sit on the bed and I'll be right in after I clean this up. Call out to me if you need anything."

Mary looked at him like he'd lost his mind. "I certainly will not sit on the bed when I'm such a mess, but I'll go sit in the bathroom and see what I can do to clean myself up without your help." Slowly, she moved towards the back of the house to the master bedroom and bath.

Only his wife would be worried about cleaning the floor or making a mess on the bed when she should be focusing on the baby she was about to birth. Man, he loved this woman. Secretly, he hoped some of her manic cleaning sessions would vanish once the baby came. If not, he'd hire a housekeeper so Mary could take a break. Even though he knew she'd probably go back and re-clean, anyway.

She already refused his proposal of hiring a nanny after the baby was born. No, refusing wasn't the right term. Her exact words were that she'd murder him in his sleep, then promote Matthews to "baby daddy" if he ever tried to bring a stranger into her home to raise her child. Matthews was more than enthusiastic about her plan. He even called her baby mama for the next few weeks.

Devon quickly cleaned up the fluid in the hall by the front door, then went to find Mary. Of course, she hadn't listened to him about resting. He found her walking around the bedroom, pulling things out of the closet and their dresser. Glancing over at the bed, her entire hospital bag, the one she had personally packed weeks ago using a checklist, was now overturned and she'd spread everything out.

Walking over, he gently placed his hands on her shoulders. "Mary, darling. What are you doing? You need to sit down."

She opened her lips and tried to talk as another contraction splintered through her sides and over her stomach, making her back feel like someone was stabbing her with a hot poker. Shooting her hands down by her sides, she grabbed onto Devon's hips, and used him to keep herself standing.

After a moment, the contraction stopped. This crazy woman continued like nothing happened. He couldn't help but stare at her, mouth gaping open.

After noticing the way her husband was looking at her, she explained what she was doing. "Well, I was about to jump in the shower when I remembered I wanted to add slippers to my hospital bag. Once I pulled the bag out, I decided to make sure I had everything the nurse suggested we'd need. After going through the bag, I decided everything was wrong, and I'd repack it quickly before you came in and noticed. That's when the contractions started more forcefully. Mind you, even though this pain made me want to vomit with each wave, they're still really far apart, so we have plenty of time."

She stopped pacing and looked around. She left the bedroom and returned with the book she was going to take down to the lake, but had never made it that far. "Here, it's the last thing I need.

Now I need to get cleaned up and then wait for these contractions to start coming closer together."

Incredible. Mary was absolutely incredible.

"Sit down, love." He gently pushed her into the chair by the window and raised a hand to stop her protests. "If you get up from this chair one more time before I'm done running some bath water, I'm going to rearrange the entire house while you're in the hospital."

She gasped with surprise; her gaze narrowed on his face. "You most certainly will not rearrange a single thing, Devon Walker! I'd have your hide."

He gestured to the bathroom door and waited until Mary nodded her head. "I wouldn't make bets right now, love. Now, I'm running a bath instead of a shower, so I can enjoy this time with you before we need to head to the hospital." Devon leaned against the door frame, a mischievous grin spreading across his face. "It's a good thing you convinced me we needed the double soaker tub when we were remodeling. It's going to come in handy today. Isn't it ironic, this baby may have been conceived in this tub, and it's going to be the last thing we enjoy together before he makes his entrance into this crazy world?"

Mary turned the scarlet shade of red Devon was hoping for. The shade intensified when Mary lifted her head to look Devon in the eyes, and he winked at her.

Yesterday was an amazing start to what should have been one of the happiest days in Devon and Mary's lives. They'd been looking forward to welcoming their baby boy into this world from the moment the two little lines showed up on her pregnancy test. It was supposed to be the day their little family of two became a loving family of three. It was, however, the beginning of a nightmare. One of many nightmares Mary had to endure in her lifetime.

Mary waited until the contractions were about four minutes apart before telling Devon they finally needed to make their way to the hospital. Admissions went smoothly, thank goodness for pre-registration. Not long after they had Mary all hooked up, things started to go downhill quickly.

The doctor was concerned Mary's heart rate was rather high, and since she had a rough pregnancy with high blood pressure, he wanted to start IV fluids to help with the dehydration that is common with delivery.

One of the nurses came in and switched her to a high dose electrolyte bag to speed up rehydration. Mary knew Devon was going to be impossible to live with after this, he'd force her to drink so much water she might as well live in the bathroom.

The contractions progressed quickly, and Mary felt like she was ready to push not even an hour after arriving at the hospital. As soon as she started pushing, everything went wrong. Devon expected bleeding, of course, but not as much as what was currently gushing out of Mary.

He was so focused on holding onto Mary, that he didn't really become concerned until Mary's aunt demanded answers from the doctor as to what was happening. It wasn't so much her questions that concerned Devon, but Patricia's tone. He'd never heard Patricia as worried as she was right now, not even when Mary was kidnapped a year ago.

Machines started going crazy, beeping and dinging, and this made the hospital staff move into high gear. The doctors' voices and their relayed orders were drowned out by the commotion. Her blood pressure had been high from the moment they checked into the hospital, but Devon watched the numbers climbing on the machine, feeling completely helpless. Nurses rushed in from every direction. The already small room grew smaller, claustrophobic in a dizzying whirlwind of motion. And yet time slowed, and it was all an impossible blur and cacophony of shrill ringing and confusion.

The towels that were placed on the bed under Mary could no longer stop the blood from spilling onto the floor. Devon stared in a shocked focus at the droplets of blood, Mary's life force, as they dropped and fell, splashing to the puddles formed on the floor below her. Looking at his wife's face, it had become so colorless it looked almost translucent, and even though she was pushing and straining, her skin was cold to the touch. Dread filled his every fiber.

The whirlwind of activity seemed to go on forever. He expected at any moment the doctors would tell him they couldn't do anything else to save Mary. He wouldn't accept it, but with everything that was happening, he expected it.

There was so much blood, and it was everywhere. Why couldn't they stop the bleeding? It was their job. Blood covered

Mary, the doctors, the bed, the floor, and all the machines hooked up to her were going crazy.

"Mary's screams that filtered through the room and down the hall suddenly stopped. For a split second, a hush descended over the room. Devon thought to himself, maybe Mary was going to be okay, but his hopes shattered when he saw the look of dismay on the doctor's face. It only took the doctors a span of a single breath to regain their bearings and surge back into action.

Mary had the best medical team. They worked together like a well-oiled machine. Devon had to believe they'd be able to save his wife and unborn child. The doctors forcefully pushed Devon out of the way, farther from Mary, making the tiny hospital room seem even smaller. He couldn't take offense to it because the doctors needed better access to Mary, and Devon was in the way.

Even at only over arms' length, it felt like he was worlds away. Helplessness coursed through every fiber of Devon's body. In the corner of the room, he dropped to his knees and prayed for whoever was listening out in the universe, to help save Mary, the love of his life.

The past thirty-six hours had been the most heartbreaking hours of his life. *What if?* Those words, even spoken in his head, twisted every fiber in body with pain. They forced him back to the unimaginable terror they went through only a little over a year ago at the hands of serial killer Jimmy Yates.

Fourteen months ago, for an impossible two and a half days, Jimmy Yates had kidnapped and tortured Mary. During those days, Devon didn't know if he'd ever see Mary again, let alone be able to tell her how much he loved her. He failed her once, and he'd gladly give up his life to not fail her again; not fail her this time. Why couldn't he protect his family?

Devon, on his knees, felt two frail hands shakily touch his shoulders. Patricia was trying to offer him comfort. Two things happened next that finally gave him hope not all was lost. Overtop all the commotion coming from the doctors, nurses, and other medical staff, the most beautiful screech reached Devon and Patricia's ears. Finally, the first hint of light in the darkness—his son was born healthy and safe.

Now, the doctors needed to save his son's mother. Devon knew he couldn't do this without her, and his son needed his mother. They both needed her. There were so many doctors rushing around, Devon still couldn't get close to his wife, but his eyes never left her face. They'd been married for only a short year; he hadn't had enough time with her. He needed more time. His son needed to meet his mother.

A few of the doctors tried yet again to get him to leave the room, but that wasn't going to happen. They'd need to drag him out before he'd let Mary out of his sight.

Though they repeatedly reassured him that his son was healthy, he argued adamantly for them to check again and keep the baby under close watch. When they announced they were moving him to the nursery so there'd be more room to help Mary, he still wouldn't give in. He knew they couldn't keep his son in the little infant warmer bed he was currently in, but surely the neonatal nurse could keep Caleb in a movable crib so Devon would be able to watch over both of them?

Mary's aunt, Patricia, got asked to leave the room as soon as Caleb was born, but she was allowed to stay in the hall. She poked her head into the room as they were moving Caleb, and trying to keep her voice as calm as possible, told Devon she'd stay with his son when he went to the nursery and would not leave his side for even a moment. With a smile she hoped he didn't realize was forced, she told Devon he needed to solely concentrate on Mary.

A steady beeping penetrated into the depths of Devon's thoughts. The doctor placed his hand on his shoulder as he sobbed, bringing him out of bleakness. Devon looked up, tears staining his face, to see Mary looking at peace, with eyes closed but smiling.

"Mary's going to be okay, Mr. Walker. We still have some work to do, but we feel confident she's going to pull through. We'll talk again soon." The doctor moved back down to Mary's lower half and continued to work. He heard words like suture and tear, but all he could focus on was his wife's beautiful face and that the doctor was confident she'd pull through.

The doctors and nurses cleared from the room, making space for him to move back to Mary's side. He slowly rose from his knees, grateful for all they'd done to save her. Devon crossed the room, placed his forehead against hers, and started crying. He never wanted to feel this dread and helplessness ever again. He'd put Mary in a bubble if he had to. Surely, he could order a bubble off Amazon.

All negative thoughts went out the window when Patricia entered the room holding Caleb in her arms. Though under any other circumstance, it would've been devastating for Mary not to hold Caleb as soon as he was born. Devon knew she'd be as glad as he was to see the person carrying their son was the woman who'd loved Mary like a daughter and was a second mother to his wife.

Mary's uncle, Robert, was at an important vote taking place on Capitol Hill when he received word Mary was in labor. He wasn't able to leave right away, but blew into her hospital room at the same time the doctor came back in to talk to Devon. Mary was sleeping, exhausted from the delivery, but he knew she'd feel better having her whole family there.

The doctor walked over to Devon, reached his hand out, and introduced himself. "Mr. Walker, my name is Dr. Chase. I'm the chief of medicine for the hospital. Would you please come with me so we can find a private place to talk?"

Dr. Chase was a very large man, over six foot, six inches tall. He appeared middle-aged with salt and pepper hair. Dr. Chase was the chief of medicine for the hospital. Mary's favorite actor was Sean Connery, and this doctor looked like he could be his brother.

Devon was silent for a moment, countless horrid scenarios rushed through his unsettled mind. Shaking his head, Devon protested, "Dr. Chase, anything you need to say to me, you can say in front of Mary's aunt and uncle. They're like her parents, and I'd tell them everything you said, anyway. So, it would be better if they heard what you need to say directly from you."

Dr. Chase nodded. "First, we'd like to congratulate you and your wife on the birth of your beautiful baby boy. We are so sorry about what happened, and understand how it could seem scary or alarming for you and your family. As medical professionals, we always consider what is the best course of treatment in any situation. Under the circumstances, we observed Mary was dehydrated and had to act accordingly. Sometimes, in the case of dehydration, anticoagulants may be administered to improve hydration. While there are risks, the documentation I have shows that the circumstances called for the use of them, which may have led to some increase in blood loss. However, our excellent staff was quick and responsive and prevented any complications. Your wife is doing very well in recovery, and we'll continue to monitor her."

Taking a deep breath, he seemed reluctant to continue. "When there is a difficult birth, tests are run to make sure the mother has not taken medication that would cause these reactions. It's usually for mothers that are on narcotics or other substances during pregnancy. We have no reason to suspect Mrs. Walker consumed those types of substances, but we'd like to rule everything out. Would it be okay to run a blood panel and see if we can find anything abnormal?"

Devon, being Mary's medical proxy, was able to agree to the blood test, knowing Mary would want all the answers when she woke from her exhaustion.

Digging around in his pockets, Dr. Chase pulled out a business card. "Here, if you have any more questions, this is the best way to reach me. My cell phone number, office number, and email are all listed on the back as well." He handed one to Devon and one to Robert.

"Mary should be waking up soon, she was completely exhausted, and the amount of blood loss she experienced would cause her to sleep harder. The lactation consultant will be in soon to talk to you about the next steps she'll need to take to feed your son. Again, I am so sorry."

Patricia was the first one to process what the doctor had said. "Some incompetent nurse almost killed my Mary. Robert, you better do something about this. I want that person's medical license. They're lucky I don't go for their head. " Her fury was evident with every word she spoke. The only thing that stopped her from leaving the room and demanding that nurse's answers right then, was that she was holding Caleb.

Robert looked to Devon and knew his composure was hanging by a thread.

"Yes, Patricia, this is far from over. I'll contact our lawyers when we leave the hospital. Right now, let's be thankful Mary's parents were watching over her and Caleb and that they both will be alright."

Devon finally seemed to snap out of his thoughts. *Caleb.* Patricia had been holding his son all the while the doctor explained why his wife nearly died.

He leaned over and kissed Mary on the forehead. "Our son is perfect, Mary. Would you like to meet him?"

He gently took Caleb out of Patricia's arms and placed him, stomach down, on Mary's chest. The moment the baby's skin contacted hers, the baby moved his fingers and started searching for his first meal. It only took a few moments before Mary's hand began creeping from her side up closer to Caleb's back. Devon let out a deep breath, and the tension he'd held instantly left his body. Tears started streaming down his face as he watched his family. This was *his* family, these two, and he'd die to protect them.

Chapter 2

Mary took in a deep breath of fresh air as she stepped out of the car. Looking towards the sky, the sun shining on her face, only two words could describe how she felt. *Ah, freedom.*

She needed this, a day out of the house. A day away from the walls that were closing in on her. It was a funny way to describe why she needed this day away so badly, since they had a lake right outside their door and she was never inside the house.

She was exhausted, both physically and mentally. Since Caleb was born, her nightmares returned in full force. The only person she'd shared those terrifying moments with was Devon, and she would've kept him in the dark if she could.

There was no hiding her nightmares from him, since she'd wake up screaming in the middle of the night, and he wouldn't just brush them off like she asked him to over and over. No, Devon liked to pry, but she knew he did it because he loved her and was worried about her. Still, it was annoying.

Every night in her dreams, the rats were back, and they wanted Caleb's blood. No matter how she tried to dissuade them or turn them on herself, the rats only wanted her son. He was there, in his car seat, down in the damp, dirty sewer. Rats climbed on the car seat and surrounded him. The first time she had that nightmare she called an exterminator even though she'd never seen as much as a field mouse on their property. She wasn't taking any chances.

The nightmares had made Mary more irritable than anyone expected a first time mother to be. Yet, neither she nor Devon would admit to anyone else the true cause of her aggression, not even to her aunt and uncle. So that's why this day out was so important to her. She needed space, and no one would give it to her.

It'd been four months since Caleb was born, and Devon hadn't left her side except to go to work, and even then, either her aunt or uncle were by her side, hovering, to make sure she didn't overexert herself. They even mentioned hiring a nanny, cook, housekeeper, and handyman. Everyone around her was plain exhausting. If she hadn't put her foot down during the first week they were home, Devon would have followed her into the bathroom every time she had to pee. It was intrusive and extremely annoying.

Matthews was at their house almost every day after work. Since the night Devon made Matthews dinner and asked him to be Caleb's godfather, he'd been coming to the house and talking to the baby about all the things he'd teach him when he got bigger. He even brought him a onesie that said, "watch out ladies, wing man in training." Mary was not amused. Devon thought it was hilarious.

Mary made it adamantly clear to Matthews that under no circumstance would he be using her son to pick up women. She even took it as far as grabbing one of Devon's specialty-forged cleaver knives from the butcher block and waving it in Matthews' face when she heard the men joking that if he took the baby to the park, he'd catch more women than if he took his dog. Matthews knew Mary wasn't really mad at him, because he saw her try to suppress a smile when Devon winked at her and gave Matthews a thumbs up.

Matthews made up for it, though, when he ordered Caleb an AC/DC sleeper and an authentic poster signed by every member in the band for his nursery. Even though it didn't match the elephant theme, Mary didn't care. AC/DC was her favorite band. Secretly, she wondered if she could take the poster to her office without anyone realizing it was missing from the nursery.

Mary loved everyone, so she didn't mind that every single person in her life wanted to visit the baby right after he was born, but she needed mommy-baby alone time. She felt like she was being smothered, and her family didn't understand.

Yes, she almost died during childbirth because of a medication mix-up, but she was fine and had been for months. This morning when she woke up, she told her husband she was going shopping, and taking Caleb, and under no circumstances was anyone else invited along.

Devon realized he screwed up when he asked if Alex, her uncle's head of security, would go along on their trip. Mary didn't even have the energy to respond to her husband's stupid ass question. She held up her hand for a few seconds, gave a quick shake of her head, then turned and walked away.

Mary wanted time to quietly walk the aisles of Target, enjoy an iced caramel macchiato, or three,and eat some chocolate-covered espresso beans, all without being rushed or judged for everything she placed in her cart. She was like most other women and couldn't go into Target for only one thing. So, she decided she'd let Target tell her what she needed, and if she wanted to spend all day there, she didn't want anyone griping at her. She was on Caleb's schedule and no one else's.

Even though Caleb had anything and everything he could possibly need or want at home, she still proceeded to purchase a magnitude of items for her little guy. Caleb and Devon were her world. She didn't feel bad about a little spoiling now and then. It was, in fact, a bit more than now and then, but before Devon, she'd never allowed herself to dream about having a family. So if she wanted to spoil her family rotten, that's exactly what she'd do.

Walking the aisles was better therapy than she could receive with a person sitting there, staring at her, asking questions. But as soon as she stepped into the bath aisle, she knew she'd made a mistake. It had been almost eight months since she had a "scald your skin off" blissfully peaceful bath, and she was going to fix that tonight. If she didn't leave that bathtub looking like a lobster, she would consider that a failure.

After smelling almost every item in the aisle, she settled on two bottles of bubble bath, four bath bombs, oil for after, and no less than a dozen scented candles to spread around her bathroom. Now, she needed a good bottle of her favorite Riesling wine, new bed sheets, and to take another spin through the baby aisles, then she'd be free to head home.

Her little spin through the baby aisle lasted almost another hour. She didn't care because there was no need to rush home. Devon tried checking on her a multitude of times, and after responding to his first text message that she and Caleb were fine, she kept responding with *"back off"* or *"everytime you bug me I add another thing to my cart"*.

As long as the baby was okay in his car seat, she was going to enjoy her time away from home, so her husband needed to stop messing with her joy of feeling free. Glancing at her watch, she knew Devon wouldn't even be home for another five hours. She still had plenty of time. He wasn't currently active on a case, and he tried to be home for dinner by six each night.

At least once or twice a week, he got hung up at work past dinner, but he worked for the FBI, so he was on their time. Today would be different though. Since most of his leadership was attending some sort of conference, he would be home on time. Maybe she'd cook up something special.

She used to only live on takeout, but that was before meeting Devon. He loved to cook. Since being married, she'd tried to learn to cook dinner and have it done when Devon got home from work.

Deciding on seafood mac and cheese for dinner, she slowly made her way back to the other side of the store to pick up the rest of the ingredients she needed. She already had the seafood at home, but she still needed some of the basics. When they finally made it to the checkout line, Caleb woke up and was ready to be fed. She quickly threw together the bottle she had prepped before leaving the house a few hours ago and fed him while waiting for her turn with the cashier.

She made it through the line quicker than expected and sat down on a bench right inside the door to let Caleb finish eating. There was no reason to sit in the hot car and wait for the AC to cool it down while she fed the baby, not when she could sit in the temperature-controlled store and they'd both be comfortable.

Caleb made quick work of the bottle and was blissfully back asleep in his milk coma. Mary knew Caleb, at this age, slept more in the afternoon, which is why she chose this time to come to the store. Sometimes, Mary wished he would stay awake a bit so she could enjoy watching his expressions light up his face each time he learned something new.

Gosh, she really was blessed. For a long time, she hadn't let herself think about having a husband, let alone a family. She used to never allow herself to dream of anything other than her career, knowing everything she loved could be taken away from her in the blink of an eye. And that's almost exactly what happened.

It was only shy of eighteen months since serial killer Jimmy Yates held her captive and tortured her for days. Nightmares still plagued her almost every time she closed her eyes, but she wouldn't let him succeed, even in death, by completely disrupting her life. If Yates would've accomplished his goal of murdering Mary, she would have never married Devon, and the world would've been denied the sunshine that was Caleb Walker. She didn't think he was special only because he was her son. Okay, well maybe a little. But it was true. Even the nurses at the hospital called him magical. He was her miracle.

As she stepped back outside and into the fresh air, she moved to the side, closed her eyes, and took a moment to allow the sun to seep into her skin. She'd always positively loved the feel of the sun on her face. When they got home, she'd take Caleb down to the lake to lie on a blanket and enjoy the rest of their day.

After taking one more deep breath, she reluctantly opened her eyes and moved down the parking lot towards her Honda Pilot SUV. It was a wedding present from Devon. He called her Toyota Camry a clunker and death trap and didn't like her driving it down the 495 Beltway.

She'd never admit it to him, but especially after having Caleb, she was very happy about the new vehicle. Nope, she'd never admit *that* to him, especially after giving him grief for almost six months when he bought it and had her Toyota taken to the junkyard without consulting her.

She was now second-guessing her decision to park all the way in the back of the parking lot. Why did she have to park there anyway? She knew the answer. It was because she liked the little walk it allotted her. It would only take her a moment more to reach the vehicle, but she decided to use the automatic start to get the AC going.

She didn't want to put Caleb in a sweltering vehicle if she could avoid it. That's one of the reasons Devon insisted the vehicle have all the bells and whistles. Anything to make daily activities easier for Mary to handle while taking care of Caleb.

Seconds after hitting the automatic start for her SUV, her world got turned upside down. The noise was deafening, glass shattered in a thunderous blast, and people screamed in shock. It was torturous, and in an instant brought her back to her time as a captive, held in the sewer, and forced to listen to that *song*. Those screams.

No. He was dead. That nightmare was over. She resisted the urge to cover her ears and lay on the ground to drown out the sound. She needed to see what happened. It was an explosion. But what blew up?

No! Caleb!

Frantically, she looked for her cart and spotted it laying on its side only inches away. Relief rushed through her as she found Caleb still in his car seat. He was screaming, and she couldn't tell if he was hurt. Her vision was blurry and it was becoming dark. No, she needed to focus and stay awake. For Caleb. Reaching around, she couldn't find her phone. Devon. Someone needed to call Devon, he'd know what to do.

She gave up looking for her purse after a few seconds, instead of calling for help, she needed to make sure Caleb was okay. She was losing her battle as the darkness consumed her, pulling her down deeper. She needed to stay awake to protect her son, to protect Caleb.

In the distance, she heard the sirens, and people around her talking, but she couldn't make out what they were saying. Sirens were good, though. Sirens meant Devon wouldn't be too far behind. Crawling on her knees, she pulled Caleb's car seat into her side right as the world turned dark.

Devon was finishing up some paperwork when he spotted Matthews rushing towards him. One look at his face and anyone could see something was wrong. His partner, who was usually Mr. Happy-go-lucky, looked like someone stole his last candy bar. Which people in the office did often.

Devon knew that look all too well because he knew where his partner hid his candy and was usually the one to steal his last candy bar.

"Grab your stuff, we got to go," Matthews said quickly to Devon, then motioned towards the door.

Devon, thinking it was a case, grabbed his badge and gun from the drawer and started to straighten up his desk. Matthews always got excited about a case, but taking one more minute to put things in order wouldn't matter. Having a tidy desk was one of Mary's compulsions, and one she drilled into his head constantly about the desk in his study. He'd never admit that she was right, but a clean desk was more functional.

Matthews grabbed his arm and yanked him away from the desk, trying to keep the desperation out of his voice. "There's no time for that. Let's go, now. I'll explain in the car. I'm driving." If he'd told him before they got in the car, Matthews knew he wouldn't be able to control Devon, and he would run to his own car and drive like a madman to the hospital.

Though excited, Devon knew this was out of character for Matthews. Despite the confusion his behavior caused, Devon went along with him all the same. Something was obviously wrong, and he was becoming more concerned about his partner with every step.

Another agent pulled Matthews' vehicle up to the front of the building. Now Devon knew something was wrong. Why wouldn't they walk to the parking lot, which would have taken them less than five minutes?

As soon as Matthews pulled into traffic, he sped up, weaving in and out, and breaking so many laws. Obviously, something happened that Matthews considered so urgent to believe traffic wasn't moving quick enough, and he turned on the lights and sirens.

"I've waited long enough, Matthews, tell me what's going on. You're driving like a maniac."

"Devon. I'm so sorry. There was an accident. It's Mary and Caleb. I'm taking you to the hospital right now. We'll be there soon."

Devon felt as if his heart had stopped, and someone had reached into his chest and ripped it out. Terror trembled through his body. His throat constricted with panic. He was sick with fear and anguish, and thankful he was sitting down. It took a moment to completely comprehend what Matthews had said. "What? What do you mean, *accident*? Are they okay? What happened? Are they okay? Did someone hit their car? What happened, Matthews? At least tell me they're alive," Devon choked out.

Matthews didn't take his eyes off the road as he explained, "Detective Miller with the MPD called me because he knows I'm your friend as well as your partner. He told me what happened. I don't have all the details, but he said that Mary and Caleb were on their way to the hospital, and he was very clear that they are both alive. Mary has a head injury and is unconscious, but she's breathing. Caleb has some scrapes, but the medics are sure he's more scared than anything. Miller said Caleb was screaming when he showed up on the scene, which may not sound like a good thing, but it really is."

"But what happened, Matthews? Did Miller tell you what happened? Did someone hit their car?" A million scenarios were running through his head. "Matthews?" Devon snapped forcefully as he slammed his fists on the dash in front of him.

There was no easy way to say it. "Damn it, Devon. Someone blew up Mary's car. The only thing that saved them was that they weren't inside the vehicle when the bomb detonated. The police pieced together that she must have used her automatic start as she was still a good distance away from the vehicle when it exploded." Matthews rushed out the explanation and punched the steering wheel.

That can't be right, Devon thought. He must have heard him wrong. The only enemy Mary ever had was dead and buried. "Someone blew up Mary's car?" Devon was trying to keep from screaming. His mouth dried, and his heart pounded to the point it was painful.

"That's what Miller said. Witnesses told him that Mary and Caleb were about eight cars away at the time of the explosion. Listen, you need to focus on your family right now. Let us worry about the investigation. Trust me when I tell you we'll not rest until we find out who did this."

Devon looked at Matthews like he lost his mind. "Are you serious? No, I'm part of this investigation. I'm going to find the bastard that tried to kill my family and I'm going to flay them alive. Don't block me on this. I'm going to be involved in every step of this investigation. You sure as hell better not keep anything from me. You're my best friend and my partner but this is my wife and my child. I know you'd feel the same way and you know it. You already know the chief is going to try to block me on this. Don't you do it too. Promise me, Matthews."

Matthews knew that'd be his response. Hell, he would feel the same way. He *did* feel the same way. He was furious, and unchecked rage boiled inside him. Matthews was Caleb's godfather, and Mary was like his sister. Avenging them was a no-brainer. He only needed Walker to focus on healing his family and keeping them safe. "Yeah, Walker. I promise. You know that, man. Anything that I know, you'll know."

Once whoever tried to hurt Mary and Caleb found out they were still alive, the chances of them trying again were a given. No one was going to harm his godson and get away with it.

Chapter 3

Devon blew into the emergency room like a hurricane. The smell of disinfectant cleaner assaulted his senses and snapped him back from a state of panic. Running right up to the nurse's station, Devon flashed his badge and demanded to see his family. To anyone within his vicinity, he probably looked like a lunatic, and that was exactly how he was acting, but he didn't care. He needed to see them now. He needed to see with his own eyes that they were okay.

After parking the car, Matthews arrived at the nurse's station just as the nurse, who was surrounded by concerned security and doctors because of the way Devon was yelling and carrying on, was waving the security away and leading Devon down the hall.

Matthews yelled out, "Hey, I'm going to go link up with Miller and check on the investigation. Call me later to let me know how they are, and I'll fill you in on what I find out."

Devon quickly raised his hand and nodded in acknowledgment as he rushed to keep up with the nurse who'd already disappeared through the double doors. Devon wanted to run right out those doors with Matthews and hunt this son of a bitch down, but his family came first. Knowing his best friend and partner would tear this city apart to help him find whoever was responsible for harming his family made it easier for him to let Matthews walk away and get back to work.

Mary and Caleb weren't in the same room. The nurse took him to see his son first in the pediatric ICU. His fear over his son's condition diminished as soon as he saw him sitting in a doctor's lap drinking a bottle, looking as content as could be.

He could see Caleb's little legs kicking over the joy of being fed. Caleb was exactly like Mary when she ate. She liked to dance around while she ate, and he called it her hungry girl happy dance.

Before he could ask any questions, the nurse spoke up. "Mr. Walker, this is Dr. Kadlec, she's on rotation in our pediatrics wing. She was on duty the night your son was born and insisted on being the one to take care of him now. She kept an eye on this brave young man until you were able to get here, and when he woke up, he was very hungry. Until we're ready for discharge, Dr. Kadlec will be his attending if you have any questions or concerns. Because everyone here knows you got that horrible Jimmy Yates off the streets, Dr. Kadlec insisted on personally taking charge of your son's care out of devotion to her patients. Isn't that right, Dr. Kadlec?"

She quietly nodded in agreement, focused on holding the bottle steady.

"And now I can take you to your wife when you're ready." The nurse paused in her explanation, but one look at her face, and

Devon could see the emotions welling up. After a moment, and a few deep breaths, she continued.

"Your son was very lucky, Mr. Walker. Your wife still had him in his carseat, perfectly strapped in, when the blast occurred. From what we were told by police, the carseat was thrown from the shopping cart, but it completely protected him. He does have a few cuts and bruises from the fall, but we did some scans and x-rays and confirmed there's no cause for concern. Let me take you to see Mrs. Walker. Then, when Caleb's done eating, he'll be returned to his crib and you can have a chance to talk with Dr. Kadlec about the course of care plan. Are you ready to go see your wife, Mr. Walker?"

Devon didn't want to leave his son but knew the nurse was right. He needed to get to his wife. Caleb was safe with Dr. Kadlec. Once he was discharged, he could stay in Mary's room, then Devon wouldn't let either of them out of his sight. "Yes, please. I know it's not normal protocol, but could we keep Caleb in Mary's room?"

Pausing for a moment, the nurse finally answered, "I'll check with the head doctor and let you know. With what happened and the added need for security, we may be able to make an exception."

Walking through the door to Mary's room brought memories flooding back. Just like the day their son was born and the awful days when he'd nearly lost her, Mary was again attached to so many machines monitoring her every vital. Devon reached up and rubbed his temples, trying to keep at bay the tears threatening to run down his cheeks. Mary looked like one big bruise. He didn't even remember the nurse was in the room until she gently placed her hand on his shoulder.

"Mr. Walker, Dr. Chase is here to talk to you about your wife's condition."

Coming forward, the doctor reached out to grasp Devon's hand. There was such a solemn look on his face it was hard for Devon to get a read on the news he was about to receive.

"Mr. Walker, first I want to tell you how very sorry I am that this happened to your family. It seems that we keep meeting under very unfortunate circumstances. Someone was surely watching over your son during this ordeal and helped him come out with only bumps and bruises. With Mary, her body took a lot more damage due to the fact she was standing when the blast happened and was not sheltered like your son was. The cuts and bruises will heal in a few weeks, but we are working with neurology regarding the contusion to the back of her head. We're monitoring it closely, and at this time see no signs of bleeding or damage. We are treating her with pain management" –he handed Devon an informational sheet– "and giving her time to rest and wake up on her own. We have no reason to expect your wife won't make a full recovery."

Feeling his knees start to buckle, Devon grabbed the chair at his side. "Thank you, Dr. Chase," was all Devon could get out. If he continued, he would surely break down.

After a quick pat on Devon's shoulder, as a sign of support, Dr. Chase turned and walked out of the room. It was at that moment, Devon finally let the emotions erupt and shred the last of his composure. For now, he'd sit next to his wife, hold her hand, and wait for the doctors to bring their son.

If anything could be said about Robert Carter, it's that he never did anything half-measure. Everyone within shouting distance knew the moment he entered the hospital and his displeasure. Congressman Carter alone had a dominating presence, but it became more apparent when his very intimidating security team followed close behind.

Devon heard the commotion in the hall and knew Robert was giving someone hell long before he saw him. He'd have to go intervene or their entire floor would be swarming with security and a very good chance, MPD. Not that any of it would matter to Robert.

The last thing he wanted to do was paperwork if one of Roberts' security went up against the hospital security. Devon had no doubt Roberts' men would come out the victors, but... paperwork. There would be a mountain of it. As soon as Devon left the room and caught Robert's attention, he pushed his way past the nurses and rushed to his side.

"Where are they, Devon? Where are Mary and Caleb? This damn nurse won't tell me anything because I'm not written down as her next of kin," he said.

It looked like Devon would need to placate Robert's strong personality and frantic disregard for the hospital's policies before he alienated the entire nursing staff. Reaching out and placing his hand on Robert's shoulder instantly calmed the congressman. "Here, Robert, come with me. This is Mary's room. Caleb will be here any minute. They were able to make an exception and they're going to bring him to Mary's room so I can have them both right here."

With every word, the congressman visibly relaxed. "What's the doctor saying about their conditions? Are they okay? Do the police have any information?"

Looking around the busy corridor, Devon noticed a few strangers watching them, and he decided they needed privacy. He took the congressman by the arm and led him into the room. "Matthews is linking up with the MPD as we speak. He'll keep us informed on the investigation. He knows that under no circumstances will I be taking a back seat in this."

Robert was nodding his head. "Yes, Matthews is a great agent. He also has great affection for both Mary and Celeb. He was vital in the return of Mary when that psychopath, Yates, was holding her hostage. I'll be grateful to both of you for the rest of my days for saving her life.

"Now, I'm going to expedite them bringing Caleb in here. I don't feel comfortable with him being out of our sight for a single moment. Whoever did this to my babies is still out there. I'm bringing my men in to be her personal security, Devon. Don't fight me. While Mary and Celeb are here, they'll have round-the-clock security. That should give you a little peace of mind. You know my men care for your family, and they are damn good at their jobs."

"I completely agree, Robert. Bring in as many men as you can spare, make sure they'll also answer to me. If I need to give them an order, I don't need the precious time wasted waiting for them to get your okay."

After a quick nod of agreement, Robert moved down the hall in an attempt to expedite moving Caleb to Mary's room. Devon got on the phone with the hospital's chief of medicine. Dr. Chase picked up his phone on the second ring.

"Dr. Chase, it's Devon Walker. I need some information, and I wanted to ask for it nicely before I officially get the FBI to request the information from a judge."

"Mr. Walker," Dr. Chase quickly responded. "If it is legally within my power, I'll help you with anything you need. If it is not within my power, I'll tell you who you need to speak with to get it. So, how can I help you?"

"I need information on every staff member that was on duty the night my son was born and when my wife and son were brought into the hospital. Call me a cynical bastard, but something isn't sitting right with me, and I want to make sure they are both safe."

"Mr. Walker, I assure you, your wife and son are safe in our facility. However, for our privacy protection, if you get me a court order I can forward you the names and titles of those employees."

After pulling out his phone, Devon dialed Matthews.

"Hey, Walker, what's the news?"

"The hospital is refusing to give me information without a court order. Do you think you could have Parker push for a warrant?"

"I was about to call the hospital CEO when you called. Let me handle this so Parker doesn't get word that you are trying to run this investigation."

"Damn it, Matthews. I can't do that, and you know it."

"Yeah, I know. I just thought I'd give it a try. Even if that try was half-assed. I don't expect you to step away, even though you really should, but let me or Scott handle the legal stuff. And Parker. Okay?"

"Makes sense. Okay. Just keep me updated."

"You know I will," Matthews said before hanging up without saying goodbye.

"Dr. Chase, You should be receiving that court order any time. My partner was just about to call the hospital with the information."

After only fifteen minutes, the doctor's computer dinged, indicating a new message. He called Mr. Walker back with an update. "I received the order to release any information regarding staffing during the periods your family was in our care. Give me about twenty minutes and I'll send that to your email. Text my phone with your email address, and I'll get that right over to you. Good?"

"Thank you, doctor. I really appreciate your cooperation."

"I told you I'd help if I legally could, Mr. Walker. I'd feel that same way if it was my family that was injured. Please let me know if there's anything else I can help with," he said and hung up.

Robert was walking back to Mary's room when Devon hung up the phone. "I just got done checking on Caleb. They said they were running some quick tests, and they'd let us know as soon as

33

they're done. The only reason I didn't push the matter was that I left two of my personal security to escort Caleb. They'll be with him for every second until either you or I go get him. I told them that they are not to let him out of their sight, even for a moment, until we find whoever was behind the attack. The doctor that was with him didn't seem so happy, but I don't give a damn. Another doctor I spoke to said they wanted to check his hearing to make sure there was no damage. So he shouldn't be gone long, but it's a good idea that they check everything to make sure he didn't sustain any injuries they didn't catch initially."

Devon nodded in agreement, his son's health came above the anxiety he felt not having him close. As they turned to enter Mary's room, Devon's phone dinged with a new email. Hitting his speed dial, he called Matthews back.

"What's up, Walker? Did you get what you needed? And I wanted to ask how Mary and Caleb were on our last call, but you were in a hurry. I don't have any new information yet."

"Caleb is fine, and Mary is stable. I have a favor to ask."

"Anything, you know that."

"Always. The hospital is sending me the names, titles, and photos of the employees that had direct contact with Mary and Caleb the night he was born and the ones on duty today. Can you contact the office and have someone check into their backgrounds? I know if I call, the chief will tell me to back off and let them handle it. I'm emailing you the list now."

"I'll get that over to IT. I'll call you when I have something. Keep me updated on Mary, and let me know if you need anything."

His Apprentice's Revenge

As Devon slid his phone back into his pocket and turned to Mary's room, an uneasy feeling swept over his body. He suspected that whatever was going on, it was only getting started.

Chapter 4

Devon received the call he'd been anticipating not thirty minutes after hanging up the phone with Matthews. As soon as his caller ID showed Chief Parker, he knew what his superior was calling about. Yes, he was expecting it, but he didn't want to hear it.

He didn't feel like being lectured right now by anyone, not even his boss, on the ethics of distancing himself from this case. There wasn't a man or woman Devon worked with, the chief included, that wouldn't demand to be included when their family's lives were threatened.

"Walker," Devon said. He wanted to laugh, to stop himself from berating the person on the other line as soon as they opened their mouth.

"Agent Walker, how's your family? What are the doctors saying? Everyone here in the office keeps asking and are keeping them in their thoughts," Chief Parker said, without an actual greeting.

Out of everything he expected to hear from his chief, it wasn't for him to skip official formalities to ask about his family. Yes, he'd become more personable since the Yates case, but he was still all work and no play. He had a strict rule about keeping his work and home life separate. Maybe Devon and Matthews were rubbing off on the chief, and he was becoming a rebel. It was unlikely, but comical to consider.

"My son is good, sir. He only has some bumps and scrapes, but Mary is unconscious. The doctors started explaining about how the brain needs time to heal and she'll wake on her own, but I'm an impatient bastard and want concrete answers. Yet, even after all that, the doctors have a good prognosis about her recovery. Thank you for asking. What can I do for you, Chief?" Devon didn't want to mention the case, hoping the chief only had called to check in on him and his family instead. Wishful thinking.

"I'm sure you're aware of why I'm calling. I'm sure that partner of yours that can't keep his damn mouth shut, or any of your other friends in this building, gave you a heads up to expect my call."

Devon played dumb. "I thought you were calling to check on my family, sir. And it was extremely nice of you to do that. I know of no other reason as to why you'd be calling me right now, truly, sir." Devon could hear Parker let out a sigh of exasperation on the other end. As annoying as his personality was, Parker was still a very sharp agent. He knew Devon was trying to avoid the topic. Or at least being a smartass.

"Agent Walker, seriously? Yes, your family's safety and health are important to me and to every one of your fellow agents, but you know that's not why I called. Are you going to cooperate, or do I need to put in a formal notice that you need to stay away from this investigation?

"You know we take care of our own. So, take care of your family, and let us handle the rest. We can't have you in the middle of this. You'd be crossing the very obvious line of being too close to the investigation. Any good defense attorney could use that against the Bureau if something ended up going to court.

"You and Matthews don't know how to do anything quietly. If I set you both free to do whatever it is you do to apprehend your target, I'd probably end up calling the coroner and not inmate containment. And that is a real conflict of interest for the Bureau, if you follow."

Devon knew this was coming, not to this extent, but he expected it, and it pissed him off. "Sir, how can you ask me to stay away from this investigation? Someone tried to kill my wife and son. If you were in my shoes, you'd be out for blood, and you damn well know it. If this was your wife and child, you'd say screw the law, and you'd hunt them yourself and burn the city to the ground in the process. I'm not asking you to put the law aside, but I won't be left out. Take a minute and think about what you are asking me to do, and what you'd be willing to do yourself. Could you completely step away and be left in the dark?"

"Yes, you're right, I would be out for blood, just like you are, and that's why you need to step back. I can say this because this didn't happen to me. It happened to you, and you're my agent. *When* we catch this person, we don't need a pencil pusher claiming any wrongdoings because you were out for vengeance.

"I'll make a deal with you. Remember, I don't even need to do this, I'm only doing this as a favor because you are my best agent and I know you'd get the information from Matthews anyway, and I don't want to lose two of my best agents. The deal is: we'll keep you informed on the case. Information only, Walker, but you are hands-off. You can do all the research you want, but you don't go near any people of interest. You know how this goes, you're a person of interest until we can clear you, and even then this was your family, you're as much part of the case as they are. So, keep your hands off, and we'll keep you informed. Deal?"

It was more than Devon expected he'd get from his boss. He thought Parker would demand he have nothing to do with the case at all under the circumstances. He understood why Parker was being as careful as he was, but he still thought it was ridiculous. "Yeah, chief. We have a deal. For now. A warning though, if there is another threat towards my family, I will put my badge down and protect them any way I need to."

"You're a snarky bastard, Walker. Just keep it legal. I'll be keeping an eye on you and Matthews. Now I'm going to get back to work. IT called and said they got some info from Matthews they are working on. We'll let you know if we need anything else from the hospital staff while you're there. I also called one of the judges at the courthouse today and gave them a heads-up that we may need a warrant for more information so we don't get pushback from the hospital. See, shared information. Let me know if you need anything."

Before Devon could respond, Parker hung up. Okay, he could work with this. At least he wasn't getting pushed all the way out.

Not that he'd ever allow that to happen, or that Matthews would allow that to happen. Like Parker said, he was a snarky bastard, but at least he was a smart, snarky bastard with resources and contacts who owed him. And right now was a great time to call in some of those debts.

Matthews was beyond annoyed. IT was taking forever to check those names from the hospital, even after he put them at the top of their priority list. Yes, it happened to be a long list, but the FBI techs were supposed to be the best in the business. Didn't they have programs that could run all that information at one time?

He bet if he pulled out his computer, he'd be able to get some information before IT got back to him. Would it be legal? Absolutely not. But when Matthews was in the Marines, he learned a backdoor way, or two, to get the information he needed.

Besides, he was going to go crazy if he sat still for even a moment longer. He needed to do something. They needed a lead. Pulling out his phone, he called Detective Miller with the MDP.

Miller answered on the second ring. "Agent Matthews, what can I do for you?"

"Hey, Miller. I was hoping you guys had something I can work with. Our bomb techs are coming up with zilch on the fragments. They're saying the bombs were made with basic supplies you can purchase from any big box store. They're still running some tests to see if there are any fingerprints or other residues we can trace, but they're not hopeful. I was hoping you could give me something from the other angles you've been working on. I don't want to call Walker back until I have something, anything, to give him."

"Sorry, Matthews, I wish I had something to give you. We pulled the surveillance videos from the parking lot, and the traffic cameras in the area, but nothing. Where Mary parked her SUV, there was such a reflection from what I'm told looks like a piece of trash laying on the ground, it obstructed the view of the security camera. I'm having the video sent to a specialist to see what she can do. I'll get back to you if I hear anything else."

"Damn. Okay. Got it. I was hoping you guys would have something we didn't."

"Matthews?"

"Yeah."

"How're Mary and Caleb doing? It scared me out of my mind when I pulled up on the scene and saw Mary laying there and the carseat on the ground. The only thing that stopped me from completely losing it was when I heard the strong lungs on that little guy and knew he was at least breathing. I met him when he was only a few weeks old, and held him, too. I couldn't take it if he was hurt worse than he was when I found him. It was hard enough seeing Mary laying there. I have a soft spot for Walker's wife. Just don't tell him, please. I'd like to keep my head intact, and I'm sure my wife wouldn't like that, either."

"I hear you, Miller. It is bad, beyond bad, but it could've been worse. Mary is pretty banged up. The doctors told Walker that she has a head injury, but they are very optimistic. Caleb was lucky and came out with only bumps and bruises. I'm telling you something, Miller, I thought Walker was scary when Yates kidnapped Mary, but no. Now you put his child into the equation… Whoever did this to his family needs to just give up now, because Walker is never going to stop hunting them down. The fury I saw in Walker's eyes would make Satan run and hide."

Chapter 5

It was coming up on twelve hours since Devon's world had once again been turned upside down. Walking back and forth at the foot of Mary's bed—waiting for any update from Matthews, Parker, or Miller—was driving him to the brink of madness.

Patricia finally couldn't take anymore of his walking in circles. Stopping her own pacing, she turned to face Devon, threw her hands in the air, and huffed as she jammed the tissue she'd been dabbing her eyes with into her purse. "I feel helpless, and I don't like knowing there's nothing I can do to help. I need to get out of this room. I'm going to go to the flower shop downstairs and get Mary some lovely daisies to brighten up her room. No one will need me before I get back. I won't be gone long. Are you listening to me, Devon? Oh never mind, I'll be back."

Patricia just said something to him, but he couldn't focus on her words. Time seemed to disappear as he ran name after name through his head to try to come up with who could have a reason to target his family. Devon found himself sitting next to Mary, holding her hand and stroking her hair. When he looked at the clock, two hours had passed since Patricia left. The only reason he snapped out of his worried trance and looked at the clock was from a ding from his phone.

The ding was a text message from Patricia.

"I'm back from the coffee shop. I'll be up soon."

Her message made him smile. His phone dinged again.

"I have food and coffee for everyone, and the security team is being persnickety about carrying it all. Please help."

Devon laughed aloud. He loved Mary's aunt; she was such an amazing woman. Always caring for others. He doubted the security team was being "persnickety." Devon learned quickly that the men hired to protect the Carters were more family than paid employees.

Incredible. Devon was downstairs in the lobby not five minutes after receiving Patricia's message, and after being part of the family for almost two years, he should have been more prepared for the sight before him. Within the short time it took him to make it downstairs, Patricia had recruited most of the hospital volunteer services for her task, which suited her security team just fine.

From what he could see, there were six pastry boxes and no less than ten to-go coffee boxes. Was Mary's aunt trying to feed the entire hospital floor? It's no wonder the nursing staff loved her. But they would love her anyway. She is just that type of person. Maybe she was trying to make up for how grumpy her husband was with the staff.

From the moment the elevator opened on Mary's floor, and the nursing staff noticed her walking down the hall, their demeanor turned from irritable and run-down to relieved and excited. One rather flamboyant nurse couldn't hold in his excitement. The moment his eyes caught Patricia, he ran over to help her, filling her with praise.

"Oh, Patricia," he said, bouncing around. "You spoil us. Not that we complain one iota. Anything you and your family need, you just ring us and let us know."

Patricia beamed with delight. "Oh thank you, Mikey, but don't you go making me blush. You know I just appreciate you all so very much. Working such a thankless job, you all are angels."

With a wave of her hands, the hospital volunteers holding the food and coffee moved forward and covered every inch of the nurse's station. After being bombarded with so many words of thanks, she took the small cup of coffee her security offered and continued down the hall to Mary's room. Wanting to allow the hospital staff to enjoy their treats in peace.

Slowly opening the door, she stopped dead in her tracks and let out an audible gasp. She stumbled back out of the room, hands shaking so hard the coffee cup fell to the floor in a deafening splash.

Devon's heart tightened and nearly stopped in his chest. Fear trickled down his spine and the color drained from his face as he assumed the worst. *Oh no.*

Patricia could barely make herself move, nevermind give a single care for the stains on the wall and puddle of coffee on the floor. She didn't even notice it had splattered all over her white pants and shoes. *Mary... Oh, Mary.*

Seconds after the gasp reached Devon and the rest of the security team, they were sprinting down the hall. Patricia's head of security, Alex, got there first. He grabbed her by the shoulders and pushed her behind his back to shield her from a possible threat.

Devon, only a half step behind Alex, had drawn his gun and slid around to enter the room. Fear and anger wrinkled his face with expectation. Then, suddenly, relief washed over him as he realized why Patricia gasped, and it wasn't because of a threat. Seeing those sapphire blue eyes locked onto his, he lowered his gun and re-holstered it, knowing he didn't need it any longer.

It wasn't fear or danger that caused Patricia to gasp but Mary, herself. She was sitting up in bed, looking confused with everything going on around her. Touching the bandages at her head, she winced in pain. Before he could even get to her side, her eyes darted around the room and she yelled angrily, "Where is my son?"

Devon couldn't help but smile. There she was. There's his girl. Momma Bear was wide awake.

Mary was panic-stricken. The only thing she knew for certain was she was in the hospital, again. The last thing she remembered was she was out with her son, being scared about something, then she woke up here. Now, Devon was standing in front of her, smiling. If something had happened to Caleb, he wouldn't be smiling. No, he'd be out of his mind with rage, but he was standing there, smiling like an idiot, and not saying anything.

Seeing the look in her eyes, he was half afraid to touch her. Knowing his wife, as soon as she felt his touch, the control over her emotions would shred.

"Oh, Mary. Oh god, you're okay."

Trying to push herself into more of a sitting position, she wasn't able to hide her pain as she involuntarily sucked air in between clenched teeth. "I'm sore, but where's Caleb?"

"I was so worried," he said, rubbing his hands behind his neck.

"Yes, I know you'd be worried. But, Devon, where is our son?"

As if answering the question her husband refused to, Patricia entered the room carrying a very fussy Caleb. She must have run to collect him as soon as she saw Mary was awake.

Walking over to her bedside, Devon reached down and grabbed her shaking hands. He was right, as soon as he touched his wife, her emotions snapped. Tears streamed down Mary's face as she watched her aunt move to her side, and since she was in a sitting position, Patricia placed Caleb gently onto the bed between Mary's legs.

His wife's quivering chin and flushed cheeks made Devon's heart skip a beat. The look she was giving their son was pure love, the love between mother and child. The tender moment was brief, then it was replaced with a look of disgust.

"Devon?" Mary choked out.

"Yes, Love," he whispered, trying to control his laughter, knowing what had her upset.

47

Without turning to look at him, she asked, "What the hell is Caleb wearing?"

Unable to tell her it was just a simple hospital onesie, he decided on a better course of action. He just laughed.

Chapter 6

Matthews and Scott were back at the office trying to make a connection with Walker's past cases and people who recently have been released from prison, when Parker got it into his head that this had to do with Yates and he wanted those two to stake out his last known residence. Matthews was sure it was a long shot that this could be, in any way, connected to Jimmy Yates. How could Parker assume this isn't a criminal with a grudge against Walker, and Mary and Caleb are collateral damage? With there being no evidence that the hit was or wasn't connected to Yates, Matthews would follow any lead.

Agents Matthews and Scott had been sitting in the unmarked car for over an hour watching the abandoned house. Matthews' mind was playing tricks on him, making him think he was seeing things that couldn't possibly be there. Twilight was the perfect time for shadows to mix with streetlights and make every dark shape look like it was a moving person.

Normally, Matthews was all "steel and grit" as Devon called him, but this time, he was spooked. After thinking about it, everything about the attempt on Mary and Caleb had the stench of Yates surrounding it, but that bastard was six feet in the ground, rotting, and insect food. He wasn't usually one to believe in the paranormal… but with the way it felt, he couldn't help but keep the possibility on the table, no matter how absurd.

The only reasonable explanation he could find for the attempt was a different suspect, someone who idolized Yates. Maybe a copycat, because there was no way Yates had somehow returned. There was nothing outside the car Matthews couldn't handle. And in the off chance there was, he'd offer up Scott as a sacrifice. That would make Walker happy because Scott was always flirting with Mary.

The sun was finally coming up, providing a better view of their surroundings, and the moving shadows faded. The last occupant of this residence, though illegally occupying the home, was Jimmy Yates. Nobody knew how long Yates had stayed in the home. The last registered occupant was one of Yates' victims years back, so he could've been living right there under the FBI's nose for years.

Matthews had been here after the Yates case concluded, but it looked completely different. When they received the orders today, both agents wondered why the chief would order them to check out the unoccupied residence of a dead serial killer. Being the good agents they were, they waited until they were alone to mention how much of a waste of time this was.

Despite it being a huge waste of time, Matthews knew better. He had the unfortunate opportunity to witness the aftermath of one of Yates's crime scenes in person, and in all his years with the bureau and the military, he'd never seen anything so sadistic. The world was inarguably a much safer place now that he was gone. But if there was even the slightest chance Yates was connected, they needed to know about it.

Matthews wished Yates would have spent the rest of his miserable life in prison, wondering every day when he'd get the needle, or walking the halls of the prison watching over his shoulder wondering if today would be the day a shiv would be driven between his ribs. His wish didn't come true because that bastard had a quick death and no suffering. Instead, it almost felt as if he'd died a psychopath's martyr.

Now the question arose, with Yates dead, who else was targeting Mary? Or was Walker the target, and in turn, his family became the targets, or did they only get in the way? Being an FBI agent, you are bound to make enemies.

After a quick search of Walker's past case files, his list of potential enemies was endless, but who was it? That was the question Matthews was determined to answer. Someone put his godson in danger, and that person was going to pay. The entire IT department was sifting through Walker's files and determining if any persons of interest were in D.C. at the time of the attack, or if they had a link to the explosive materials used to blow up her SUV.

Agent Scott grew impatient, bouncing his legs and tapping his foot. He checked his watch for the hundredth time and decided he couldn't sit still any longer. Reaching for the door handle, he said, "Matthews, I'm just going to take a quick look around inside. Per the report, this house has been unoccupied for over a year. If we're going to learn anything, we need to get inside. We aren't going to gather any information just by sitting here on our asses."

He quickly agreed, knowing Scott was right. "Just call it in to dispatch while I grab some gear. We need to make sure we do this by the book."

Opening the trunk, Matthews pulled out the gear he thought they'd need. The house was supposed to be vacant, but he wasn't one to take unnecessary chances. Who knows, there may be harmless squatters living inside, or someone with a sick fascination with serial killers who gets a kick out of being in their home.

He saw firsthand the lengths serial killer groupies, as they called themselves, would go to feel close to the psychopaths they idolize. Matthews learned long ago to expect the unexpected, and that's how he strived to handle every situation since joining the FBI. If you expect the unexpected, you are less likely to get caught off guard and more likely to make it home alive. Complacency kills, and he's seen it happen too many times to people he worked with to allow it to happen to himself.

Scott signed off the radio and swiftly moved around the car to the trunk. Looking around at the dark homes and empty front yards, everything seemed to be quiet. He learned the hard way not to depend on appearances, as they could change in a blink of an eye. Scott reached inside the trunk and picked up the bulletproof vest Matthews set aside for him.

As a fresh-out-of-the-academy agent, Scott understood the importance of always wearing his vest. Even though it was supposed to be part of their uniform when entering a scene, some agents considered the few seconds it took to apply a vest as a waste of time. He'd never forget the day he'd fallen into the same lazy and complacent mindset.

His second call as an FBI agent was for an active shooter at an office building. Scott ignored his partner's demand to wait for backup and went to check if a side door to the office building was unlocked before donning his protective equipment. As soon as he jiggled the handle of the door, the shooter on the other side fired two rounds through the door, and one found its way into Scott's abdomen. From that day forward, he'd never go on another call without his vest. The scar, however, was a great conversation point when picking up a woman.

Closing the trunk and setting all the gear on the ground, Scott pulled out the blueprints to the home again and spread them out so Matthews could see them. It was supposed to be abandoned, but that was no reason not to be completely prepared.

The home's layout was a ranch-style with no attic. The main level had three bedrooms, one and a half baths, kitchen, dining room, family room, and laundry room. Pretty easy and common for being built in the early 50's. The blueprints also showed a good size unfinished basement, which is where the home's furnace and hot water heater were located. Again, straightforward and easy.

Scott pulled out the radio and double-checked the channel. "Dispatch, this is Agent Scott. We will be moving to do a sweep of the residence. We're going to go radio silent incase of occupancy."

"Hold please," replied the dispatch operator. "Negative. You are to stay in your vehicle until backup arrives. This is an order from the chief. Do you copy?"

Typical of their boss. He wanted them to wait to make entry until he could arrive and micromanage them. At least they expected it would be Parker that made an appearance. Both Scott and Matthews knew the congressman was making waves with the top brass, and rightfully so, but Parker would do anything to make himself out as the hero. So waiting was out of the question.

Leaning against the car, Matthews called out. "Let's go, Scott. We aren't waiting for backup. I want this search done by the book and won't tolerate anyone messing up possible evidence that'll lead us to who is targeting Mary and Caleb.

Scott rolled his eyes but quickly agreed after seeing the look on Matthews's face. That look told him that if he didn't agree, Matthews would likely handcuff him to the steering wheel and search the home himself. Scott quickly double-tapped his radio, muffling his response with static noise, "dispatch... and... there.. .no...."

"Please repeat the last transmission," the dispatcher ordered, but Scott wouldn't respond.

When, at last, dispatch had given up and stopped responding, they knew backup would be only minutes away. But if the blueprints were correct, they'd have the house clear before the others arrived.

The last thing they needed were more bodies tripping over each other, when they'd be able to run through the house in only a few minutes. With a last check of equipment, the agents, in perfect unison, moved towards the house. Having to trust they had each other's backs, they proceeded without the ordered backup.

Hopefully, they did the right thing, and nothing was lying in wait to surprise them.

Chapter 7

T he closer Matthews came to the abandoned home, the more evident it was that the likelihood of anyone occupying the home was nil. But they'd still keep their eyes out for squatters as they entered the home. It looked like the city kept the grass cut around the sidewalk, but there was no other upkeep.

Parker had called in a request for verification of ownership from the city and got a woman in desperate need of a vacation or a coffee. From experience, Matthews knew how understaffed and overworked they were down in the county city buildings, so he didn't expect the information any time soon. And if the woman running Parker in circles was the one he thought it was, she was far from pleasant and would keep him tied up for hours. No wonder Parker sent him and Scott down to check the place out.

On the outside, there wasn't much to see. It looked very similar to every other house in this neighborhood, except a little more run-down. The home was more than likely part of a big push of manufactured homes on a new plot of land. Neighborhoods like this were commonly reproduced in the 50s, 60s, 70s, and 80s.

The home's driveway was overgrown to the point the concrete parking space was barely visible. Leaves and overgrown moss filled the sagging gutters which draped low in some places from the weight. It was surprising to Matthews that they were still attached to the house with as bad of shape as they were in.

Roots and weeds protruding at all angles from the base of the home cracked the foundation, tipping the house at a slight angle. The windows were long broken, with not even boards or plastic wrap to keep the elements, or intruders, from gaining access to the space within. Glancing quickly at the windows, not even one full or partial screen was still present in any of the frames.

Matthews knew it had once been a nice family home, meticulously taken care of. It was the home of Mary's childhood neighbor, Mr. Smith. The same Mr. Smith that inadvertently saved her from being found by Yates the same day he murdered her parents.

Mr. Smith's murder had remained unsolved until Yates admitted it to Mary while he had her held captive. He was murdered because he interrupted Yates that day inside the Anderson home. Matthews always thought it particularly disturbing how Yates went so out of his way to get to Mary. Even killing someone outside his MO. They never connected the murder to Jimmy Yates because Mr. Smith still had his face when his body was discovered.

As they reached the house, Matthews and Scott decided not to split up, with one going in front and one going around the back. They'd both use the back door instead. There were fewer windows around the back of the house, and they were less likely to be seen there. Even though they were FBI and on an official case with court documents, the moment any of the neighbors knew someone was entering the home, the more likely there would be a crowd waiting for them when they exited.

After testing to make sure the door was locked, Matthews dropped to one knee and made quick work of picking the lock. They could have easily kicked in the door—hell, a hard shove with a shoulder would have splintered the door frame—but they wanted a quiet entrance on the off chance there was someone inside.

"Now listen," Matthews started, "we confirmed on the blueprints that this layout is going to be close-quarters with not many open areas, I feel we need to clear each room as a team. If we separate, it would leave us open to ambush."

With a quick nod, Scott agreed. "Got it. Even though we aren't expecting anyone to be inside, there's no reason to take chances. My dog will be pissed if something happens and my mom needs to take care of him."

Exasperated with Scott's immature comments, Matthews went back to focusing on the door. Once it was unlocked, using speed to their advantage, Matthews led the way into the house and into the laundry room. Quickly scanning his sector of the room, moving forward only when feeling the tap on his shoulder from Scott, they cleared the laundry room, and then the kitchen, dining room, a half bathroom, and living room in under a minute before they advanced on the hallway.

Agents referred to hallways as fatal funnels. They'd need to take more care on the way to clear the rooms at the end. Hallways are likely ambush points, and Scott personally knew more than one agent killed in the line of duty while clearing a house and being stuck in the hall.

Thankfully, both agents made it to the bedroom with no issues. At the first door, Matthews stopped, "Once we breach these doors, we need to be silent and quick. There wasn't intel on what we can expect, so always expect the worst. Ready?"

Scott slowly nodded. Not taking his gaze from the window next to the door.

Matthews held up three fingers and counted down to one. On one, he, as quietly as he could, swung the door open and Scott quickly entered the room, sweeping from one corner to the other for threats. They repeated this motion until they cleared the other two bedrooms and bathroom. Now they only had the basement to check.

Clearing basements is dangerous because you are initially open and vulnerable during the descent down the stairs. Matthews, during his training with the Marines, participated in similar training but with paintballs instead of bullets. During those first few sessions, he'd leave the training area hardly able to tell the original color of his uniform.

Being hit multiple times was the point of that exercise. They wanted to drill it into the Marines' heads just how dangerous descending stairs in a hostile situation could be. That was training he'd never forget, and one that came in handy more times than he could count.

After opening a few closet doors, they finally located the stairs leading to the basement. Like the rest of the house, someone must have been oiling the door hinges, because there was not one squeak when they opened the door. It suggested someone had been in the home recently. For about thirty seconds after opening the door, Matthews and Scott didn't move a muscle. They didn't even breathe. For those few seconds, they listened for any indication someone was below, listened for any hint that they weren't alone.

Confident no one was lying in wait, but still not willing to take the chance, Matthews pulled a non-irritant-filled smoke grenade from his vest, pulled the pin, and tossed it down the stairs. After it completely saturated the basement and no coughing or yelling came, both agents slowly descended the stairs. They moved back to back and side-stepped down, each facing a different direction as they moved lower. Once they hit the bottom, the smoke was dissipating, and they headed toward the only light in the room which came from a very small window located at the top of the far wall. They crouched and waited for the smoke to clear.

The good thing with the smoke Matthews used, is it was a small canister, roughly a quarter amount of what is used for riot control. Each agent's vehicle had a few of these small canisters for situations just like this. Fortunately, because of the small size, they only had to wait another two minutes or so until the room was completely clear and no trace of smoke lingered in the air. Since the basement was only one room, and surprisingly uncluttered, they could see it was otherwise empty.

On a small table in the corner were some loose papers, but there was nothing of immediate interest. Scott walked away, leaving Matthews to finish re-stacking the papers. He wanted to walk the wall, just in case they missed something, but nothing was jumping out at him. This was a bust, just like they thought.

Matthews and Scott were about to give up searching the basement for any indication someone else may have occupied the house since Yates' murder, when something caught Matthew's eye. Next to the stairs leading to the outside was a large built-in shelf covered in dusty, old, canned goods. At the bottom right corner of the shelf, there was a barely noticeable scrape on the concrete floor. It was fresh compared to the dingy, dirty layers of crud covering every other inch of the basement floor which looked like it hadn't ever been swept or mopped.

"Hey, Scott, bring the flashlight closer down here. What do you make of this?" Matthews squatted next to the mark.

After seeing the indentation on the floor, Scott knew exactly what it was. "That's not a normal shelving unit. This one swings out. They are usually used for hidden rooms."

Matthews looked at him incredulously. "How would you know that, Scott? Did you have a case with one before, or see it in a movie?"

Scott grinned from ear to ear. "I know about them because I have one in my house. It hides my very well-stocked liquor and porn collections. Some people have man caves, I have a hidden room."

Groaning, Matthews said, "Of course you do, Scott. I shouldn't even have asked. Only you would have something like that in your house. I don't know why I'm even surprised." Matthews gestured at the shelving unit. "If you know so much about these things, have at it. Why don't you show me how they open?"

Scott shined the flashlight over the shelves. "These are built on a hinge system. We need to find an object or latch that will move slightly if touched but is attached to the shelf." Without even considering how it sounded, he added, "My lock object is a photo of me and my mom from the day I graduated from the academy."

Matthews stopped, shined the flashlight directly on his face, and stared at him for a moment. "You're sick, Scott. The key to open the room that houses your alcohol and porn collections is a picture of your mother. We need to wrap this case up fast; I need Walker back as my partner. At least he doesn't have any weird fetishes. You worry me, Scott. You need therapy."

"What?" He shrugged. "I never saw the issue with having a picture of me and my mom as the key. Only you'd think of it in some perverted way. If anyone needs therapy, it's you."

"No, Scott. Anyone would think it was repulsive, not just me. You really need to change that."

"Fine, whatever. I'll change it to a picture of Maxine, my German Shepard." Scott broke off his conversation as he started speaking into his radio.

"Dispatch, this is Agent Scott. I need a forensic team at my location."

"Copy. A forensic team is being dispatched now to your location. Backup should almost be there. It's good to hear your voice after your radio issues a bit ago," the dispatcher added with humor in her voice.

Making sure to stop laughing before he responded, he took a few deep breaths. "Dispatch, it's good to hear your voice too. I'll get my radio checked when I get back to headquarters."

"Heard, Agent Scott. Yes, please get that looked at, we don't want it to happen again." The radio cut out, but not before a few seconds of giggling came across the channel.

Matthews was just shaking his head, knowing that all the dispatchers knew Scott's humor and were not fooled by his "faulty" radio. Backup and forensics would be here soon, and he wanted this door open before they arrived.

After three painstakingly slow minutes, Scott finally found the lever hidden on the bottom shelf, with a disgusting piece of brown cloth covering it to make it look like part of the dirty wall.

Matthews stood to the side with the flashlight in one hand and his weapon drawn in the other, ready in case anyone was waiting until they opened the door. Scott held up one hand and counted down from three. On one, he threw open the door while simultaneously drawing his firearm.

"Oh, shit!" Matthew shouted. There was no one hiding, waiting to spring on them, but what they found in the room was even more disturbing.

There was a shrine dedicated to Yates, with candles that had long past melted down the table and new ones placed on top. Small bones, that he didn't know if they were human or animal, were scattered around. Pieces of jewelry, presumably from his victims, were piled high in an ornate chalice that had spots on the handle that looked like dried blood.

The picture smack dab in the center disturbed Matthews the most. It was of Yates with a young woman. She was holding a severed face and had a gruesome smile. With a trembling hand, he completely disregarded forensic protocol and tore the photo from the shrine and shone his light on it. Matthews knew that woman, her golden brown hair and green eyes were hard to mistake. The photo was of a young girl, but he saw her recently, and he'd seen her holding his godson. "That Bitch," Matthews bellowed. Fear mixed with rage churned through him, as he frantically reached for his phone.

Quickly, he dialed Walker. Even though Parker ordered him to keep his partner out of it, there was no way he was going to do it. Especially when that woman could be with Caleb right this minute. This just became more serious than they could've ever imagined.

Matthews yelled for Scott to get everyone available to the hospital, now. He had a dreadful feeling that the backup wouldn't be able to make it to the hospital in time. Even if he got reprimanded, Matthews was going to warn Walker about what they found.

Chapter 8

Devon picked up on the second ring. "Hey, Matthews. Did you guys find anything out? I'm going crazy sitting here—"

"Walker, shut up for a second," Matthews yelled.

Hearing the urgency in his voice, Devon stopped.

"It's the doctor, Walker. The one that was in his nursery, Dr. Kadlec. Caleb's pediatric doctor is the one that tried to kill Mary and Caleb. We found proof she was in a twisted partnership with Yates. Get to Caleb and get Mary, and I'll call for backup," Matthews yelled more forcefully than necessary.

He heard the phone drop, and bounce a few times, then chaos ensued. Devon yelled at whom Matthews could only assume was a nurse or doctor. "Where's my son? Don't shake your head at me. Find my damn son right this second or I'll have you arrested. A nurse said he was going for another test. Find him."

With all the commotion happening through the phone, Matthews wasn't able to hear the response from whomever he was talking to, he only heard Devon.

"The nursery? Why is he in the nursery and not in my wife's room? Call security and get to my wife's room, and don't let her out of your sight. You go into that room and you lock the door. You don't let anyone in there until I get there. I don't care who it is, no one, not even another doctor."

The line disconnected, but Matthews was already running up the stairs and out of the house. Scott was only steps behind him when Matthews started barking out orders. "Scott, you stay here and secure the scene. We need to get as much information about this bitch as we can. Now that we have a face, we need to get an idea about where she's hiding. We need to make sure she doesn't get another chance to get close to Walker's family. Make sure forensics goes over everything with a fine-tooth comb. I'll give you an update as soon as I make sure Walker's family is safe."

As much as Scott wanted to argue and go with him, he knew Matthews was right. Both of them couldn't leave the scene before it was secure, and Matthews should be the one to go to Walker's side. That was his partner and best friend. Matthews would lay his life down for Walker and his family.

Devon slammed through the double doors to the nursery with such force they bounced off the walls. The whirlwind of activity around him and the vulgar yelling from confused parents outside the room barely penetrated his concentration. His focus was singularly on finding his son, and nothing else mattered.

Looking around the room, he was oblivious to the sound of all the screaming babies he'd just woken up. It shouldn't be hard to find Caleb, Mary wanted him to wear a bright green froggie outfit on his first day out into this world, but when they woke up that morning, it had been too warm for him to wear it.

Devon had found the bright green matching hat in the diaper bag when he was searching for a new set of clothes for his son to wear after being cleaned up after the explosion. Because he knew it would make his wife happy, his son had been wearing the bright hat all day. Mary was still mortified that he was wearing a hospital onesie when she'd woken up, but at least he got the hat on him.

Time seemed to stand still, but he found Caleb in the center of all the other screaming babies, bright green hat still on his head. Doctors, nurses, security officers, and concerned parents descended upon the nursery at the same time.

People rushed about to soothe the upset infants, while others talked over each other, pointing in Devon's direction and demanding answers as to what was going on and questioning if their children were in danger. Devon picked up Caleb, and the baby instantly started calming down. A nurse rushed over and offered to take the baby back out of Devon's arms, but one look from Devon made her slowly back away.

It was at that very moment, Dr. Chase rushed through the doors and over to Devon, the security team surrounding him. "What's going on, Agent Walker?" the Chief of Medicine demanded.

Looking him right in the eyes, Devon simply stated, "Dr. Chase, you have a doctor that's wanted for two counts of attempted murder. Dr. Kadlec isn't who you think she is, and until she's apprehended, this hospital is on lockdown by order of the FBI."

Before the doctor could respond, Devon turned and walked out the door holding his son, heading to Mary's room. One of the nurses assigned to the nursery quickly ran ahead of him to scan her badge before the alarms started blaring, notifying staff and security that a baby was on the move. Neither Caleb nor Mary were going to leave his sight until Kadlec was dead or behind bars. Now that he had a name, he also had a target. He finally knew who tried to take his family from him.

Devon was about to enter Mary's room when he saw Matthews rushing out of the stairwell. Matthews' step faltered when he saw him holding Caleb but quickly righted itself. He hurried to Devon's side and placed a shaking hand on Caleb's tiny head. "Hey, little guy."

It warmed Devon's heart every time he witnessed his hardass partner melt like ice around his son. He knew Matthews would move heaven and earth to protect Caleb, and it made their friendship even stronger. But as comforting as it was for Matthews to be there, worried for his family, Devon's attention returned to the matter at hand.

He knocked on Mary's door and gestured to the nurse through the small window, the one he'd yelled at while he was on the phone with Matthews. "Thank you for watching my wife, you can go. Agent Matthews will be staying with her now."

"Matthews, take Caleb and go sit next to Mary. Under no circumstance do either of them leave your sight. They don't go for any tests, and no one enters this room until I get back. I don't give a damn who it is. I'm going to call Chief Parker and fill him in, I'm also calling Mary's uncle. He left only thirty minutes ago and is going to rush back with his entire security force when I explain what is going on. I ordered this hospital on lockdown, and I want every floor, room, and closet searched. That is going to take time.

"I need to know Mary and Caleb are protected while the hospital is searched, and I don't trust anyone more than I trust you. So again, the only people allowed in here are you, me, the Chief, and Mary's aunt and uncle, plus his security. No doctors or nurses at all, I don't care if they make a scene. I need to go find Dr. Chase, and I want this Dr. Julia Kadlec located. I don't care how many toes I need to step on. I'm going to find the bitch that threatened the lives of my family."

Chapter 9

Julia stood behind a tree that only covered about half her body. If anyone looked in her direction, they'd be able to see her instantly. But no one would see her because they were all blatantly self-absorbed. She stood only yards away from the emergency room entrance as dozens of police and FBI vehicles came screeching around the corner, surrounding the hospital.

It was like a game to her, seeing if just one of the many people pouring out of the official vehicles would do their jobs and canvas the surrounding area, but not a single one of them did. Not a single one of them looked at the gangly trees only fifteen feet away. They were entirely focused on the hospital.

All the officers rushing through the doors, holding up their badges and trying to look badass, were too late. They were never going to find her. Did they think she was stupid enough to still be somewhere inside?

Even with having the highest level of respect for her mentor, she was so much smarter than Jimmy ever was. Though she never would've admitted it to him when he was alive. Jimmy liked to stay up close and personal and watch his handy work; Julia had more common sense and believed in self-preservation. Even though she thoroughly enjoyed a little blood on her hands.

Julia had installed listening devices all over Jimmy's house, so she knew the moment it was violated by those dirty FBI agents, putting their undeserving paws all over her idol's most cherished possessions. It took all she had not to snap those little bastard's neck when she heard the two agents talking in the basement and realized they were about to find his trophy room.

No, she decided keeping her composure was the best course of action. She had placed the baby in the nursery and calmly walked out of the hospital. If she tried to walk out of the hospital with the baby, the band on his ankle would trigger the alarm, and she'd be caught. She didn't have the tools to remove the band, or the clearance to request it be done. That hospital had a policy in place to never grant those privileges to new staff.

Mary was still admitted to the hospital but was surrounded by security or her pain-in-the-ass husband around the clock, so she wasn't able to go in and finish the job. Julia wanted Mary to know Yates won when she took everything away from her.

She wanted her to see her world crumble before her eyes, so Julia would need to wait... for now. Placing the baby back in the nursery was beyond hard, she'd rather have snapped his neck right then, but she wanted Mary to watch her as she took her son away from her.

Biding her time and making a new plan was the road she now needed to follow. However, instead of leaving right away and returning to her safe house, she decided to stick around and watch the show. She wished she could be a fly on the wall in Mary's room and see Agent Walker's face when he realized he caused this threat to his family when he allowed the best serial killer the world has ever seen to be gunned down by a coward.

If Agent Walker had done his job and protected Jimmy, he'd still be alive and Julia wouldn't be after his family. No, she'd have waited until she was able to spring Jimmy from prison before allowing him to exact his revenge.

If Jimmy would've made it out of that hospital and to court, the jury would have seen he was doing the world a favor by cleansing it of future evil. It was that bitch that tempted the FBI agent into letting him be murdered before he received his day in court. They'd both pay, and Jimmy will be avenged even if it was the last thing she did.

She had one more thing to do before leaving the hospital grounds. Julia reached into her pocket and pulled out her cell phone. Just one quick call would achieve her goal, and they wouldn't have a moment's peace again.

The deafening commotion coming from outside the emergency room doors reached Congressman Carter. How the hell had the media heard what's going on so quickly? There's no way it was a coincidence they were converging on the hospital not thirty minutes after the FBI made the connection between Dr. Kadlec and his niece. Either someone in the hospital tipped off someone in the media, or Kadlec called in the tip herself.

Either way, he wasn't going to wait around to find out. Those vultures weren't going to get anywhere near his niece or his great-nephew. He needed to make sure no one got near his family ever again. Pushing through the crowd, Robert and his security team made their way to an elevator blocked by an MPD officer. After a quick check of his ID against a list provided by Devon of approved individuals, they were on their way up to Mary's room.

As soon as Mary was well enough to travel, with or without Devon's permission, Mary and Caleb would be placed into protective custody until any and everyone connected to Yates was either eight feet in the ground or behind bars. The time for playing by everyone else's rules was over.

The media surrounded the hospital with lightning speed. Every entrance and exit were covered within five minutes of Julia tipping off the news outlets about a threat against the congressman's family and she'd hinted at revenge for Jimmy's death. Which, on all accounts, that information was correct. No news outlet got the exclusive on Jimmy's murder, so every station was determined to be the first ones to report anything new regarding Jimmy Yates.

Thinking of Jimmy made Julia want to rush back to her apartment and greet her little friends she knew would be excitedly waiting for her to return. When she went back down to the sewer to retrieve all Jimmy's equipment after he was apprehended, she took a few friends home with her. Not knowing they'd soon be one of the last links she had to her Jimmy.

Waiting at home for her were six beautiful, yet aggressive, sewer rats. These were the amazing creatures that fed on Mary when she was providing Jimmy with his much-needed vengeful release. Since the day they came home with her, she'd nurtured their blood lust, feeding them a regulated amount at every meal. She gave them just enough to keep them wanting more.

Mary would be ecstatic to be reunited with her little friends, and they would certainly be ready for their next encounter. Sewer rats have a lifespan of around two years, so this would probably be their last hurrah. She'd make sure to give her little friends a chance to go out in style. Bloody, carnage-covered style.

Chapter 10

Congressman Carter walked into Mary's room. Tension radiated off Devon's partner, Agent Matthews, as he was in full agent mode. He could tell the difference between fun-loving Matthews, and wanting to hunt everyone down, Matthews. And this was not fun-loving Matthews. Far from it.

Robert scanned the room. The tension wasn't coming only from Matthews; Devon was wound tight, too. His jaw was locked and his focus on his family, while the silent gears turned in his head.

Devon gave one last glance to Mary, laying in her bed, and Caleb, sleeping in Patricia's arms. She'd shown up only moments before the media and wasn't about to put Caleb down for anything. He then motioned to Robert to head back out the door. The two agents were waiting for Robert to get to the hospital before Matthews would tell Walker everything they'd found in Yates' old home. There was no use repeating himself, when they knew Robert would demand to know every detail.

Matthews had it in his head that he needed a buffer and was determined the congressman would be just that. Although Mary's uncle was just as likely to burn D.C. to the ground to find out who was targeting his family, it was a fifty-fifty toss-up if the congressman would be a help or a hindrance.

Without saying a word, they made their way down the hall to an open conference room. When the three were inside, Walker closed the blinds, then turned to Matthews, waiting for him to tell them what he'd found.

Matthews moved to the other side of the room and leaned against the door, knowing it was the only way to keep Walker from storming out after he revealed what he and Scott found in Yates' old home. It would at least slow him down, unless Walker decided to throw him out of the way. Which he'd actually done in the past, once.

"I wanted you both here to give you all the details about what we found this morning so we can formulate a plan for Mary and Caleb's safety before their location is leaked to the press. They are going to go into a frenzy when they get this information. So, we need to move quickly. Parker is already making plans, since you haven't been answering your phone for anyone but me, he's just waiting on the call from you, Walker, or you, Congressman, for confirmation."

Matthews took a deep breath. He dreaded being the one to give them this news. "Today, besides coming to the astounding realization that Yates did in fact have a partner, we also... we found where Yates stashed his trophies."

Robert bounded to his feet, upset, and rightfully so. His sister's face, like so many others, had never been recovered. Every atom in Devon's body twisted in pain. Bile slowly creeped up his throat. Mary was going to find out her parent's faces had been displayed on a damp, dingy basement wall of these years. He wanted to run from the room, pick up Mary and Caleb, and take them to a deserted island. Once the story hit about what was found in that home, every crackpot, sicko, and Yates's groupie would be trying to witness Mary's reaction to the news.

Bile was threatening to rise in Robert's throat as he asked for the information, but he needed to know. "Give us as much detail as possible. We have to know what we are up against."

Robert took a seat at the small conference table and put his head in his hands. Never before had Devon seen him look defeated, even after Mary was kidnapped and tortured. Twenty years of pain and emotion came back with only a few words and were tearing him apart.

Matthews, staying posted against the door, pictured the basement room in his mind. It wasn't likely he'd ever forget anything he saw down in the dingy room. He'd even remember the smell until the day he died, but he didn't want to miss any important details.

"Yates really didn't want the items he collected from his victims to be found. In all honesty, if it wasn't for Agent Scott, I would've missed it and would've had to wait for forensics to hopefully find my mistake. In the basement, there was an old bookshelf, and something looked off to me, but I couldn't figure out what it was. There was a tiny scrape on the ground, but I didn't know what made those marks. What it ended up being, was a room hidden behind what looked to me like a built-in storage shelf, but Scott knew after looking at it for a split second that it was a shelf that moved on hinges. A Murphy door.

"The shelf was used to hold dusty, dirty canned goods that looked like they hadn't been touched in years. But when Scott saw that mark on the floor, he knew it moved. Apparently, Scott has one of these types of shelving systems in his home." After seeing Walker's questionable glance Matthews shuddered, shook his head, and said, "Don't ask. I regret asking him why he had one, and now I'm going to have images in my head for life that will give me nightmares.

"Back to the basement. After making quick work of the lock mechanism, we checked for booby-traps and entered the room. It wasn't a large room, but it was jam-packed with items that would give anyone nightmares." Looking over at Robert, Matthews already knew the answer, but he wanted to ask anyway and give him an out. "Congressman, what I found is disturbing. Why don't you go back and sit with your niece? We'll be right down once I'm done talking to Walker."

Robert shook his head. "You had all that time before I got to the hospital to debrief him, but you waited on me for a reason. Do I want to hear what I think you are going to say? No, I absolutely don't want to hear it, but if it will help protect my niece and great-nephew then you damn well better not spare any details. Got it, son?"

Matthews nodded. "Yes sir, I promise I won't hold anything back. Where was I? As we entered the room, we found what Yates had been hiding for years. The entire left-hand wall was covered with the missing faces of his victims, hung up with nails, in neat rows, and labeled with the names of the victims and the date of their deaths. Before you ask, we didn't examine them close enough to view every name so I can not confirm if Mary's parents were there. At the time, I was more focused on what was on display in the middle of the room. On the right-hand side, was a collage of photos. Very gruesome, very detailed photos of his crime scenes.

"A mantel was placed at the center wall. Melted candles upon melted candles covered the top of the table, it looked like just a pile of wax—indicating this room had been used very often, and very likely recently. Right in the center of the altar, was a blown-up photo of Yates and a younger Doctor Kadlec.

"As soon as I saw that picture, I called you, Walker. Then I ran out of the house, leaving Scott to deal with the backup that was already pulling up to the location and the forensics team that was on the way. My only focus was getting here to you and your family. You needed to be notified right away that Caleb's doctor was in cahoots with Yates.

"Between the two of you, you need to figure out how you are going to handle security around your family. Unless you want the FBI to do it. I'll warn you now, when Scott and I were in the office, before he gave us the order to watch the Smith residence, Parker was on a tirade and announced that he wants Mary and Caleb packed up and shipped out of the country. Those were his exact words.

"You know he's still sour about Yates being shot and killed before we could get him secured in prison. He knows it's his fault the transfer failed because he called for him to be moved too soon without properly securing the area around the hospital. When he was ranting about the nightmare this has once again become, he even mentioned bringing in his superior if either of you decide to cause waves and not allow the FBI to take over completely or provide ample security yourselves. It's like he doesn't know either of you at all.

"He's determined not to let anything like what happened with Yates happen again, especially when it directly involves one of his agents, again. I'll text Parker and let him know I gave you both the rundown on what we discovered and that you'll call him soon with a game plan on how you want security handled. You know, Walker, it may not be a bad idea to leave for a while. Your family is my family, don't doubt that for a single minute. Let us hunt down this bitch, you go disappear. I'll keep you in the loop."

It wasn't a bad idea, but Devon knew Mary, and she'd never go for it. "What if we sent Caleb and Mary away with Patricia and a full team of security? Robert, do you know somewhere we can send them where they'd be isolated and safe until we can handle this situation ourselves?"

That was it; Robert was done. The last shred of patience he was holding onto finally snapped. He was putting his foot down, or he was going to put his fist through Devon's face, family or not. Slamming his palms down on the table he leapt up and stalked over to Devon, jammed his finger in his face, and started shouting.

"Now listen here, Devon. You need to step away and stop thinking like an FBI agent and start acting like a husband and father for one gosh dang minute. You are talking like it would be nothing to send your family away without your protection when there is, yet again, another psycho out there that has already tried to kill them, not once, but twice."

Robert lowered his finger but didn't step away. "How you're behaving is unacceptable. So, I'm going to tell you what's going to happen. Either you're going to help me take Mary and Caleb to a safe house and you'll keep your ass there to see to their protection, or I'll take them away and you'll never know where they are. If you decide not to go with us, you will not see them until Kadlec is apprehended and the threat against them is neutralized. And when I tell Mary that you decided to prioritize the case over your family's safety, she might decide you won't see them even after Kadlec is apprehended."

He quickly held up a hand when Devon went to open his mouth to protest. "Before you go spouting that, 'but you can't do that' bullshit to me, know that I can, and I will. I love you like you are my own son, but I'll not risk Mary or Caleb's life even a fraction to allow you to play both agent and husband. As a man, I know you want to be their hero, that you feel you can't trust anyone else to successfully capture the person trying to harm your family, but for once in your life, just check your ego at the door and put them above everything else.

"This is your choice, but you have my counter. Don't make the mistake of thinking I'm bluffing. I'll be in Mary's room waiting for your answer. Don't keep me waiting long, or you might not find us there."

Matthews moved away from the door to let the congressman by, too shocked to stop him or stand in his way. Damn, he'd never heard anyone speak to Walker like that. Ever. If the look on Walker's face was any indication, he knew he was correct in his assumption. It was nice to see him put in his place occasionally, especially when he agreed with Robert. This was one time Devon needed to trust his fellow agents to do their jobs.

Devon couldn't take exception with the ultimatum Mary's uncle placed before him, but how dare he pressure him to make the decision he wants with the promise to hide his family from him. He was already planning to ship them away; far away. Yes, he wanted to be both husband and agent, but there was no way he'd be able to let them out of his sight until the threat was eliminated. Mary and Caleb were his world, and one too many times, somebody had threatened their safety. No more.

Since his partner was in the office when Parker ranted about the danger to his family, he'd already guessed about his plans to take his family away. That had to have been the reason he was nodding his head when Robert gave his ultimatum. Devon wanted to punch his friend for just standing there, watching Robert yell at him worse than his own father ever had. It was utterly embarrassing, and Matthews looked to be thoroughly enjoying every moment of Devon's torture. *What a great partner.* Devon would find the perfect time and then he'd get even.

Devon already had another agent checking into safe houses and security teams available for round-the-clock protection, the only thing he didn't work out was how he'd also be able to work the case. Robert took that choice away from him.

One thing he learned about Robert in the short time he's known him was he didn't bluff, ever. If he felt Devon wasn't entirely invested, he'd do exactly as he'd promised. No doubt about it.

Chapter 11

It was the first time in hours that he'd been out of that basement, but Agent Scott needed some fresh air. He felt as if he was suffocating, and the mustiness absorbed into his every pore. The tiny house was crawling with federal agents and every available forensic technician assigned to the D.C. field office. Even a select few MPD were allowed at the crime scene. Every MPD officer was on the original Jimmy Yates case eighteen months ago. Of course, they had to be re-approved by Parker before being allowed to cross the yellow tape. What an ass.

Matthews had called him a long time ago and let him know Walker's family was safe and secure behind a blanket of security provided by Mary's uncle, a few FBI agents stationed around the hospital, and MPD assigned a few plain-clothed officers around to try to get eyes on the doctor.

Scott had a well-needed laugh when Matthews told him how Mary's uncle went toe to toe with one of the newly assigned FBI agents. Apparently, the agent felt it was beneath him to be stationed out in the hall and thought it was more his level to be in the room with the victim. When the agent attempted to breach the room, Alex, the congressman's head of security, blocked his way. The FBI agent threatened to put him in handcuffs if he didn't move, and didn't take kindly to a lowly security guard snickering at his threat.

Agent Matthews sat in the corner during the confrontation, of course, and watched with a smile on his face. Alex stood his ground and told the agent he was not allowed inside Mary's room, which he didn't like. And when the agent reached for Alex's hand, Alex moved so quickly he had the agent on the ground before he could start to read him his rights.

It was then Matthews finally moved from his chair next to Mary's bed. The only reason he decided to get involved was because the agent was starting to yell, and if he woke Caleb up, he'd have to toss the agent down the hall himself.

Matthews hadn't made it to the door to break up the confrontation when the congressman grabbed the agent by the back of the collar and pulled him out of the room. Alex followed, pulling the door shut behind him. Giving a quick glance back to Mary and Caleb to assure the commotion hadn't woken them. The agent was bringing up his fist, turning to confront the threat behind him, when he saw Agent Walker standing with the person who'd grabbed him.

Before Devon could say anything, Congressman Carter had his phone pulled out, dialed Chief Parker, told him to come get his "pup", and hung up the phone. Then he proceeded to lay into the agent and tell him if he ever placed a hand on one of his employees again, he'd not just lose his badge, but never even be able to get a job as a rent-a-cop.

A few times, the young agent looked to Walker for help, but none was given. When the congressman was done with his beratement, he turned toward Mary's door, and Alex opened it and let him pass. Without even saying a word, Walker and Alex followed him into the room and shut the door, leaving the agent jaw-dropped, looking questionably at the door.

Dang, Scott wished he could've seen that interaction. Hopefully, he'd be able to join them at the hospital soon and help with the search.

Smitty shouted for Scott from the basement as everyone else was packing up. "Scott, get down here!"

"What do you have, Smitty?"

Smitty hopped excitedly from one foot to the other. "We hit the jackpot, Scott. We not only have incriminating evidence against that doctor you were looking for, but there's tons of evidence against Yates. Not that it matters anymore because Yates is dead, but the stuff we found will help us to understand his motives better."

Without even stopping for a breath, he continued. "Everything was so well hidden, the techs almost missed it. It was only found with the help of some fancy, very expensive equipment the chief can't bug me about being a waste of money any longer. In the back corner of the basement is a very old access hatch to the chimney. It was packed over with dirt, so they almost missed it.

"You'll never believe what we've pulled out so far, and we barely scratched the surface. The chimney is packed to the brim with things, it will take us a while to sort through it all. There has to be another access port somewhere upstairs feeding into the chimney because of how these items are stacked on top of each other. I sent some guys upstairs to start looking around to see what they could find. I just thought you'd want to be here with us as we bring everything out in case anything stands out as time sensitive."

Scott slapped him on the back. "Smitty, you're amazing, a freaking rockstar. Yes, you're absolutely correct, I want to look through everything you pull out. Anything to help them catch the person threatening Agent Walker's family. Let's go. If you're correct, we're going to have a lot of evidence to sort through."

Everyone was energized; the space filled with activity. The forensic techs were moving around the basement, never stopping for a moment. Within minutes, tables were placed in every open area and covered with sanitized cloths, and flood lights illuminated every nook and cranny until the basement looked like it was bathed in sunlight.

Agent Scott was about to call his chief when Smitty interrupted him, calling him over to a table where a new box had been placed.

"Hey, Scott. You might want to get your partner, or hell, everyone, back over here. From what I remember about the Yates case, I think you guys vastly under-analyzed how many people he murdered."

Scott moved to see what Smitty was talking about and almost became ill when he saw what was being spread out over the table. There had to be hundreds of Polaroid pictures, and each one showed a clear image of a dead body missing its face. Smitty knew instantly these were Yates's victims because they all had his signature. His sadistic, demented signature. The number of pictures dramatically outnumbered the amount of faces on the wall. Could Yates have another hiding place?

One of the techs came over to the table holding two more dirty cardboard boxes. As he gently lifted the lid of the first one, Scott could see even more pictures inside of the same thing, and some different. Damn it.

The second box was in a little better shape, but what the box contained was just as disturbing. There were photos of Yates and what looked to be the doctor Matthews went over to the hospital to warn Walker about and in turn, arrest.

After donning a pair of gloves, Scott laid out the pictures from the second box on a clean table. It looked like the theory about Yates never taking a partner just got blown out of the water. There were pictures of the doctor going back to when she was possibly a teenager.

Could this woman be related to Jimmy Yates? He didn't think so. When they had pulled the background on him, they found no living relatives. They also knew for a fact he'd never been married or claimed any children.

In quick time, Scott, Smitty, and the rest of the technicians had all the tables in the room covered with cardboard bankers' boxes. Each was filled to the brim, containing horrors that shouldn't exist in a civilized world. Yet here they were, and every piece of evidence would need to be gone over with a fine-toothed comb, and then gone over again, and finally cataloged.

Smitty set down a few boxes, of what he felt was high-interest evidence, on a table directly under three spotlights. One of the boxes had writing on the side, but it was so old and dirty, it was no longer legible. The items on the inside, however, were clearly marked and gave Smitty the chills.

He carefully picked up the first Polaroid of a little girl in pigtails and red lipstick, riding a bike with the biggest smile on her face. The haunting part was it was taken right in the street right in front of the house they were currently searching. Smitty knew this had to be Mary as a little girl. Who else could it be?

After gathering up and laying out enough pictures to cover most of the tabletop, he knew he found the surveillance photos Yates took of the Anderson family after he decided they were his next targets. It was a good thing Yates was already dead because if Walker ever saw these, he'd want to kill him all over again.

Smitty hesitatingly pulled out his phone to call Chief Parker, who picked up on the second ring.

"I hope you found something, Smitty. I have the brass breathing down my neck because you guys are on the live news."

"Oh, we found something all right. We found the motherload of disgusting murder memorabilia. Yates kept everything, and I mean so much that he could be classified as a hoarder. He mustn't have cared about being caught with incriminating evidence, because if he were still alive, there would be no beating these charges."

"So tell me what you found," Parker cut in, exhaling loudly to convey his eagerness.

"We found everything from the missing faces to actual photos of families he had to have taken when he decided they were his targets. There are also photos of Mary that start from when she was a child and go into adulthood. I'm having all the evidence packed up and we'll be heading back to the office with the first load presently. I've already called ahead and am having an area staged and ready to receive us.

"Good," Parker said quickly before disconnecting the call.

After giving a quick peek into another box, Smitty knew he'd need much more space to analyze the evidence they'd found. The dingy basement wouldn't hold nearly a fraction of what they were pulling out of the chimney and the hidden room. He needed to move everything back to his lab, and he'd need help. He'd need lots and lots of help.

Chapter 12

It was crazy how fast an entire area could change and be repurposed when an emergency arose. By the time the forensic vans were loaded and made the trip across town, the FBI field office's parking garage was emptied and turned into a temporary staging area for all the evidence Smitty and his team retrieved from the house where Yates stored all his sadistic trophies.

When he left the parking garage not many hours ago, the space before him was dingy and dark, and never a place he'd remotely consider safe to store evidence. Now, it was like a miracle occurred. In place of the fluorescent lights that barely allowed you to read a report you were holding in your hands, there were state-of-the-art crime scene portable lights that made the parking garage brighter than high noon in an open field.

There also wasn't a single vehicle parked within the walls. Smitty's van was parked at the entrance, where the evidence was unloaded, then moved by hand cart. In every open space, a table was set up and ready to be filled with evidence, and that's exactly what Smitty was going to do.

After opening the first few boxes, Smitty refused to let anyone else help him lay out the items and directed them to start sorting what was already on the tables on the other side of the room. As sickened as he was by every item he touched, he had an overwhelming need to quickly examine every single item before anyone else laid eyes on them. Once he had them spread out on the tables in a predetermined pattern only he understood, his technicians instantly knew what needed to be done without additional orders.

Smitty had only ever had this unreasonable reaction to evidence once before, and that was during the case of a missing girl and her younger brother. He felt only he was capable of solving the case, which was complete bullshit and he knew it. In the back of his mind, he knew his team was top of their fields, but he couldn't explain what had come over him. This was the same feeling, and no matter what he did, he couldn't shake it.

It took hours, but all the boxed contents were finally on display. After Smitty laid the final VHS tape onto the corner of the table, he bolted over to the trash can and proceeded to expel anything and everything his stomach contained.

Knowing he wouldn't be able to explain the sight before him, he opted to just pull out his phone and send Matthews a message. The message was simple:

Evidence is ready, you need to see ASAP, bring Walker. Warn him it's bad.

One of the technicians was standing off to the side holding out a bottle of water. Smitty took the bottle, grateful to rinse his mouth, and for the drink, before heading back to the tables. He'd get to work instead of waiting. Knowing they wouldn't take long to get there, he wanted to have something to tell them when they arrived.

Mary slept peacefully in the hospital bed, Caleb held in her arms. Patricia hovered close with her hands always nearby. She was worried poor Caleb would move and fall from Mary's arms. Devon had seen her do this same thing when Mary fell asleep with Caleb in her arms not long after he was born.

At the time, Patricia would sit on the floor below Mary in preparation to catch Caleb since they often fell asleep together on the sofa. Only once had she ever taken him from her arms, and that was only because Caleb started to stir, and Mary needed to rest. Or at least that's what Patricia told Devon when he started to laugh at her protectiveness.

Devon made sure to catch moments like that on camera for his wife so she'd be able to cherish them for the rest of her life. He was secretly putting together a photo album for Caleb's first birthday as a surprise to Mary.

He himself said a thank you every day for the two loving people that raised his wife and helped her overcome the most horrific time of her life.

Matthew's phone gave a soft ding in his pocket. One glance from his partner and Devon knew whatever was in that text message wasn't good. Matthews gave a quick nod of his head and moved towards the door. Handing his phone to Devon, he said,

"You don't need to go. Stay with Mary, and I'll fill you in on what they got."

Matthews knew it was futile to argue when Devon started shaking his head.

Devon walked over to Mary, leaned over, and gently gave her and Caleb each a kiss on their foreheads.

Robert joined them, not wanting to be left out. "What's going on?"

Devon and Matthews shared a quick glance before Matthews began to speak. "I just received a text from our head of forensics. There's some evidence he pulled from Yates' old house, and he's asking I meet him at the office right away. And before you ask, he didn't tell me what he found, only to get there quickly."

"Okay. Then I'm going with you."

"No, Robert," Devon said. "Stay here and I'll call you when we find out what's going on. You know I won't keep anything from you concerning our family."

After Robert gave a curt nod in understanding, Matthew and Devon turned to leave. Robert grabbed hold of Devon's arm, stopping him before he could walk out the door, fury back in his eyes. "I want your answer before you walk out the door, Devon. What are you going to choose? Are you going to choose this investigation, or do I take Mary and Caleb away and make them safe?"

Devon's shoulders tensed. He had to remember Robert only had Mary and Caleb's safety in mind. "Robert, my family is the most important thing in the world to me. If Mary asked me this second to quit the FBI, I'd walk down there right now and turn in my gun and badge. I've already been working on safe houses and security for them, we've just been very busy.

"As soon as she is released from the hospital, neither one of them will be anywhere near D.C., and neither will I. Matthews will keep me updated on the case because he's my best friend, Caleb's godfather, Mary's friend, and my partner. So as soon as we leave D.C., I'm hands-off. Right now, I'm going to see what forensics found and see if I can be of any assistance. Good?"

Robert gave a quick nod, and visibly relaxed. "Good."

Without another word, Devon walked out the door Matthews was holding open for him. Of course, his partner couldn't keep anything serious. He ruined the mood as soon as he opened his damn mouth.

"Aw, so you really feel that way, Walker. We're best friends, truly? Can we have matching friendship bracelets? Or tattoos? What about pictures? Can we get pictures together for my Christmas card this year? My parents will be so proud."

Devon punched the down button on the elevator. "Really, Matthews. You're going to make me regret ever admitting that you're my friend."

"No, Walker. Not just friends. You called me your best friend. To do take backs would be rude, and impossible, because I have a witness that heard you say it. Plus, you'd hurt my feelings."

The sigh Walker let out was loud enough the people outside the elevator probably heard him. "You're an ass, Matthews. How anyone puts up with you, I'll never know."

Matthews kept his mouth shut but didn't even try to hold back his grin.

Chapter 13

Devon and Matthews walked into the FBI parking garage and then stopped in their tracks. After the cryptic text message from Smitty, Devon expected a few tables with the morbid trophy items from Yates's murder sprees. What he was not expecting was for almost every foot of space to be occupied with tables. There was only enough room to walk single file between them. "Every crime scene light they had in stock was constructed and strategically placed around the area, further congesting the space.

"Holy shit," Matthews said under his breath. "Where was all this hiding?"

"What is it?" Devon asked, confused.

"I can't believe they found all this at the Smith residence. When I was there, Scott and I only found the secret room that held a creepy ass altar and the wall of Yates' victim's faces. I didn't see a single box while we were clearing the house."

"I've seen the blueprint of that house. I wonder where Yates had all this stashed. Surely it wasn't all in that room."

"No, I would've seen if this was all in there. Granted, I was focused on the picture of that woman, but all of this" —he waved his hands around— "had to be hidden somewhere else."

From across the room, Matthews spotted Scott who had a clipboard in hand, meticulously cataloging every single item on his assigned table and then marking it with a little silver flag. That was Smitty's personal process of cataloging extreme amounts of evidence so not a single piece was ever missed. Cases are lost in court on mistakes as minor as a single typo on an evidence log, so Smitty was insane about his paperwork.

Matthews made a beeline across the room, and though it was funny, it also wasn't, when Scott jumped nearly three feet at the slight tap to his shoulder. "Damn it, Matthews. Are you trying to give a guy a heart attack?"

Confused, Matthews looked to Devon for assistance but found none. "Sorry, Scott. I wasn't trying to sneak up on you or anything. I thought you heard us walking up. What has you so jumpy, anyway?"

Scott waved his hands around, indicating everything in the room was the cause of his attitude. "This crap is the reason I'm jumpy. I've seen shit like this in movies, but I never imagined seeing it in real life. Maintenance has had to empty the trash cans so many times I've lost count because everyone keeps throwing up. Yates was even more of a psychopath than anyone could ever imagine. Walker, when the threat to your family is over, you really should let Mary take a look at all this. She'd be able to spend the rest of her career just analyzing one of these boxes."

Devon picked up the photo closest to him and shuddered. "Mary might agree with you, and I know for a fact she'd be interested, obsessed may be a better description, but there's no way in hell she's getting close to anything in this room. She'd never get the images out of her head or stop thinking about what could've happened with her parents. No, hell no. She'll never even hear about any of this. You mention it to her, Scott, and I'll make sure you're on traffic duty for the next year."

Scott put his hands up in defeat. "I understand, sorry I mentioned it."

Looking around the room, Smitty was nowhere to be seen. Matthews was very curious about what he found, and why he insisted he brought Walker. Every agent was informed that Walker was supposed to be hands-off on the investigation, but they'd have a better chance catching air with a butterfly net than keeping Walker completely off of this case.

"Hey, Scott. Where's Smitty?" Matthews asked.

Scott ran his fingers through his hair, shaking his head. "He's locked in his office. It's the weirdest thing. He had an old VHS player dug out from the basement and hooked up to the TV in his office. He won't let anyone else inside. His poor intern tried to see if he needed anything and Smitty practically ripped his head off yelling to go away and tell everyone not to disturb him."

Devon and Matthews shared a look of bewilderment. In all the years either of them has known Smitty, they've never known him to raise his voice, even remotely, unless it involved sports. And now he was yelling at interns. Something was going on, and they were going to figure out what. Apparently, Smitty had found something, and Devon wanted to know what it was.

The two agents, ignoring questions from other forensics technicians, quickly left the parking garage and made their way to Smitty's office. Devon carefully jiggled the doorknob and found Scott was correct. Smitty had, in fact, locked everyone out.

Devon wanted to see what Smitty was up to and didn't want to give him time to hide whatever he was watching on that old VHS player. With a quick nod to Matthews, his partner dropped to his knees, pulled out his lock-picking kit, and made quick work on the office door. There wasn't a lock yet that Matthews wasn't able to break.

No matter what Devon was expecting Smitty to have found in that basement, nothing could have ever prepared him for the images on the screen and the horrific screams coming from its speakers. Devon's knees buckled, and he barely registered Matthews' hands under his arms, supporting him, and guiding him to a chair next to the door.

Smitty's eyes grew wide with shock as he turned around at the noise and saw the two agents had entered the room despite the door being locked. He quickly registered Devon's distress. He was such a fool; Devon never should've seen what was on the screen. That's why the damn door was locked. How could he forget that Matthews was an expert at picking locks?

On the screen before them was Devon's beautiful wife, chained to the cold, wet, floor. A plastic bag covered her head, and Jimmy Yates stood over her. He was laughing while Mary fought for her life. Pure enjoyment spread across Yates' face.

With one glance at the video, anyone could see that she was trying to fight back, fight for her life, but being restrained, she couldn't. She had told Devon about her time with Yates, and he knew that during the moment playing on the screen, Mary thought for a fact she was going to die, and almost did.

Smitty jumped up to cover the screen as he fumbled for the power button. Stammering out an apology, he said, "Agent Walker, I'm so sorry. No one told me you were here. How did you get in here? Why didn't you knock?"

Devon couldn't respond. He scarcely lifted his head enough to look Smitty in the eyes.

"What the hell was that, Smitty? No. We know what that was. Where did you get that, and why the hell are you watching it? Better question, why are you watching it in a locked room?" Matthews asked, unable to keep the outrage from his tone.

Smitty hung his head with remorse. "It was in a banker's box in Yates's chimney, and it's not the only one. I'm assuming you both already saw the tables full of evidence, there are four boxes that I have in here full of VHS just like this one. Apparently, Yates videotaped everything he did. He taped the stalking of his victims, the preparation he conducted before the murders took place, the murders themselves, and even the cleanup."

Pointing to some boxes in the corner, Smitty continued, "Those two boxes were from the time Mary was kidnapped. I had the door locked because I didn't want anyone else to see what I was watching because of who was on the video. Everyone in the agency knows Mary, and I wanted to keep these private except for notifying Chief Parker and only those with need to know. That's why I texted you, Matthews, and told you to get over here and bring Walker. Again, Walker, I'm so sorry you had to see this without me preparing you. I wanted to be able to tell you what was on them, not for you to see them yourself."

Walker was about to explode. Even with the TV off, the images were still playing over and over in his mind. Those images were going to haunt him for a very long time.

Devon knew at some point, he'd force himself to watch those tapes in their entirety, but not today. Right now, he needed to get out of that room. He'd do the last thing anyone would expect him to do, he'd go help Scott catalog evidence.

Once Matthews saw Walker push through the door at the end of the hall leading out of the forensic lab, he turned back into the office, closed the door, and replaced the lock. Smitty was standing by the TV, looking anxious to resume the video he was watching. If Matthews didn't know Smitty so well, he'd think he was acting creepy, but he knew his mind was reeling with unanswered questions.

Smitty could feel the anger pulsating off Matthews. After a few moments, he finally got the nerve to look up and meet his eyes.

"I could wring your scrawny neck, Smitty. What the hell would possess you to send me a message to bring Walker here to see this crap? You should've called me, so I could've discretely come over here without him. What were you thinking? No, no. I got it. You weren't thinking at all. You're an idiot. I thought you were smarter than this. Hell."

With every sentence, Smitty inched further away from Matthews. He was afraid of what the agent was going to do to him. He and Walker were more brothers than partners, and when you made one mad, you better watch out for the other one.

Putting his hands up in surrender, he tried to explain. "Listen, in my defense, I had my door locked for a reason. Neither one of you were supposed to see these videos. Chief Parker is going to have my ass. He told me not to let Walker see these without being briefed first."

Wrong words, wrong words. The moment the words left his mouth, he realized it was the wrong thing to say because Matthews started walking towards him again with fire in his eyes.

"So, this is our fault? You were the one that called us down here. All your technicians plus agent Scott were telling us how concerned about you they are because you seemed to have shut yourself away from everything going on with the other evidence, so we wanted to make sure you were okay. Just take responsibility and tell me what the hell is going on."

"You're right, you're right. Sorry. Yes, I called you both down here, but I only wanted you to see everything else we recovered regarding Mary. I never intended on Walker seeing these videos. I didn't even start the first one until after I sent you that message. I need him to take a look at the pictures on the tables. Both Yates and Kadlec were obsessed with Mary, there may be something here that helps you figure out where she is hiding out."

Matthews moved to the door, unlocked the bolt, and held it open. "Well, if you wanted us to see these photos, let's go see these photos."

"What? Right now?" Smitty looked longingly back at the TV.

Matthews snapped, "Yes, right now. I don't know what has you so transfixed with those videos. I'm hoping it's you just doing your job. Right now, we are going to go look at what you called me down here to look at. I don't care if I need to drag you out of here kicking and screaming because I will, and right now, I'd enjoy dragging you up those stairs by your hair. Don't test me right now, Smitty."

Admitting defeat, Smitty walked to his desk, picked up a clipboard, and went out his door. He made sure to huff as he passed Matthews, letting him know how annoyed he was.

Matthews closed the door behind him, then moved to lead the way to the parking garage. "Suck it up, buttercup. Let's go."

Chapter 14

The parking garage was bustling with activity. Chief Parker had finally arrived after briefing his boss, and unfortunately, so had Congressman Carter. Matthews noticed the arrival and after quickly scanning the room, found Walker standing next to a table, wearing evidence gloves, holding a Polaroid picture in his hands. The look on his friend's face was a mix of confusion and sorrow.

Being so focused on the image in his hands, Devon didn't even see or hear Matthews approach. He only became aware of his presence by the hand that now cuffed his shoulder in a show of support.

"She's never going to be safe, is she Matthews? No matter what I do, I'm never going to be able to keep my family safe. First, it was Jimmy, now this crazy doctor. When will it ever end? When will Mary be able to stop looking over her shoulder and just enjoy her life?"

No words he could say would help his friend from feeling completely helpless. Reaching over, he clasped Devon on the other shoulder in a silent show of support. A response wasn't needed at that moment for Devon to know Matthews would be right there with him, doing everything within their powers to protect Mary and Caleb.

Matthews looked over and spotted the congressmen wrapping up his conversation with Parker. He gave a nod and then made his way toward Walker. Yes, the congressman had every right to be as infuriated and distressed about the items laid out on display, but after the verbal lashing he gave Walker earlier, he didn't believe his friend was up for another round. Maybe he'd be able to intercept him and direct him to the other side of the room, giving Walker some space.

All his worrying was for nothing.

When Robert was no less than five feet from Walker, Walker put a hand up. "Stop right there, Robert. I know exactly what you're going to say. I'm warning you right now that I'm not in the right headspace to hear a lecture, especially after walking in on the video the lead forensic agent was viewing earlier.

"I checked with my people that were trying to secure a safe location for me to take my family when they are released from the hospital, but they haven't come up with any that meet my approval yet. So, I'm asking for your help. I don't care if we need to hire a doctor to take with us, but Mary and Caleb will get moved within the next twenty-four hours. If I need to kidnap Doctor Chase, that's exactly what I'll do. But I guess I shouldn't be admitting that while standing in the FBI building. I also want that house so jam-packed with security that we'll be tripping over them. I want them so close that one is within reaching distance at all times to Mary and Caleb. I'm going to go tell Parker my plans, then I'm going home to pack. Let me know what you arrange."

Robert turned to Matthews, looking completely confused, as Devon walked away from both of them without another word. "Well, that was unexpected. But I'll get it done. He'll get everything he asked for, and more if I get my way." He was already pulling out his phone to call his head of security.

In Matthews' experience with Alex, he'd be able to get everything on Robert's list in a few hours. Alex had more connections in D.C. than even Matthews did, and that was a long list.

Matthews turned to walk away when Robert stopped him. "Matthews, what video was Devon talking about?"

Smitty had just returned to his office and was about to turn the TV back on when there was a pounding on the door. A pounding that suggested the person on the other side was enraged. He hesitated, allowing himself one deep breath before he answered. "Chief Parker, what can I do for you?"

The chief never came down here. If he needed anything, Smitty was always summoned to him. Whatever the reason for his visit, it wasn't good.

Parker pushed his way into the small office. "Smitty, you are my best forensic scientist, but I just heard something disturbing. I want some answers, and I want them now. Agent Walker made an off-hand remark about a certain video you were watching, but he happened to make this remark to Congressman Carter. From what I'm told, the video was about Mary, whom you know is Congressman Carter's niece and Walker's wife. You better tell me what's going on because it took all my authority to keep him from storming down here himself and tearing your office apart. I had to remind him that this was an ongoing investigation, and I could have him removed from the building unless he got a court order. Now, tell me I didn't just piss off a very powerful man for no reason."

"Yes. Yes, Sir." Smitty quickly stammered. "Of course. Please know that I wasn't doing anything unethical or immoral by bringing these down here and locking the door while I viewed the videos. These are videos that absolutely shouldn't be viewed in the common evidence room, especially with the connection to Agent Walker. After noticing a pattern on multiple banker's boxes, I assumed what these videos contained. The boxes that seemed to contain early pictures and news articles about Mary and her family were marked with a red x in the lower right corner. After opening a few more boxes, I found what looked like his surveillance pictures and marked videos from the time he came back to D.C. to stalk Mary and they continued up until right before he died.

"There were a few boxes that were marked with bigger red x's, but the videos weren't marked, but the pictures that were inside were of the time Mary spent alone with Yates after he abducted her. Seeing the pain and fear in her eyes made me want to pass this investigation on to someone else. But I couldn't do it. I couldn't fathom the idea of another agency coming in and taking these videos and putting them in storage somewhere when there may be vital information about catching the woman that is threatening Agent Walker's family. I read the report of his interview in the hospital and knew if I was correct about what was on the tapes, I needed to find whatever evidence I could. Someone had to watch them, and I'm a professional, so it had to be me. I couldn't let one of the new guys do this, it is my job. I'd never forgive myself if something was missed and someone was hurt because of me.

"Then something got me thinking, how would these pictures and videos end up with the rest of his items when he conceivably didn't have time to take them back to his house and hide them between the time he performed these heinous acts and when he was apprehended?"

"That's great thinking. It had to be the woman that moved them and placed them in that chimney where you found the rest of the items," Parker concluded.

"Yes, exactly. And while the rest of my technicians were dusting every item for fingerprints other than Yates or Kadlec, I just needed to make sure there wasn't another player. We need to make sure that after this last threat against Mary is neutralized, the Walker family can finally be at peace.

"I never wanted anyone else to see these videos. I, of course, was going to give you a full report, but anyone that has a relationship with Walker and his family would find the images on these videos impossible to ever remove from their minds. Walker and Mary don't need people to look at them with pity, so the less people that see these videos, the better."

Parker, looking at the TV, nodded in agreement.

"I will tell you this, Chief," Smitty said. "After watching the few videos I have, I've come to the conclusion that Mary's the strongest woman I've ever met. Anyone that thinks otherwise is a damn fool. This Kadlec was lucky with the bomb because she was a coward and didn't approach Mary face to face. After seeing her fight for her life in these videos, I, for one, would bet on Mary any day of the week."

Chapter 15

Devon wasn't at the hospital when Robert returned from speaking to Chief Parker at the FBI building. Robert walked into Mary's room and found her playing with Caleb in the bed and then noticed Patricia was nowhere to be found. The only other person in the room was Patricia's head of security, which made her lack of presence all the more questionable since he never leaves Patricia's side. By Robert's orders, of course.

Alex was one of Robert's closest friends. So, when Robert contacted him, after he entered into politics, and asked him to take on the dangerous task of protecting his wife, Alex jumped at the opportunity and never made Robert question his decision a day of his life. Alex was as much a part of the family as Mary was. Robert and Patricia were even godparents to his children. So, for him not to be in the same room as Patricia when there was a security risk was alarming.

After greeting his niece and great-nephew with a kiss on the forehead, he addressed his friend. "Alex, where's Patricia?"

If Robert wasn't watching, he'd have missed the pleading glance shared between Alex and Mary. "Well, Sir," Alex started to explain, but Mary interrupted.

"Now, Uncle, when Aunt Patricia demands something, you know she gets her way. Alex was just following her orders to stay here."

Robert shook his head, trying to follow what Mary was talking about. She was playing games, taking her time getting to the point. She had always done this, ever since she was a little girl, when she was trying to keep something from him.

"Where, Alex?" Robert asked again.

"Well... That's the thing. We don't exactly know, sir," Alex stated, barely above a whisper.

Whipping his head to meet his friend's gaze, unbelieving what he just heard, Robert roared, "What the hell do you mean you don't know where she is? Your number one job is to keep her in your sight at all times. Are you telling me you lost my wife?"

Mary's laugh unsettled her uncle. "Oh, do calm down, Uncle, you're upsetting Alex, and I won't have it. She has the other four security guards with her, she's in no way alone. She got a call from Devon, kissed my forehead, ordered Alex to stay here and protect me, then rushed out the door. She didn't even give poor Alex time to argue. He'd have to have tackled her to get her to stay in this room. If he would've chased after her, it would've left me completely alone. The only reason he let her leave is that Devon sent him a message that he was picking her up downstairs and she stated she was taking the rest of the security team that was stationed in the hallway. Which I can bet Devon was not all too happy about. I'd love to have seen his face when they all started climbing into his car."

That made Robert smile. As much as he loved Devon, he also loved watching him squirm. The question now was, what were Devon and his wife up to? He knew Devon was in rare form after witnessing what was pulled from Yates's house. Hell, so was he. Seeing pictures of his sister and brother-in-law, taken only days before their death, spread all over a table, had brought back so many feelings he'd been fighting for years to control.

His composure damn near snapped when Chief Parker told him what the lead forensic scientist had found in another box of evidence. Robert couldn't even imagine the emotions Devon was feeling after seeing what happened to his wife. Of course, Mary told him every detail of what had occurred, but seeing a video of her actual torture was worse than the images he must have created from her story.

After talking to Parker, it made complete sense why Devon handed control of finding a safe house over to Robert and his security team. Devon wanted his family moved, and he knew Robert had the right strings he could pull to make it happen. Robert was pulling his phone out to give Devon a call to figure out where the hell he took his wife when Dr. Chase walked in the door.

"How are my two favorite patients doing today?" Dr. Chase said.

Mary's cheeks turned scarlet, and Robert instantly knew why. Dr. Chase had an uncanny resemblance to Sean Connery, her favorite actor. "We are good, Doctor. Caleb is ready to bust out of here, and so am I. Please tell me you're here to give us our discharge papers?"

Walking to the side of her bed, Dr. Chase pulled up Mary's chart on the computer and started to read. "Caleb is fit and ready to go. Your husband just wanted to keep him here as long as you were still admitted. Which I agreed upon. You are looking good, but the nurse indicated you are still having bouts of dizziness, and only picking at your food. That is perfectly normal and to be expected with the head injury you received."

Taking the penlight out of his pocket, he started slowly moving it back and forth in front of her eyes asking her to follow the light. "Your husband called me a little bit ago and requested both your and your son's medical charts be sent to his official FBI email. It's a little unorthodox, but I learned not to question your husband. He also has power of attorney, so it was completely legal. He explained that within the next day, he would be demanding discharge papers, so for me to get you ready to leave.

"I requested a few more days for observation, but he explained a retired nurse friend of your aunts was going to be staying with you for the foreseeable future. He wouldn't tell me more than that, he said for security reasons. Because of the threat to your and your son's safety, I approved the transfer and made sure he had all my private contact information in case he needed to reach out."

During the evaluation, Robert leaned against the wall next to Alex and remained silent, realizing how serious Devon was when he gave him the twenty-four-hour deadline to find a safe house. As it seemed, Devon was already well on his way to fulfilling his end

113

of the deal by obtaining a live-in nurse, so now Robert needed to step it up.

Dr. Chase was still speaking to Mary when Robert received a text message. As Robert glanced at the screen, Alex saw Robert's brows scrunch together.

"Is everything okay, Sir?"

"Everything's fine, Alex. Patricia just wants to know where the keys to the RV are and she's asking if I want the four-wheelers in the garage or taken to storage. What is this woman up to?"

Alex let out a chuckle. He'd been friends with Robert and Patricia longer than he's been working for them, so he knew Robert wouldn't take offense. "I would never assume to know what any woman is thinking unless she is so inclined to tell me."

"That's the best advice I've ever heard, Alex. Please tell that to my husband next time you see him," Mary called from across the room. Dr. Chase nodded, agreeing with Mary.

Alex couldn't keep a straight face; he'd never really tried to keep serious with Mary. Except with her safety. He'd watched Mary grow up from the moment she was taken into the Carter household. Then he watched out for her when he became employed as the head of security. She always was a cheeky little girl.

"Miss Mary, I'll be more than happy to tell that to Mr. Walker next time I see him. If you ever think he needs to be knocked down a peg or two, please keep me in mind. I'd love to go a round or two with your husband."

"How many times have I asked you to just call me Mary? You don't need to be so formal."

"At least a thousand. You know I can't help it. I've been calling you that since you were a little girl, and you can't make me stop."

The room filled with joyous laughter, a sound neither Alex nor Robert had heard in a long time. "Oh, Alex. You're such a dear one." I would never let you go up against my husband in a fight, even one just playing around. It may not seem like it all the time, because he can infuriate me to no end, but I do actually enjoy having him around. I've seen what the other men look like after training with you, and I don't feel like nursing Devon back to health or listening to him whine."

"As you wish, Miss Mary." Alex laughed as he replied. "But the offer will always be on the table."

When Patricia got an idea into her head, Devon learned the hard way to just stand back, take orders, and not question a single thing. From the moment Devon picked up the picture of Julia Kadlec kneeling next to one of Jimmy Yates' victims, he realized the level of crazy that woman could reach. He knew she was dangerous, hell, she tried to kill his family when she blew up the car, and he had a feeling she had something to do with Mary's traumatic delivery. But now he had concrete proof she liked to get her hands dirty with the crimes and wouldn't hesitate to get close to Mary and Caleb. This, Devon could not allow.

In an instant, he decided Mary and Caleb would leave right away. Caleb was already healthy enough to come home, and that just left getting the care he needed for Mary and the details of packing what they'd need for their trip. Patricia was the obvious choice to facilitate any and all decisions regarding both Mary's care and what Mary and Caleb would need necessity-wise.

Patricia had her fingers in so many different charity organizations and had made so many friends and contacts throughout her life, it was no surprise to Devon when he asked for a recommendation on an in-home nurse, she had one lined up in less than five minutes. Patricia held up her finger, pulled out her phone, called her friend Charlotte, and secured what she called the best retired nurse in the entire city to provide round-the-clock care for her niece. Charlotte agreed to live at the safe house for security purposes. Amazing was the only word to describe Mary's aunt.

The next task was to get down to packing. Neither one of them were sure about the accommodations Robert would be able to find on short notice, except that they would be safe. Because of this, Patricia was determined to pack damn near Caleb's entire nursery. She simply stated, "It just isn't reasonable for him to be without his toys if you guys don't know how long you'll be gone. We don't want the poor boy to be bored, now do we? So, we'll just take whatever I think he'll need."

Devon shook his head and left Patricia and two of her staff to pack up Caleb's room. He knew if he protested even one time about the number of items she wanted to take, he'd be hearing about it for years. He decided it best to pick his battles. It also helped that there was no way they had something to transport everything she intended to bring, so they'd have to downsize anyway.

He was wrong.

Packing was completed quickly and efficiently. Devon had a total of four bags, and none were very large. Mary always made fun of him for his packing style, since he had to separate everything. His bags consisted of one for work, one for everyday wear, one for workout and sleeping, and his toiletry bag. Nice and efficient. As he was placing his last bag by the front door, Patricia came down the stairs and joined him.

"Oh, Devon." She waved her hands at the bags. "What's this?"

"These are the bags I packed for myself. I figured I'd go start on Mary's items next."

The look of disgust on her face didn't faze him in the slightest.

"No, darling. I'll see to Mary's packing. Why don't you go see what items you've missed packing for yourself? The RV will be here soon to collect these items and be on standby to deliver them to whatever address Robert decides." She turned and walked away before he could ask any of the many questions rushing through his brain.

Will, one of Patricia's security team, waited until she was out of the room before he started laughing at the expression on Devon's face.

Turning to face him, Devon asked, "Did she just say RV?"

Trying, and failing, to hold in his grin, Will said, "Yes, sir. She did. She called one of the staff at her house to clear out and ready the RV to be brought over here to load all the luggage inside. She was worried that you'd make her leave some baggage behind if she didn't personally provide adequate transportation. Those were her words exactly."

"Well, son of a bitch. That's exactly what I was going to do."

Chapter 16

After doing another once over to see if there was anything he missed packing for himself, Devon took his bags outside. There was so much stuff piled in the driveway, Devon would've been surprised to find anything left inside the house. It seemed Patricia had cleared everything out. After heading back inside, Will helped Devon pack up Mary's painting supplies, a hobby she'd picked up after finding out they were expecting Caleb. She said it helped calm her mind. When Devon snapped the last case shut, he turned to Will. "It looks like we're packing to never return. If it were up to me, we'd each have an overnight bag and nothing more. We aren't going on a vacation. I'm hiding my family from a psychopath trying to harm them."

They laughed together about it until they noticed Patricia standing in the doorway with her hands on her hips. Will immediately stopped laughing and straightened his posture. Devon just gave her a smile, acting like a child trying to make nice to avoid punishment. The young security guard acted like royalty had entered the room, and in all honesty, Patricia deserved all of the respect in the world. But Mary's aunt was not amused by Devon's opinion about what was necessary to pack or not.

"I'm going to assume the stress of the day has addled your brain. If you think for a moment I'd let my niece and great-nephew live out of an overnight bag for any time longer than a single night, you are out of your mind. Who knows how long you guys are going to be gone. I'm going to ensure you have every comfort. If I could, I'd damn well pack up your entire house. Do you doubt me?"

Suppressing a smile, he said, "No, ma'am. I don't doubt you at all. And if that is what you wish, I'll try not to complain."

A polite chuckle escaped her lips. "I don't believe that for a single moment. You'd complain all you please, Devon. You just wouldn't do it in front of me or where you think I'd be able to hear you." Without another word, she turned and walked down the hall towards the front door.

"Patricia certainly has a way of getting her point across without raising her voice," Devon muttered, and then let out a deep sigh of defeat, accepting his fate to pack far more than he would have otherwise planned.

"Come on, Will. Let's make Patricia happy and collect all the bags that have already been packed but need to be moved outside. She's right, especially during this trying time, I'd rather my family be comfortable and surrounded by their own items so it may bring them a little bit of joy. And maybe distract them from the real reason they are in hiding. Not that Caleb will know the difference. But having his toys around will help keep him entertained."

Nodding in agreement, Will picked up the two bags Patricia left at the painting studio's doorway and added them to the pile in the driveway, waiting to be loaded up when the RV arrived.

His wife was astonishing. When she wanted something done, she didn't waste time making it happen. Robert arrived at Devon and Mary's house as the RV pulled up to the curb outside their home. Robert parked in front of the RV. Every other available spot was filled with luggage, boxes, and items that were too large to properly pack. So, this is why Patricia wanted the RV. He should've known she'd do something like this.

Robert was surprised Devon allowed Patricia to virtually pack up their entire home, but after thinking about it for more than a second, he found he wasn't surprised at all. Unless it was something of dire importance, Devon would never deny the women in his life anything they wanted that was within his power to provide. Patricia was no exception.

As if she was able to sense his presence, Patricia appeared and leaned against the front entryway door frame. The love and joy on her face matched the way she looked at him when they first met. Even after all these years together, their love had only flourished, never fading, even after all the trials they'd endured. He stepped out of his car and struggled to navigate the mess covering the driveway.

Leaning down, he tilted Patricia's chin up and kissed her. She put her arms around him. "Hello, Darling. I see you've been busy. You have your security team running around all over the place."

From inside the house, a voice yelled out, "Like chickens, Sir, but we don't mind."

"Will!" Patricia exclaimed with humor in her voice. *He is such a cheeky devil*, she thought. Devon set down another box as he stepped up behind them. He glanced back to Will and then to Patricia, chuckling at their exchange.

Patricia and Robert shared a glance of gratitude. Devon needed more laughter in his life, especially now. Neither of them had heard him laugh in what seemed like forever. Hopefully, soon, they'd be able to have happiness back in their lives again. It was a rare thing to see unmitigated joy since the day Mary's car exploded, and it was a welcome change.

The joyful moment was interrupted when Robert's cell phone rang. For a split second, he was tempted to ignore the call, but he'd set the specific ringtone to an old friend who was searching for a safe house for his family. Holding up a finger, he whispered, "I'll be right back," to Patricia and Devon, as he pulled out his phone.

"George, what'd you have for me?" Robert asked.

"Mr. Carter, I got some great news. I have three very secure locations available right away. Two of them have everything you asked for, the last one doesn't have as many rooms. I'm going to send you the information on the first two now and let me know if you need the information on the last one. I still have feelers out for other options and will keep them out until you give me a final decision. Let me know what you think, and we can get your family relocated quickly."

"Thank you, George. I'm sorry I've not kept in touch the last few years; you must think I'm a horrible friend. When this is over, I'd love for you and your wife to come for a visit, and we can reminisce about the good old days. You haven't seen Mary since she was in elementary school."

"That would be great. Life gets in the way; we all know this. Yet as we get older, we miss how things used to be. Like how we never needed to worry about our family being targeted by psychotic murderers. I'll send this over to you right away, let me know what you think."

"Thanks, George. Talk to you soon."

One thing Robert never left home without was his laptop. Not five minutes after retrieving the computer from the car, Devon and Robert were seated at the dining room table, looking at the safe houses George sent. The two locations were as different as night and day, and they both knew immediately which one Mary would prefer.

Devon pointed to the screen. "That one, Robert. We need to go with location number two. If Mary ever found out we had a chance to stay at a home with its own personal lake in the middle of nowhere and we didn't choose it, I think she'd disown the both of us. Either one is going to require a large amount of security, but with location number one, I don't like the proximity of the neighbors. Neighbors are nosey, and the last thing we need right now is for either you or her to be recognized and end up on someone's social media page."

Robert nodded. "Yes, I agree. We'd be more secluded with the second option, therefore on our own, but I'd rather rely on our own men. The less people that know our location the better. With location number one, it looks more like a suburban neighborhood, though more spread apart than most. I agree, I don't want Mary and Caleb to be locked inside all day on the off chance someone would recognize them. With how much news has surrounded Mary in the last year, it is very likely someone would recognize her and leak a story. I want Caleb to be able to run around outside and play. Yes, location two it is. I'll give George a call right away and get everything else in motion."

Chapter 17

The next morning, what should have been an easy day turned out very demanding. Even though Patricia and her security team had almost everything set up in what was going to be their home for the foreseeable future, Devon could see and feel the stress radiating off Mary as they left the hospital. Her eyes darted everywhere, looking for threats.

He wanted his carefree wife back. He wanted her not to have to look over her shoulder every moment of every day. As they walked towards the parking lot, she held Caleb so tight he started wiggling to break free from her grasp. She wasn't even aware of what she was doing. Devon had asked her if she wanted him to bring his car seat up, and she refused, stating she wasn't letting go of him until they were safe in the car.

His wife had experienced more trauma and horrors in her short years than most people do in their entire lives. Hopefully one day, she'd be able to just live her life without worrying about stepping out the door or looking at every face she passed on the street. That day wasn't today. Though he'd do everything within his power to make sure she was able to breathe easily in the future.

The safe house was only forty-five minutes from the hospital, but it took them almost two hours to reach their destination. Patricia insisted on Devon utilizing Alex as his driver for the day, but Matthews assumed he'd be the driver. Devon didn't correct either one of them when both men walked into Mary's hospital room and announced the SUV was downstairs and ready to go. Alex and Matthews didn't come out and say anything, but they looked at each other like the other one was crazy.

Mary looked back and forth between them, then finally caught Devon's wink. She knew her husband's body language well enough to know when he was up to something, and he was *definitely* up to something. Alex and Matthews were very large, intimidating men. They were people Mary would never like to meet in a dark alley. Unable to hold it in any longer, Mary burst into laughter. Tears ran down her cheeks by the time she was able to gain her composure, and everyone turned to look at her. "Sorry, boys. I was just thinking about the old MTV show with the Claymation figures in the wrestling ring and the guy yelling 'let's get it on,' and thought to myself that you both look like you want to go a few rounds in the ring over who will drive us. I'm flattered, of course."

Alex, true to his nature, was the first to concede. He slapped Matthews on the back and walked over to where Devon piled Mary and Caleb's bags. "Now, Miss Mary. It's actually a good thing that you have both of us. Since Devon here is good for nothing, one of us will drive and one of us will watch for dangers." Before anyone could comment, he grabbed the bags and left the room, straight-faced.

Devon, on the other hand, looked like his jaw would hit the floor at any moment. How did this turn around on him? Matthews' full belly laugh made Caleb jump a little and his wide eyes seemed to search for his Godfather.

"Hey, Mr. Good-for-nothing, are you ready to go?" Matthews called out to Devon.

Devon shook his head in disbelief. "Matthews, you dick. You're supposed to be on my side. Always."

"Nope. I'll always have your back. I'll always protect your family. But anyone that can make fun of you like that—they become my new best friend."

Sputtering, Devon couldn't seem to put a sentence together.

Mary was thoroughly enjoying every moment of the show. "Don't worry, Matthews, I'll make sure Devon still feeds you."

"You always were my favorite, Mary," he said, giving her a wink.

"Like hell. He won't even get scraps," Devon grumbled as he stalked out the door.

Mary and Matthews looked at each other and chuckled.

The rest of the ride was blissfully silent. Devon's bad mood seemed to disappear as he watched the smile slowly spread across Mary's face and tears come to her eyes as they got closer to the safe house.

Based on the pictures, Devon knew this place was perfect. Hopefully once Mary saw everything the home came with, she wouldn't feel like this place was a prison but maybe a tiny vacation instead. Wishful thinking.

Patricia, Robert, and a team of security waited on the large wrap-around porch when the black SUV pulled up to the house. Patricia came bounding down the steps, holding one of Caleb's stuffed animals in her hands, hoping to grab up the baby and take him for a walk to get some fresh country air. She'd make sure both Mary and Caleb stayed outside as much as possible after being pent up in the hospital for three days.

Matthews, after exiting the passenger seat, opened the back door and offered his hand to assist Mary down from the SUV. Devon, on the other side of the vehicle, was unbuckling a sleeping Caleb and handing him to an impatient Patricia.

Mary was in awe of the view. If it was at all possible, the view of this lake was even more breathtaking than the one at her home, but she'd never tell Devon that. Completely enamored with watching the water, Mary tripped and gasped as Matthews threw out an arm and caught her around the waist.

After placing Caleb into Patricia's outstretched arms, Devon called out to Matthews. "My wife is on her feet now, Matthews. You can get your paws off her."

Hearing the annoyance in his friend's voice, Matthews leaned down and swept Mary up into his arms instead of letting her go. "Now, Devon. What kind of friend would I be if I let her trip and fall? No, this way is much more pleasant, for both of us. Wait... I mean safer, for Mary."

Mary dared to look up at Matthews, and he winked at her. It took all her power not to let her husband hear her laugh. She knew Devon was already in a rare mood, and his friend was poking at him and making it worse. But it was so much fun to watch the two banter back and forth.

"Matthews, I'm warning you now. I'll get you back for this. Mark my words. I'll never forget." Like a little kid, Devon stalked towards the house.

All eyes were on Devon's back. As soon as the front door slammed shut, Mary, Matthews, Robert, Alex, and the rest of the staff burst into laughter. Picking on Devon was so much fun.

Robert suggested everyone make their way inside and get comfortable, but Mary decided to sit on the porch and enjoy watching her aunt walk near the lake with Caleb. The two were trailed closely by Will and another guard. She wanted to enjoy the fresh air, and it was still hard for her to let her son out of sight. Robert glanced at Alex, who instinctively knew what he was asking and gave a slight nod, acknowledging he would stay on the porch to keep an eye on Mary.

After making sure Patricia and Mary were covered, Robert and Matthews made their way into the house where they found one hell of a racket coming from the kitchen. It sounded like pots and pans were flying everywhere. But no, it was just Devon angrily cooking dinner. He may be annoyed that his friends and family were getting immense enjoyment out of teasing him, but he'd never sink so low as to let them starve, or worse, eat a bad meal.

Linkin Park was blasting from Devon's phone when Matthews walked into the kitchen. "Dude, don't you have anything on that playlist from this century?" he called out.

"Linkin Park is fantastic," Devon responded with clenched teeth. "Get out of my kitchen," he said as he chucked an onion at Matthews' head.

The accuracy was impressive since Devon never once lifted his head from whatever he was peeling on the cutting board in front of him. After a quick glance to see where the onion landed, Matthews turned back to find Devon holding a very large knife and using it to point to the door.

"Everyone out. Now. Come back in forty-five minutes and not a second before," Devon said before he blocked everyone out again and was moving around the kitchen trying to find everything he'd need to make a decent meal. This was the first meal he'd cooked for his wife since the accident, and he was determined to make it freaking delicious.

Matthews knew Devon was stressed, and there were four ways he worked out his frustrations: gun range, wrestling mat, running track, or kitchen. At least when he chose the kitchen, Matthew got a good meal out of it instead of either running miles or having bruises for days. Being the good partner he was, Matthews was usually right there with him when he needed an outlet for his stress. Like a great friend, Devon did the same for him.

Exactly forty-five minutes later, everyone quietly waited in the doorway to the kitchen. Trying to suppress smiles, they watched Devon work. No one was going to enter the kitchen until

Devon noticed them and let them know it was okay to come into his domain.

As his last timer beeped on the oven, he pulled out the garlic bread. Instantly, the aroma filled the room and a collective sigh filled the air. That's when Devon noticed he had an audience.

"Don't just stand there. I cooked, someone else can come set the table."

Everyone moved at once. The food smelled so amazing. They all had eaten Devon's food before and knew how good it was; they wanted to dig in as soon as possible. Mary hung back and waited until everyone else had rushed past. Holding Caleb, she slowly made her way over to Devon, pushed onto her tippy toes, and gave him a tender kiss on the lips.

"Boy did I miss your cooking. I think I've lost twenty pounds eating that garbage at the hospital for the last three days. It smells amazing, baby. Thank you for cooking for everyone."

The praise from his wife meant more to him than if it came from a master chef. Mary loved him to the ends of the earth, this he never doubted. Sometimes it felt like she'd rather tease him than give him a compliment, but teasing was her love language. She said it was because she didn't want him to become more conceited. Which he had to admit, did keep him in line a bit.

Dinner was a surprisingly uneventful affair. There was no teasing Devon, only moans of pleasure for his cooking.

As dinner was winding down, Mary noticed it was already 9 p.m. All throughout dinner, Caleb was passed from person to person. Everyone wanted their share of snuggle time, but her son needed a bath before settling for bed.

Patricia quickly jumped to her feet when Mary announced she was taking Caleb for a bath and offered to do it for her. Mary's aunt was a miracle. She was the surrogate to the grandmother Caleb would never have. Mary couldn't stop the tears from falling down her cheeks as she nodded okay. She'd get Caleb's nursery ready as her aunt gave the baby a bath.

Two hours later, the kitchen was cleaned up and the baby was bathed and put to bed. All seemed well, yet Mary couldn't seem to shake her unease. It was a feeling she'd lived with for a while, as if waiting for her peace to be disturbed.

She'd try to make the best out of their situation. Her family had turned this safe house into a temporary home for her and Caleb, and she was grateful.

As Mary made her way down the stairs, she could hear the laughter coming from outside and went to investigate. Never in a million years would she have expected to see her husband and Matthews racing around the yard, apparently seeing who could catch the most lightning bugs. Everything was a competition with those two. All she could do was shake her head as she made her way over to sit on the steps next to her uncle. Seeing these men so carefree made her heart swell. She decided she'd enjoy tonight and worry about the horrors surrounding her family tomorrow.

Chapter 18

It had been three days since Mary and her spawn disappeared from the hospital. Even after hacking into the hospital security cameras to check the parking garages, ATM cameras across the street and within a three-block radius from the hospital, and traffic cameras, Julia couldn't gather any more information as to where they went. It was as if they'd simply disappeared.

Nobody can disappear into thin air in the age of technology, but Mary had her agent husband and corrupt politician uncle to whisk her away to parts unknown. Just because the cameras didn't pick anything up, didn't mean there were no clues to be found. Julia would just need to dig a little deeper. It would take a little work, but surely she'd be able to figure out what credit card companies they used and she'd just follow the money. Money trails never lie.

How could it be that everyone hovering around that bitch for her entire life had suddenly disappeared and no one is gossiping about it? When she was pretending to be a doctor, those nurses and residents lived to try to one-up each other on gossip, but the security cameras in the break rooms and outside the on-call rooms weren't picking up any chatter about Mary or her goon squad. *Weird.*

Everyone was trying to hide her, but Julia was smarter than any of them realized, and that'd be their downfall. She had to find the pattern; everyone had a pattern. Not one single person on the planet was completely untraceable. Hell, if the police or FBI would've done their damn jobs years ago, they would've been able to find her and Jimmy within days or, if she gave them the benefit of the doubt, weeks.

Doing a quick mental inventory of her supplies, she realized the first thing she needed to pick up was more equipment. Right after her attempt to blow the bitch up failed, and while everyone was occupied with Mary and her spawn in the hospital, Julia took the opportunity to place many cameras, inconspicuously, around the congressman's property. Which left her short-handed on equipment.

After watching and cataloging everything the FBI removed from Yates's home and loaded into their vans from afar, she was confident they hadn't found her technology stash. Still, it wasn't safe to return to the house to retrieve it, as it was surely being watched, but that was okay. She had access to all Yates' offshore accounts, and those funds were damn near limitless.

Jimmy was more than an expert serial killer; he was a master thief too. As a result, he was able to sufficiently support himself for years without a nine-to-five office job. She chuckled at the thought of the police never once questioning it. What, did they think he moonlighted as an investment broker? Morons.

No, after Jimmy fantastically murdered his deserving victims, he went around their houses to gather cash and other items he'd be able to sell on the black market that wouldn't attract any unwanted attention. This included stocks, bonds, and investment accounts his hacker friend could log into, transfer the funds into an untraceable account, take his twenty-five percent cut, and then send Jimmy the rest. It was the perfect partnership.

Julia thought Jimmy was crazy the first time she witnessed him shoving vintage toys into one of his canvas bags. That was until she saw the amount transferred into a dummy bank account by the person selling those items for him. The amounts were insanely large even after the seller took his cut. It became a game between the two of them—who could find the most valuable items to sell to keep their lifestyle going.

Jimmy always made sure money wasn't an issue, and for that, Julia was eternally grateful. She didn't need to worry about trying to hold a steady job or steal money for the things she needed. No, with access to Jimmy's bank account, she'd be able to have all fun and no work for the rest of her life. Now, to get to shopping for the necessities. Having her preferred surveillance cameras, microphones, and other necessities pre-saved on her phone, she added ten more items to her cart and hit buy. With the expedited shipping, they'd be delivered to her PO box tomorrow.

For today, she'd scope out the locations to strategically install the cameras for the most likely chance of catching repeat behavior and therefore have a target, or at least a lead to follow. Thinking about it, she jumped back online and ordered a few more gadgets for once a target was acquired. Every girl needs a basic bionic ear portable dish listening device. If people realized they had zero privacy with the technology anyone could get from the internet, they wouldn't feel safe, even in their own homes. But their ignorance was to her benefit.

It had only been three days since she'd left the hospital and come to the safe house, but Mary was already about to murder her husband. At least when they were back home, he'd leave the house to go to work or let her go into her office to work. From the time she was eight months pregnant, she's been teaching via video to her students at the university. Here, Devon was home all day long. Hovering. He didn't understand the need for personal space when he believed her safety was at risk, but who was going to be able to get her all the way out here other than him?

Last night, before bed, she'd told him she was going to the bathroom to brush her teeth. Not two minutes later, while she was on the toilet, the door flew open. Finding no threat, he had the audacity to lean against the door jamb and try to strike up a conversation. Widowhood was looking more and more appealing.

It happened again this morning. Apparently, she wasn't where he expected, and he almost bellowed the house down. This wound up waking their son, who had already spent most of the night awake and had just fallen back asleep.

Mary was in a rocking chair on the front porch with a good book and a cup of coffee, enjoying the fresh morning air, when she heard her name shouted from inside. Not shouted, *bellowed*, over and over again. Thinking something was wrong with the baby, she tossed her book, missed the table when she went to place her coffee cup down, and rushed inside, leaving the scattered pieces of her cup to clean up later.

Devon came marching down the steps, yelling her name once more as she opened the door. He cut off mid-scream when she came into view in the doorway, a look of confusion on her face.

"Devon, what's wrong?"

"I couldn't find you. Where were you?"

Fury spread to every fiber in her body the moment the words left his mouth. Then came the screams from her son's nursery. Caleb had also heard Devon shouting and was now awake and ready for attention.

"Are you telling me that instead of taking a moment to look for me like a normal human being, you just decided to scream like a fiend? Now you woke our son up, and I have a mess to clean up outside. Gosh! You need to get back to work even if I have to call Chief Parker myself and beg him to get you away from me. You go get Caleb. I'm going to go clean up my coffee. And I swear to you, if my book is damaged from me flinging it in my rush to get inside, you are buying me ten more for the emotional damages incurred.

"Don't you ever do that again unless something is wrong with our son, this house is on fire, or there is an actual emergency. Because I'm warning you now, Devon Walker, I won't divorce you, but I bet I could get some people to help me bury your body in the backyard. I know I could come up with a whole damn list of people that would help me dig a hole."

"Damn it, Mary. I was worried about you. I woke up and you weren't in bed. Can't you just stay where you belong?" From the look on his wife's face, Devon knew those were the wrong words, and he'd screwed up majorly. "Wait, I didn't mean it like that!" His hands shot up, either in a puny attempt to protect himself or a sign of surrender.

"Oh really, Devon. Then how did you mean it? Do you want me to notify you each time I leave a room, or do you want me to tell you exactly where I think you belong?"

Hanging his head in shame, he decided he needed to grovel. "I'm sorry. When I rolled over and you weren't next to me, I panicked. Maybe next time wake me up before you leave the room."

Wrong words again.

"You dick. I was trying to be considerate and let you sleep. Neither one of us got a good night's sleep since Caleb decided he wanted to play in the middle of the night. Now go get our son and calm him down. I'm going back outside, just so you know where I am. Don't come near me again until you have your head out of your ass." She slammed the door behind her as she made her way back to the front porch.

Devon hadn't seen Mary that mad since he told her she was no longer allowed to swim in their lake because she was too far along in her pregnancy, and he didn't want anything to happen to her. That went over like a lead balloon.

"Allowed?" Was all Mary had said to him before she turned and walked into their bedroom, changed into her swimsuit, and went swimming to spite him. Then she didn't talk to him for two days. Now, he had a feeling she wouldn't talk to him unless he made amends, and quickly. Maybe he'd have one of the security guys grab something special from a bakery in the city and bring it out. His wife loved her sweets.

For now, he'd do what Mary demanded and go calm down their son. As he was coming down the stairs with Caleb in his arms, Alex called out to him from the kitchen. "Devon, I made a new pot of coffee, why don't you make her a cup and take it out to her? And apologize for ruining her first cup of the day."

"Apologize? I was worried about her, and you think I should apologize for that?" He looked at Alex with a dumbfounded expression.

"Yes, you oaf. You get on your knees and ask forgiveness if that's what it takes. I witnessed your little freak-out, and even as protective as I am towards this family, I wouldn't just bellow Mary's name unless absolutely warranted."

Devon was now shuffling from foot to foot. Alex loved to watch his squirm.

"Maybe you're right. Here, take Caleb. I better try to soothe her anger now, since, apparently, I was in the wrong."

"Damn right, you were wrong. And hopefully, she never lets you forget it."

Gently placing Caleb in Alex's arms, Devon grabbed two mugs of coffee and went to check on his wife. He stopped dead in his tracks as his hand was lifted to open the front door, realizing he was just manipulated by Alex. *Damn, he's good.* He wondered if he'd ever be able to hire Alex away from Mary's aunt and uncle. Alex's quick thinking helped to alleviate Mary's aggravated mood. Anyone who knew Mary more than a day knew to never get between her and her coffee. Alex would be an asset to have in his employ.

Chapter 19

It was Aaron's second day on the job with the private security company, and he wanted to impress his new employers. This was his dream job, and he was lucky to have even landed an opening. The day before, he spent his first day at the capitol building being briefed on the situation the congressman and his family were currently involved in. Before starting this position, he'd heard about serial killer Jimmy Yates but didn't connect it with what was going on currently in D.C. now that Yates was dead.

Aaron may be new to the private security sector, but he wasn't new to law enforcement and security. After being injured on the job as a police officer in Chicago, he had moved back home to be closer to family and recover. Once recovered, he decided to stay and bought a house, keeping him close to his nieces and nephews.

When he was ready to return to work, it was a friend who'd set him up with an interview. If he was interested, there was a position available on Congressman Carter's security team. His friend was the head of the South Carolina Congressman's security, and an interview with Congressman Carter was an opportunity he couldn't pass up. Aaron was warned the position wasn't going to be all foot chases and stakeouts like it was with the Chicago PD. So, when he received a message to go to any bakery in the vicinity of downtown D.C. and pick up some items for someone in the doghouse, he wasn't fazed and was determined not to disappoint. However, that same text message left him perplexed about his new position and what he'd be walking into when he finally made it to his station at the safe house.

First, they needed him to make a stop at the Walker residence and pick up a package delivered there by mistake. All of the Walker's mail should be forwarded to the congressman's work office. Afterward, he'd head over to a small mom-and-pop bakery where his mom always got him and his siblings treats on Saturday mornings. Those pastries would be able to get anyone out of the doghouse with a single bite. He was thinking either a fluffy, powdered sugar-topped beignet or vanilla cream filled choux.

Traffic was light and he made good time from the Congressman's home to the Walkers'. He saw the package at the front door. Immediately after picking it up, he knew something was wrong. Years of training and intuition said as much once the box was in his hands. He gently placed the box back on the ground, being careful not to shake it, make any sudden movements, or touch it any more than necessary.

He needed to ask what the protocol was for these kinds of situations. Did they handle this in-house? Did he contact the MPD in case they wanted to send a bomb squad or bomb dog? He knew internally he was most likely being paranoid, but after the brief he received on the horror surrounding the congressman's niece, Aaron wasn't going to downplay the smallest suspicious item. Pulling out his phone, he pressed one on his speed dial.

"Alex," the voice on the other line said forcefully.

"Sir, it's Aaron. I received a message today to stop and pick up a package before heading for my shift at the safe house, but there's something wrong. There is something very suspicious about the package, and I feel it needs to be checked out by another unit before it's moved. I don't have the proper equipment in my vehicle to determine if it is safe to move."

A brief moment of silence met Aaron from the other end of the phone. Alex's heavy footsteps echoed as he moved to a quiet, private place to speak. His voice lowered, a growled hush through the phone, urgent as he spoke again. "What's wrong with the package, Aaron?"

"We were briefed that all mail carriers were notified to forward any correspondence until further notice. I didn't question the message I received this morning because the postal service isn't perfect, and mistakes happen. However, I noticed as soon as I picked up the box there was no label on it, anywhere, not even a barcode. So, it couldn't have been delivered through the mail, it's not possible. I did pick up the package, but as soon as I noticed the missing label, I placed it right back down, gently, without jarring it. And I certainly didn't open it. Did you need me to contact the police to try to get any fingerprints or anything from the package?"

"That's a great job, Aaron. Very observant. Don't call the police. The FBI is leading the protection of the Walker family, so we'll contact them. If they want to have the MPD handle the evidence, they can make that determination. Stay there, and don't let that package out of your sight. I'll contact Agent Matthews. I'll also send you his contact information in case you need it. Call me as soon as the package is secured by the FBI or MPD. And Aaron, again, great job."

About forty-five minutes later, the sound of a car door shutting carried up the driveway and heavy steps rushed towards the porch. Aaron moved from leaning next to the front door to a full position, set to face any possible threat. He was taken aback when a teenager, with hair that looked like he had just rolled out of bed, rushed closer, carrying something in his hand.

Pulling his taser from his belt, Aaron braced himself. "Stop," he shouted.

Smitty stopped dead in his tracks. He hadn't seen the man leaning against the porch. He had tunnel vision on the package, thinking some idiot had left it unsecured.

The logo on the stranger's polo shirt identified him as one of the security members hired by the congressman. "My name is Smitty. FBI. I'm head of forensics for the D.C. field office. I'm here to secure that package until Agent Matthews or Chief Parker get here. They should be right behind me. Would you like to see my ID?"

How could this kid be FBI? Were they hiring them right out of high school now? "Yes. Keep one hand where I can see it and slowly reach for your ID. Don't make any sudden movements, son, and there won't be any problems."

Son? It took all of Smitty's power not to laugh. He had probably already been with the FBI when this kid was still in diapers. Though, he did get comments about his youthful appearance often. His wife called it a blessing, not a curse, but it was a curse when he looked close to the same age as his almost grown children.

Slowly reaching into the collar of his shirt, he pulled on the chain with his lab ID. Most of the lab technicians kept their IDs in their back pockets, but Smitty had always found it easier and quicker to keep it around his neck, especially when his hands were full of evidence and he needed his badge to enter every single door in the FBI building.

As Smitty held his badge up for Aaron to inspect, Agent Matthews pulled up to the house. As he exited his vehicle, he didn't know what to make of Smitty seemingly going toe to toe with one of Carter's men. After assessing the scene, he burst out laughing. "Smitty, what trouble are you into now?" Noticing the taser in the security agent's hand, Matthews said, "You can go ahead and tase him, we've all wanted to do it at least a dozen times or two. He does look suspicious, doesn't he? No one would blame you. If you are going to do it though, will you give me a minute to get my cell phone out so I can record it? The rest of the agents would pay me a bundle to get their hands on that video."

Who did this guy think he was, a comedian?

After spotting the badge on the front of Agent Matthews' belt, Aaron holstered his taser. Alex had warned about him, and he was right, he thinks he's a real joker.

Smitty put his ID back into his shirt, turned towards Matthews, and gave him an ear-to-ear grin. "We don't need any of your snide remarks, Agent Matthews. I must look dangerous or he wouldn't have pulled a weapon. This security professional was just doing his job and securing the scene and must have felt threatened. He must not have felt threatened by you, since he holstered his taser when you walked up. He knew you were no more dangerous than a flea."

Aaron did not look amused in the slightest. Matthews would need to tell Alex to prepare his guys a little better for the FBI's apparent morbid sense of humor.

Matthews slapped Smitty on the shoulder as he passed him and walked up to Aaron, hand stretched out in greeting. "Agent Matthews, FBI. Alex gave me a call and told me you found something that may interest me, and I rushed right on over. Now why don't we let poor Smitty get to work doing his boring science stuff and you and I can talk. Alex and I have a friendly rivalry going on, and I'll buy you a bottle of your favorite alcohol if you help me get one up on him. I'd love any dirt you can give me on Alex."

"Agent Matthews, if you are done messing around, can I get to work?" Smitty asked, exasperated.

"Sure, Smitty. Go ahead and get your science on. Who am I to get in your way?"

Smitty rolled his eyes as he walked back past Matthews. He went to his vehicle to get his complete forensics kit. When he had first reached the property, he was singularly focused on securing the package, but now that he knew it was secure, he wanted to get to work.

After quickly grabbing his large, rolling forensics case from the car, Smitty strategically laid out the equipment he'd need. He needed to take advantage of the thirty or so minutes he had before the bomb squad showed up and took the package away. It was likely to never be seen again after that.

All his swabs for explosive residue came back negative, and there was not one single fingerprint on any of the sides or top of the box. Smitty was careful not to disturb the box and decided to wait for the bomb squad to arrive before he checked the bottom.

Matthews walked up to the porch. "Smitty, the bomb squad is right around the corner. Carefully, pack up your equipment so we can give them all the room they need." As he was reaching for his fingerprint brush to put back into his bag, he noticed a small spot of red liquid coming from the corner of the box that wasn't there just a few minutes ago.

"Agent Matthews, you need to see something," Smitty yelled as Chief Parker arrived.

Both the agent and the chief joined Smitty, who was still looking at the corner of the box, shining a high-powered pen light on the spot. They both crouched down to get a better look at what had his attention. Parker was the first to speak. "Damn, Smitty, that's blood."

Parker jumped up and ran over to the explosive ordnance disposal truck still sitting in the driveway. "Get this package scanned now. I need to know what's inside," he yelled.

At the same time, Matthews pulled out his phone. After a single ring, Alex picked up. Skipping the greeting, Matthews started, "The bomb squad is here with the portable scanner. Smitty found blood on the box, but it hasn't been cleared to open yet, so we can't confirm what's inside. You need to do a headcount of everyone, and I mean everyone, at the safe house. And make sure your men are on their A-game. Like you'd allow anything else. Message me when that is complete so I can let Parker know."

"Got it," was all Alex said before disconnecting the call.

Almost fifteen minutes later, the package was finally placed on the portable scanner EOD carried with them. While they waited, Parker hadn't stopped once in trying to bully the EOD captain to hurry along and Matthews was ready to slap a muzzle on him. Matthews would never try to prove it, but he had a feeling the EOD captain was also sick of hearing Parker bitch and had moved even slower just to annoy him more.

After a quick scan, it was confirmed there were no electronics or explosives in the package. But there was organic matter, and the EOD tech was happy to explain it was way too small to be a human head.

Rubbing the back of his neck, while taking and holding some deep breaths, he tried to ward off the frustrating anticipation of what they were going to find in that box. Matthews almost didn't want to know what was waiting for him in this mystery package. Parker, however, was done being patient. He pulled out a pocket knife and cut open the box. Pulling the flaps back, Parker grimaced, reeling away. Now Matthews was intrigued. Smitty, donning a new set of gloves, carefully pulled apart the flaps that had fallen back into the box and gagged when he saw the contents.

Matthews was next to look in, and he immediately recognized what was inside. He'd never be able to forget his first confrontation with the evil, blood-thirsty rats that looked exactly like the ones now dead and laying at the bottom of the box.

The rats weren't only dead, they were decapitated. Just as Matthews was pulling away from the box, a glint of metal caught the sunlight. In the bottom of the box, held in place by each rat carcass, were two tiny collars. Each collar had a name engraved, and upon seeing the names, his blood turned cold as ice. "Mary" and "Mr. Agent Man."

Chapter 20

Worthless. Every single one of them should have considered themselves worthless. There were three wannabe law enforcement men in one location and not one of them noticed the flashing red light from the tree not even twenty feet from where they were standing.

To make matters worse, the camera was practically at eye level. For how half-assed Julia had placed it, someone should have seen it. The government's finest, that's what they called themselves. Bullshit. No wonder Jimmy had eluded them for so many years, especially if every one of them were as sharp as the ones at the Walker residence.

The likelihood of Julia's mission succeeding skyrocketed if all the people attempting to protect Mary had the same level of intelligence as these mouth breathers she was watching through the surveillance camera. She had not witnessed one ounce of professionalism during the time they analyzed the gift she left Devon and Mary.

Realization quickly set in. The hopes that this day would be productive went down the drain. Today would not be the day she'd be able to move on to the next step in her plan. But she would gather plenty of information she didn't otherwise have, at least there was that.

The failure of this part of her plan was unfortunately her fault, but unlike a lot of people, she learned from her mistakes, and she'd never make the same one again. Though it was a stupid, minor mistake, it still set her back. If only she'd remembered to put the obligatory shipping label on the package, then she'd be on her way to finding that bitch and her spawn by now. She could've found a million images of a fake shipping label online and just slapped it on the package. It was an unfortunate oversight. It was only a matter of time before they found the tracking device she shoved down into the carcass of the female rat. At least they were untraceable back to her, she knew they'd know exactly who sent them. And that was okay with her.

Mary was going to be safe for a little while longer, then the chase would officially begin. It's not that Julia didn't enjoy the chase, she just wanted this to be done and over with. She wanted to move on and finally make a name for herself. She didn't always want to be known as the person Jimmy trained, or "Jimmy's apprentice" as the newspapers were calling her.

If she was honest with herself, she was getting sick and tired of cleaning up Jimmy's mistake. But she had a debt to pay, and even though Jimmy was gone from this earth, she knew she'd meet him again one day. When she did, she wanted to rub his nose in having taken down his biggest adversary; the apprentice succeeding where the master failed. She could just picture it. When they finally meet up again, Jimmy would be green with envy over her accomplishments. She'd moved hell itself to see Jimmy even remotely envious of one of her kills. The only thing that would make it better would be if she could bring him Mary's face when she met him in hell.

Making sure this damn debt from when he took her in and trained her was paid was the last thing she needed to do before she could leave this forsaken city. Hell, maybe she'd leave the country. It'd probably be easier hunting in a country with less "big brother" surveillance on every corner.

Surely, she'd be able to do a quick search and find which countries had the most violent crimes per capita, and that's exactly where she'd go. Somewhere she could do what she loved, what Jimmy taught her to do, and she'd be able to blend in.

Julia closed her laptop, not wanting to watch those three clowns any longer. Julia knew the security guard wouldn't return to the safe house today. While he was on the phone with Alex, he said he'd head back to the office and write up the report and email it to him before his shift ended, and then start again tomorrow.

Yes, tomorrow. They'd all get a new start tomorrow.

Now she had faces for her list of names, and that was one of the most important parts of knowing the enemy. With her computer software, as long as she had a name and a photo, any photo, she could access CCTV anywhere and track a person's patterns.

She'd rather rely on her own surveillance, but the CCTV was always available as a last resort. Oh, how she loved the advances in technology. No one could really hide anymore, not truly. Not that anyone could really ever hide from her anyway. She always found her target.

A growling sound came from the small table on the other side of the room. A smile spread across her lips. Her friends were angered, and when they were angry, they became lethal. From all the noise, it sounded like they could tell their friends were gone. The excitement seemed to make the other rats in the cage become combative, like they were trying to break out of their confinement. As she stepped up to the cage, in unison, they all began hissing, clawing and the cage, and snapping at each other when their bodies made contact. Anguish surged through her as she thought about the sacrifice two of her babies just had to make to further her cause of finding Mary. How many more would need to die before Mary's life was finally ended? All of them if that's what was needed. And if they could talk to her, she knew they'd tell her they'd all gladly sacrifice their puny existence for a chance for her to gain her revenge.

Most of the rats were gnawing on the cage. Maybe they were just hungry and wanted their afternoon treat of blood. Julia only had two vials left, and she'd need to ration it out.

While she was charading as a nurse, she had collected six vials of Mary's blood. All under the guise of needing to run tests. With these being the same rats that fed on Mary just over a year ago, she knew they'd recognize her blood and hoped it would drive them into a frenzy.

She became giddy, thinking about the first time she honored her rats with a taste of enemy blood. The first few drops from the vile that were placed into their food dishes had the rats showing their bloodthirsty side. The rats threw themselves against the cage in a tiny show of desperation of needing to consume every drop, and wanting more. Julia quickly obliged.

Sadly, with her blood supply dwindling, she had to sacrifice the two rats with the bloodiest appetites. Rat Mary and Rat Mr. Agent Man gave their lives for the greater good. After watching the worthless agents on the monitor scramble and recoil as they opened the box, Julia felt a warmth in her chest that their deaths were not in vain.

With the little bit of blood left, she would continue to rile up the rats as she made her plans. Then, when they were made, she would split what was left with each rat as a generous last meal. The rats were coming close to the end of their life expectancy, so instead of allowing them to suffer, as they become too old to have fulfilling lives, they'd go to the end doing what they loved. Enjoying the delicious taste of blood. Now, Julia needed to figure out how to reunite Mary and her rodent friends.

Chapter 21

The next morning, Julia had a little more pep in her step. She started the day with a nice run through downtown D.C. She loved running around the capital and watching the faces of the politicians as she ran by, dreaming of how nice they'd look tacked up on Jimmy's wall of trophies.

If some of these people in power realized how close they were to becoming one of Jimmy's victims, they wouldn't be walking around so carefree. They'd surround themselves with security, or live in hiding, or piss their pants every time they heard a car backfire. Jimmy had a "decoration" wish list, he'd called it. He was very particular about whose faces would adorn his wall.

Not long after Julia came to live with Jimmy, she sat in the corner of the basement trophy room in complete humbleness at being in the presence of a master. The corner was the closest he'd allowed her to his wall of success, as he listed all his potential targets and placed sticky notes with the names exactly where on his wall their final placement would be. If it wasn't for his obsession with Mary, she had no doubt he would've completed his list. It was all because of one stupid newspaper article that their world changed.

She'd never forget the day her world came crashing down. Jimmy just finished gathering his latest victims and corralling them into their living room when he started shouting a bunch of expletives and throwing furniture. This was very out of the ordinary for him, he was usually so composed when the kill was imminent. Not this day. He was so out of control, if someone happened to come close to the house, they would've heard the commotion and glass breaking inside. Because he couldn't control his temper, Jimmy could've gotten caught long before he was viciously murdered in cold blood outside that hospital.

Laying on the coffee table was that day's newspaper. The paper was open to an article about a multistate forensic psychology convention at Georgetown University and the headlining speaker was Dr. Mary Anderson. Paired with the article was a large closeup of Mary, which is what had caught Jimmy's attention. Dr. Anderson would be giving a presentation on common misconceptions surrounding serial killers and the mistakes they make that aid the police in their apprehension.

Jimmy had been tortured with the idea that he failed so many years ago and was unable to completely cleanse the Anderson home. Yet, after reading that article, Jimmy turned completely obsessed and stopped their fun, hunting adventures. She'd never forgive Mary for ruining her fun.

Julia would repay her debt to him, but then she's gone. So, she'd finish this as soon as possible. Now she needed to get her head in the game and refocus.

Her run had dredged up old negative feelings, which was not at all how Julia wanted to start her morning. She needed some good news in her life. She deserved a break. After a melt-your-skin-off shower, she called in her normal order into her normal coffee shop, conveniently called "The Shop", down the street and grabbed her bag of surveillance equipment.

As she picked up her cream cheese bagel and coffee, she smiled at Troy behind the counter. Even though her photo had been plastered all over the news the last few days, she never had to worry about anyone in this coffee shop running to the cops and turning her in. Everyone in this shop, especially the owners, had criminal records longer than her own. That's why this was one of her favorite places in the city. It was the one place where it was always safe, and no one ever asked questions. With a final flirtatious wink to Troy, she sauntered out the door, exaggerating the movement of her hips as she walked. Knowing he wouldn't be able to keep his eyes off her ass.

Back in her car, she ate her breakfast in blissful silence as she finalized her plans for the day in her head. Julia maneuvered out of the D.C. traffic and carefully into the overpriced neighborhood where Congressman Carter lived. Since his neighborhood was mostly politicians and dignitaries, it took little effort to find a property close to the congressman with a family that would be away or out of the country for a few weeks. Drones are an amazing thing, especially ones equipped with heat sensors so she could determine which homes had higher chances of being vacant.

She pulled in front of the second home of a senator from Idaho. The only person that should be at the residence at this time of day, should be the live-in maid. As long as Julia didn't trip the security system that bordered the house at ten feet from the structure, the maid would never even know she was there. As luck would have it, when the senator built their children their tree house, it just happened to be outside that ten-foot security perimeter, so she'd perch inside, unable to be seen by others.

She was surprised the senator's security team never told him how very unsafe the structure actually was, not being covered by his security sensors, but she was glad they were so incompetent because in this moment, it helped her serve a purpose. That purpose: revenge.

Congressman Carter's security team, like most other politicians in Washington D.C., held their base of operations centrally located to the person or object that they were hired to protect. In this case, it was originally Congressman Carter and his family. So, it only made sense that the base of operations was a building attached to the back of the Carter's home.

The small building housed two walls of cameras and another wall of rotating photos of persons of interest that every security team member was briefed on daily to be on the watch for. With the congressman moving his family to a safe house location, the smart thing would have been to change the base of operations, but Julia deduced that Carter wasn't very smart at all.

Since the congressman's security team at his residence was maintaining contact with the security team at the base location, she'd be able to gather all the information she needed to track down Mary. There were only two security men Julia knew she had to watch out for, ones that seemed to be semi-intelligent, but she hasn't seen either of them since Mary's disappearance. The likelihood was that they were assigned to keep Mary safe. That would mean she'd need to plan the final attack down to the tiniest detail, but their absence would at least make finding Mary simpler.

Julia had been in the tree house for about thirty minutes, the normal amount of calm down time she allotted to make sure no alarms were triggered with her arrival, and no one had seen her climb the ladder attached to the tree. As soon as her watch vibrated, notifying that her thirty minutes were up, she pulled her canvas supply bag closer and started gathering her new equipment.

She loved when she got new toys in the mail. Jimmy never liked what he called "newfangled technology." He was such a party pooper. Jimmy was old-school, and while Julia appreciated his talent, she wasn't going to let his lack of technological progression land her behind bars.

The first new toy she pulled out of her bag was her new bionic ear portable dish listening device. Yes, it was only the basic model, but she could only transfer little bits of money to her accounts at one time to avoid suspicion.

Unlike a man, she read the instruction manual cover to cover last night so she would be prepared to use her new listening device. She didn't want to be fumbling with a book if she needed to troubleshoot her equipment. Especially if something was happening and her looking through a book for information caused her to miss an opportunity to find Mary.

Time for the magic to happen. Headphones on, cord plugged in, point dish in the direction of the senator's house to test it out, and power. Instant gratification.

Just as Julia suspected, the only person she could hear in the senator's home was the maid, and from the sounds of it, she was on the phone with another female complaining about her boss and how much of a slob he and his family were. *Nice.* A disgruntled employee would be a complacent employee. It was less likely she'd get caught if the maid was busy gossiping about how unhappy she is with her employment.

Since her listening device worked, it was now time to put voices to the faces she's been watching.

Julia pulled out her laptop and opened the camera program. Yes. Every camera she'd previously placed on the property was still active. Like she said before, the congressman was paying for nothing because every single one of his security men were worthless.

Reaching into her pack, she found the last cable she needed before she'd finally be ready to get this show on the road. She plugged the cable from the portable listening dish into the output jack on her laptop. Now she'd be able to record long-range sounds to match her video. She was a genius. She wanted to be able to go back later and watch everything just in case something was missed. It was always smart to have a backup, that's why she needed to record everything.

After hours of sitting in the cramped kids playhouse, the sun was starting to set, and packing up for the night started sounding better and better. Somewhere down the street, someone was cooking on the grill, and Julia's stomach reminded her that she hadn't eaten since her bagel after her morning run.

She was just about to pull off her headphones when the phone in the security building started ringing. She'd listen to this last phone call, then call it a night. The stars aligned; this was what she'd been waiting for. She recognized the voice of the security guard that followed the congressman's wife around like a lost puppy dog.

The guard in the building addressed him as Alex. She quickly jotted that down, it would be useful information. Realizing he had to be an important part of the Carter household, she'd need to do research on him later. Maybe she'd target some of his loved ones to get him out of the way. He'd have to leave the Carter family's sides if she painted some homes with blood.

Alex said he'd be sending someone to the house in two days to pick up an important package. He didn't say what was in the package, but now she had a date when someone from the safe house would be on the move to a confirmed location, then returning to the safe house. To Mary. Julia had to be ready to follow them.

Hopefully, this means something was finally going to go right. Like, really, it shouldn't be this hard to kill one helpless woman and her useless spawn.

Chapter 22

Forty-eight hours later, on the dot, the security guard, whom she found out is named Alex, pulled up to the congressman's house. The package he was coming to retrieve must have been extremely important, because on the last phone call, Alex had indicated he was going to send someone else, not come himself. The only time Julia ever saw this "Alex", was when he was personally shadowing the congressman or his wife.

Julia was on her A-game. She wasn't taking any chances on missing this arrival, so she had been parked three blocks away, watching the security cameras intently from her laptop, for about three hours now. The only time she'd taken a break was for coffee and bagels. Which were from her favorite criminal coffee shop, of course.

She'd just popped the last piece of her plain bagel with cream cheese into her mouth when the sleek, black town car pulled up in front of the Carter home. She knew instantly it was either the congressman himself or one of his security. She assumed this because it was the exact make and model that was usually parked outside their house, or around back next to the security building.

Quickly clearing the clutter from around her lap, she readied her car to move. Julia watched Alex make his way from the town car and around the back of the house to where the security building was located. Once inside, it was now a waiting game. She wouldn't be able to hear what they were saying because she felt following them to gain their location was more than grabbing fragments of information. She also wasn't in any position to pull out her portable listening device.

He wasn't inside with the other security men for very long. Whatever was said inside that building, Alex seemed to be in a good mood when he walked out. Maybe that would put him on less of an edge, and he'd be less likely to notice her following his car. In his right hand, was a metal briefcase that was very evidently locked. Interesting.

Finding Mary was the primary task, but if she got a chance, she wanted to know what was in the briefcase. Maybe it was money, or government secrets. Either way, there might be something inside she could sell or use for blackmail.

She'd only been following the black town car for a few moments when she realized where they were heading. As soon as they turned onto Wilson Blvd, she knew they were heading for the 110, which linked to the 395, that would take them into the heart of D.C. "Shit, shit, shit!" Julia slammed her hands on the steering wheel. It would be next to impossible to track them in this traffic.

After what seemed like hours of weaving in and out of traffic and almost wrecking eight times trying to keep the vehicle in her sights, she realized she drives better than any NASCAR driver ever could. She almost thought they caught on to the fact they were being followed when the black town car pulled into somewhere Julia couldn't follow. The car pulled into the Hall of The States Parking Garage.

If Julia tried to pull in behind them, they'd immediately spot her. If they didn't see her, one of the many FBI or Capitol Police officers that patrolled the area most definitely would. She would need to park across the street and wait for them to come back out. Then she'd start her pursuit all over again.

If Julia had to guess, they were probably delivering whatever was in that fancy briefcase to the capitol building. Maybe that's where they were hiding Mary. Why not? It would be next to impossible to get in there undetected, and she'd be surrounded by twenty-four-hour security.

No, too obvious. Plus, she wouldn't be able to take that brat with her. Well, she could, but he would be all pent-up and miserable. So it was very likely that she was being held someplace else, and Julia was going to find her.

Two hours had passed when the realization slapped her in the face. They weren't coming back out, or they already had and had switched vehicles. *Shit*, she knew this one guy, Alex, was smart, but she wouldn't let him make a fool of her. Reaching over, Julia pulled her laptop from the bag on her passenger seat. Pulling her dashcam down and placing it on the center console, she plugged it into the laptop. After rewinding all the way to the beginning, she was quickly able to get a clear image of the town car's license plate. Score, she had a crystal-clear image of the plate.

She waited until streams of vehicles were leaving the parking garage and heading straight into rush hour traffic, before slipping inside unnoticed. As she looked around, her head started to pound. Of course, there were black town cars everywhere, this was a parking garage for federal employees. A little challenge wasn't going to deter her from her goal, she needed to stop whining and find that license plate. Then it hit her, why the hell was she wandering around like a lost puppy? She had skills for tasks like this. After some master hacking into the parking lot's cloud, she found the parking assignments and knew what section to look for. The congressman had four spaces in this parking garage, on floor D.

After starting to understand the pattern between groups of vehicles for individual politicians and vehicles randomly parked in the garage by staff, it made searching a lot easier.

Finally, there they were.

In the back, in the north corner of floor D, sat two black town cars—one with the matching license plate—and one black suburban. She knew a black town car did not leave the exit she was watching, so that meant there was one more vehicle unaccounted for.

Reaching into her back pocket, she pulled out her phone. She hit speed dial number four. Her black-market contact picked up on the second ring. "Yeah?"

"Hey, it's Julia. I need to place an order, and I need it within a few hours."

She heard his fingers flying over his keyboard. "What do you need?"

"I need four trackers for vehicles. They need to be top-of-the-line and very discreet. They are going on government vehicles, and I need to assume the vehicles will be checked daily for devices."

Silence and typing were all that could be heard for a few minutes. "Okay, I found what you need. I have an old CIA contact that got canned and is salty about it so he's willing to part with all his old equipment. The cost is going to be astronomical. Do you care?"

Letting out a chuckle she said, "You should know better than that. No expense spared for what I need to get done. Jimmy was the cheap one, not me. You know, though, that if I find out you are taking advantage of me, I will add your face to Jimmy's wall."

"Yeah, yeah, I know that. Both you and Jimmy threatened me with doing just that so many times, and believe me, I know you'd do it. I'll text you the total, just wire the amount to the normal account and I'll go pick up your product. I'll drop it in your PO Box by midnight. It's still the same box, right? It's the only one I have a key for."

"Yes, same PO Box." She disconnected before he could ask any more questions. Their relationship had always been a professional one, and neither ever worried about pleasantries.

Glancing at her watch, she had four hours until her trackers would be ready. Hopefully, things would progress quickly once they were placed. She'd use this time to shower, pack some provisions, and resupply the stock of items she'd need if she's able to get her hands on Mary. She'd at least need lots and lots of duct tape.

Nicole Keefer

Chapter 23

Two o'clock in the morning in downtown D.C. still looked as it did in the middle of the day, only more shadows for the epitome of immoral politicians to slink through. One of the more entertaining differences found at this time of day were the influx of intern whores looking to climb the corporate ladder, who traded in the business style dress for something that could quickly be hiked up in a back alley.

Didn't they know their brains were more powerful than what was between their legs? That if they played their cards right, they could entrap and captivate any man just by whispering what they wanted to hear, then use it against them? Apparently not.

With all the hustle and bustle in the streets, it was easy for Julia to sneak back into the parking garage where she had located Congressman Carter's vehicles earlier that day. Still in his designated spots, there were parked two black town cars, one suburban, and an empty spot. She'd need to come back later and make sure she placed a tracker on that last vehicle. Details were key. She couldn't leave any stone unturned. That single vehicle may be what leads her to Mary.

Her small stature was advantageous in situations like climbing under the cars. She shimmied under each vehicle until she was directly in the center. Pulling out the GPS trackers—which were the best in the business since they were waterproof and in a plastic shell making them hard to detect—Julia added a few drops of quick dry epoxy, and reached up and placed it directly on the underside of the body. If she placed it on the chassis, someone looking under the vehicle with one of those mirrors on a stick may be able to see it, and that would be unacceptable.

Pulling out her cell phone, Julia took pictures of the license plate and VIN numbers of each vehicle, plus her placement of each tracking device. This was another little trick Jimmy taught her during her initial training.

There were lots of faces from heads of criminal empires, and even some federal attorneys, on Jimmy's wall, so he was always meticulous about his tracking and preparatory legwork. Over the years, he perfected his placements so they were less detectable by eye or machine.

One of the many "tests" Yates had her complete consisted of her placing tracking devices on a vehicle, and every time Jimmy found one, that was a kill Julia had to sit out on. Needless to say, she mastered that task rather quickly. Besides knowing that Jimmy was disappointed in her, she had been jealous. Knowing his victims were being denied seeing her face before their end was an even more productive motivator for her to practice and succeed in all his training. Listening to Jimmy gloat about seeing the fear in his victim's eyes and experiencing the scent of death in the air made Julia push herself to become the apprentice he'd be proud of, and finally allow to be more hands-on.

As a fail-safe in case one of the security guys found her little devices, she placed a cheap camera with long battery life facing the tracker. She needed to know if the trackers were touched. If they were found, it didn't matter who found them, she'd need to put her next plan in place.

She'd seen too many crime shows where trackers or bugs were found by the intended victims, then turned around and used to capture the ones just trying to complete their job of ridding the world of toxic scum. She wasn't going to be one of those people that got caught because of her own clumsiness, like Jimmy was.

Julia was getting ready to place the last camera when she heard footsteps coming her way. *Who the hell would be in the parking garage at this time in the morning?* Whoever was coming wasn't trying to be quiet. The footsteps quickened, then giggling reached Julia's ears. Ah, just a typical politician with either his whore or his mistress, and they were trying to hide whatever torrid affair they were having by meeting in a semi-dark parking garage.

Rolling under the car, she quickly snapped a bunch of pictures of the pair as they stumbled to a limo parked in the back corner, and quickly disappeared inside. Once she got home, she'd anonymously send these to the tabloids.

Hey, no one could ever say she never did any good deeds in her life. You are very welcome, Mr. Politician's wife. Now, back to work.

Chapter 24

Julia sat at her kitchen table, drinking a large coffee, and eating her normal bagel with cream cheese. Leaning back in her chair, her legs propped up and ankles crossed, she was totally relaxed.

Troy personally delivered her breakfast to her this morning when she called it in, and since she was in such a good mood when he arrived, she gave him a very enjoyable tip.

Troy's family had their fingers in half of the criminal activity in the city, so it was always beneficial to keep her prospects open, even if that meant occasionally opening her legs. Ever since Julia found the coffee shop, Troy had been very vocal in his attempts to get her into bed. Until today, she'd always blown him off, but also always insinuated that he should keep trying.

Everyone in the world knew of Jimmy. Anyone who was anyone knew of her association with Jimmy, so that elevated her status within the criminal community. The first day she walked into the coffee shop, every conversation immediately stopped, and all eyes turned to her. The owner of "The Shop" came from the back room to personally welcome her to his establishment and let her know that if she ever needed anything, anything at all, to just ask. He would hold her strictest confidence.

Focus.

Pushing that morning's activities to the back of her mind, it was time to get down to business. After a quick trip back to the parking garage the night before last, she was able to install the final tracker on a black suburban that had not been there previously. Now that the trackers have been on the four vehicles between twenty-four and forty-eight hours, all she needed to do was analyze the data for patterns.

The program her contact gave her with these trackers was top-of-the-line and took all the leg work away from her. Anything that lessened error margins cost a fortune but was worth every penny in the long run. Each tracker on the screen is color coded, and each stop where the vehicle ignition was turned off is marked with a different symbol than if the vehicle is just stopped for a traffic light. Really, they were dummy-proof.

The program was very easy to understand once she read the manual cover to cover and drew a color-coded diagram on a dry-erase board she had picked up at the corner store. After clicking some buttons, the program ran a triangulation algorithm. It pulled GPS coordinates with multiple pings at the same location.

The graph that appeared showed each location's GPS coordinates, the number of times it pinged, and what kind of stop occurred. The order of the coordinates descended from highest number of pings to lowest.

Score. The program indicated that in forty-eight hours, there were five locations that had multiple stops that resulted in the vehicle ignition being turned off. After a quick Google search, Julia was able to eliminate three of the five locations. Those three locations consisted of the parking garage where the vehicles were normally parked, the congressman's house, and the Walker home.

The fourth location, after some digging, looked to be an old laundromat turned into a Chinese restaurant. Maybe someone had an obsession with greasy food. She'd keep that location as a backup. Maybe someone inside knew something, she'd love to try out her interrogation techniques. Admittedly, they were a bit rusty. Jimmy had his own special ways of making people talk, and she was rarely allowed to practice her own skills on their victims. Jimmy liked to get his hands dirty, or bloody. He was all show and pomp, and she was more about breaking the mind before breaking the body. There was nothing in the world like having a person begging for death without even drawing one drop of blood. It was an art form, one she was looking forward to perfecting on Mary Anderson.

It was the fifth location that interested Julia the most. That location had the most pings and the vehicles were stationary for hours and hours at a time. However, she was having the hardest time finding anything online. It's like those GPS coordinates didn't exist.

That wasn't discouraging, though, it was actually a very, very good sign. Jimmy taught her that if someone wanted to hide something hard enough, they'd find a way to bury the information deep. He proved this point when he went after one of his victims that happened to be a paranoid doomsday prepper. Jimmy's intended victim and his entire family lived in an underground bunker. They only left to go to the grocery store and other places like the library, where Jimmy had his first run in with them.

They had an exciting two weeks of playing cat and mouse with a man that seemed to disappear into thin air every time he went into a specific wooded area. The area was right on the other side of a covered bridge. It was so damn frustrating.

Apparently, this prepper had millions of dollars and had put that money to good use. He was able to disappear and throw us off his trail by hitting a button which triggered a garage door that looked like a rock wall to retract into the mountain, then he'd drive his vehicle inside and close the door. Pure batman bullshit.

Hopefully, Mary wouldn't be hiding somewhere with such intricate security. From the financials Julia pulled on the congressman, he was very wealthy, but not millionaire status like "doomsday prepper man" was. Jimmy never told her the victim's names, and she's never been able to find out anything online about them. Pity, she'd love to be able to leak that it was her and Jimmy's handy work.

She needed to stop reminiscing and get back to work.

When she pulled up the coordinates to the fifth location in google maps, it was just a photo of an open field. Why would multiple government vehicles be parked, sometimes overnight, in an empty field?

She knew the answer. That has to be the location of the safe house where that bitch was being hidden from her. Of course, the government would be able to get google to put whatever picture they'd want at any location. The government considered everyone else their bitches, and they could get everyone else to do their bidding. Now, she'd just need to go check the location out for herself to confirm, but she knew she was right. She finally found her, and her debt was about to be repaid.

Bibbidi, Bobbidi, boo. Mary, I'm coming for you.

Chapter 25

Nothing could ruin Julia's good mood. She even caught herself whistling "It's a Small World" to herself repeatedly. Jimmy used to whistle to himself when he was happy, and it drove her crazy. Maybe it drove her crazy because the only time Jimmy would whistle that specific song was when he was thinking about everything he wanted to do to Mary freaking Anderson.

Now, she was whistling it while thinking about Mary freaking Anderson. The difference between her and Jimmy was that there was no way in hell that Mary freaking Anderson was going to be the basis of her demise. No, she was too smart to be caught by that bitch and her substandard protection detail.

Reminiscing about Jimmy was making Julia feel emotions that she fought against expressing for as long as she could remember. When she was sitting home alone, and the news broadcasted the death of Serial Killer Jimmy Yates, Julia wasn't sad, no, she was pissed. Anger surged through her, and for a single moment, she hated him for being caught. Even after the information sunk in that he was never coming back, she still didn't cry over his death.

The last time Julia cried was when she was six years old. Her father had just finished chasing her around the backyard with a baseball bat and finally caught her. He connected the bat to her legs a total of eight times; one smack for each minute he had to chase her around the yard.

Julia's coward of a mother came and found her long after dark, still laying in the middle of the yard and unable to move. Even though the beating had happened hours earlier, tears still streamed down her face when her mother walked up to her side and knelt down.

"Listen here, Julia, because I'm only going to say this one time. Your father responds to emotion, so if you deny him the satisfaction of shamelessly displaying your every emotion, he will soon become bored and move on to torturing someone or something else."

Quickly looking back at the house to make sure Julia's father was still sitting on the porch drinking his beer, she continued to speak to her daughter. "Now, you can either take my advice or not. But know this, I won't help you anymore. I can't. From here on out, you are on your own."

Fury raced through every fiber of Julia's body as she thought about everyone that's wronged her. Jimmy had promised to add their faces to his trophy wall, but he never got the chance to fulfill that promise of killing everyone on her hit list. It was all her fault—Mary freaking Anderson.

None of that mattered now, the finish line was in sight. She would finally get her revenge. Julia dropped to her knees in front of her closet. Shoving her hands forward, she pushed things around and tried to reach the back of the storage space. That damn canvas bag had to be there somewhere. When she had to hastily leave Yates's home, she'd grabbed two canvas bags. One she used for her surveillance equipment, and the other one she used to hold her "stalking" necessities, as Yates had called those items.

Reaching back as far as her arms could reach, her fingertips finally brushed against what she believed was the bag. Not caring about anything else, she started tossing things from the closet left and right. Yes, it was the bag she was looking for, and dang, it was heavier than she remembered.

Dragging it over to the middle of the living room, she sat cross-legged on the carpet. She started to pull everything out and lay it out nice and neat on the floor. Everything would need to be cleaned and inspected. Nothing could go wrong when she stalked her prey.

Julia was hardly able to control her excitement because things were finally progressing in her favor. As she bounced up and down in the driver's side of her car, she knew she should probably compose herself, but screw that shit. It was almost midnight, and she was parked at a truck stop only five miles from where the vehicle tracking devices had been pinging, and where one was currently located. She knew in her gut she had the right location, and she was allowed to be excited.

She would give it ten more minutes before she'd move her car just a little closer. Since she had waited until closer to midnight to make her move, she had lots of time to look over maps and satellite imagery of the surrounding area. Bordering the safe house's wooded area was a federal game reserve. Federal safe house attached to a federal game reserve; she was not surprised. Yet, it was just another coincidence that made her believe she had the right location.

After looking at the satellite imagery for a while, she found a service trail that was less likely to be patrolled since it was near a residential neighborhood. She'd park her car there and hike the rest of the way in. By her estimation, she'd need to hike about four and a half miles. Hiking that distance with night vision goggles should take her just over an hour and a half.

If luck was on her side, which she knew Jimmy would be sending her all the luck she needed, she'd be near the safe house before two a.m.

The hike to the coordinates ended up being blissfully easy. Jimmy made her practice with night vision goggles so many times, so navigating the flat, wooden area between where she parked, to the assumed location, was a piece of cake. Moving quickly, but also being very careful to not step on twigs that would alert the security of her presence, she knew she was getting close as the night vision goggles shined brighter in her field of vision. This indicated she was approaching lights.

Arriving at the brightly lit house that wasn't supposed to be in the middle of the field, she immediately noticed the license plate on the black suburban SUV parked not far from the front door. Her mission wasn't a complete success until she got eyes on Mary, but she was at least able to confirm that the congressman's men were inside.

Complacency is a bitch, but in her case, Julia was happy these guards felt comfortable enough with their floodlights blaring away to not feel obligated to check the tree line. Not once in all the hours she was watching the house, did one guard ever come close to finding her. Their error in judgment gave Julia all the opportunity she needed to watch the roving guard, time their spacing, mark their patterns, and map their movements. They didn't even see her moving tree to tree placing cameras.

It was almost seven in the morning, and Julia knew she was already pressing her luck by not leaving, so she told herself if nothing new happened by seven fifteen, she'd leave and come back tonight. She'd do the same recon tonight just to make sure nothing changed in the guard's routines before she made her move.

Step by step, she slowly started retreating into the woods when a movement by the front door caught her eye. The big security guy, Alex, from a few days ago emerged onto the porch, carrying a tray, and he was laughing. Right behind him, stepped out FBI Agent Devon Walker. Every fiber in Julia's body tensed, ready to strike. She wanted to rush across the yard and rip his throat out. He was the reason Jimmy wasn't with her anymore, him and that bitch.

Speaking of that bitch, Agent Walker was reaching his arm back into the doorway, and she emerged, holding his hand. Yuck! Bile raced up Julia's throat, but she had to choke it back down. If she got sick now, one of the guards might hear her, then all her planning would be for nothing.

Agent Walker leaned down and kissed Mary on the forehead, said something to the guard, then raced off toward the water. Dressed how he was, it was safe to assume he was going for a run. The security guard waited for Mary to sit down on the swing at the end of the porch. Once Mary was settled, he handed her a cup from the tray, before taking one himself and having a seat next to her. If only she had her sniper rifle, she'd take the shot right now.

Look at them all, eating out of the palm of her hands. Jimmy was right, she put all the men around her under some sort of spell. A witch, he had once referred to Mary as, and Julia could see it. Now, it was up to Julia to rid the world of her bewitchment; she couldn't let Jimmy down.

Presently, she needed to go home, regroup, and prepare to come back tonight. Maybe she'd strike tonight if everything looked the same, or maybe she'd just watch the guards again to confirm the patterns. Either way, she needed to get some sleep, then plan, plan, plan.

One thing was for certain, now that she found her, Mary wasn't going to get away. This was going to end here, at this house. One way or another.

Chapter 26

After the euphoria of finally finding that bitch started to wear off, Julia needed to get her shit together and get down to business. Verifying every moment and every detail of the security agents' routine and schedule would be vital for her mission to succeed.

As soon as she walked in the door this morning, she immediately looked over her notes to make sure she didn't forget to write anything down about the guards' activities. Confident with her notes, she plugged the tiny camera that was attached at her shoulder into her laptop.

The video confirmed everything she'd written down. Damn, she was good.

There were eight floodlights that surrounded the house, and they were on at all times during the night, not connected to motion sensors. The floodlights were positioned: three in the front of the house, three back of the house, and one in the middle of each side. They were powered by moveable generators, like those found at a construction site, so they offered her some cover for noise.

From the tree line where Julia had been watching, she was able to see guards at the two corners of the house that were visible, so she needed to assume some were positioned at the other two corners as well. This was a safe assumption, because every thirty minutes on the dot, they rotated in a clockwise motion around the house, ending up at a new corner.

In addition to the guard positions on the house that she could see, there were three guards that roved the property. Their patterns took most of the night to figure out, but she had finally done it.

Guard one would rove in a pattern from the front porch, down to the lake, over to a small, shed-type building next to the driveway, and back to the front porch.

Guard two would rove in a pattern from a barn that had zero activity so she'd presume that besides possible vehicles, it was empty. Then they moved what looked to be a guest house, or where they were housing the rest of the security, to down and around the vehicles, then back to the barn.

Guard three would rove from the back porch, all the way around the house, close to the tree line, down to a different part of the lake near a little, tied-off boat, and back to the back porch.

Each guard would complete a rotation once every forty-five minutes or so. Only once or twice, did a guard not complete the rotation in that allotted time. When that happened, Julia noticed a convergence of flashlights to a different area on the property. This probably indicated the guard needed something checked by his superior before they could continue on with their route.

Watching the videos over and over again, she found one point of entry that showed promise. Right in the back of the house, there was a willow tree that was large enough to conceal her presence in shadows, and it was close enough to the house that she should be able to get onto the second-floor ledge from a close branch.

The house was older, so if any of the windows on the second floor had loose sash locks, she'd easily, and quickly, be able to get inside the house well within the thirty-minute window of guard changes. Now, if the window didn't have loose sash locks, she'd take her glass cutter with a suction cup and move quickly. Either way, she'd get inside that house.

Now that she had her plan of attack down pat, she was starting to feel a little melancholy. Maybe those feelings were starting to surface because she was so close to fulfilling Jimmy's dream, and he wasn't here to witness it.

Jimmy wasn't here to see her victory against possibly dozens of armed, trained guards. She was about to prove her vast superior intellect, and no one was going to be around to witness it. Except, one day, her name would be in the history books alongside Jimmy's for all eternity.

Shaking her head, she couldn't hold in the laughter that now echoed throughout her mostly empty apartment. In that instant, she knew Jimmy was looking at her from wherever he was with disdain over her behavior, but she didn't care. He promoted composure at all times, even though he failed to keep his own composure when it came to Mary. Oh well, it's not like he was able to berate her now.

Giggling, she jumped from the couch and skipped over to the electric fireplace in the center of the living room wall. Reaching down and carefully moving the fake rocks out of the bottom of the fireplace, she pulled out the plastic bag she had hidden the first day she moved into the apartment.

Inside that simple plastic bag were some of her most prized possessions. It held the first pictures she'd ever taken of Jimmy, when she was the hunter and he was the hunted.

Anytime you walk down the street, the chances you are walking past a killer are higher than anyone would like to believe. It would be wishful thinking to expect that all murderers looked like deranged psychopaths with dirty clothes and hair sticking up every which way. It's quite the opposite, actually. Which was exactly the case with Jimmy Yates.

Julia will never forget the first time she saw a picture of the infamous serial killer. She was eighteen, working at a hole-in-the-wall bar, as a bartender, using a fake ID, when Jimmy's picture flashed on the screen highlighting his latest killing spree. The first thing that caught her attention was how much this supposed dangerous killer looked like he could be a stripper.

The news anchor described Jimmy's identifying features as a six-foot three-inch male, with black hair, a deep voice with a British accent, and a master of manipulation. That's the image that jump-started Julia's fascination with Jimmy.

Three years later, the fascination turned into an obsession. Her obsession soon began to cause interruptions in her daily life. On more than one occasion, Julia was written up at work for daydreaming and completely ignoring customers. Her daydreams featured a sexy six-foot three-inch, dark hair, mystery man that made her tingle in all the right places.

Slamming her hand down on the bar, she finally made up her mind that she needed to find Mister tall, dark, and scary. Maybe he'd be the one to finally make her feel something again. When she finally found him, Jimmy made her feel something all right, but it wasn't with sex. What he made her feel was even better. There is nothing more pleasurable than physically feeling the life leaving a person's body while their eyes stare at you, like they are pleading for mercy.

With so much care, Julia placed the photos back into the plastic bag. If anything ever happened to those pictures, Julia would burn the world to the ground. These pictures show a timeline of her time with Jimmy, the most enjoyable years of her life. The first pictures she had were of the time she was trying to track him down. After some time of being a "team," Jimmy allowed her to take pictures of his successful murder scenes, as long as they didn't show his face directly. Like anyone wouldn't be able to take one look at the polaroid and know instantly this was the work of the infamous Jimmy Yates. Wiping a single tear from her cheek, she went back to placing the pictures in their protective spot, where they'd never be found by anyone but her.

After making sure every fake rock in the fireplace was replaced perfectly so you could not see a hint of plastic, Julia moved back to the couch to finalize the checklist of equipment she'd need to finally make her move against Mary.

As much as she wanted to take the rats with her, right now was not that time. After figuring out how she'd get into the house, it just wasn't feasible to take those bloodthirsty creatures with her. How would she carry them anyway? Yes, she'd feed them blood, but she wasn't going to carry them around in her pocket. That was just psychotic. No, she'd execute her plan and use the rats later to torture Mary's little spawn. Using them on the child would make her revenge that much sweeter.

With her perfect plan in place, nothing could go wrong. Nothing was going to get in the way of her revenge.

Chapter 27

Never in a million years would Mary have thought she'd be able to find peace living in a place where she and her family were forced to live due to a threat to their lives. However, since her uncle found them a house that so closely resembled her own, besides the fact that someone was trying to kill her, it was not really stressful at all. Well, to be completely honest, her husband stressed her out more than anything.

For the past few mornings, Mary had been waking up earlier, sneaking out of the room while Devon was still asleep, enjoying a cup of coffee on the porch, and simply watching the sun come up. She loved her family beyond measure, but there was nothing like having a few moments of peace and quiet. Some time when there wasn't someone demanding her attention or relying on her to keep them alive.

The first few days of this new routine, the men that her uncle paid to protect them, for which she now considered her friends and some even close enough to call family, stayed away. It was only after a little coaxing on her part, bringing an extra cup of coffee with her and practically begging, would one of them finally begrudgingly sit with her on the porch swing.

On the third morning, Alex walked out to see Will sitting with Mary on the swing and drinking coffee. Will had been so worried that Alex would berate him, that he'd jumped up so quickly he jarred the swing and almost spilled his coffee all over Mary. After a menacing glare from Mary, Alex let out a booming laugh, which let Will relax minutely. Then Alex nudged Will out of the way and sat down next to Mary, grinning widely up at a baffled Will.

"There's something you need to know, Will. I grew up with Alex watching out for me, making sure no harm came to me, so the relationship we share is different from the relationship I share with anyone else. Alex was the first person to catch me sneaking out my bedroom window to go to a party when I was in high school." She was unable to hold in her laughter when she dared to steal a glance in Alex's direction and he had a huge scowl on his face.

"Alex earned my love when he didn't go directly to my aunt and uncle but instead drove me to the party and stayed in the background just to make sure I was safe before driving my drunk ass home. Even after I threw up all over his car, he never tattled on me or got me in trouble."

Looking between the two grown men, Mary witnessed Alex mouth "ha ha" to Will. All she could do was shake her head.

"Children, you are both children. Sometimes, I swear that Caleb has better manners than every grown man that currently resides in this house," Mary said with laughter in her voice.

Anyone could tell by the exasperated look on Mary's face, that she was in fact joking and not trying to hurt the men's feelings.

After leaving Alex and Will on the porch to bicker like preschoolers, Mary decided to head inside to refresh her coffee. Alex was arguing that he and Mary have had a twenty year friendship, and Will was arguing that it didn't matter the time they were together, all that mattered was keeping her safe. She had been enjoying the back-and-forth banter going on between the men too much to focus on drinking her coffee, and in turn, she'd accidentally allowed it to get cold.

Mary opened the door to a house wide awake with activity. If the racket coming from the kitchen was any indication, she'd think there was a party going on before nine a.m. When she walked on the porch this morning, everyone seemed to be sleeping peacefully, but not any longer.

Before reaching the kitchen, she could already hear Devon and Matthews arguing over Devon's taste in music. In most cases, Mary and Devon agreed on almost everything, but not this. This was one topic Matthews was one hundred percent correct on, and Devon deserved any mocking he received on his taste in music.

Trying to be as quiet as possible, Mary went into the dining room, which was attached to the kitchen. They'll still be able to see her, but they'd need to look in her direction, which she doubted they'd do if she didn't make any noise or sudden movements.

Her heart almost stopped from being full of love at the sight before her. Devon was holding Caleb in his arms, gently swinging him around. Baby giggles radiated from Caleb's little chest, while

Devon sang his favorite song "Come Sail Away" alongside the music playing from the Alexa on the counter.

Matthews was throwing a fit. If Mary didn't know any better, she thought Matthews was about to put his hands on his hips and stomp his feet. If only she had her video camera. "You're ruining my Godson's eardrums with this garbage. How does Mary put up with this being played in her house? Around her son? The horror."

Devon stopped dead in his tracks. He might have thrown a punch at his friend if it wasn't for the fact that he was holding his son. "Garbage? How dare you? Styx is one of the best bands ever. If I ever hear you talk such blasphemy again, I swear to you Matthews, I'll never cook for you again."

It took everything in Mary's power to not bust up laughing and give away that she was watching what was transpiring between the two men. They'd stop immediately if they knew they had a witness. Man, she wondered if she could make it to the porch to get her cell phone and record this interaction without being caught. The rest of the guys at the bureau would love to see this.

Devon always threatened to take his cooking away from Matthews, and the threat always carried weight. Mostly because Matthews loved to eat, even though he was a fanatic when it came to working out. His motto was, "Run ten miles a day, so I can eat and drink whatever the hell I want to."

Matthews was reaching out to Caleb, arms stretched, fingers wiggling. "Come here, Caleb. Come to Uncle Mikey." Caleb giggled and reached for Matthews.

Matthews knew Devon wouldn't keep Caleb from him, especially when Caleb was reaching back for him.

It was in such a low voice but Mary read the movement on Devon's lips when he said, "Traitor."

"Alexa," Matthews called out. "Play 'It's a Long Way to the Top' by AC/DC."

Devon gave a hearty laugh. "You and Mary are exactly the same. AC/DC is her favorite band. She only ever admitted that to me one time, long before we were married, but I catch her singing it to Caleb all the time. She sings it to him like a lullaby."

Giving Caleb some bounces, Matthews said, "See, buddy. That's another reason your mother should have ended up with me and not your dorky dad over here."

Mary had been quiet long enough, so she gave up her hiding spot and made her way over to her son. "Yeah, yeah, yeah. Mr. Comedian over here. He thinks he'd actually be able to handle me. Give me my son, Matthews, and stop trying to corrupt him. Yes, you sing him good music, but stop filling his head with bologna. Devon can barely handle me, what makes you think you could? You wouldn't even swim next to me in your boxers. No, I don't think you could handle me at all."

Turning away from the men, she called out, "Alexa, play 'Walking on Sunshine' on max volume. It's time for me to harness my inner Charlie Bradbury and get this day started the right way. Let's go, baby boy."

Grabbing her son from Matthews, she didn't wait for either man to respond to her declaration before dancing with her son out of the room while singing one of her favorite songs. She got what she wanted though. A few seconds later, the sound of laughter followed her outside. That's what she liked to hear, laughter. These days, it was a sound that was heard so little, except from Caleb.

Maybe, while everyone was in a good mood, she'd be able to convince them to join in a game of poker tonight. Pulling out her phone, she quickly sent a message to her uncle, asking if he'd be able to have the travel table and chips delivered by tonight.

Seconds later, she saw her aunt and uncle come around the house. They must have gone out the back door and gone on a morning walk by the water. That had become her aunt's favorite thing to do. Her Aunt Patricia told her that after the threat was over, she was going to try to convince Robert to buy this house because just like Mary had with her own home, Patricia had fallen in love with the lake on the property.

Patricia admitted to Mary one night while it was just them sitting out on the porch, well, with Alex of course, that she was trying to convince Robert to retire and take her traveling. Mary agreed wholeheartedly that it was an amazing idea, and she'd try to help in any way she could to convince her uncle that it was time to step away from politics.

"Good morning, sweetie," Robert said to Mary as he walked up the steps. He leaned down, and gave Caleb a kiss on the head, then gave her a kiss on the cheek. "Those items are already here and are being stored in the summerhouse out back where my men sleep. I was wondering when you'd get around to showing these men whose boss. It's your game, but I'd love to sit in. That is, if Patricia is okay with being on baby duty tonight?"

Patricia slapped Robert's shoulder, let out a laugh, and walked over to pluck Caleb out of Mary's arms. Since everyone was temporarily living in one house, Mary rarely got one-on-one time with her son. She would never complain about that fact, for it meant Caleb always had someone watching out for him.

"Of course, I'll watch over this precious boy. As long as I can peek in every once in a while. I love to see my two favorite people in action. I still remember the first time I walked into the study and found you teaching Mary poker. I was furious, to put it mildly. I felt that poker was not at all ladylike, and Mary didn't have any reason to be learning such a skill. You both have proven me wrong over the years. A woman needs any and every skill she can obtain. So go get'em, darlings."

Chapter 28

Devon was curious about what his wife was up to when at dinner she announced she wanted to play poker and asked who was courageous enough to take her on in a game. Mary winked at him when he gave her an eyebrow flash look. He's played against his wife; she's a shark. He knew she was up to something. Should he pull her aside and ask her, or just sit back and enjoy the game?

Alex and Will eagerly looked to Robert before agreeing to play. Since they were on the technical day shift, the nights were theirs for whatever they wanted to do. Alex would keep his radio next to him, of course, but was excited to take any chance he could to destroy Devon and Matthews. Smug bastards needed taken down a peg, and he enjoyed it immensely any time he was able to be the one to do it. He wasn't sure, however, if he'd be able to humiliate Mary during the game. No, he couldn't do that to her, he'd just focus his wrath on the guys, and let Mary play her own game.

Devon helped Mary set up the table later that evening, chuckling the entire time. "Are you sure you want to do this, love? Better question would be, why are you doing this, Mary?"

Without looking up from setting out the chips, she shrugged. "I don't know exactly what you mean. I just thought it'd be a fun thing to do. I was a little bored and thought a game of cards sounded like a fun way to pass the time." Reaching down, he grabbed her hand to stop her from setting the table. "That's bullshit, and you know it, sweetheart," Devon said, laughing so hard tears almost streamed down his face.

"What?" she asked, trying to sound innocent. She pulled out of his grasp and continued what she was doing.

"Are you kidding me, Mary? The only time you ask to play poker is when you've had a bad day and need to feel empowered by humiliating someone, usually me. You always get what you want, too. Not that I'd have any choice. I've tried and tried to beat you in poker. Matthews and I have even practiced, but you still kick my ass. No, you are up to something. Now spill."

Mary walked over to her husband and poked him in the chest. He could tell she wasn't mad but was still trying to act intimidating. "You take all the fun out of things, Mr. Walker, you know that? Now you listen to me, tonight is going to be fun. We are going to enjoy being with friends and family. We are going to eat pizza and drink beer and tell stories. Don't overanalyze things. And if you leave your agent mentality at home, maybe I'll let you use that authority in the bedroom later. This is your only warning. And I swear on everything, if you even try to warn the others that

I may be just a little bit good at poker, I'm withholding sex for a month. I dare you to test me and see if I'm joking."

Pulling her into his arms, he gave her a quick but passionate kiss. As he released her, she swayed a little, bracing her fingertips on the back of the chair for balance before turning away. She wasn't able to make it very far before Devon took a step and slapped her ass.

Looking over her shoulder, she said, "I'll remember that, Mr. Walker, and I won't take it easy on you tonight." They both started laughing as the door opened and the rest of her unknowing victims filed into the summerhouse behind the main house, ready to lose their proverbial shorts.

The group had been playing for hours when Will finally threw his cards down on the table and glared at Mary. "You're lucky I have a soft spot for you kid, or I'd think you were taking advantage of us."

Matthews, who sat next to Will, slapped him on the back and laughed out. "Oh, Will, you could only wish someone like Mary would take advantage of you one day."

"I hope you realize you're not as funny as you think you are," Will shot back.

Instead of responding back, Matthews just slapped Will on the shoulder before pouring him a shot.

After all this time together, Alex noticed Will still didn't realize Matthews had a tactless sense of humor. Walking around the table, Alex handed Will another beer. When Matthews held his hand out for one, Alex slapped it, giving him a high five.

Sitting back down, Alex decided to stir the pot a bit. "Devon, deal the damn cards. Will, did you ever hear the story about how Devon here made Matthews wear a dress to his and Mary's wedding?"

Will spit out his beer. The room filled with a mixture of yelling from Devon and Matthews as they jumped up and down, spilling beer all over the cards and table. Uncontrollable laughter came from Mary and Robert upon hearing Alex call what Matthews wore to her wedding a dress.

"Now, Alex," Matthews started, "If you're going to tell the story, you have to tell it right." Leaning back in his chair, he propped his feet up on the table, slowly sipping his beer. "I remember it just like it was yesterday. Devon came to my house, sweating bullets that he finally decided to ask Mary to marry him. He said she's too good for him, and like the best friend I am, I wholeheartedly agreed with him." Everyone laughed, except Devon.

"Little did I know that he'd try, and I emphasize *try*, to get back at me for making him doubt himself in his time of distress. Knowing that he'd never be able to make it through that day without me, he had no other option than to ask me to be his best man. Trying to get a little payback, he told me I'd have to dress similarly to him, in his native ceremonial outfit. I wasn't scared, I mean, have you seen this body?" He waved his hands up and down his body in a gesture. "This tall drink of water looks good in everything, or nothing. Dealer's choice."

After winking at Mary and taking a long drink of beer, he continued his story. "What I didn't realize was that I would be asked to wear a Scottish kilt for the ceremony. Apparently, it's rude to ask a Scotsman what he's wearing under his kilt because traditionally they didn't wear anything. So what do you think happens when someone tells me I can't do something? Devon tried using his big boy voice and told me that under no circumstances could I go commando at his wedding. It was rude to ask though, so right before he went into the ceremony, I had to show him what was under my kilt. No one can resist these tactical buttcheeks, but they do look better in jeans. More emphasis on the shapeliness. Anyway, I may or may not have ruined his wedding night. I can, however, confirm that I made the night of some of Mary's bridesmaids."

Devon slammed his head down on the table. The visual of Matthews' ass had resurfaced in his mind. Only seconds passed before Devon whipped his head back up and bellowed, "Damn it Matthews... Wait, some of Mary's bridal party were members of my family. Matthews, damn it, did you sleep with any of my cousins?"

"It's very ungentlemanly to kiss and tell."

Mary was wiping at the tears streaming down her face. "That's why your face was so red when I got to the altar, you liar. You said it was because of the heat. But, in fact, Matthews' ass made you blush."

Devon shook his head, completely exasperated with Matthews. "Yes, Mary, I'm a liar. I wasn't going to tell you, mind you in front of the minister, the reason my face was bright red was because Matthews just showed me his ass cheeks." Before Matthews could react, Devon turned and punched his shoulder causing him and his chair to fall backwards. "That's also the reason Matthews' attire was a bit disheveled. After he mooned me, I tossed him like a caber into a nearby table. He hit it so hard the flower vase fell off, splattering water all down his shirt, tartan, and bare legs."

Mary grumbled as she moved towards the door while Alex helped pick Matthews off the floor. "Children, all men are children." Robert glanced at where his niece was going and noticed his wife standing in the doorway holding Caleb. Her eyes were filled with humor, and he realized she heard the interesting parts. His Patricia was quite the wild one in her days, but he still tried to shelter her from what he considered "locker room talk".

Patricia moved into the room, trying to keep a hold of a squirming Caleb. "I decided to bring this bundle of joy down here to say goodnight. Don't any of you get him dirty, I just spent the last hour giving him a bath, and I swear I ended up wearing more water than what was left in the tub. I'm not doing that again tonight. He's going to be a soccer player, mark my words. Give your hugs and kisses and I'll be on my way and get this young man to bed."

The rest of the night passed in endless, enjoyable banter. Mary was blessed. Looking around the room, these men were no longer just friends or professionals hired to keep her safe, she considered them family.

Devon and Matthews stood as Mary pushed back from her seat and stretched her arms above her head. "Well boys, I for one had a great time whooping your asses tonight, but I'm going to call it a night. One of us needs to be coherent when Caleb wakes up in the morning, and you boys drank enough beer that I doubt any of you will wake before noon."

Leaning down to kiss her forehead, Devon whispered in her ear. "Remember, you said I can play special agent when I come to bed. I played nice tonight with these boys, so I don't have to play nice with you later."

"Down boy." She tapped his arm. "You just have fun here and I'll see you in a bit. We have all the time in the world. Enjoy some boy time."

Looking around at the droopy-eyed men, Devon knew it was time to wrap it up. "I'm going to help clean up here, then go check on the guys outside and make sure everyone's where they need to be and freshen up their coffee, then I'll be up to bed. Okay? "

"Yes, love." Turning to look at the rest of the guys, the night was exactly as she knew she needed when she planned it and was satisfied. "Goodnight, guys. Alex, Will, I'll expect one of you guys to have coffee with me tomorrow. You can rock, paper, scissors to figure out who it will be, but one of you better be on that porch swing when I bring out the morning coffee. I'll even make it extra strong, just as a peace offering for embarrassing you all a little bit tonight."

Stepping out the door, Mary's skin instantly tingled, and not from the cold. Her senses were suddenly on high alert. She felt as if she wasn't alone, and it wasn't the same feeling as having the security agents watching her. This was like when Yates was on the loose, but that's impossible, he's dead. There was only one other person out there that wanted to hurt her, but her uncle's security was too well-trained to let her get close.

Maybe she should go back into the summerhouse and tell Devon about her feelings, but Mary decided against it. There was no way Julia Kadlec could find this safe house, let alone get close enough to be a danger to them. Mary picked up her pace. She would feel better once she checked on Caleb and made sure he was okay.

Mary's imagination was running wild, and it was all because she'd allowed herself a few hours of pure, uninhibited peace. She'd talk about her feelings with Devon tomorrow. Tonight, she wouldn't worry him by letting her anxiety get the best of her. She'd go to bed and tomorrow would be a new day.

Chapter 29

It seemed like hours since she'd left the poker game, and Mary was exhausted. She just couldn't seem to shake the feeling that something was off, so she did a walkthrough of the house, checking every window and door to make sure they were locked. Of course, Devon and every single security agent would do exactly the same thing, but it made her feel slightly better to physically do it herself.

The last thing she had to do before she'd finally allow herself to relax for the night was check on Caleb. Making sure to open the door as quietly as possible, she only stuck her head inside before she knew her son was snug and warm in his crib. Her anxiety being on the rise didn't give her the right to disturb his peaceful sleep. Quietly, she backed out of his room, and when the door was shut, she placed her back to the door and took a few deep breaths before moving down the hall to her bedroom.

Mary was finally pulling the covers back to get into bed when the security bracelet Devon insisted she wear day and night started going off. At first, she didn't know what was happening since she wasn't physically wearing the bracelet when Devon showed her how it worked. Vibrations pulsed against her wrist, and the red light on the side flashed like a strobe light.

Once the meaning registered, she knew exactly what was going on. There was an immediate threat. The bracelet going off meant that someone was entering the house, uninvited.

Quietly sliding out of bed, she decided against putting on her slippers, opting to be as quiet as possible. Opening the bedroom door slightly, she quickly noticed how quiet the house was. The lack of noise coming from the living room meant the security team her uncle hired to protect them at the safe house were already at their posts for the night, and that Devon wasn't back yet.

With no one moving around downstairs, that meant the alarm system would be activated, and no one should be entering the house. Glancing over to the office connected to the bedroom and seeing no lights, she confirmed Devon wasn't back yet from the poker game. His bracelet should've been going off also, so where was he?

Chills ran down her spine as a thought came to her, Caleb. Someone was entering the house and Caleb was alone in the nursery. She ran over to the safe Devon had placed in the closet when they first came to this house and grabbed her Glock 9mm pistol then ran down the hall, no longer caring to be quiet.

If there was, in fact, someone trying to breach this house, there was no way in hell they'd get to her son. They'd need to go through her first, and in the past year, she's become quite deadly with her pistol. Devon and her uncle made sure of that. Mary was never going to be a victim again.

Carefully, and as quietly as possible, she opened the nursery door. The night light on the table in the corner still projected moving stars across the ceiling, allowing Mary to see that Caleb was sound asleep in his crib.

Maybe she was mistaken and the alarm was triggered by one of the security officers by accident. No, either one of them or Devon would have come and told her. They wouldn't let her worry needlessly, especially since they were already in a safe house because some psychopath was targeting them.

She was just about to pull out her phone to call Devon when a noise came from the adjoining bathroom. The creak of the window opening was undeniable. Someone was trying to make their way into the nursery through the bathroom window. None of her guys would ever come through the window, so this was, in fact, a threat.

Looking back and forth between the bathroom and bedroom doors, she made the hardest decision at that moment. Without knowing if there was anyone else in the house, or where the security agents were, she'd need to protect her son in the nursery. With every fiber in her being, she'd protect her son.

Moving quickly but quietly, Mary grabbed the travel bassinet she used when Caleb napped on the porch from the corner of the room and placed it on the floor of the walk-in closet. She then placed a thick blanket in the bassinet and ran to the crib to pick up Caleb. Whoever was coming through the window was moving slowly, obviously trying to make as little noise as possible.

Caleb didn't even make a peep when Mary snuggled him down into the bassinet inside the pitch-black closet. Thankfully he was exhausted from spending hours with her aunt outside this afternoon. She sent up a quick prayer that her son would sleep through whatever was about to happen next. Although it was unlikely he'd be able to retain memories this young, she knew about trauma and never wanted her son to have nightmares like her.

She wrapped the blankets around Caleb, lovingly placed a kiss on his forehead, and gently shut the door so as to not alert the intruder that anyone was in the nursery. Sweat dripped from her brow, and her heart skipped a beat as she worried over her son's safety during the confrontation that was bound to happen soon. She was just about to run back to the crib to place a stuffed animal under the blanket to make it look like Caleb was still sleeping when the bathroom door started to slowly creep open.

Internally, Mary was seething with fury over someone having the audacity to break into her home and threaten her family, again. Her son had already survived more trauma in his short life than anyone should ever need to endure. No one else was ever again going to threaten his safety. Moving back into the shadow of the dresser, she waited to see who would emerge from the bathroom. Thankfully, from where she was hiding, she'd be able to see the person's face, because the night light was shining towards the ceiling and angled away from the crib towards the bathroom.

Devon warned her of who tried to take her and her son's life that day at the store, but it still shocked her to see Doctor Julia Kadlec creeping into her son's nursery. When Devon first told her that they found evidence Dr. Kadlec was working with Yates and was the one that had targeted them with the car bomb, she was shocked, to say the least. The pediatric doctor was present when her son was born, and she had been told Dr. Kadlec was there to comfort him after the explosion.

Devon explained his suspicions that Dr.Kadlec was the one that gave Mary the blood thinners that almost caused her to bleed out during childbirth, but they haven't been able to prove that it wasn't an accident. One thing was for sure, they were one hundred percent positive that she was a danger to Mary and Caleb.

This wasn't an accident; you don't break into someone's home by accident. This woman purposely broke into her home and was now right in front of her, creeping towards her son's crib. Mary had every legal right to defend her life and the life of her child.

When Julia discovered Caleb wasn't in his crib, her expression started as surprise, and in a blink of an eye, turned to black-out rage.

Julia's spine straightened, and she squinted her eyes to try to see better in the dimly lit room. Where was that damn kid? She needed him to use as leverage to get Mary to leave the house with her. That stupid bitch would do anything for her son. It was quite pathetic. She knew that for a fact from watching them in the hospital together when she was in and out of the room charading as a nurse. No matter how many times Julia tried to kill Mary, she just kept coming back, and all because she was fighting to return to that little brat. *Shit.*

She caught a small movement out of the corner of her eye. She wasn't alone. "Shit."

Before Julia could realize what was happening, Mary was on top of her, knocking her to the ground. Julia barely registered the attack before Mary's hands were around her neck, squeezing the life out of her. No, this wouldn't be the way she died, she needed to avenge Jimmy so she'd be able to gloat when they were finally reunited. Using her knee, she jabbed upwards, connecting with Mary's stomach and temporarily knocking the wind out of her. The blow caused Mary's grip to loosen enough that Julia was able to get her arms between Mary's and break her hold on her neck.

Pushing Mary away, Julia scrambled to her knees and tried moving towards the bathroom door. If she reached the bathroom, she could lock the door and get back out the window to regroup and plan her next attack. Kidnapping wasn't a good idea, she'd need to go for a quick kill next time.

Mary, under no circumstances, was going to let Julia leave this nursery. Where the hell was Devon? He should've noticed she wasn't in bed and come looking for her. She also knew that he always looked in on Caleb before going in to bed. Shit, couldn't anyone hear the commotion coming from the nursery? What if Julia did something to Devon?

No, that couldn't be possible. She'd never be able to get the jump on him. Mary needed to clear her mind of everything but the task at hand. She was the only thing standing between this psycho and her son.

Mary lunged and grabbed a hold of Julia's ankle as she crawled towards the bathroom door and gave a big yank. She couldn't move her very far, but it threw Julia off balance just enough to give Mary a little advantage. Remembering that she wasn't defenseless, Mary looked around the room for where she'd placed her Glock.

It only took her seconds to find it sitting over by the closet door, then she remembered Caleb. The last thing she wanted was to use the gun in such close proximity to Caleb. And what would happen if Julia was able to overpower her and use the gun against her? No, she needed to use all other options before reaching for the Glock. Since Julia hadn't noticed the gun yet, she figured she wasn't completely out of options.

Julia wasn't going to give her the time she needed to formulate a plan to subdue her until she was able to get help. In the span of only seconds, Julia turned into a raging maniac. That's what made the decision easy for Mary. Knowing she was the only thing standing between this psychopath and her son, Mary needed to think quickly.

In one swift motion, Mary grabbed Caleb's lamp, yanked the cord out of the wall, and swung until it connected with Julia's head. It must have been the adrenalin, but Julia was barely phased by the hit to the head. Her eyes, however, swung towards the door as the lamp crashed to the ground.

The noise. She was worried about the noise. Mary could hear shouting coming from downstairs. Thank goodness, finally, someone heard them. Devon or one of the security agents must have come into the house and heard the loud crashing.

Mary's concentration wavered for only a moment, but that was all the time Julia needed. Julia gave Mary a well-placed karate chop to the side of her neck, hitting the vagus nerve, causing Mary so much pain she fell to the ground. As soon as

Mary started to crumble, Julia rushed over and locked the bedroom door before running to the bathroom and jumping out the window.

Only seconds passed, even though it felt like minutes, but Mary finally heard pounding on the door. The loud noise must have woken Caleb because suddenly wailing came from the closet.

Devon was already frantic, but as soon as he heard his son's cries, he pushed the security agent attempting to use a lock pick set to open the bedroom door aside, and with one kick, splintered the frame into pieces.

With a gun drawn, Devon and three other agents rushed into the room. Instant relief filled Devon when he saw Mary kneeling on the floor blocking the closet door, which he deduced from the noise was where Caleb was located. She was safe, and his son was safe.

Mary, with tears running down her face and her body ready to spring and attack, started yelling to Devon. "She went into the bathroom. That bitch came through the window. She came after our son. Don't you dare let her get away."

Devon started barking orders to the three agents in the room. As much as he wanted to run after Dr. Kadlec himself, he needed to make sure his family stayed safe. His phone buzzed in his pocket, indicating a message. Two of the security officers stationed on the grounds were in pursuit of Kadlec, and he'd be notified as soon as she was in custody.

Deja vu washed over him. Devon slowly walked towards Mary, hands in front of him. "Mary, are you hurt?"

Leaping to her feet and reaching behind her, she pulled the door to the closet open. "No, Devon, I'm not hurt. I'm pissed. That bitch dared to enter our home; enter our son's bedroom. His. Bed. Room. If you hadn't insisted on me wearing this ugly-ass bracelet thing, she could've kidnapped our child. I want to find that bitch and gut her. I swear with every fiber in my being, she's not going to get near our son again."

Her fury was stoked further upon the sight of Caleb's tear-streaked face. She took a single deep breath, straightened her shoulders, placed Caleb into Devon's arms, and walked past him towards the door. Alex was in the doorway blocking her escape.

"Alex, if you don't get out of my way, so help me, I will put you on your knees."

Looking over the top of Mary's head, Alex could see Devon shaking his head no. "Sorry, Mary, I can't let you leave this room."

Tears streamed down Mary's face, but she was completely unaware of their presence. The tears were not from fear or sadness, they were out of fury.

If these men think they are going to stand in her way of going after Dr. Kadlec, they better think again. She made Mary feel trapped and helpless in her own home. The suffocating feeling of hyperconscious and restraint, like when she was being held captive by Yates, came flooding back. She'd be damned if she allowed someone to rule her life the way Yates did in the days he tortured her. She's done feeling this way. She's the master of her life, not some murderers.

If Devon and Alex wouldn't help her, she knew her uncle and her aunt would. They knew what she went through and wouldn't deny her anything. To get her point across, Mary walked across the room, ripped Caleb's Alexa from the wall, and chucked it at Alex's head.

Alex looked at her like she'd lost her damn mind, and in a way, she had. If Alex hadn't anticipated what she was about to do and moved at the last second, the Alexa would have done some major damage to his face. Mary's aim was right on target.

She walked right back up to him and said just one word. "Move."

Rolling his eyes, Alex stepped aside but followed her out of the room. As hard-headed as she was, he wasn't going to let her get herself killed trying to chase after Kadlec when the rest of his guys were already hunting her down. So, he'd keep her within two steps until Devon or Robert told him it was all clear.

Chapter 30

W hen Mary left the nursery, she didn't try to go far, or even try to run out of the house and track down Julia herself like she originally wanted to. Instead, she walked room to room, looking out the windows for any hint that Julia had been apprehended, before heading downstairs.

There was no one else downstairs besides Alex and Mary, and Alex wanted to give Mary as much space as he could, so he stayed by the steps with a clear view of her. It chilled him to the core to think about all the trauma this poor girl had endured in her short life. He'd been with the congressman for almost twenty years. He became employed with the Carter's not long after Mary's parents were killed, so he watched Mary grow into the amazing young woman she is.

Alex applied for the position of head security with the Carters right out of the Army, where he had served as a Captain with the Rangers. Alex's father went to school with Robert, and Robert called Alex about the opening when he heard he was thinking about leaving the Army. It was the job of a lifetime, so he quickly agreed and joined Carter's security team as soon as his contract was complete.

Looking across the room at a statue-still Mary, Alex was concerned about what lasting effects tonight's attempt on Caleb would have on her. Would she become so consumed with worry that Caleb would never be out of arm's reach, paranoid he'd be lost at any moment? Or would she become withdrawn? Currently, she was standing in the middle of the living room, staring out the window. She had not moved a muscle in over ten minutes, not even to shift her feet. Was she in shock? Like always, he'd keep a close eye on her.

The outside flood lights made it look like it was midday, and all that light poured right into the house. Because everything inside was also illuminated, Alex was able to see Mary as clearly as if she were standing in the sun. It wasn't her posture that worried him, it was the look in Mary's eyes that caused Alex concern. He's seen that look in a soldier's eyes before, and it always meant trouble.

Someone was coming down the stairs, and they were trying to be quiet. Alex heard the footsteps behind him and turned to intercept whoever it was before they could enter the living room and disturb Mary. Thankfully it was Devon because they needed to talk.

Alex placed a hand on Devon's shoulder, and he stopped in his tracks. After a quick glance at his wife, Devon nodded to the small alcove by the front door.

"What's wrong, Alex?"

He peeked back around the corner, wanting to check again to make sure Mary was out of earshot. "I'm worried about Mary. I've seen that look in men's eyes before, but usually in combat. I've known Mary for almost twenty years; I've watched that girl grow up. I'd never suggest that I know her better than her own husband, but I do know her very well. I think you should know that I'm almost one hundred percent sure that she's going to do something stupid. I think tonight was her breaking point— when the danger revolved around Caleb and Mary was actually the one defending his safety. I care for your wife, Devon, we all do. We consider her our family, our little sister if you will. You just tell us what you need, and you got us. We know you're the law, but when it comes to family there is no law. If you have an issue with that, you need to step away. You got me?"

No response was needed. Devon gave Alex a quick tap on the shoulder as a sign of agreement, then moved to stand with his wife.

Silence was all around them. Lights and movements from outside slowly pulled Mary from being lost in thought about all that recently happened. She didn't see nor hear Devon come into the room, but she'd been aware of his presence for some time. Caleb pulled the rest of her concentration when Patricia carried him into the living room. He was dressed in new pajamas, smiling ear to ear, sucking on a bottle of warm milk.

She realized in that instant, the fierce, protective emotions her parents must have felt the night they were murdered. Her parents knew they were about to die when Yates invaded their home, and yet they did everything they could to give her a fighting chance at survival. Looking into her son's eyes, she knew, without a doubt, she would lay her life down for this boy. And she might do just that, if she could get away from her husband and the rest of the men that have sworn to protect her. This wasn't their fight any longer. This was between Mary and Julia. It was going to end, one way or another, and ideally before that bitch had the chance to regroup and take another shot at Caleb.

Patricia kissed Mary on the cheek, then leaned her forehead against hers, holding it in place. "I got this little prince all settled down. I had Will move the pack-n-play into our room for the night so I can watch over him. I'm going to take him upstairs and get him down before he sucks down all this milk and thinks it's time to get up and play again. Do you need anything before I take him up, darling? Some hot tea, a bath, something to eat?"

Tears sprang to Mary's eyes. "No, thank you, Aunt Patricia, but thank you for protecting my son. He couldn't be in better hands. No matter what happens, protect him, always. He's just a little boy. He needs everyone watching out for him, and he needs to know he's loved."

Patricia was confused, wasn't the threat over? Something in her niece's voice was very concerning, and she'd mention it to Robert and Devon first thing in the morning. "What are you talking about, darling? Everything will be okay. I know it was a horrible night, but please try to get some sleep. We'll talk about this tomorrow, okay? I love you."

Hugs were exchanged, and Patricia took an already almost sleeping Caleb back upstairs. It was going to be a long night, so Mary needed coffee. Apparently, the men had the same idea because when she walked into the kitchen, she found Devon, Robert, Alex, and Will standing at the counter with cups of coffee in front of them and a new pot already brewing.

Alex was the first person to notice Mary standing in the doorway and slowly walked over to stand by her side. Without saying a word, he placed an arm around her shoulders, gave her a squeeze, and guided her to the kitchen table. Will approached and set a fresh cup of coffee in front of her and placed a hand on her shoulder, wanting to also show his support.

Hours seemed to pass in silence, even though it was only minutes before the dreaded call came in over the radio. Julia Kadlec had escaped the property, and there was no trace of her. Everyone would continue to search for the smallest clue, but they wouldn't be making an arrest tonight. That call started the four men discussing what should happen next. The anger everyone was feeling was evident in the tone of their voices. They were snapping questions at each other, but the rage was all directed at Julia Kadlec. Even the mention of her name seethed fury.

Mary tried to pay attention but only caught bits and pieces as she played the events of the night repeatedly in her head. She did hear Devon call Matthews at some point, which was expected since she assumed he probably was still driving home after their evening of poker.

Arms wrapped around Mary's shoulders from behind, and she knew then that Matthews had arrived. How long had she been lost in thought?

"Matthews, get off my wife," Devon called out from across the room, instantly halting all conversations.

He gave Mary one last squeeze before releasing her and walking towards the fridge to get a beer.

"Anything?" Devon asked as Matthews approached the table.

"No, she was long gone by the time we found her tracks. She came prepared for a quick escape. But don't worry, she won't be able to get past us again."

Robert slammed his hand on the table. "That bitch shouldn't have been able to get onto this property, let alone into the house. Alex, bring in all the men. They are needed here, not at our house."

"Yes, Sir," he said, and he pulled out his phone, typing quickly.

When he was done with his message and put his phone back into his pocket, everyone started speaking at once again, and it was a unanimous consensus, the safe house was compromised and they would be moving in the morning. Matthews wanted Mary and Caleb placed back under twenty-four-hour surveillance in a new unknown location, just like she was when Yates was alive. Devon agreed, and Alex mentioned adding Patricia and sending the three of them out of the country.

To hell with that idea. They were not about to ship her away and exclude her from bringing that psychopath to justice. The time for being reasonable and calm was over, Mary was determined to get them to listen to her, or else she'd handle the threat herself. She had sat at the table long enough listening to everyone around her making plans that didn't include her.

Jumping to her feet, she pushed back from the table so hard and fast that her chair fell over. Slamming her hands on the table, she shouted, "Enough is enough. You're talking and making plans as if I'm not a part of this. If anything, I need to be front and center. I'm the one she wants. I'm the key to unlocking her rage. *Use me.*"

Protests came from every man at once. Devon grabbed her shoulders and started to shake her. "Absolutely not. You're not getting within fifty feet of her. We've decided that you, Caleb, Patricia, and Alex are going away for a bit. At least until this is all over."

Mary pulled back and out of Devon's grasp. She looked around the table and noticed all the men were nodding in agreement with what her husband was saying to her. "So, you've all decided what I'm going to do? Hell no."

Mary shook her head, straightened her back, lifted her chin, and tried to calm her voice. One look at her and all the men could tell she was furious, but damn it if she wouldn't try to keep a semblance of decorum.

"I'm going to say this once, and only once, so you all shut your mouths and listen up. I have lived my *entire* life in fear. Since the day Jimmy Yates tainted my existence, I've lived in fear, always looking over my shoulders. The twenty-three years between my parent's murder and when Yates finally found me, I lived in fear every single day. Every day for those twenty-three years, I never knew if I'd live to see the sunrise the next morning. Now, Yates brought this bitch into my life, and she not only threatened me but the life of my child. I will not stand on the sideline and allow any of you to tuck me away so you boys can play protector any longer. You are all talking about not including me in whatever plan you make to finally catch her, but you are going to change your plans."

Robert looked as if he was about to cry. Alex and Will looked ready to go on a rampage. Devon, though, looked completely devastated. He knew Mary well enough to know that there would be no changing her mind, especially when it came to their son. Matthews, on the other hand, was the only one brave enough to attempt to argue.

"Now, Mary…" Matthews started to say.

"I swear on everything you love, Matthews. If you don't shut up right this instant, I will make it so you can never have children. Do you doubt me? I'm not above Lorena Bobbitting you with the mood I'm in right now."

That got Matthews to shut up and Alex to crack a grin.

"Now, where was I? You are going to use me as bait. I'm the only pull strong enough to draw her out and you all know it. If you cannot agree to my terms, I'll walk out of here and find her myself. If you'd try to stop me, I will cut you all out of mine and Caleb's lives. Drastic? Abso-freaking-lutely. This psychopath is smart, too smart. She got so freaking close this time; she was in Caleb's nursery. If I wasn't wearing this stupid bracelet, my son would have been kidnapped. So, if it's a fight she wants, it's a fight she'll get, but she's not ready for one with me. Mama bear has been activated, and I'm going to tear her limb from limb."

Chapter 31

Silently, the men watched as Mary left the room. None of them tried to stop her nor did any of them mention the tears that poured down her cheeks the entire time she had spoken. All the men in the room knew how strong of a woman Mary was, and they knew that those tears were not of sadness, but of frustration and rage.

The emotions that flooded through Robert could only be described as devastation. He could see and feel the pain and outrage in his nieces' eyes. Yes, he lost his sister, but the feelings he experienced from her loss were only a fraction of what his Mary endured. How could she ask them to allow her to put herself willingly back in harm's way? Well, she hadn't asked, she demanded. Robert knew that she got her stubbornness from him, and most of the time he appreciated her fire, but this time he was terrified her fire would cause her to get burned. They needed to take her threat seriously.

One thing about his niece is that she isn't a confrontational person, and didn't normally make threats, so when she does, people need to take it seriously. Robert knew Devon would be able to make one phone call to his boss at the FBI and they would whisk Mary and Caleb away to safety, but at what expense? They'd both lose Mary and Caleb if they didn't agree to her terms instead of forcing her onto the sidelines.

Would Devon put Mary and Caleb's safety first, damn the consequences, and try to make up for it later?

The only noise in the kitchen came from a clock that hung above the stove. The clock, like an annoying beacon, ticked away the seconds, letting everyone know they didn't have much time to make a decision. Mary wouldn't give them much time.

Robert was the first to speak. He stood, shaking, with tears in his eyes. With one look, Devon could tell that whatever Mary's uncle was about to say was tearing him apart.

"Now, boys. I'm going to take a page out of my niece's playbook, and I need you all to hear me out before you start your arguing. I'm the elder here, at least give me that."

In unison, the other four men all nodded in agreement.

"Everyone in this room cares for that woman outside and that precious baby upstairs. Every one of us would place ourselves in the line of fire before allowing either of them to be harmed, if it was our choice. But this time, the choice is out of our hands. Fate has decided to play a sick, demented game with my family, and I can't just stand by and watch them continue to be threatened. Mary gave us an ultimatum. She said we needed to allow her to be the bait to draw Kadlec out so she can finally be neutralized, or she'll take Caleb and disappear."

Taking a second to compose himself, Robert walked over to the sink, grabbed a washcloth, ran it under cold water, and held it to his face. With the washcloth in hand, and after a few deep breaths, he slowly walked back over to the men waiting for him at the table.

"My niece does not make threats, she makes promises. I truly, with my entire heart, believe she will leave us all if we cut her completely out of this case. As much as she loves all of her family, her son is her world, and his safety will forever be her number one priority. Personally, I can't lose her. When I lost Mary's mother, my sister, it almost destroyed me. So I'd rather her hate me for the rest of my life than for her to lose hers."

As the men started to protest, Robert slapped his hands on the table, and the talking stopped.

"It is my hope that Mary would one day forgive me, but I'd be okay with just knowing she's alive. My plan is that I'm going to take her and Caleb away. Just me. Along with some very capable men I'm going to borrow from some friends of mine. You four, are going to put all your efforts forth and catch this bitch so Mary can come home. Now, Patricia can't know about this, so I need you to protect her or put her somewhere safe. Alex, my wife's safety is in your hands. Can you guys please agree to this?"

Alex was the first to lunge to his feet. "Absolutely not. Robert, Mr. Carter. You can't be serious. Do you know what this will do to the relationship you have with Mary? I have been in your employment for twenty years, and in every way that matters, you are Mary's father. It would kill her not to have you in her life, or to even feel any resentment towards you for keeping her away from getting her revenge. No, I'll take Ms. Mary away. I'll be the one that she is mad at. She and I are friends, but you two are family."

Will, until now, had been sitting quietly at the table. He hadn't been with this family long, but he already knew the love they had for each other. Will considered Alex not only his superior, but also a good friend, and he could see that the decision to take Mary away so Robert didn't have to was devastating.

"Alex, no," Will said, also standing up. "I'll take Mary away. She doesn't know me as well as the rest of you, but with the men Mr. Carter's friend is going to provide, we will keep her safe. I promise. It won't hurt me as much as the rest of you to lose her friendship. Let me do this for you guys."

Devon silently watched these men before him argue about who would practically kidnap his wife and child and, in turn, ruin their relationship with her. He couldn't sit back and let that happen. Not when, against his better judgment, he actually agreed with his wife.

Mary needed to do this, and she was tougher than everyone seems to think. She could do this and win, Devon had to believe that. Now, he had to convince everyone they needed to give in to Mary this time. She made a valid point, as much as he hated to admit it.

While the other men argued in the kitchen, Matthews walked over to the front door. From the little window built into the door, he was able to see Mary sitting on the front step with her head in her hands. Only a few steps away stood one of Alex's security guards who was keeping a close eye on her.

"Shit," Matthews said to no one in particular. He'd grown to care very much for Mary, and it hurt him to see her being mentally torn apart. She was right; she wasn't going to have peace until Kadlec was either behind bars or rotting in the ground with Yates. Now how was he going to convince his best friend and partner that he needed to put his wife in danger?

Only years of training allowed Matthews to detect the faint footsteps of Devon making his way to his side at the front door. "Can you see her? Does she seem to be okay? "

"Yeah, I can see her. She's sitting right outside on the steps. Security is watching her closely, she's okay. You know better than anyone else how tough Mary is. She's a survivor." Turning to his friend, Matthews could see the strain of everything very evident on his face. "You know she's right? She does have a stake in all this. As much as we hate to admit it, her stake is higher than anyone else's. If we take this away from her, she'll be looking over her shoulder every day of the rest of her life."

Letting out a long, jagged sigh, Devon responded, "I know, man, but how can I let my wife put herself in danger? I swore to protect her, and we have no idea what Kadlec is capable of."

Matthews placed a reassuring hand on his friend's shoulder. "We plan this down to the last detail. We plan for every contingent. Nothing is foolproof, but we make it as safe as possible. We make sure that Mary can defend herself against the person for whom she harbors so much rage. We make it so Mary can finally let her demons go after this is over. Okay? "

"Yeah. It has to be okay because I don't think we have another option." Devon moved towards the door. "I'll go out and get her, can you gather everyone in the kitchen? Maybe put on a new pot of coffee. It's going to be a very long night. We don't stop planning until every detail is hammered out to everyone's approval and Mary's in agreement to not deviate from the plan."

A few minutes later, Devon and Mary walked back into the kitchen. Once seated at the table, Mary began to speak. "When I was sitting outside, I had time to think. I know how I'm going to draw her out and make her furious enough to make mistakes. So here's what I'm going to do…"

Chapter 32

Tonight was a freaking disaster. How in the hell could she let that woman overpower her? Julia worked out like crazy and trained like a fiend just to keep up her strength. If Jimmy was here, he'd make her walk him through the night and analyze every step over and over again until she could see what went wrong. So that's what she needed to do.

Hours later, the only thing Julia could come up with as to why Mary could possibly be able to overpower her was simply adrenaline. Mary had to have received a burst of adrenaline when Julia threatened the life of her child. It's the only conceivable explanation for her failure.

The adrenaline hormone makes your heart and lungs work faster and harder, which sends more oxygen to your major muscles. Because of the extra oxygen to your muscles, your body gets a temporary boost of strength. Yes, that must be the only reason she wasn't able to complete her mission. Next time, Julia would go for a quick kill, and not a long, drawn out, satisfyingly painful torture session.

She wasn't able to plan long. Her laptop started dinging, indicating movement on the cameras she set up around that worthless safe house.

"Why is she leaving the house? That's the only place she's remotely safe," Julia said out loud to herself as she watched the camera, which she was able to place in a driveway to their not-so-safe house that faced in the direction of the buildings. Watching her computer screen, she saw Mary walking down the steps to the house, holding her child in her arms, while looking around her as if to make sure no one was watching her leave. What was she up to?

It dawned on her, Mary was running away and taking the child with her. Pure satisfaction hit Julia like a rainbow. She had Mary so scared with her intrusion last night that she must have lost confidence in her law enforcement husband and was running away. This might be her one and only window of opportunity to make her move. With Mary having no protection, and having her child, she'd be vulnerable. Easy pickings.

Now where would she run to? She'd need supplies to run away, right? She'd need to make at least a pit stop at her home, and she'd need to be quick if she was to get away before her husband knew she was gone. Julia needed to move now if she wanted any chance of catching them. Mary and the spawn in one swoop, with no police interference? It was shaping up to be her lucky day. If anyone was due to have some luck thrown their way, it was her.

Realizing the time of day, she cursed under her breath. She'd get stuck in rush hour traffic and might not be able to make it to

Mary's house in time. A thought popped into her head, Troy drove a very nice Ducati Monster in rosso red, and he parked it out back at the coffee shop. The question was, would he let her borrow it?

Troy just needed a little persuasion, and a quicky in the back room, and the motorcycle was hers. Of course, she did need to promise a much longer reward later tonight when she returned the bike back to him. If she was able to achieve her goal, she'd be so turned on that she'd need the kind of release Troy was guaranteed to offer her. He could be violent when she allowed, and damn was he hot when he let go. Yes, she'd reward him big time for allowing her to get to her prey in time and exact the revenge Jimmy dreamt about for years.

Pulling into traffic, after feeling the power between her legs, she knew she'd be able to make time up quickly. Knowing the roads between the coffee shop and that bitches house by heart, Julia would be able to get there in just under forty-five minutes, even less now that Troy allowed her the use of his bike. Since Mary only had about a twenty-minute head start from the safe house, so long as she drove the speed limit, Mary would only beat her to the house by less than ten minutes. She had the kid with her, so she'd probably be driving cautiously. That meant, there was no way Julia would miss her this time. This time she'd have her revenge.

Looking out the window, he saw his wife pulling out of the driveway, and fear coursed through his every fiber. "What the hell is she doing?" Devon asked Robert, who was standing by the coffee machine.

"You knew she wasn't going to sit idle any longer. She told you those exact words last night. The only thing we can do now is trust that she will be safe and come back to us. She left us no other choice." Even as the words left his mouth, he couldn't help but feel there was impending doom on the horizon.

Devon and Matthews had drilled every single detail of their plan into Mary's head until she was ready to scream. Yes, it was her plan on how to catch Julia, and she gave them the ultimatum to use her or she walked, but she had given them the leeway to plan the details. Maybe that was a mistake. No, not a mistake. If anyone could plan this with the best outcome possible, it was her husband and his partner.

Julia Kadlec never should have been able to find the safe house, and the FBI was still trying to figure out how exactly she did it, so they couldn't take anything for granted. They needed to assume she had the ability to use some very high-tech equipment or there was a leak.

In retrospect, the plan was perfect, but Mary wasn't going to leave anything to chance. So the plans changed. Knowing the moment she left the protection of the safe-house, she needed to cut all communication, her son and her family were all that was on her mind. How could she keep them safe? She couldn't stay behind the protective walls a moment longer, not doing anything. As

Mary pulled up the driveway, it took all her power not to scan the tree line, checking for any sign of danger. She wished Devon was close. Not to help with what she had planned, but having him close kept her calm. Calm was the last thing she was feeling right now. That woman came after her son, so Mary would burn everything she held dear to the ground. Things were finally coming to an end, and she was terrified. Terrified something would go wrong and Caleb would grow up without a mother.

Thinking back to their planning, Mary knew Julia was most likely watching the house, so she needed to act frantic. Not that it would take much acting on her part. She left the car running and rolled the windows down halfway so you still couldn't see inside, but it looked like she had them open because the baby was in the back seat. She popped the truck as if preparing to place their bags inside and paused to talk to the empty back seat that was supposed to contain her son before heading towards the house.

After running up the porch steps, she unlocked the door, gave a quick glance at the car and the still-empty driveway, and ran inside the house. As soon as she crossed the threshold, she dropped to her knees and tried to control the overwhelming need to sob. She's the one that wanted this, so why was it that at this very moment, all she wanted to do was run back to the safe house and Devon?

"Mary?" She heard a familiar voice whisper from the bottom of the steps. "Mary, we can still call this off. We can walk out of here right now and figure out another way to catch her. It's not too late to back out. You just say the word and we'll walk out together.

We'll find a safe place for you and your son, and we will catch her. I promise you, Caleb will be safe."

No, she'd come too far to give up now. Forcing a smile, she said, "I'm good, Alex. I got this. This ends, here and now. I'm good. I promise you. It was just a moment of weakness."

Alex was now standing beside her. He leaned down and placed a kiss on the top of her head. "Here, kid." He placed a familiar item into her hands. Looking down, it was an expandable baton. It was the first weapon Alex trained her on when she turned fourteen. It was the weapon he gave her that was small enough to carry in her backpack to school, though it was illegal. It was the weapon she carried every day in college, and even when she started to teach at college. She had only stopped carrying one when she married Devon.

She couldn't stop herself, she gave him a quick hug before walking out the door. "Thank you, Alex, for everything."

Mary couldn't stop pacing near her car in the driveway. The waiting was driving her to distraction. What was taking so long? Shouldn't they have seen a sign of Julia by now? Maybe they had it all wrong, maybe she wouldn't make a move this soon. "I'm going to take a quick walk down by the water. I'll be back soon." She said out loud so Alex could hear her through the earpiece he required her to wear.

Still inside the house, Alex placed a hand on the front door. "I don't think that's a good idea. That's too far away from both Matthews and myself if you need my help."

"Alex, I wasn't asking permission. I was telling you what I am going to do. You can listen through your earpiece and give

Matthews a heads-up when he's on. I don't think she's going to show up. I'm going to take a walk by my lake, my happy place. Then, when I'm done, we can head back to the safe house so I can hold my son and make a different plan of attack. Okay?"

He wasn't happy about it, but unless he was going to hogtie her, they'd just have to make it as safe as possible for her. Removing his hand from the door, Alex quickly gave Matthews a heads up that Mary was being stubborn and was on the move. Mary smirked at being called stubborn.

A triad of curses came through the earpiece, none directed at Alex, or Mary. All indicating how Devon would drown both of them in the lake and let the fishes eat them if even one hair was out of place when Mary returned tonight. There was even a comment or two about how Devon was never going to cook for Matthews again after this, so how dare Mary do this to him.

Being near her lake was exactly what Mary needed. Thankfully, there was a breeze this morning. The wind whipped Mary's hair around her face, which was something people always thought she was crazy for enjoying. Lifting her face to the sky, she breathed in deep, taking a second to enjoy the freshness of the air around her. Why people would rather live in the city, she would never understand.

Mary was just taking her third deep breath when she faintly heard a sound in the distance. She knew that sound. The roar of a wide-open throttle and throaty growl of the engine was a sound very common on campus. Taking one more deep breath, she turned to face whatever was coming head-on.

Still far away, but making its way quickly up her driveway, was a red motorcycle. The only person she knew who drove a motorcycle was Matthews, but his bike was black, and he was in the tree line to her right, so it wasn't him. It was Julia, it just had to be. A tightness in the pit of her stomach told her this was what she was waiting for, and Mary was ready.

Moving away from the water, Mary intentionally made herself more noticeable. She could just imagine Matthews yelling at her from his hiding place, but he wasn't saying anything into the earpiece. The person driving the motorcycle suddenly veered away from the house and gunned the bike toward the water; she saw Mary.

Yes, and just as Mary thought. It was Julia.

When the motorcycle was about fifty feet away from Mary, a shot rang out from the tree line. Matthews. The bullet didn't hit the rider, it hit the front tire, instantly laying the bike down on its side. As if she'd practiced this before, the rider didn't miss a beat and she hit the ground, tumbled a little, then jumped to her feet and kept running directly at Mary.

"Shit! Get to Mary! I don't have a shot," Matthews yelled as he shimmied down from the tree. Mary's focus was taken from Julia's fiery gaze by a glint of steel at her side. Julia had a knife in her hand. So, she was ready for a fight? After what she put her son through, Mary would take pleasure in finally getting her hands on this woman.

Mary held her retracted baton behind her back and watched Julia charge. When Julia was within feet of Mary, she pulled the knife up above her head. Just a few more seconds and Mary would be ready to strike.

Just like Alex taught her, once Julia was within striking distance, Mary flicked her wrist, opening the baton. Mary's reflexes were fractionally quicker than Julia's, which allowed her to connect her baton with Julia's wrist and knock the knife out of her hand. A roar of rage erupted from Julia.

In the background, Mary could see Matthews coming from the wooded area, and Alex bursting out the front door and rushing down the driveway towards them. Julia took advantage of Mary's lack of focus and swept her feet. Mary went down hard but kept hold of the baton. Striking out, her baton connected with Julia's left shin, and they heard a sickening crunch.

Grunting, Julia lost focus and instinctively reached down to cover her shin. Mary took advantage since she was still on the ground, and kicked up with her right foot, aiming for the side of Julia's head. Mary's black Under Armour running sneaker connected only slightly with the side of Julia's temple. "That's for my son, you psychotic bitch."

The kick grazed Julia's head, but was still hard enough to put her on her knees. Shaking her head as if to clear away the fog, Julia prepared to lunge but never had the chance. Alex ran up from behind and tackled her to the ground, quickly reaching into his pocket and pulling out his handcuffs.

Matthews helped Mary up off the ground and rubbed his hands all over her body to check for injuries.

Out of nowhere, Mary burst into laughter. Both Matthews and Alex looked at her like she lost her mind. Maybe she had.

Matthews asked, with worry in his voice, "Mary, what's so funny?"

"Oh, Matthews. If only Devon could see you now. Feeling me up the way you are. Remember, my husband is a very jealous man. I remember when you wouldn't even swim with me in your boxers, now you were just feeling every single part of my body. Oooooh, you're in so much trouble, mister."

As soon as the words were out of her mouth, she started shaking. Matthews was suddenly concerned that she was going into shock. Alex picked up on Matthews' concerns and nodded towards the house. Matthews gathered Mary in his arms and rushed towards the house. Yes, he had a reason to worry; Mary just leaned into his arms and didn't put up a fight.

"I got you, Mary. You're safe. You did it. You won. Your son will never have to worry again. You're a hero. His hero." Matthews kept whispering words of encouragement, hoping it would help keep Mary from going into full-blown shock.

In the distance, he could hear sirens. Good, help was on the way. Mary may have taken down her enemy, but the fight was far from over.

Chapter 33

*F*inally, an update, Devon thought, as his phone rang. Looking at the caller ID, it wasn't from a number he recognized. "Walker," he said promptly.

"Walker, it's Scott. I'm calling from one of the medics' phones. The mission was a success. Julia Kadlec is in custody and on her way to FBI headquarters now with a very large escort. Parker is heading the convoy so he can be right there for the interrogation, and two of our vehicles, plus a few MPD are tagging along. Parker wrangled up everyone in the vicinity because he didn't want any mistakes."

Taking a deep breath, he asked the question he's been holding back. "What about Mary? You didn't mention her, Scott. Where is my wife?"

"Sorry, Walker. Mary is here. She's in the house with Matthews. Matthews won't let anyone in the house but the medic team. Parker's calling me, so I have to go. Let me know if you need anything." He disconnected the phone before Devon could ask more questions. Why wouldn't Matthews have called him himself? Something didn't go to plan, so he needed to make sure everyone was okay and they weren't keeping anything from him.

No, they wouldn't keep something like that from him. Right? His colleagues told him Mary was safe. He'd just need to believe them until he saw her with his own eyes. Yeah, right. That was easier said than done. He flicked on the lights and sirens of his unmarked car and slammed on the gas. He wouldn't be able to calm down until his wife was in his arms.

Sliding to stop in his driveway, there were still some official vehicles hanging around. Not even taking the time to remove the keys from the ignition, Devon turned the car off and ran into the house. He slid to a dead stop upon finding Mary in the living room, laying on the couch, eyes closed, her legs propped up on pillows, and her body wrapped in blankets.

Matthews sat on the couch with her head touching his leg but not in his lap. His eyes were closed. He was stroking her hair. A medic sat on the floor next to her, looking to be taking her pulse.

"Mary," Devon said, barely above a whisper.

Matthews' eyes flew open and the look of relief on his friend's face was evident. "Hey, Walker. Come sit here. She's just tired. Our girl here had quite a day."

Devon knew there was more to the story. "What happened?"

The medic slowly started to stand. "I think we are out of the woods now. Agent Walker, Agent Matthews, will fill you in on what happened. I was just treating your wife for signs of shock. We can still take her to the hospital if you'd like, but in my professional opinion, I think she's going to be just fine. Agent Matthews assured me that he knows the signs to be on the look out for, and it was actually him that was spouting orders to me as I walked in the door.

Shaking his head, Devon replied, "No hospital. She's had enough of them to last a lifetime, and both of us know the signs of shock and will watch out for her. I won't let anything happen to my wife." She'd also be leaving for the safe house soon, and there was a retired nurse there helping with Caleb. Mary wouldn't want to go back to the hospital if she had a choice.

The men were whispering about everything that happened that day, when Mary started to stir. "Mary, love. I'm here." Devon leaned down so she'd be able to see his face. She looked exhausted. Hopefully, now that Kadlec was behind bars, she'd finally be able to rest.

"Devon?" Mary said, barely audible.

"Yes, love?"

"I have to tell you something."

"It's okay, baby. Matthews told me everything that happened. You really kicked her ass, didn't you?"

"Oh good. He really told you everything?" she asked.

"Yes, baby. He did. Now, why don't you get some more rest? Your uncle will be here soon to pick you up and take you to our son. Matthews and I need to go to work, but I'll keep you informed about what's going on. I promise, I won't keep anything from you. The danger has passed, now we are just going to get information."

Mary became unreasonably annoyed. She was going to be left alone again. "Oh, so he told you everything, did he? Did he tell you how he ran his hands all over my body and liked it?" Before

Devon could say a single word, she pulled the covers up over her head, turned towards the back of the couch, and fell back asleep.

Looking around the room, all Julia could think was that it was a literal cliche. A row of incandescent bulbs installed directly above a stainless-steel table provided the only light in the cramped interrogation room. What she could only assume were once white walls, providing an area no more than ten feet by ten feet, surrounded her.

Not that she'd ever admit it, but the enclosed space was starting to make her anxious. Knowing that they were watching her from the two-way mirror that replaced most of one of the four walls, she was determined to not show a shed of anything but sheer boredom.

There was no clock on the wall, but she knew what they were doing. The FBI threw her into this room and thought that if they left her alone for an extended amount of time, she'd break down and confess all her sins. They had no idea who they were dealing with. She wasn't just some punkass criminal they picked up off the street. She was Julia Kadlec, apprentice to Jimmy Yates. No matter what they did, they'd never break her.

Scott knew it had to be killing Walker not to be allowed into the interrogation room with Kadlec, but at least Parker even allowed Walker in the building. Scott was sure Parker wanted to order Congressman Carter to keep Walker under an unofficial house arrest after the incident at their house. Parker was infuriated that he was not made aware of their plan until after the fact.

Scott heard from Matthews what was said in the hospital room between Walker and Carter when Carter threatened to hide Walker's family from him unless he put their safety above everything else. Matthews and Scott were working their own investigation on the side, but after Kadlec broke into the safe house, Matthews called Scott and told him there would be no more holding back from Walker on anything. Scott agreed.

Matthews could see what having Kadlec invade his friend's home and getting so close to his wife and son had done to him. He worried that if they tried to keep Walker out of the interrogation, Walker would find a way to talk to her anyway, damn the consequences.

When Walker couldn't act on anything important going on in his life, he was like a caged animal. That's what his partner had been like these past weeks while sitting at that safe house with his family. Every time he or someone else dropped off supplies, he could see Walker's demeanor changing, and not for the better. He needed to be involved in this case, one hundred percent. He knew his partner could separate personal and professional feelings. He'd proven that when Yates was apprehended.

Finally, two men walked into the pathetic little room, but neither were the agents Julia wanted to see. Even they knew better than to let him in the room with her. The entire time they left her alone, all she'd done was think of more ways to torture Agent Walker before she needed to do what had to be done. Maybe, if she played around with these two for a while, they'd finally let the big boy in to see her.

One agent walked over to sit across from her at the stainless-steel table while the other decided to observe from the corner next to the two-way mirror. The one sitting across from her had the presence of a kiss-ass, or someone attempting to be in charge.

"Ms. Kadlec, my name is Chief Parker, and the agent standing by the door is Agent Scott."

Bingo. She nailed it.

"You've already been read your rights, and you've waived the right to have an attorney present. Just so you are aware, this room is both video and audio recorded at all times to protect the rights of both parties. Do you understand?"

"Sure do," she cheerfully said. Her words oozed sarcasm.

Chief Parker ignored her tone and continued on. "You are being charged with breaking and entering, assault, stalking, harassment, and two counts of attempted child abduction. And those are just the ones that we have hard evidence to connect you to right now. We are still confident that after we finish our investigation, we'll be able to get you on four counts of attempted murder; two for giving Mrs. Walker potentially deadly medication when she was in the hospital, then two counts for blowing up her vehicle. Both instances, you failed in what you set out to do. What would Yates think of this little prodigy now?"

Scott could see Kadlec's composure slipping. Parker was doing exactly what he set out to do. He wanted to rile her up so much that she exploded.

Julia smiled. "Do not speak his name with disdain in your voice. You know nothing about Jimmy, so stop talking like you do. He was smarter than everyone in this building combined. He never would've got caught if it wasn't for that bitch, Mary Anderson. He should've just taken her out quick and easy before anyone knew he was even back in D.C. But no, he wanted Mary scared and worried about her insignificant life. But she'll still get what's coming to her. She and that devil spawn still have to pay for what you people did to Jimmy. You are all murderers."

Scott and Parker both knew Walker and Matthews were behind the glass, probably seconds away from rushing in here and strangling the life out of Kadlec. Good thing Parker anticipated just that and stationed four agents in the span of five feet between the observation room door and the interrogation room door. They were all under orders not to let Walker in this room under threat of one year traffic duty.

"You make Yates sound untouchable, but that's not true. Because if he was as all-powerful as you seem to think he was, he wouldn't be rotting in the ground right now, bugs crawling all over his body, eating him from the inside out. Isn't that right, Ms. Kadlec? If Yates was as good as you have this delusion he was, he would've taken care of Mary *so* efficiently, and he'd still be here. Then the two of you would be off somewhere still wreaking havoc on the world as a serial killer duo. But you're not; he's not. He is rotting in the ground, and you'll spend the rest of your life without him, behind bars."

Julia was starting to lose her patience. How dare he speak about a legend with such blatant disrespect. Long after this useless excuse for a man was gone from existence, Yates would still be striking fear into the hearts of everyone that read about him in the history books. Jimmy would live forever, as the boogeyman.

Scott thought to himself that if this woman wasn't such a psychotic maniac, he'd actually admire her ability to control her temper. Yet what they needed right now was information, so they needed her to either get her to lose her composure enough to let something slip, or play into her delusion. Then maybe she would start talking.

Matthews must have been thinking the same thing because when Scott felt his phone vibrate and checked it, he found a message that read, "She is an idolater and psychopath. You need to play into those."

After four hours of Kadlec refusing to speak, Parker and Scott left the room. Matthews and Walker came out of the observation room to meet them in the hall. Matthews was the first to speak up.

"What is your next move, Chief?" he asked.

Everyone turned to Walker. "We're going to give her what she wants. Agent Walker, she wants you. Just try not to kill her. That's a lot of paperwork, and I hate paperwork. Got it?"

Chapter 34

From the moment Agent Walker entered the room, he was met with an unwavering hostile glare. Kadlec's expressions alternated between baring her teeth, and her face contorted with rage.

She looked across the table at the agent who was unprofessionally slumped in his chair, crossing his arms across his chest. It took a while, but Walker finally gave in and spoke first. "Listen, Ms. Kadlec, I can see you are all worked up. Hell, anyone would be that was in your current situation. We have more important things to discuss right now, so do you think we can work together?"

When she continued to just glare at him, he continued to speak. "I think you have a story to tell. A story that you have to tell, that is eating you up inside. And it's a story that I want to hear. So what do you say? Do you think we can have a civil conversation, one where we both benefit?"

Kadlec just stared at Walker, deciding if she should give him the information he asked for. She knew he was just playing her. How could any of this benefit her? Not that any of it really mattered anymore. And maybe she did want to tell her story. It was a hell of a story.

Over the last few hours, she's come to the conclusion that there's no way out of this for her. Prison? That's the end game for the FBI. But did she want to spend the rest of her life behind bars until a jury decided they were ready to stick a needle in her arm? She wasn't sure yet. What were the chances she could get Agent Walker to just shoot her here and now? Then she'd be able to go out just like Yates did. They'd have to wait and find out if she could annoy him enough to get him to do it.

"Okay, Agent Walker. I'll give you three questions, and three questions only. So, ask question number one. But I'd really think carefully before speaking if I were you."

Straight to the point.

"How did you get mixed up with Jimmy Yates?"

"Great first question. Bravo. Even when I was a little girl, no one ever understood me. Ever. Except Yates, but even that came later. Since the moment my all-righteous mother married her second husband, I just became an inconvenience. Some called me trouble, most called me a sinner, but I considered it a product of my surroundings.

"The entire time my mom dated hubby number two, old daddy dear had eyes for me, not her. He only got with my mother so he'd have access to me, that dirty old man. Mommy walked in on us the night of my sweet sixteen party. All the blame, of course, was placed on my head. She blamed him for nothing, not one little infraction. Apparently, I seduced him. That's the only thing that made sense to her.

"Later that night, I found my mother in my room, packing my bags, and a set of airline tickets sitting on my bed. At six the next morning, I was supposed to get on a plane and go live with my grandparents in Alaska. Mom wanted me as far away from her husband as possible. She couldn't even take a moment to think that this grown ass man was the one to seduce me. She was correct in her assumption that it was all my fault, but she didn't even ask me. She just wanted me shipped as far away as possible from her picture-perfect life.

"I didn't get on that plane as my mother intended. She didn't even have the decency to walk me, her own daughter, to the ticket counter. She just dropped me off at the curb, with my bags and tickets, and told me her parents would call me when I was settled in Alaska. But that call would never come. I walked to the ticket counter, and I told them I wouldn't be able to make my flight. I returned the tickets for only a fraction of what dear old mom paid for them, but it was enough to keep me on my feet for a few weeks. Apparently, mom was willing to pay any amount to get me out of Atlanta and last-minute tickets weren't cheap. Pity.

"No matter what a child has done, how does a parent abandon their sixteen-year-old? Especially for a man. So, if anyone is to blame for how I turned out, it's her. Yates must have seen the evil in my mother because just a little over two years later, he murdered her lovely new family. That was before I even had the pleasure to meet him. So you see, it was kismet that we met and united.

"It wasn't until years after their murder that I even found out what had happened to them. Up until that day, I just imagined them miserable in their big suburban home, regretting the day they kicked me out, but luckily, I was so wrong. So there I was, celebrating my twenty-first birthday in some dive between Dalton and Chattanooga when an eerie silence spread over the bar. The infamous serial killer Jimmy Yates was presumed to be back in Atlanta after not being apprehended after some killing spree three years before. The TV screen lit up with the faces of the Atlanta victims, and low and behold, there was dear old mom, my handsy stepfather, and my two stepbrothers. Needless to say, I bought a round of shots for the bar in celebration.

"It was that night that I made what most people would consider a dumb decision, but it would actually be the best decision I ever made in my entire life. I decided that night that I would track down Yates and thank him for murdering my family." Seeing the looks on the two FBI agent's faces was priceless. They looked at her like they couldn't believe she'd want to intentionally find Yates, or that she truly succeeded where dozens of law enforcement agencies have failed.

With a big smile on her face, she continued. "That's right guys, for years we've watched you blunder trying to track him down, like it was actually hard. I tracked him down to a run-down motel outside of Raleigh, North Carolina just about six months after I saw that news story. Six months was all it took me, and you couldn't find him in twenty years. I was only twenty-one with zero law enforcement or investigative experience, and I found someone on your most wanted list like it was child's play. I'd say you're all quite pathetic.

"When I found Yates, I knew the moment I laid eyes on him that he was magnificent. He was what all men should strive to be. He was perfection. All the pictures I've seen of him, they never could come close to doing him justice. They'd never be able to capture the essence that oozed out of his every molecule. He was perfect not only with his body but in mind and spirit as well. I had my work cut out for me proving to him that I belonged in his presence, but I was prepared for the fight ahead.

"The moment his name came out of my mouth and he realized I knew who he was, he threatened to slit my throat. I think what impressed him was that I proved in that initial moment that I wasn't afraid to die. After he threatened to slit my throat, I reached into the small of my back and handed him a knife. He stared at it in my hands for a while, looking back and forth between the knife and me, before finally shaking his head and stepping aside so I could follow him into his hotel room.

"Jimmy had a God complex, so I used that information and expanded on it. I proved to him how invaluable I could be to him by taking some of the risk off him and placing it all on my head."

"Besides taking some risk off of him, he also pawned all the shitty jobs off on me with the excuse that I needed to 'earn my stripes'. He was very impressed that the first time he tossed a severed face in my direction, I didn't even flinch. I just grabbed it from the air like a baseball and told him 'sweet'.

"One of my many new jobs included embalming his victims' faces before he added them to his wall of treasures. He said that it wouldn't make them last forever, but it would help them last long enough for him to get as much pleasure out of them as he needed.

He explained that by the time they were too rotted for him to discern the features, he'd have another one to swap it out with.

"I tried a few times to explain to him there were new ways to preserve them so they'd last forever, like placing them in epoxy resin. He just didn't want to try anything new; he wanted to keep to his old ways. His problem was he didn't want to evolve with the times, so I did the best I could with what he had, and I just sucked it up and made him happy.

"That was the beginning of our beautiful working acquaintance. I guess I wouldn't technically call it a friendship, because for all the years I lived with Jimmy, he repeated over and over that we weren't friends. At first it hurt, coming from my idol, but I quickly came to realize it was his way to protect his feelings. In the beginning, he refused to let me call him Jimmy, but after about a year, he stopped throwing knives at me whenever I'd slip and call him by his first name. That's when I realized he finally began to like me."

Silent moments ticked by, signifying to Walker that Kadlec was seemingly done with discussing that first question. Walker studied her expressions as he waited to see what she would say next. She was tapping her fingers in some sort of rhythm on the table, but he couldn't quite figure out the tune.

"Okay, Mr. Agent Man. What is your question number two? Make it good. I won't answer any more."

"The FBI knows why Yates targeted Mary, but after he was killed, why didn't you just disappear? If you would've never come after Mary, we may never have known of your association with Yates. So why not just leave D.C.?"

Something in his question triggered an explosive emotional response. Kadlec started bouncing her leg under the table, her eyes pinched together, and her posture became rigid.

"Why would I let that bitch run me out of D.C.?" She seethed between her teeth.

Matthews watched from the corner and Kadlec tried her hardest to bait Walker into losing his cool. From the way his partner was flexing his hands as she disrespected his wife, he'd guess Walker was using every trick in his book to keep his cool and not leap across the table and bash her face into a bloody pulp. Maybe Matthews would do it for him.

Devon knew the moment he asked the question pertaining to Mary that he'd need to put personal feelings aside when Kadlec answered. No matter how impossibly hard that was going to be, the question needed to be asked, and if he couldn't keep it together, Parker would kick him out of the room. Right now, he needed to be an FBI Agent and get the answers they needed to build a completely airtight case against her.

"Yes, Julia. Why didn't you leave D.C. before we could connect you to Jimmy Yates?"

"You really want to know why? I'll tell you why. Because I was finally going to do something that Jimmy was never able to do. I was going to watch and wait, and at the right time, I was going to make Mary suffer. And I did all of those things. Now she's going to live the rest of her life a screwed-up little mouse, always looking over her shoulder.

"Now she's always going to be worried to even let that son of yours leave the house or be worried if he'll make it home from school each day. Can you just imagine the fear she'll feel each time she starts her car? I can. Every time she turns that key or hits her auto start, she'll be wondering if it will be her last. She'll be wondering if her car will explode.

"Yates and I may not have killed her, but together, we've ruined her life. I almost got her this last time too. If that dick in the corner over there and his friend hadn't come to her rescue, she would've been mine. I was so looking forward to adding her face to Jimmy's wall, but oh well.

"I still didn't lose, not by a long shot. Going forward there's not going to be a single day that'll go by that she doesn't think of both me and Jimmy. We'll consume her nightmares and rule her every move. How do you think she'll cope when your poor son grows up, if he lives to grow up, and wants to move out? She will go insane with worry. Yes, I believe I'm the winner.

"And yes, I guess I could've just flittered off into the sunset and maybe you never would've known of my involvement with Yates, but where's the fun in that? Now, whenever someone thinks of the name Jimmy Yates, it will be associated with Julia Kadlec. Our names will be side by side in the history books."

This woman was delusional. First off, yes, history books will add Jimmy Yates to the list of infamous serial killers. Mary had told him some of her college classes had already touched on his criminal history. She's always been excused from those lessons because she lived them, of course, and it was up to her if she wanted to teach them or even talk about them in her classes. Yet Kadlec would always be listed as a minor accomplice, so at most, there would be a very small blurb with her name. Should he tell her and get her all riled up? Maybe he'd keep that up his sleeve for later. He really should try to play ball for now.

Leaning forward, Julia placed her elbows on the table and her chin in her hands. In all honesty, she looked like she was having the time of her life. She was either completely delusional and couldn't understand that she'd never leave prison again, or she had something up her sleeve that the FBI knew nothing about. Devon was becoming more apprehensive by the minute, and from the corner of his eye, he caught a slight hand gesture from Matthews, indicating he was thinking the same exact thing.

"Agent Walker, did anyone ever tell you that your eyes are gorgeous? I mean, damn, a woman could get lost in all that lovely greenness." Julia dramatically signed as she made the statement.

"Ms. Kadlec, I want to talk about you and how smart you are."

"Tsk, tsk, tsk. Now who's the liar agent? But since you recognized my brilliance, I'll let that lie slide and you can ask your third question."

"Thank you, Ms. Kadlec. As I said, you are a genius. You outsmarted the FBI, the MPD, and so many other law enforcement agencies in other states over the years. So, we'd like to know how you found the safe house. Please. If you'd be so kind as to explain it to us."

This is the question Parker needed answered. Devon's chief was worried about a leak within the FBI. If that was the case, they needed that name. Even if it meant playing into Kadlec's fantasies, then he'd do what needed to be done to get the answers they needed.

"Oh, yes," Julia said. "But this is what you want to know for question number three? Boring. Last one? Final answer? Okay. You tried to run and hide your family from me, agent. That wasn't very nice of you, now, was it? It took me a while to piece together who you all may have contact with once you were hidden away. All it took was a little bit of money for some high-tech equipment, some that I think the FBI could benefit from. Just saying, you guys might want to think about linking up with the CIA, they get better equipment than you do. Alas, I was finally able to find her. The little mouse, as Yates called her, had finally been found.

"Come to think about it, anyone that has access to the internet could've figured out how to track you guys. Some of your guys are sloppy, you may want to look into that. Not you though, Agent Green Eyes. No, you were harder to get around. But I'm getting ahead of myself.

"Let me get back to how I found you. I ordered a basic bionic ear portable dish listening device from the internet. Once I figured out what security firm her uncle hired for extra manpower, I just had to sit and wait to intercept some phone transmissions. After a few days, I knew I had the right guys, so I started to follow them. I watched where they met up to switch vehicles, pick up food deliveries, then finally to where you were trying to hide from me.

"Once I found your little home away from home, your schedule was a bit harder to anticipate. You kept me on my toes, agent. Bravo. Your men, however, kept to the same time frame when they did their rounds of the grounds. You had a different schedule; it was always changing. You used random times to check to make sure the men were keeping your little family safe. The only reasonable thing for me to do was to strike at night.

"The only thing I was able to somewhat figure out, was about how long you stayed outside at each single time. That's how I knew how long I'd have to sneak into your little spawn's room, grab him up, and leave back out through the window. Everything would've gone perfectly if your bitch would've gone to bed at her normal time. I watched the cameras I planted for two days, and her bedroom light went off at the same time each night, but not the night I made my move.

"I should've had roughly forty-two minutes to climb the ledge to the second floor where the baby's room was. You really should've chosen a safer room for him. Any crazy person could climb the tree on that side of the house that led to the windows above. Look how easy it was for me.

"But alas, it wasn't meant to be. Now, I get the pleasure of knowing Mary will never rest easy again. Anytime she hears a noise outside her son's window, she'll be worried about someone trying to break in. Her heart will race when a stranger gets close on the playground for fear of him being kidnapped. No, she's going to make him live in a bubble, and he will grow up to resent her. I win.

"Oh, I had grand plans for your son, but I think this is a more fitting revenge. There'll never be a day that passes where she'll be completely at peace. And that'll only intensify when he's old enough to leave the house. Yes, I'm very happy with this turn of events."

Unable to contain it any longer, Devon laughed in her face.

Julia did not react well. "You think your wife's pain is humorous? Well, so do I. I'll find pleasure in her pain every day for the rest of my life."

Shaking his head, Devon said, "No, I think it's funny that after all this time of you and Jimmy watching Mary, you don't know her at all. Tonight, she is going to sleep peacefully knowing you are behind bars. She even texted me right before I came into this room that she wants to start planning a vacation to take Caleb to Disneyland. Mary is hands down the strongest person I've ever met, and your mistake was that you underestimated her. Game over, Julia. You lose."

Julia went ballistic. She tried jumping from her seat and lunging for Devon, but she was still handcuffed to the table in front of her.

Devon casually stood up, ignored all the insults Julia was screaming at him, and walked right out the door.

Chapter 35

*D*amn it. Damn it. Damn it.

Julia's fist slammed into the cold steel desk. How dare he speak to her like that. Her fury ignited with every strike. She couldn't seem to catch her breath because she was so breathless with anger. Her rage threatened to consume her, and if she had the ability to free herself from this table, she'd burn this building to the ground with everyone inside.

He was just trying to taunt her, right? There's no way Mary would be able to brush off everything both Julia and Yates have put her through and expect to live a normal, non-paranoid life. It's impossible. No one can live through that much trauma and not be scared from the inside out. No, Agent Walker was lying. Right?

What was going to happen next? Jail? No, not for her, she had her contingency. She'd planned for this. Well, Yates had planned for them both. Yates came up with this idea but didn't have the time to properly implement it for himself before he went off script and kidnapped Mary prematurely.

She was ready to take her fate into her own hands. She's never been afraid of death, and this time was no different.

Carefully, she ran her tongue over the back of her teeth. She felt where the cap was fitted over her last molar. This wasn't how she wanted this to end. She'd always imagined going out in a hail of bullets, but at least she'd be with Jimmy again. She failed her last mission, so would Jimmy be happy to see her? No, this wasn't her mission to fail, Jimmy's the one that failed at killing the bitch. It wasn't her fault at all. Damn you, Jimmy.

The agents stepped out only a few minutes ago and would be back at any time. She needed to work fast. She refused to rot in some prison cell until they decided to stick a needle in her arm. She'd decide how it would end, and it would be on her terms. These terms.

She was finally able to get her tongue under the small cap and felt it fall away from the tooth. The tiny pill that was embedded inside fell gently onto her tongue. Even though she knew the pill weighed next to nothing, it felt like her tongue now weighed ten pounds. There was no going back now, she could already feel the casing of the pill dissolving in her mouth.

With one quick bite, she broke the cyanide pill in her mouth. Looking up at the bright lights, she was filled with relief. She hasn't had an easy life, and she'd finally be able to spend eternity with the only man that truly loved her, the man that made her whole again, the man that gave her a second chance. She'd be able to spend forever with Jimmy, the best serial killer in history, and no one would be able to convince her otherwise.

Seconds turned to minutes, and still, nothing happened. What the hell? Why wasn't anything happening? She felt a powder leave the broken pill casing, and Jimmy told her the cyanide would take effect immediately. However, she didn't feel even slightly different.

Realization hit her hard. That bastard, he lied to her. He never gave her a quick way to end her life if she was apprehended, he gave her an excuse to make herself a martyr in case it was between him or her. He knew she'd sacrifice herself to keep him safe. He knew she wanted to be remembered forever. She was such a bloody fool.

Rage pulsed through her body. That bitch, Mary, had won after all. The screams that tore through her body could be heard throughout the entire FBI floor. It sounded like a tortured animal was in their interrogation room, not a psychopathic woman.

Devon leaned against Matthews' desk. Both agents were waiting on Chief Parker to finish with his phone call so he could tell them how to proceed with Ms. Kadlec. The pair were joking about running off and taking their families to the Bahamas when this was finally over. They were in agreement that they both deserved a nice, long vacation after this.

"Women in little bikinis, unlimited drinks, and not having to wear shoes for a week, I'm completely there," Matthews joked, nudging Devon in the ribs.

"Yeah right, man." Devon leaned over and punched his friend in the arm. "If we go to the Bahamas, you won't be chasing girls; you'll be chasing Caleb, and you know it."

Matthews shrugged but had a huge smile on his face. "Hey, I can't help it if I'd rather spend my time with that little man. He doesn't cause drama, and you know how I hate the drama. Now, his father, he brings drama wherever he goes, but I put up with it because he feeds me."

They were still joking around and laughing like loons when Parker left his office and beelined towards the two agents. "Transport is on its way. Let's get this psychopath out of my building. Listen to me carefully, we need to get her onto the truck. Once we transfer custody, she's out of hands. She's the Virginia Department of Corrections' problem until the trial. I will not have what happened to Yates happen to Kadlec."

Devon knew what Parker was saying, Kadlec needed to make it out of the FBI building alive. Yates's transfer should've been planned better. He should have lived to stand trial and pay for his crimes. The moment he was murdered by that sniper, he was relieved of his suffering and he got off easy. No, Kadlec would not get off easy.

Every agent that was available was already in the office. From the moment the operation was set to try to trap Kadlec, almost no agent had left the immediate area. In the FBI, every agent, man and woman, were family. Therefore, their families were family. So, when one of their own was attacked, everyone felt attacked.

Even though Kadlec was behind bars, everyone was here for Devon, to support him and his family. Most of these agents were present when Mary was kidnapped, so they felt a kinship with her, which Devon appreciated.

Chief Parker wouldn't allow Devon into the interrogation room with him when he informed Kadlec her ride to pretrial detention would soon be arriving. From the sounds of the screaming coming from the room, Devon assumed Kadlec was taking the news rather well.

The screaming didn't let up as Parker led Kadlec from the room in handcuffs, it even escalated. Kadlec didn't like the fact that every agent in the hallway kept a stone-cold expression and didn't react in any way. She didn't scare anyone anymore. She'd lost everything.

Once the building doors opened to reveal the open back doors of a white Virginia Department of Corrections vehicle, Julia's screaming tantrum came to a sudden halt.

"Don't worry, Ms. Kadlec," Chief Parker said as he pushed her towards the open doors. "The other inmates are going to welcome you with open arms when you get to your new Supermax home."

She wasn't stupid. She knew the other inmates wouldn't be waiting with open arms, but she didn't expect them to be openly hostile. She'd make sure these women knew who she was. Weren't they supposed to idolize serial killers? She was a serial killer, technically.

Julia had only been in the general population an hour when she noticed two inmates had been watching her more than the rest. The only weird thing was that it was only after speaking with one of the security guards. Oh well, she'd take whatever fan club she could get.

That security guard was back again, walking around, being nosy. Julia made the decision that once the guard left the area again, she'd walk over to the other inmates and assert dominance. The guard stopped right in front of Julia, slowly looked her up and down, and shook her head with a look of disgust on her face. How dare she? Glancing quickly at the guard's name tag, she saw her name was Miller.

Damn, she hated that name. Detective Miller with the MDP was the one that apprehended Jimmy, and in turn was the reason for her being locked away in here. There was absolutely no way they could be related, right? Miller was a common enough name.

The guard finally walked away and out the door. That was weird. Looking around the room, Julia noticed that all the guards were actually gone. She'd never been in prison, but did they really leave the inmates alone? Oh well, she'd make the most of this time and head over to her admirers.

They seemed to be waiting for her, and that was a good sign. They watched Julia walk towards them, with their arms crossed over their chests. They didn't look threatening at all. Julia, however, didn't even get a single word out of her mouth before she felt the sharp pain enter high in her abdomen. Looking down, she saw the blood start to spread across her shirt.

"Why?" she croaked as she slowly fell to her knees.

More women surrounded them, blocking the view to the doors. One of the women Julia thought was an admirer stepped closer to tower over her. "We don't allow child killers to pollute our prison. Go to hell, bitch." With one swift kick to the chest, Julia was flat on her back, laying in a pool of her own blood.

The only image she could see as her vision faded to black, was the backs of the women surrounding her. They wouldn't even watch her as she died. She was nothing. She had always been nothing. She would die... a nothing.

Chapter 36

Mary finally stopped pacing by the front door after it felt like she was about to wear a path into the hardwood. Devon had messaged her about an hour ago to let her know he would be on his way home after he finished one last report.

Reluctantly, and against Chief Parker's wishes, her uncle had kept her informed about everything that had happened at the FBI building and some of the interrogation. Devon had been periodically calling Robert with every detail, and Robert refused to keep that information, no matter how disturbing, away from Mary.

After checking her phone a hundred times and recalculating how long it would take him to drive from the field office to the safe house, her wait was finally over. She knew without seeing him that he'd just pulled into the driveway because she heard him lock his car, then lock it again.

His damn OCD ass, she loved every inch of it. With tears in her eyes, Mary all but ripped open the front door and then made herself stand in the open doorway. It was a beautiful sight, watching Devon make his way up the path towards her. He told her often that he'd always find his way back to her, no matter what.

Devon must have sensed her watching him because he looked up and smiled. He's always told her that he could feel when she was close. She called him crazy, but she was able to feel it too. It wasn't some psychic thing, but she couldn't explain it, and she wouldn't try to. Because for her to get an explanation for her feelings would take all the mystery away.

Without stopping, Devon closed the gap between them in only a few strides and pulled her into a big hug. Burying his head into her hair, nuzzling his mouth against her neck, he breathed in deeply.

He would have been content to just stand there and hold her all night. The last few weeks had put a terrible strain on Mary and their entire family. Hell, since he met Mary, her life has been under one big strain. But no more. There were no more links to Jimmy Yates, and the threats against her were all gone. Gently, he reached up and started stroking her hair. Any excuse to touch her, he took.

"Mary, the nightmare's over. It's done. Kadlec is no longer a threat."

Her shoulders visibly relaxed, and she heard herself let out a deep breath. Until that very moment, it hadn't yet hit home as true. She needed to hear the words come directly from her husband's mouth for them to completely sink in.

That's how he was hoping she'd react. He wanted his wife to feel in that moment, instant peace.

"Are you sure, Devon? Is it really over? Is there a chance, any chance, that she can beat these charges? You should know better than anyone what a lawyer is capable of. Uncle Robert told me she was on her way to prison, but is there a chance she can fight the charges? What if they find her incapable of standing trial due to insanity?"

Gently, he grasped her shoulders and looked her in the eyes. "No, Mary, listen to me closely. It's completely over, love. Miller called me on my way home. His sister is a corrections officer in the prison Kadlec was sent to, and she didn't last even a few hours after an inmate found out who she was. She's gone."

Giving her a second to process, he continued to explain when he saw the doubt in her eyes. "Even criminals don't like people that hurt children. It's over, sweetheart. She's never going to be able to hurt you again. Tomorrow, we'll pack up and head home. I don't know about you, but I miss my bed and my lake. I want to see Caleb in his own room where he belongs. I miss privacy. I want to be able to walk around my house naked if I want to and not have to worry about running into a security guard around every corner." Reaching into his back pocket, he pulled out two plane tickets. "Here, love."

Curiously, she grabbed the tickets from his hands. "Mr. Walker, what is this?" she asked, chuckling with excitement.

"Those, Mrs. Walker, are two plane tickets to Belize. It was the closest I could get to your secluded island on an hour's notice. I'm taking you away for a much needed vacation. Patrica and Robert already agreed to watch Caleb."

Throwing her arms around his shoulders, she kissed him passionately. "Thank you," she whispered against his lips.

Once she pulled back, he reached down and cupped her chin, looking deep into her beautiful sapphire eyes. "Before we head off to parts unknown, we need to go home."

"Home," she said wistfully. "It seems like forever since we were able to all be at home without some pending threat hanging over our heads. Caleb's been adjusting fine, but I want to be surrounded by our things, just like you said. This house that my uncle stashed us in is nice, but it's not ours. There's just something about having your own things within reach that has a calming effect. Home."

"Home," he said softly. He lifted her chin to meet her eyes. "Let's go home, love."

"Yes, home. Though I was thinking, unlike you, I still walk around this house naked, and if I run into a security guard, oh well."

Letting out a full-hearted laugh, he reached around and slapped his wife on her pert rear end. "Home, now. No other man is ever going to see you naked ever again."

Walking hand and hand up the stairs, Mary started chuckling. "Okay, I promise, no other man will ever see me naked. Now that you are in a good mood, I've been thinking, now that the threat is over, how about we work on giving Caleb a brother or sister?"

Devon gave a booming laugh. This was just like Mary. "Love, the threat's only been gone a few hours. You had to have been thinking about this longer than that."

She was silent for a moment. "Of course I've been thinking about it longer. I love being a mother, and any child would be lucky to have you as their father. What do you say? Could we give Caleb a sibling?"

Grinning from ear to ear, he said, "It would be my pleasure, literally. Let's get started right now." There was nothing in the world he'd ever deny Mary.

He pulled her up the stairs and down the hall towards their room. Quickly checking the baby monitor and confirming Caleb was still fast asleep, Devon threw a giggling Mary onto the bed and proceeded to show her just how pleasurable her request could be.

Acknowledgments

I owe my gratitude to my team at Flick-It-Books, Publishing. My publisher, Misti, who gives all her authors the support we need to share our stories with the world. Nothing I say could express the level of gratitude I have for you and your company.

To my two editors, Glysia and Sage, thank you for hard work and support in making this book become everything I dreamt it would be.

A big thank you to Cassie, my cover designer from Booklytical Designs. You've made the Jimmy Yates Duology come to life in the form of two stunning covers.

To my amazing husband and daughters – you three give me a reason to keep going every day. The support you provide, is unimaginable. I love you!

And finally, thank you to my readers and everyone that's supported me in this journey. Without your support, writing more books wouldn't seem possible. You are the reason I keep putting my stories to paper.

Thank you, everyone!!

About the Author Nicole Keefer is a writer whose military experience and educational background in criminology and forensic psychology provide her with the vast inspiration and insight she needs to create riveting characters. Writing a novel was always on her bucket list, and eventually, with MY SAVIOR, it became a reality. When not reading or writing, Nicole enjoys spending time with her family. Nicole lives in Michigan with her husband and daughters. HIS APPRENTICE'S REVENGE is the conclusion of her first serial killer duology.

Milton Keynes UK
Ingram Content Group UK Ltd.
UKHW042158031123
431935UK00003B/40

C000233781

A to Z
HEALING
TOOLBOX

*A Practical Guide
for Navigating Grief
and Trauma
with Intention*

Susan Hannifin-MacNab

ISBN 13: 978-1-63489-084-7
eISBN 13: 978-1-63489-085-4

Library of Congress Catalog Number: 2017948466
Printed in the United States of America
First Printing: 2017
25   24   23   22   21   6   5   4   3   2

Cover design and interior design by Dan Pitts

Wise Ink Creative Publishing
807 Broadway St. NE, Suite 46
Minneapolis, MN 55413
wiseink.com

To order, visit site www.a2zhealingtoolbox.com.
Reseller discounts available.

PRAISE FOR A TO Z HEALING TOOLBOX

"Get out your highlighter and sticky notes because this book will take you on a healing journey from broken-down to breakthrough. *A to Z Healing Toolbox* will change your life in ways you never thought possible and will become your go-to companion for years to come." —Paula Stephens, MA, creator of Crazy Good Grief and author of *From Grief to Growth: 5 Essential Elements of Action to Give Your Grief Purpose and Grow from Your Experience*

"*A to Z Healing Toolbox* is the book I wish to give to all of my clients who are in the throes of grief. This practical, relatable, and deeply meaningful book is everything a bereaved person could want when needing some healing fast."—Claire Bidwell Smith, LCPC, grief therapist and author of *The Rules of Inheritance* and *After This: When Life Is Over, Where Do We Go?*

"With humility and perseverance, Susan Hannifin-MacNab navigates the world of grief and trauma with the brain of a social worker, the heart of a teacher, and the love of a mother. *A to Z Healing Toolbox* is a shining beacon of hope in the darkness." —Christina Rasmussen, author of *Second Firsts: Live, Laugh, and Love Again*

"*A to Z Healing Toolbox* is a guide that provides holistic, practical, and invaluable information for any griever. Susan's unique blend of professional expertise and personal grief experience makes this book relatable. I'd recommend this book to grievers at any distance from their loss and from any walk of life. Every person who picks up this guide will find enrichment, validation, and hope." —Michele Neff Hernandez, founder and executive director of Soaring Spirits International

"Susan Hannifin-MacNab does exactly what she set out to do in *A to Z Healing Toolbox*—she makes life 'a little easier' for anyone moving through grief and trauma healing. Susan lights the way with quotes, personal stories, practical definitions, honest explanations, doable exercises, and love. I wish I'd been given this book after the death of my husband and two sons. Every page is full of hope and demonstrated resilience. This book will be shared often!" —Nancy Saltzman, PhD, educator, and author of *Radical Survivor: One Woman's Path Through Life, Love, and Uncharted Tragedy*

"*A to Z Healing Toolbox* is a gift to anyone who is undergoing the effects of trauma or the pain of loss. Susan Hannifin-MacNab's book is unique in its approach, which is simultaneously deeply personal and extremely practical. She skillfully invites the reader to see her resilience, and in doing so, Susan shines a light on a healing path for us all." —Mary Lee Moser, MA, certified instructor for Journal to Self® and SoulCollage®

"Susan Hannifin-MacNab has created a practical guidebook that anyone can use with ease. It is personal and heartfelt and encompasses many of the leading interventions the field of grief and trauma have to offer. *A to Z Healing Toolbox* gives survivors the knowledge and hope necessary to find grounding while on the roller coaster ride of grief." —Lydia Lombardi Good, LCSW, BCD, grief therapist and hospice bereavement consultant

"Social worker Susan Hannifin-MacNab's *A to Z Healing Toolbox* is a must-have guide for anyone living with loss. This book shines with genuine care and wisdom. The innovative format invites readers to explore the Toolbox without feeling overwhelmed—or alone in their reactions. I highly recommend this insightful and helpful book." —LeslieBeth Wish, EdD, clinical psychotherapist and author of *Smart Relationships: How Successful Women Can Find True Love*

"Gifted writer-practitioner Susan Hannifin-MacNab grabs you on the very first page with her own story of traumatic loss, and doesn't let you go until you've absorbed a good, healing dose of practical wisdom, inspiration, and tools for moving forward—always offered with the most gentle and impeccable respect, kindness, and just the right dollop of humor. Make no mistake: this is not just a clever list of things to do; it's a road map, where you get to choose the elements of your journey and the sequence that works best for you. The whole thing is made coherent and compelling by the depth, authenticity, and generosity of this courageous author, who leads by example." —Belleruth Naparstek, ACSW, author of *Invisible Heroes: Survivors of Trauma and How They Heal* and creator of the Health Journeys Guided Imagery library (www.healthjourneys.com).

"*A to Z Healing Toolbox* will be one of my first recommendations to clients who are navigating their grief journey. Susan's suggestions are straightforward, accessible, and heartfelt. If you are looking for a book to offer to a friend or relative who is grieving the death of someone dear, or if you are in the midst of your own grief journey, this is the book for you." —Kath McCormack, MS, LMHC, founder and former executive director of Seattle's Healing Center

"When someone we love dies, we are thrust into the wilderness. We wonder what to DO to find our way out of the wasteland of grief. We wonder if it's possible to live again. Susan Hannifin-MacNab is providing what grieving people all over the world are asking for: a road map for what to DO. In this book are life-changing suggestions, beautiful prose, and encouragement. Susan shows us that we can live lives with even greater purpose than we thought possible. *A to Z Healing Toolbox* is a game changer and a tremendous gift to this world." —Jessica Lindberg, founder and executive director of the Ethan M. Lindberg Foundation and creator of Restoring a Mother's Heart

To Brent:
You showed me love and commitment.
You guided me to action and adventure.
You taught me to never give up.
This book is for you.
I love you forever.

To Jacob:
You showed me resilience and laughter.
You guided me to hope and healing.
You are the reason I never gave up.
This book is for you.
I love you forever.

Contents

FOREWORD

by Tom Zuba

Is healing possible? Healing your broken heart? I believe it is. But I don't think healing is always a destination at which we arrive. For many of us, healing becomes our way of being in the world. We heal a little bit more every day. And I'm okay with that. Are you?

Healing our broken heart, no matter what the cause, requires hard, hard work. Susan Hannifin-MacNab understands that. She's lived that. She continues to live that. Day by day. Now, with her ground-breaking, one-of-a-kind book as your daily companion and guide, you can live that too. You can go about the work of healing your broken heart. Every day. If you are ready. To heal.

Following the "monumental life shift" that occurred for Susan in 2012—the sudden death of her husband, Brent—slowly, but surely Susan gathered the knowledge, wisdom, and tools that are necessary to heal. From her social worker's heart, she's offering all that and much, much more to you because she wants her life to make a difference in your life. She's done the work in hopes of making your journey lighter. A tad easier. Not quite as painful. She's offering you hope. And light. And a path through—which will lead you out. Ultimately. Into the biggest, boldest, most powerful version of you.

The you you came to the planet to be. If, and when, you are ready. To heal. Or you wouldn't be reading these words.

This is the book I wish I'd read after my eighteen-month-old daughter Erin died in 1990. I wish someone had gifted it to me in 1999 following the sudden death of my forty-three-year-old wife Trici. And had I found it in 2005, after my thirteen-year-old son Rory died, I'm certain that journey through grief would have been different. But Susan Hannifin-MacNab had to live it first. All of it. Before she could write *A to Z Healing Toolbox.* For you. And for me.

And boy did she live it. Susan dove right in.

I first met Susan in March of 2016 in a Tampa, Florida hotel lobby. We were both facilitating workshops at a conference for widows and widowers. Standing on the staircase, we shared a little about the events that brought us there. Brent's death and Trici's death. But we spent most of our time talking about life. Life after death. Susan talked about the ups and downs and ins and outs of her new life with her young son Jacob. I talked about my new life with my son Sean. We agreed on many, many things. That the work of healing is hard. Really, really hard. Harder than we'd imagined. We shared that the isolation and the loneliness and the feeling of being abandoned by so many family members and friends was surprising. And confusing. We talked about stumbling. A lot. And getting back up. And taking another step. In the direction of healing. We talked about hope. And possibility. About realizing that time alone did not and would not heal our wounds. But rather, that what mattered, was what we did with our time. And we discovered that we both believed in the power of intention.

Setting the intention to heal. Even when, especially when, we weren't quite certain that healing was even possible. We talked about the importance of holding a vision of what healing looked like. So we would know it when we arrived. At a place of healing. And we talked a lot about taking action. Doing something. With the intention of healing.

In order to heal, you have to work at it. Every day. Many times throughout the day.

I attended Susan's workshop that weekend. An introduction to some of the healing tools included in her fledgling A2Z Healing Toolbox steps. Following a powerful two-and-a-half-hour workshop I shared these words on the conference evaluation form. "I had the good fortune of participating in the hands-on workshop facilitated by Susan Hannifin-MacNab of A2Z Healing Toolbox. She is offering concrete steps you can take and things you can do every day in order to heal. Susan knows her stuff. It is hard-earned, well-researched, and lovingly offered. Say YES to Susan's work!"

I supported Susan's vision of compiling all her gathered tools into a book. "Hurry up though," I said. Many times. "Hurry up. We need it now!" And here it is. *A to Z Healing Toolbox: A Practical Guide for Navigating Grief and Trauma with Intention.*

Put this book on your nightstand. Open it first thing in the morning as you plan your day. With intention. Put another copy on your desk or kitchen table. So you can refer to it throughout the day. And make sure you have extra copies in your car. So you can pass it on when you "randomly" meet the next person ready to heal. Their broken heart. No matter the cause of the break.

Susan has laid the path out for us clearly, gently, and thoroughly. She introduces us to other people like us who are doing the work. And healing. It's all here. Your job is to say yes. Every day. Many times throughout the day. Your job is to realize you're not a victim, no matter what you've lived through. And with. You're actually a co-creator. And Susan offers you the tools necessary to co-create a glorious life.

There is a new way to do grief. It involves diving in. Head first. Heart open. Believing, trusting, that healing your broken heart is possible. It's not easy. That's why so many don't do it. Yet. Let this be your guide. Your companion. Your beacon of light. Say yes today.

You did not come to this planet to suffer. And neither did I. We came here to be radiant. Not in spite of the fact that someone we love has died. But because of the fact that someone we love has died. Let this powerful, transformational, love-filled book be your guide. To healing. To being radiant.

Thank you, Susan. For being a teacher. For doing your part to change our world. For teaching a new way to do grief.

Much love always,

Tom Zuba,
author of *Permission to Mourn: A New Way to Do Grief*

INTRODUCTION

Man is a tool-using animal. Without tools
he is nothing, with tools he is all.

—Thomas Carlyle

This book happened quite by accident. I had no intention of becoming an author. I was completely content with my chosen profession. Twenty years of working as a teacher and social worker on behalf of children, youth, and families had been extremely fulfilling. But life has a way of shifting things. Sometimes the shifts are monumental. Sometimes they alter the course of life. Sometimes they propel one to take action.

My own monumental life shift occurred in 2012.

I was forty-one years old. I was a wife and a mother.

Until my husband went out for a Sunday drive and didn't show up for dinner. Until he didn't show up for breakfast. Until he was silent. Until police and investigators were involved and he was declared a missing person. Until the search began. Until weeks went by and his vehicle was discovered. Until his body was recovered in the wreckage. Until he never returned home.

Somehow, in an instant, my entire world spun off axis and sent me careening into an invisible pit of darkness and despair. Falling down. Unable to breathe.

Unable to move. Unable to see. Not a thing in the world made sense anymore. **One moment** *I had been living overseas with my preschool-aged child and international business professor husband. We were in transition, moving across the world to settle back in America. Our personal belongings were en route, on a container ship bobbing across the Pacific Ocean.* **The next moment** *my husband—best friend, co-parent, athletic adventure buddy, travel partner, house chef, family comedian, devoted dad, creative artist, talented musician, brilliant young surfing professor—was . . .* **dead?** *Impossible. I sat ravaged, immobilized, and completely alone in that pit of darkness and despair for an eternity.*

Until something bumped against me. Was I really alone? It was a young child. Our five-year-old son. He was in the pit too. I didn't care about myself, but I did care about him. How could I save him? How could I get him out of here? I needed to save myself first. But where should I begin? My life was already in flux: no house, no car, no job, no community, few friends. And now I had a distressed child, a dead husband, unimaginable grief, indescribable trauma, and little desire to keep living. Where would I even **begin?**

At first I thought time would help us heal. But time marched on. And we felt worse. Something was missing.

Action.

Intention.

I was propelled to act, both personally and professionally, to find resources that would help me intentionally restore, renew, and rebuild a new life.

As a seasoned social worker, I had been trained to research, organize, and connect other people to resources in their community. Certainly I could find some tools to help *myself?*

As a credentialed teacher, my heart had been trained to love, support, and provide the best care for children. Certainly I could dig deep to help my *own* child?

So I went searching. Actively. Intentionally. For tools that would help us heal.

And I found them.

They are gathered here, in this book. The book I wish I had been given when my life shattered into a million pieces and I began a desperate attempt to crawl toward any sliver of light.

A to Z Healing Toolbox is a collection of powerful and action-based A-to-Z tools, resources, and personal stories compiled to accompany and accelerate the healing journey of those living with grief and trauma. The tools are organized alphabetically for clarity and convenience.

You may start on any chapter you choose.
You may skip around in the book.
You may focus on one chapter per day, per week, or per month.
You may visit sections when you feel like it.
You may return to pages that resonate with you.
You may share information with family and friends.
You may move through the toolbox with your therapist.
You may write in the book.
This is your own guidebook to personal healing.

A to Z Healing Toolbox is full of positive and practical tools and resources that have been studied, researched, recommended by professionals, and tested by thousands of peers, mentors, and colleagues. Integrating these tools into my new life has been part of my own active healing process, and it can be part of yours.

A to Z Healing Toolbox can help you restore, renew, and rebuild your life one small step at a time. There are a range of tools for you to use on your journey. It doesn't matter where you begin. Just begin. These are lifelong tools that can be integrated at any point in your healing process. Start on any page. Take a small, hope-filled step forward.

A to Z Healing Toolbox is the result of my personal experience, professional knowledge, and humble desire to make this challenging time in your life just a little bit easier. My hope is that this book can be your guide and roadmap—a lantern to light the pathway of active, intentional healing—as you gather appropriate resources for your own journey. My hope is that you don't have to spend copious amounts of time and energy discovering what can assist you because there are so many grief and trauma resources already in your community. My hope is that you choose active, intentional healing to benefit your mind, body, and spirit.

Because waiting for time to heal is not enough.

Over the past five years, I have been invited to live and work with a remarkable community of friends, peers, mentors, supporters, and colleagues, all of whom are tackling the hard work of intentional healing while living with profound grief and trauma. Collectively we grieve our spouses, partners, children, parents, siblings, extended family members, best friends, lives, and former selves. We have experienced trauma by accident, illness, stillbirth, suicide, addiction, murder, war, abuse, assault, terrorist attack, natural disaster, serious medical condition, occupational duty, and other life-altering circumstances. Perhaps you are now, unexpectedly, part of our community.

- Has your own life shifted in a monumental way?

- Are you unsure how to begin anew?

- Would you like to take proactive steps in the grief and trauma healing process?

- Would you like a new set of tools and resources to help you restore, renew, and rebuild your life?

- Are you wondering if there is anything that can possibly help you heal mentally, physically, socially, psychologically, and spiritually?

If you answered "yes" to any of these questions, this book is for you.

Welcome to the *A to Z Healing Toolbox* community.

As you get up each day, know that there are thousands of us walking alongside you on your journey, sending support and encouragement (and tools!) along the way.

With much love in the days to come,

Susan ☺

GRIEF

*Grief is a process that is better thought of as
a journey. It's just one foot in front of
the other.*

—DR. TIM CLINTON

Have you heard the story about the woman who almost burned down
her kitchen with two gigantic bags of flaming popcorn? No? I would
love to explain.

I've never been much of a chef. That's why I have been known to use
my empty oven as a pantry. In a small kitchen, it's the perfect storage
unit for extra-large food items, boxes of plastic utensils, paper towel rolls,
cleaning supplies, and bulky grocery store purchases that won't fit in the
cupboard—like popcorn. My oven storage workaround had always worked
out very nicely, until my husband died and my brain stopped functioning.

One day, our young son asked me if his friend could sleep over. I
said yes. I said we would pick up his buddy and we would cook pizzas. I
said we would watch a movie and have fun. We picked up his friend and
came home, but that's when the cooking began and the fun ended. Two
minutes after I turned the oven on to preheat, it happened. Pungent smell.
Billowing smoke. Fire alarms. Shooting flames. Kids screaming. Mom

running. Coherent thoughts coming like molasses. *Fire. Fire? What? Why? How? Where? Do we have an extinguisher? Brent, where is the fire extinguisher? Why aren't you answering me? Oh, you're dead. Okay. No extinguisher. Flames. Water. Pans. Throw water at the oven. Okay. Is the fire out? The fire is out. It's okay, boys. Everything is okay.*

Well, sort of okay. Maybe not okay. No, most definitely not okay. I almost burned down the kitchen with two gigantic bags of flaming popcorn inside my oven storage unit because I forgot they were in there. I forgot. I just forgot.

Other grievers forget too. Some refer to it as "grief brain."

Kelley Lynn Shepherd had grief brain. Kelley, comedienne and author of *My Husband Is Not a Rainbow: The Brutally Awful, Hilarious Truth about Life, Love, Grief, and Loss*, does a very funny stand-up comedy routine at yearly conferences for grieving communities. She remembers going to work one day, not long after her husband died, and wondering why so many people were looking in her direction as she walked from her apartment to the parking garage. *Oh well*, she thought. *Just a typical busy morning in the New York/New Jersey area.* She then crossed the busy street full of buses and pedestrians, walked through the bustling parking garage, unlocked her car door, and slid into the seat. As she leaned over to buckle her seat belt, she realized that she has forgotten something. Her pants. She had forgotten to put on pants. And now, embarrassed and aware, she had to retrace her steps—out of the parking garage, through the busy street, back into her apartment complex—to find some pants.

In addition to forgetfulness, grief can coincide with other massive internal shifts—physical, emotional, behavioral, mental, social, and spiritual. A snapshot of my grief includes:

- Isolating myself from anyone who didn't have a forty-three-year-old musical-surfer-professor husband with big muscles and brown hair who died in a car accident.

- Nearly punching the elderly lady at the gym who complained about her live spouse snoring next to her in bed.
- Spending four hours a day crying, wailing, screaming, and beating pillows on the bed.
- Feeling nauseous all day and all night with no relief in sight.
- Shrieking obscenities at God while driving around perfectly manicured suburbs.
- Failing to put coherent sentences together, even after years of graduate school.
- Discovering one evening that I had been walking around all day—school, grocery store, medical appointments—with a smashed green earplug embedded in my hair, a remnant from the previous night's failed attempt at sleep.

But I didn't care. About any of it. I was standing and breathing. Wasn't that enough?

WHAT IS GRIEF?

Initially, I had complete misinformation about the term "grief." I always thought grief was the very brief period of sadness that immediately followed the death of a grandparent who passed away peacefully at the age of ninety-five. I had no idea this term could and would apply to me and my life. I realize now that of course grief applies to my peers who are sad after their grandparent dies at the age of ninety-five. But it also applies to my community members who collectively mourn the deaths of young spouses, school-aged children, teenage siblings, middle-aged parents, and college best friends. They grieve shattered marriages, unmet hopes, broken dreams, and financial instability; they struggle with addiction, infertility, physical pain, and legal woes; and they assist family members living with congenital heart defects, incurable genetic disorders, long-term illnesses, and fatal diseases.

We are all unique individuals with varying biologies, psychologies, and life experiences. The details of our grief stories and grief reactions may differ.

But we all belong to the same grief community.

WHAT DO THE EXPERTS SAY?

A) "An unimaginable, indescribable loss has taken place," explain Dr. Elisabeth Kübler-Ross and David Kessler, authors of *On Grief and Grieving*. "It has inflicted a wound so deep that numbness and excruciating pain are the material of which it is made. Your world stops. You know the exact time your loved one died, or the exact moment you were told. It is marked in your mind. Your world takes on a slowness, a surrealness. It seems strange that the clocks in the world continue when your inner clock does not. Your life continues, but you are not sure why . . . you will survive, though you may not be sure how or even if you want to."

B) "Grief is wild and messy and unpredictable and uncertain and ever-changing and unsettling and unnerving," describes Tom Zuba, life coach, speaker, and author of *Permission to Mourn: A New Way to Do Grief*. "And as much as I'd like to tell you that grief will be orderly, neat, tidy, and predictable and unfold in five stages, it will not. Period. You may feel confused, sad, anxious, desperate, angry, frightened, lonely, nauseous, numb, dazed, dizzy, to name just a few of the ways that grief expresses itself seemingly all at the same time."

C) "Grief is the normal and natural reaction to loss of any kind. Therefore, the feelings you are having are also normal and natural for you," state John James and Russell Friedman, founders of the Grief Recovery Institute. "The problem is that we have all been socialized to believe that these feelings are abnormal and unnatural. While grief is normal and natural, and clearly the most powerful of all emotions, it is also the most neglected and misunderstood experience, often by both the griever and those around them."

D) "An essential breakdown in how we've been taught to grieve is the culturally accepted idea that we have 365 days to grieve, then we should be ready to move on," says Paula Stephens, wellness coach and author of *From Grief to Growth: 5 Essential Elements of Action to Give Your Grief Purpose and Grow from Your Experience*. "If we are to understand grief over the loss of a loved one as the result of deep love, then we can no more put a timeline on it than we can for love of a living person. The reality is, grief knows no deadline because love knows no bounds."

It seems there are no containers massive enough to hold the physical, emotional, behavioral, mental, social, and spiritual changes that can accompany grief.

And yet . . .

There are powerful and effective tools and resources available to help carry, support, and accompany the grief-healing journey.

WHAT NEXT?

A to Z Healing Toolbox can be your guidebook and roadmap—a steady lantern to light the pathway of active, intentional healing as you gather appropriate resources for your grief-healing journey.

But first:

1) An Invitation: Become familiar with your grief reactions.

2) An Assignment: Take a few minutes to complete the following worksheet, **Common Grief Reactions in Adults**. This will assist you in understanding that your grief behaviors are normal, guide you in navigating your next days with clarity and compassion, and aid you in gathering appropriate tools and resources for your own unique healing journey.

3) An Acknowledgement: I first completed this worksheet during the darkest part of my grief. I circled 95 percent of the reactions and behaviors listed. With action and intention, that list has dramatically changed. Your list will change too. You will heal in the days, weeks, and months to come.

Exercise:
COMMON GRIEF REACTIONS IN ADULTS

This exercise will take 5–10 minutes. Here are some **common grief reactions** in adults.
Circle all that are true for you at this time.

Physical
upset stomach
pain
exhaustion
sleep changes
appetite changes
dry mouth
muscle tension
clumsiness
low energy
shortness of breath
tightness in chest
tightness in throat
agitation
sensitivity to light, smells, sounds

Emotional
shock or numbness
sadness
guilt or regret
anger
emptiness
relief
irritability
restlessness
listlessness
insecurity
betrayal
resentment
desire to join loved one
feeling helpless
feeling out of control

Behavioral
crying
sobbing
wailing
difficulty crying
sitting quietly
staying busy to avoid emotion
avoiding situations that provoke grief
talking aloud to loved one
channeling energy into activities
looking at photos and videos of loved one
keeping a home altar
carrying loved one's belongings
wearing loved one's clothes
repeatedly visiting ash site or cemetery

Mental
denial
disbelief
forgetfulness
confusion
disorientation
difficulty concentrating
shortened attention span
minimal motivation
retelling story of death
memories of past losses
dreams or images of loved one
expecting to hear from loved one

Spiritual
mystery and wonder
questions about afterlife
and mortality
questions about God and
higher power
affirmation of spiritual/
religious beliefs
doubting spiritual/
religious beliefs
questions about the
whereabouts of loved one
sensing the presence of
loved one

Social
difficulty relating to old
friends
making new friends
isolation
alienation
shifting roles
new responsibilities
not wanting to burden others
withdrawing from activities
low desire for conversation
holding grief in to help others
difficulty relating to those who
aren't grieving

Resources: San Diego Hospice, *Men Don't Cry, Women Do: Transcending Gender Stereotypes of Grief*
(Martin & Doka), and *How to Go On Living When Someone You Love Dies* (Rando).

TRAUMA

*Trauma is hell on earth. Trauma resolved is
a gift from the gods.*

—Dr. Peter Levine

I met the biggest cockroach of my life one spring evening in Kingston, Jamaica. It was my senior year of college and I was on a volunteer service trip with a handful of other students from my university. Daytime hours were spent working in impoverished neighborhoods that housed shelters, schools, and care centers. Evening hours were spent getting to know our incredibly generous Jamaican host families. They served us breakfast with fresh juice made from the fruit trees growing in their yards, opened their lives, and shared their music and culture. The family I stayed with owned a home with an indoor-outdoor cold-running shower. Even though I stood showering indoors, the cut-outs in the cement shower slabs allowed me to see the birds in the papaya trees and feel the tropical breeze from outdoors. The cutouts in the cement shower slabs also allowed various crawly creatures to come in and out of the house at their leisure. But that was okay by me because I loved the outdoors and all things nature.

One evening, as I sat on the toilet facing the shower, I reached back to grab the toilet paper roll sitting on the back of the toilet tank. As I held the roll in front of me, a dark brown head with two long feelers popped out from inside the roll. In slow motion, a cockroach the length of the entire toilet paper roll proceeded to climb out—inch by inch—of his secret hiding place and crawl toward my hand. I freaked out. I jumped off the toilet seat, hurled the roll and the roach across the bathroom, and jumped up and down about twenty-five times. For some reason, I didn't scream, but my body shook in quiet shock and disgust as I watched the gigantic cockroach scurry through one of the openings in the shower slab and escape into the night.

I clearly remember thinking, "I've just been traumatized by a cockroach!"

There are three parts of this story I would like to highlight:

1) I met Mr. Giant Jamaican Cockroach more than twenty years ago, but to this day, I always peek inside toilet rolls if they have been sitting alone on the back of the toilet tank. I don't care if I am using the bathroom stall at a five-star hotel. I always look. *Because even small experiences can stay with us forever.*

2) My body shook in quiet shock and disgust. *Because sometimes there are no words.*

3) Being startled by a cockroach was stressful and surprising. Not all stressful events are traumatic. *But all traumatic events are beyond stressful.*

I learned the true meaning of trauma in 2012 when my husband went out for a summer afternoon drive, went missing, and never returned.

Weeks of confusion, chaos, horror, searching, silence. Then a knock on the door. The police detective hands me my husband's wallet and wedding ring and tells me a local nature photographer was in a field taking pictures, overlooking a beautiful lake in a dangerous mountainous area, when he noticed a vehicle in the ravine below. I'm so sorry . . . I'm so sorry . . . Today is your wedding anniversary? Tomorrow is your birthday? I'm so sorry.

Happy anniversary to us. Happy birthday to me.

You too may have a trauma story that has knocked you to your knees.

WHAT IS TRAUMA?

Initially, I had complete misinformation about the term "trauma." I thought trauma and its aftermath, known as post-traumatic stress disorder (PTSD), was reserved for people who had survived violent situations like rape, abuse, and combat. I had no idea this term could and would also apply to me and my life. I now realize that of course trauma applies to my peers who were raped in college, were abused by family members, and fought in wars. But it also applies to my peer group, who collectively have had to bury stillborn babies, perform CPR on dying children, clean wounds for spouses battling cancer, witness siblings undergo massive medical interventions, organize search parties for missing loved ones, rehabilitate bodies after accident and injury, and maintain professionalism in the line of duty as emergency first responders.

Additionally, I had no knowledge whatsoever about another term that could and would apply to me and my life: traumatic grief. Traumatic grief refers to the combined experience of grieving a significant loved one while experiencing their traumatic death, usually by sudden, violent, or accidental means. "Survivors who suffer through traumatic bereavement have to cope with the trauma and any resulting stress in addition to the death and the grieving process. Having to deal with posttraumatic stress as a result of traumatic loss can interfere with the grieving process," state Yuval Neria and Brett T. Litz, authors of the article "Bereaved by Traumatic Means: The Complex Synergy of Trauma and Grief." The term traumatic grief applies to many in my peer group, who collectively grieve immediate family members who died by auto accident, drowning, gunshot, motorcycle collision, suicide, and terrorist attack, all the while being traumatized themselves.

We are all unique individuals with varying biologies, psychologies, and life experiences. The details of our trauma stories and trauma reactions may differ.

But we all belong to the same trauma community.

WHAT DO THE EXPERTS SAY?

A) Trauma is "a metaphor for life-events that tear at the psychological skin that protects us, leaving us emotionally wounded," describes Dr. Stephen Joseph, psychologist and author of *What Doesn't Kill Us: The New Psychology of Posttraumatic Growth.* "When we experience trauma, our bodies go into shock and our minds are overwhelmed. Imagine a Christmas snow globe. Shake it and the snow flurries; over time, it settles. How long the snow remains unsettled depends on how vigorously the globe was shaken in the first place. So it is with the trauma that shakes up our mental world."

B) "Suddenly there's no place to stand. It's as if the world has broken its promise, revealing itself to be capable of devastating chaos and cruelty," explains Belleruth Naparstek, psychotherapist and author of *Invisible Heroes: Survivors of Trauma and How They Heal.* "The trauma carves a painful dividing line in the survivor's personal narrative, a line that splices his life in two: there's the person he was before, and the person he's become since. Profoundly undermined, he is lonely, fearful, disoriented, and unnerved by the certainty that he is not who he thought he was, and indeed the world is no longer amenable to past interpretation."

C) "Trauma is the most avoided, ignored, denied, misunderstood, and untreated cause of human suffering," says Dr. Peter Levine, psychologist and author of *Healing Trauma*. "People often ask me to define trauma. After thirty years, this is still a challenge. What I do know is that we become traumatized when our ability to respond to a perceived threat is in some way overwhelmed."

D) The American Psychiatric Association's *Diagnostic and Statistical Manual of Mental Disorders* (*DSM*) lists two conditions that must be present for medical professionals to begin evaluating and treating an adult for PTSD:

1) the person experienced, witnessed, or was confronted with an event or events that involved actual or threatened death or serious injury, or a threat to the physical integrity of self or others

2) the person's response involved intense fear, helplessness, or horror.

It can seem as though there is absolutely no container massive enough to hold the anguish, misery, agony, torment, and suffering that come with trauma experiences.

And yet . . .

There are powerful and effective tools and resources available to help identify, manage, and accelerate the trauma-healing journey.

WHAT NEXT?

A to Z Healing Toolbox can be your guidebook and roadmap—a steady lantern to light the pathway of active, intentional healing as you gather appropriate resources for your trauma-healing journey.

But first:

1) An Invitation: Become familiar with your own trauma reactions.

2) An Assignment: Take a few minutes to complete the following worksheet, **Common Trauma Reactions in Adults**. This will assist you in understanding that every trauma behavior is normal, guide you in navigating your trauma with more clarity and compassion, and aid you in gathering appropriate tools and resources for your own unique healing journey.

3) An Acknowledgement: I first completed this exercise during the early stages of trauma. I circled 95 percent of the reactions and behaviors listed. With action and intention, that list has dramatically changed. Your list will change too. You will heal in the days, weeks, and months to come.

Exercise:

COMMON TRAUMA REACTIONS IN ADULTS

This exercise will take 5–10 minutes. Here are some **common trauma reactions** in adults. Circle all that are true for you at this time.

- Were you exposed to an event(s) that involved actual or threatened death/serious injury OR a threat to the physical safety of yourself/another? (Yes/No)

- Did your response to the event(s) involve intense fear, helplessness, or horror? (Yes/No)

Behavioral

startling easily

jumpiness

feeling on edge

over-alertness to danger

feeling detached or withdrawn

fearfulness or nervousness

anger outbursts

irritability

sleep disturbances

avoiding thinking about trauma

avoiding people, places, activities, thoughts, feelings, conversations associated with traumatic event(s)

Mental/Emotional

difficulty experiencing emotion

mentally shutting down

emotionally shutting down

guilt or shame

difficulty concentrating

sadness or anger

flashbacks

nightmares

disturbing memories or images

Physical

shallow breathing

muscle tension

headaches

nausea

hot or cold sweats

vomiting or diarrhea

trembling

fatigue

Social

wanting to isolate from others

avoiding social interactions

feeling not understood by others

strained relationships

strengthened relationships

anxiety being with others

Resources: *DSM IV* (American Psychiatric Association), *Healing Trauma* (Peter Levine), and *What Doesn't Kill Us* (Stephen Joseph).

A

ANIMALS

*A cat purring on your lap is more healing
than any drug in the world, as the
vibrations you are receiving are of pure love
and contentment.*

—St. Francis of Assisi

HEALING POWER

When Brent died, I could barely function. It was a Herculean effort just getting out of bed each morning, much less taking care of our young son. I knew about the therapeutic benefits of pets, but there was absolutely no way I could think about taking care of a live creature. So I started introducing animals into my home with one ten-dollar beta fish. I put it on my bedside table and watched it swim. Months later, I began borrowing friend's dogs. I would sit on the floor and play with them. Eventually, I remembered I loved horses. So I tried infusing holiday vacations with horseback riding trips that gave me moments of grief and trauma relief. I would close my eyes, breathe in time with the horse, and smile when overhearing my son and his friends laugh over the volume of urine a horse can release.

Two years into my healing process, I was ready to investigate getting our own pet. I am allergic to hamsters, rabbits, guinea pigs, cats, and most farm animals, so I made a list of every quality I wanted in a dog: non-shedding, easily trainable, calm temperament, friendly with children, stamina for trail hikes, adventurous for water sports. When I showed my list to a local dog trainer, she took one glance at it and declared, "What you are looking for is an Australian labradoodle!" *Say, what?!* I couldn't believe it. First, Australia was where we lived right before Brent died. Second, Australia was where our son was born. Third, I was a dog lover and had never heard of this breed (it turns out some Australian dog lovers decided to mix four breeds together in the 1980s: Labrador retriever, poodle, Irish water dog, and American cocker spaniel). Anyway, we got the perfect dog for our family. We named him Kai.

Kai, a chocolate brown Australian labradoodle, is our personal therapy dog and living symbol of integration—merging my old life with new life. Kai is the Hawaiian word for ocean, and Hawaii was where Brent and I made our home together for many years. Kaimana Beach, at the base of Diamond Head on the south shore of Oahu, was our favorite beach. We got married there, gave our son his name there, and it is in that kai where Brent's ashes and mana (spirit) commingle with the waves at his favorite surf spot.

Kai has immensely helped in our family's healing. He brought joy and laughter into our home, gave us respite from intense emotions of grief, calmed my rampant anxiety, counteracted my depressed mood, and helped to stabilize my breathing. I would lie on the floor next to him and try to match his relaxed, grounded breath. Kai has also become an integral part of my resocialization process. I lived in a cocoon for years, feeling isolated and alienated from the non-grieving/non-traumatized community. I felt I had nothing to say, nothing to share, nothing in common. But pets are wonderful icebreakers. Having Kai has allowed me to interact with the children at my son's school (*How old is your dog? What's your dog's name?*), strike up conversations with other dog owners while on hiking trails (*Which veterinarian do you use? Where did you buy that collapsible water bowl?*), and engage with other volunteers in the community as part of the Love on a Leash certified pet therapy team.

I wonder if animals might assist you on your healing journey.

Why consider animals?
Human physiology is positively altered in the presence of animals. Therapists, medical professionals, hospice workers, hospitals, and veteran recovery programs have introduced pets to provide comfort and healing to those living with grief and trauma. Over the past decade, many doctors, dentists, veterinarians, and health clinics have added freshwater aquariums to their waiting rooms because of the meditative effects of hearing bubbling filters and watching fish swim. Whether large or small, with fins or fur, animals are natural healing resources.

How do animals promote healing?
- By decreasing feelings of loneliness and isolation
- By relieving symptoms of anxiety and depression
- By increasing the level of the "happy hormone," oxytocin
- By improving overall heart health

SINGLE SMALL STEPS

If you would like to integrate animals into your healing journey, here are some single small step suggestions you may be able to use.

Is there one that resonates with you?

1) **Play**: Spend twenty to thirty minutes a day playing with your own pet.

2) **Borrow**: For twenty to thirty minutes a day, borrow a neighbor's pet (walk their dog, play with their cat, etc.).

3) **Volunteer**: Once a week, volunteer at a local animal shelter, veterinarian clinic, or pet store.

4) **Buy**: Integrate a new animal into your own home. Can you add a single beta fish? Or a rabbit? Or a guinea pig? Or a turtle? Or a cat? Or a dog?

5) **Qualify**: Have a medical or mental health professional help you determine whether you qualify for an Emotional Companion Animal or a program in Pet Therapy or Equine Therapy.

Here is one single small step I may be able to take in the future:

_____

_____

_____

_____

_____

_____

_____

HEALING STORIES

My father died when I was five, and I knew we needed something else in our lives. After I begged for weeks, my mom finally gave in and we went to the pet store. We walked into the small, tucked-away place, just like the place I felt I was stuck in. But as the dogs starting barking, I could tell I broke the barrier. The barrier of death. We asked to see the black dog and then a second dog popped her head out from behind the other one. The pet store man asked us if we wanted to have them in the pen with us and we said, "Yes, of course." Right then I knew we'd have new company in our life. When they were put in the pen, one went straight to me and one went straight to my mom, and that was when it clicked. We were getting both dogs, and I told her these dogs were going to help us heal.
—Oliver, age twelve

My husband and I both adored dogs. When we first met, we often hung out at the local shelter where I volunteered as a dog socializer. When Steven bought a Chihuahua, I told him she was to be his *dog. I was done caring for animals—or so I thought. But when Steven passed away after a two-year battle with cancer, it was suddenly just me and Maggie the Chihuahua. I seriously considered moving and running away from it all, but I knew I needed to try something different. For the last year now, it's been "dog days of summer" at my house. I have started my own pet sitting, dog walking, and day care business. I love all my new furry friends. Animals have brought so much new life into my home that I can't imagine where I'd be if not for them. I believe Steven is just loving the new life we've chosen!*
—Sarah

I've been living with the deaths of three vital people. I've moved cross-country three times and have felt overwhelmed, depressed, dazed, and confused. The difference with my last move is that it's just me—no one to take care of but me—still grieving, needing to redefine myself. I thought working with animals would help center me more, ease me into the community, and provide some

much-needed love. So I recently found a cat adoption center that functions on volunteers and donations. I'm not ready to get overly involved with people, so this seemed like a good compromise. I volunteer for a few hours a week with about thirty-five cats and kittens on the floor. These fur babies have been abused, abandoned, or thrown out. When I am struggling, the benefits of caring for animals are amazing. It's a chance to shut off my mind, focus on something outside myself, and experience unconditional love and gratitude. The cats play, cuddle, purr, and fall asleep at my touch or in my lap. Ultimately, it brings relief from heartache and grief.
—Margo

My wife couldn't have children, but she would have been a good mother. Instead, we got two big dogs, Giselle and Amanda, our Borzois (aka Russian wolfhounds). Thus began almost a decade as a family with dog-governesses and other dog-moms and doggie dates at the park with other Borzoi friends. Laurie loved her dog-children more than life itself. Then Laurie suddenly died, and the world stopped. This may sound silly, but pets are proxy for family and children at home. Giselle and Amanda enforce a structure and rhythm to my life. They must be fed and walked every day. They remind me I must get out of bed, whether I want to or not, workday or not. They are intuitive and understand my emotions. Most nights after dinner, one of my pups comes over and plops onto the sofa head to head so that I can rest my arm on her and give her a scratch and a pet. While I can't take care of my wife anymore, I can continue to take care of the things that were important to her.
—Stephen

RESOURCES

If you would like to integrate animals into your own healing journey, here are some resources that can help you get started.

Article

"Easing the Way in Therapy With the Aid of an Animal" by Jane Brody *(The New York Times)*

Books

Chicken Soup for the Pet Lover's Soul by Jack Canfield, Mark Victor Hansen, Marty Becker, and Carol Kline

The Healing Power of Pets: Harnessing the Amazing Ability of Pets to Make and Keep People Happy and Healthy by Marty Becker

Booklet

"Get Healthy, Get a Dog: Special Report," Harvard Health Publications

Organization

National Service Animal Registry
www.nsarco.com
Facts related to owning Service Animals and Emotional Support Animals (ESAs).

NOTES

Use this section for any notes related to animals.

_____

_____

_____

_____

_____

_____

_____

_____

_____

_____

_____

_____

_____

_____

_____

_____

"It's not one huge step that promotes healing . . .
it's many intentional single small steps."

B

Breathwork

*Just breathing can be such a
luxury sometimes.*

—Walter Kirn

HEALING POWER

The man I married was a cross-cultural professor by training, but a cross-cultural musician at heart. Brent played a variety of unique woodwind instruments, including the Great Highland bagpipe, Mexican pan flute, Irish tin whistle, Hawaiian nose flute, and Australian didgeridoo. Honestly, the guy had quite a pair of lungs. So it was ironic that, when he died, I completely lost *my* ability to breathe. I couldn't get any air. I felt suffocated, panicked, and fearful, and became prone to anxiety attacks, which I had never experienced before.

On a whim, I signed up for a grief healing retreat cofacilitated by a yoga and meditation instructor. In one exercise, we placed both of our hands on our abdomens. Our instructor wanted us to see and feel our hands rise and fall with our breath. She wanted us to practice deep, slow, intentional "belly breathing." So I tried it. Nothing. No abdomen movement whatsoever. *Well, this is just perfect. My belly isn't moving. No wonder I feel so horrendous.*

I'm not even breathing. Then I learned that I was breathing with and through my chest—not my diaphragm. My breath was short, labored, tight, erratic, and taking place high in my chest. I was making minimal use of my lung capacity. I needed to be taught how to breathe again.

After the retreat, I practiced regulated breathing through drinking straws. I focused on my breath during yoga classes and downloaded free breathing applications on my phone. I also spoke to a doctor who suggested I might want to participate in a few biofeedback sessions while hooked up to electrodes. *Fine. Hook me up. Wait, bio-what?*

Biofeedback is a noninvasive technique that taught me how to bring my autonomic nervous system under conscious control. (The autonomic nervous system manages many bodily functions that we usually don't think about, including our heart rate, blood pressure, muscle tension, and breath.) A biofeedback practitioner attached electrical sensors to my fingers, stomach, and chest while I reclined in a comfortable chair. Then we watched a computer screen, which resembled a huge heart rate monitor, as it gave us feedback about my nervous system. I could see on the screen why I had been feeling anxious and panicked for months—my heart rate and breath rate were completely disorganized, unregulated, and out of sync.

I participated in six biofeedback sessions, which were covered by my health insurance provider. While hooked up to a computer and electrodes, the biofeedback practitioner guided me through regulated breathing exercises in the office as we watched the screen. I received regulated breathing exercises as homework, and I eventually matched my breath to the ebb and flow of my heart rate. I learned to have conscious control over my autonomic nervous system, therefore minimizing episodes of anxiety and panic.

I have slowly learned how to breathe again.

I wonder if breathwork might assist you on your healing journey.

Why consider breathwork?

Intense emotional and physical responses to grief and trauma may cause rapid, shallow breathing, which takes place high in the chest. This can heighten physiological reactions of anxiety, panic, and feelings of suffocation. In contrast, deep, slow, regulated breathing from the abdomen ("belly breathing" or "diaphragmatic breathing") can help calm the mind and relax the body. Experts in meditation, instructors at yoga studios, nurses in birthing centers, and therapists in session all incorporate breathwork to regulate the body. Any time of day or night, breath is a natural healing tool accessible to all.

How does breathwork promote healing?

- By reducing blood pressure and heart rate
- By relieving symptoms of post-traumatic stress
- By improving physical and emotional health
- By calming an anxious and ruminating mind
- By promoting more restful sleep

SINGLE SMALL STEPS

If you would like to integrate breathwork into your healing journey, here are some single small step suggestions you may be able to use.

Is there one that resonates with you?

1) **Air**: Practice Straw Breathing:

- Find a drinking straw; any size will do.
- Hold the straw gently and put one end lightly between your lips.
- Take one full breath in through your nose.

- Blow slowly out through the straw until all air has been exhaled.

- Repeat three times. Inhale through your nose and exhale through the straw.

- Practice several times a day to begin calming the nervous system.

- Keep straws handy—in your car, in your backpack, in your purse, in your office drawer.

2) **Apps**: Download free breathing applications onto your phone or device.

3) **Audio**: Listen to guided CDs that teach a variety of breathing exercises.

4) **Attend**: Find a yoga class in your community that emphasizes grounding breathwork.

5) **Apply**: Work with an experienced biofeedback practitioner in your community.

Here is one single small step I may be able to take in the future:

_____

_____

_____

_____

_____

_____

_____

HEALING STORIES

When it all implodes, explodes, hits the fan, comes to Jesus, goes to hell,
unravels, derails, blindsides us, sideswipes us, bowls us over,
or pulls us under, the breath is still there

starting with the pause after the exhale
that moment where we decide to keep breathing
to keep living

it invites us to sit with the nothingness
to see how it is big enough to hold everything that was
and everything that is

it asks us to allow silence where their words used to be
to listen to all it doesn't say for as long as we need to until
we finally hear the soft beat
of our own heart

until we remember how it has never left our side
not even for a moment

it introduces us to the tick-tock of this moment
until we see how the hand of Now reaches for ours

not to replace theirs or to pull us away from them
just to be with us
here where we are
as we are
right now

—Monique Minahan, author of *The Unedited Heart*

The day my sixteen-year-old son died of suicide, I felt like a huge part of me died too. My grief and despair would often grip me so hard that it was difficult to breathe. I would often go into a full-on panic attack. Nearly a year later, I have learned how incredibly healing mindful breathing can be. It has been documented that as little as three minutes of mindful breathing can calm the nervous system, and just a few minutes of mindful breathing can set the tone for my entire day. I have found that breath is the sacred link between my body and soul. It allows me to feel emotionally centered, alive, and present, and it's drug free. I am so encouraged by breathwork that I am now seeking my yoga instructor certification, and I hope that someday I can share its healing powers with others. Mindful breath is a wonderful coping tool. I am certainly better equipped to handle the grief journey if I simply remember to just breathe.
—Stacie

One of the most effective and powerful tools I have in my arsenal of self-care has turned out to be breathing. Yes, we all do it, but sometimes it needs to be done with intention. I didn't seek out learning to breathe—I was looking for anything that would give me some peace after my father's death. Eventually, I found a Meetup.com group that taught me about central-channel breathing. Basically, I picture a tube running vertically through the center of my body and take the breath in from the top of my head and push it (with some force) through my tailbone. I have found that it is ridiculously calming. I visualize the air coming through and being expelled, and it takes away my thoughts long enough to settle me down. Whether anxiety, fear, anger, sadness . . . it gives me a break. Sometimes breathing is all that's needed.
—Janie

My personal journey with breathwork began thirty-five years ago with a home yoga practice using tapes and CDs. My life stressors consistently grew with constant change, frequent job relocations, complicated children's issues, parental loss, and the inevitability of an empty nest. How has breathwork worked to help me through the many mental and physical challenges of life? I believe the yogis call the results "centering" or "calm." A few breathing techniques (called pranayama) that regenerate energies of life are cleansing breath, alternate nostril breathing, cooling breath, breath of fire, three-part breath, humming breath, belly breathing, diaphragmatic breathing, essential breath, lion's breath, mantras with breath, long deep breathing, rhythmic breath, and many more. Air (or prana) stimulates mental clarity as we breathe, so if you need healing, discover samplings of these Kundalini yoga breathing techniques by finding a quite spot to sit and spend time with yourself. Breathwork awakens my tattered spirit and enables me to face adversity head on.

—Donna

RESOURCES

If you would like to integrate breathwork into your healing journey, here are some resources that can help you get started.

Audio and CD
The Breathing Box by Dr. Gay Hendricks
Set includes CD, DVD, photo cards, and study guide on effective breathing techniques.

Breathing: The Master Key to Self-Healing by Dr. Andrew Weil
8 different breathing exercises to reduce anxiety and promote overall wellness.

Books
The Breathing Book: Good Health and Vitality Through Essential Breath Work by Donna Farhi

The Healing Power of the Breath: Simple Techniques to Reduce Stress and Anxiety, Enhance Concentration, and Balance Your Emotions (CD included) by Richard Brown and Patricia Gerbarg

Organization
The Association for Applied Psychophysiology and Biofeedback (AAPB)
www.biofeedback.org
General facts and information about biofeedback, including how to locate a practitioner.

Websites
Health Journeys
www.healthjourneys.com
Find a variety of resources on breathwork and healing.

NOTES

Use this section for any notes related to breathwork.

---

*"It's not one huge step that promotes healing . . .
it's many intentional single small steps."*

COUNSELING

*Time and time again, people transcend
the paralyzing effects of psychological pain
when they have sufficient contact with
someone who can hear them empathetically.*

—MARSHALL ROSENBERG

HEALING POWER

When I was in my teens, I thought a lot. I remember listening to a local news station one evening while the reporter covered a story about authorities rushing to the scene of a local bridge. Someone was about to jump off. My young mind was confused. *Authorities? Why are the police involved? Are they taking the person to jail? That person needs help, not to be locked up.* I didn't understand the intricacies of mental health, but that was my first memory of being interested in how the human mind worked, why people behaved as they did, and what could help individuals when they weren't feeling their best.

When I was in my twenties, I learned a lot. I worked and studied within the fields of education and social work. I read about behavioral, educational, and psychological theories. I volunteered with disenfranchised communities in Kingston, Jamaica, and spent a year with a national volunteer corps in the Pacific Northwest. I began collecting friends and future colleagues who were studying to enter the helping professions: teachers, nurses, doctors, firefighters, paramedics, psychologists, psychiatrists, school counselors, and social workers.

When I was in my thirties, I helped a lot. I focused on making sure my own clients had all the possible resources to make their lives a little bit easier. I taught in classrooms for abused and neglected children in California, facilitated health and wellness programs for foster teens in Hawaii, worked with special education elementary school students in Canada, advocated community support systems for families with disabilities in Australia, and instructed college students on best social work practices at two different overseas universities.

When I was in my forties, I healed a lot. But first I kicked and screamed and raged a lot. I also thought I could somehow singlehandedly "fix" my situation, like I had done for so many clients. But I quickly realized my son and I would never survive the aftermath of Brent's death without some of our own serious interventions. So I began to chase after every tool, resource, and person that might help us. In the name of pure desperation and intentional healing, I sought out every helping professional I knew, participated in every therapy session that might help, and looked for every social support system I had ever researched, taught, or mentioned to previous clients. I started social-working my own life.

Qualified counselors were the first invited into the aftermath of my husband's death, and they immediately started to pull us out of the darkness. Over the last four years, I have enlisted help from psychologists, psychiatrists, marriage and family therapists, social workers, and mental health counselors. My son and I have utilized various therapeutic modalities on our healing journey, including animal-assisted therapy, art therapy, cognitive behavioral therapy (CBT), eye movement desensitization and reprocessing (EMDR), narrative therapy, play therapy, sandplay therapy, and somatic experiencing.

I have listed a few general definitions of the various counseling-related therapies that have helped me move through grief and trauma processing and healing. But this list is not exhaustive; there are additional therapies available. I invite you to do more research to see what resonates with you and speak with local counseling professionals about their personal areas of expertise.

Animal-Assisted Therapy: This type of therapy uses several types of animals—dogs, cats, horses, dolphins—to assist individuals in their emotional and psychological healing and functioning. For example, my son's counselor had a highly trained therapy dog in her office to help grieving and traumatized children feel calm, safe, and emotionally stable in therapeutic sessions.

Art Therapy: This type of therapy uses various creative supplies—colored markers, finger paint, oil pastels, soft clay, textured beads, tissue paper—to assist individuals in their emotional and psychological healing and functioning. For example, during my first year of counseling, I made a double-sided mask out of papier-mâché. The mask enabled me to visualize, process, and integrate the massive discrepancies between my internal world (*I don't recognize myself, I have been completely altered in every way possible*) and external presentation (*I still look the same to others, I am a tall woman with blue eyes and long brown hair*).

Cognitive Behavioral Therapy (CBT): This type of therapy has been used for decades to effectively treat depression and other symptoms similar to those exhibited in grief. In CBT sessions, individuals explore the relationship between their patterns of cognition (thinking) that create certain feelings, which in turn lead to specific behaviors (actions). Changes can then be made to the thought process to create more positive feelings and behaviors. For example, I used to believe that no one else could possibly understand the magnitude of my husband's death (cognition); this made me extremely lonely and angry (feelings), and I would intentionally isolate from others (behavior). After CBT work, I chose to believe that other people could understand the magnitude of my husband's death (cognition); this made me feel empowered, acknowledged, and hopeful (feelings), which in turn encouraged my action to lead a peer support group for the widowed community in my city (behavior).

Eye Movement Desensitization and Reprocessing (EMDR): This type of therapy is used by both veteran and civilian communities as a method to assist the mind and body in healing from distressing images and bodily sensations associated with PTSD. The EMDR practitioner assists individuals in coming to a more peaceful resolution of trauma by using bilateral movements to help desensitize and reprocess the trauma experience. For example, for many months my brain repeatedly and involuntarily recalled disturbing images related to Brent's death. As I recalled an image in counseling sessions, my EMDR therapist methodically moved her hand, two fingers pointed up, back and forth in my field of vision. My eyes followed her hand as it moved: left, right, left, right, left, right. If I was sobbing hysterically and couldn't focus on her hand, she would instead incorporate the bilateral movement onto my knees, alternatively tapping the same pattern. Other EMDR therapists integrate bilateral reprocessing by having individuals use handheld buzzers that vibrate alternatively. By the completion of my EMDR sessions, the incapacitating images I saw in my head were no longer screaming at me in full color at the forefront of my mind. The images and sensations are much harder to retrieve; they have been desensitized, reprocessed, and stored in another part of my brain.

Narrative Therapy: This type of therapy uses an individual's personal story to rebuild, empower, and expand their identity. Narrative therapy assists in reframing life stories and life purposes by looking at new ways a challenging experience may be helpful rather than hurtful. For example, Brent and I moved around the world for his job as an international business professor. His job and our lifestyle helped me feel secure in the world: emotionally, physically, financially, spiritually. When he died, I felt directionless, adrift, and completely insecure. *No more international moves? No more university life? No more double income? No more dual parenting? No more secure partnership in marriage?* A weekend retreat with a narrative therapist helped me to honor my "old story about security" and envision a "new story about security." The colorful, creative cover page of my continued book of life: *The New Narrative* by Susan Hannifin-MacNab. "My Security Comes From My Soul: God's Unconditional Gifts of Life, Heart, Breath, and Connection" now hangs on my office bulletin board.

Play Therapy: This type of therapy uses a child's natural affinity to communicate through symbolic play to assist them in coping, processing, and expressing feelings that come along with difficult life situations. A play therapist may provide toys, art supplies, sand trays, dolls, play houses, tea sets, puppets, theater costumes, and games in order to help the child resolve conflict through play. For example, my son's play therapist immediately recognized his love for vehicles and his fascination with their engineering. Each time we entered the therapy room, he would gravitate toward the shelf of cars, trucks, trains, and boats. She even let him put together a new ambulance to add to her collection. Playing with familiar toys, while engaging his sense of self-efficacy, made him feel safe and comfortable enough to express—and eventually resolve—the anger, fear, and confusion he had over his father's death.

Sandplay Therapy: This type of therapy uses the power of symbolic imagery to provide individuals with a safe space to connect with their subconscious mind, move through overwhelming feelings of grief, and process traumatic experiences. Sandplay therapy is done by creating scenes in a tray of sand with miniature trinkets, symbols, statues, and figures. For example, my sandplay therapist always handed me an empty basket when I entered her room. She invited me to choose three to five items from the office shelves, which contained hundreds of miniature items: people, tents, buildings, balloons, dragons, cars, trash cans, steeples, rocks, butterflies, snakes, fairies, etc. I didn't have any idea what I was going to put into the basket when I began the process. I just scanned the shelves until something resonated before placing it in the basket. One day I grabbed three figures and placed them in the sand tray: a female army soldier holding a machine gun, a female warrior princess wielding a long spear, and a female child sitting atop a blue fire-breathing dragon. As I sat and stared at the tray of sand, I realized those figures were all representations of me. I was the soldier. I was the warrior princess. I was the child atop the dragon. And I was in "fighting mode," symbolic guns, spears, and fire helping me heal.

Somatic Experiencing (SE): Like EMDR, this type of therapy is also used by both veteran and civilian communities as a method to assist the mind and body in healing from the distressing images and bodily sensations associated with PTSD. The SE practitioner assists individuals in trauma resolution by assisting in the release of residual physical tension that has been locked into the body and causes physiological disruption. (SE theory suggests that negative energy that was not fully discharged at the time of trauma disrupts the balance of the nervous system.) For example, my SE practitioner invited me to lie face up on a massage table, encouraging me to relax and breathe deeply. Inevitably, a vivid, traumatic memory related to Brent's death came to my mind. As I alternately sobbed and froze, the practitioner's hands lightly rested on various parts of my body—head, neck, shoulder, feet—and allowed my body to discharge the energy locked inside. With no control or intention of my own, energy released from my body; my hand would begin to twitch, my foot would start to shake, my stomach would get a flash of warmth, and my breathing would suddenly become less restricted.

I wonder if counseling might assist you on your healing journey.

Why consider counseling?

There are numerous types of mental health practitioners who have specialized skills and training to assist those working toward healing the emotional and psychological effects of grief and trauma. Qualified counselors go by many names: licensed professional counselor (LPC), licensed mental health counselor (LMHC), marriage and family therapist (LMFT), licensed clinical social worker (LCSW), psychologist, and psychiatrist. These practitioners have a master's degree or PhD in their field of study, hundreds of hours of supervised clinical therapy experience, and a combination of modalities to assist clients. Counseling is an effective tool to use while moving through the various stages of healing grief and trauma.

How does counseling promote healing?

- By assisting in "old life" and "new life" integration
- By helping the mind and body restore balance and equilibrium
- By offering positive ways of processing grief, traumatic grief, and trauma
- By tailoring therapeutic options toward individual life experiences
- By providing a safe and welcome space for all thoughts, feelings, and emotions

SINGLE SMALL STEPS

If you would like to integrate counseling into your healing journey, here are some single small step suggestions you may be able to use.

Is there one that resonates with you?

Choosing a counselor can be a process. Sometimes it requires an interview, a consultation, and a bit of shopping around. Try to get a referral from someone you know who has used a particular practitioner. At your introductory meeting, make sure your personalities mesh, the conversation is easy, the environment is relaxed, and there is some agreement on the purpose and process of your future sessions. Here are some interview questions you can use to help you find a counselor who is right for you.

1) Do you accept my health insurance payment plan?

2) If not, do you offer a sliding fee scale? What are your rates?

3) Do you currently have clients who are working through similar issues to mine?

4) How long have you been practicing?

5) What type of training and licensure do you have?

6) What approaches and techniques do you use in counseling sessions?

7) What are your strengths as a counselor?

8) Do you lead the sessions or do you follow my lead?

9) Ask yourself during and after the interview: "Do I feel heard by this counselor?"

10) Ask yourself during and after the interview: "Do I feel comfortable with this counselor?"

Here is one single small step I may be able to take in the future:

_____

_____

_____

_____

_____

_____

_____

HEALING STORIES

I started seeing a grief counselor a few months after my daughter died in a car accident. My therapist uses a combination of talk therapy, guided imagery, cognitive reframing, and animal-assisted therapy. Counseling has helped me develop new coping skills and effectively learn how to keep living and breathing. I am learning how to fully embrace my new life and move with my daughter's death. Working with my counselor has been hugely beneficial. Therapy has also encouraged me to find ways to celebrate and honor the memory of my daughter. There is no guidebook on how to do this ugly thing called grief, but having a good counselor is like having a good coach. They are there to guide, teach, listen, and help you master the skills and techniques to "do grief" in a healthy way.
—Trish

My sister suffered two major strokes at the young age of twenty-nine that left her physically handicapped. We almost lost her multiple times. In the blink of an eye, I quit my job and lived in three different hospitals over the course of four months to be her advocate. I didn't realize throughout the course of this bad dream that I would end up suffering from PTSD, but it makes sense now. I eventually started seeing a marriage and family therapist. Going to counseling allowed me to share my feelings, let myself be sad, and sit in that moment. The therapist helped me realize that I didn't have to be strong for everyone. I had not allowed myself to grieve the sister and family that I once knew. My therapist helped me to accept my sister's injury and deal with this loss over time. I worked through the sadness and anxiety that had manifested. Instead of being the rock all the time, I focus on the actions I can control.
—Stephanie

I did none of my wife's cancer experience alone. For myself and our girls, I sought help from trained experts who knew the territory and had guided others before: social workers, psychiatrists, and psychologists who had worked with people losing a loved one or who had lost a loved one themselves. Our girls went weekly to a play therapy group for families dealing with cancer. After my wife died, the girls moved to a similar group for kids who had lost someone to cancer, and I moved to a weekly group meeting for people who had lost a loved one. The weekly sessions were a place to stop all the things I was doing, stop all the work calls, all the emails, and just focus on what I was thinking about and tell someone. Someone who listened and remembered over time, whose job it was to listen and who didn't have to run after fifteen minutes. Someone who had specific training and experience in helping people like me sort through the worries, frustration, anger, wishes, or sadness that came up, spurred by random events or connections.

—Tom

RESOURCES

If you would like to integrate counseling into your healing journey, here are some resources that can help you get started.

Book

Little Ways to Keep Calm and Carry On: Twenty Lessons for Managing Worry, Anxiety, and Fear by Mark Reinecke

Organizations

Association for Behavioral and Cognitive Therapies
www.abct.org
CBT information, resources, and help locating a therapist in your area.

Good Therapy
www.goodtherapy.org
General counseling information and help locating a therapist in your area.

EMDR Institute Inc.
www.emdr.com
Eye movement desensitization and reprocessing information and help locating practitioners.

Somatic Experiencing Trauma Institute
www.traumahealing.org
SE information and help locating practitioners.

NOTES

Use this section for any notes related to counseling.

_____

_____

_____

_____

_____

_____

_____

_____

_____

_____

_____

_____

_____

_____

_____

_____

_____

_____

_____

_____

_____

"It's not one huge step that promotes healing . . .
it's many intentional single small steps."

DOING YOUR HOMEWORK

Knowledge is power.

—FRANCIS BACON

HEALING POWER

After the atomic bomb of sudden death blasted into my life, I poured myself into reading. My brain wasn't functioning well at all—horrible concentration, inability to focus, extreme difficulty retaining information—so I read material in small doses. I got my hands on every published book, article, journal, brochure, handout, and online blog that reviewed the effects of grief and trauma to help me understand what was happening to my internal and external worlds. Everything had shifted—physically, emotionally, behaviorally, socially, mentally, and spiritually—and I somehow had to wrap my brain around it, little pieces at time. When I eventually stumbled upon the theory of post-traumatic growth, I felt the tiniest bit lighter—like I might, in fact, be able to survive the destruction and despair of my new life. I didn't *believe* it was possible, but I *hoped* it was. Hope was all I had left.

So I kept reading.

I learned that post-traumatic growth (PTG) can be the result of a life-changing incident that initially causes post-traumatic stress. PTG refers to the *positive* changes experienced resulting from a person's internal struggle with a major life crisis or traumatic event. I began to internalize that if I was somehow able to rebuild a new life—instead of trying to force the pieces of my old life back together—that I might have a chance of not only surviving, but thriving. *Thriving? How could that even be possible?*

> *"When adversity strikes, people often feel that at least some part of them—their views of the world, their sense of themselves, their relationships—has been smashed. Those who try to put their lives back together exactly as they were remain fractured and vulnerable. But those who accept the breakage and build themselves anew become more resilient and open to new ways of living. Focusing on, understanding, and deliberately taking control of what we do in our thoughts and actions can enable us to move forward in life following adversity."*
> —Dr. Steven Joseph, *What Doesn't Kill Us: The New Psychology of Posttraumatic Growth*

According to the PTG Research Group at University of North Carolina–Charlotte, a person's growth following adversity tends to occur in the five general areas below. I have discovered through lots of intentional healing work that I have grown in each of these areas:

1) New opportunities emerge from the crisis, trauma, or struggle.

2) Relationships with others change (e.g., "I feel closer to others who suffer").

3) There is an increased sense of personal strength (e.g., "I can do anything now!").

4) There is a greater appreciation for life in general.

5) There is a deepening of one's spiritual or religious life or a significant change in one's belief system.

I wonder if doing your homework might assist you on your healing journey.

Why consider doing your homework?

Gathering and understanding information related to grief and trauma—including normal reactions, behaviors, and processes—can assist individuals in applying helpful tools and resources to their healing process. Doing grief and trauma homework is similar to doing self-guided "bibliotherapy," which refers to using books, articles, journals, magazines, videos, websites, and brochures to support positive outlook and change. Intentionally moving toward healing various components of our lives, whether physical, emotional, psychological, behavioral, social, or spiritual, allows room for the business of restoring, renewing, and rebuilding lives.

How does doing your homework promote healing?

- By increasing the understanding that the personal effects of grief and trauma are universal
- By decreasing personal isolation, helping you realize that no one is alone on their healing journey
- By allowing recognition of possible steps to take to promote processing and restoration
- By integrating positive new ideas, habits, and thought processes into life rebuilding

SINGLE SMALL STEPS

If you would like to integrate doing your homework into your healing journey, here are some single small step suggestions you may be able to use.

Is there one that resonates with you?

1) **Bundle Up with Books**: Grab a blanket and head to the couch to learn more about grief and trauma through the writing of others.

2) **Lie and Listen**: Lie down and listen to helpful information via audiobooks and device applications like livestreams and podcasts.

3) **Click the Computer**: Check out informative websites that offer stories, advice, resources, reassurance, peer mentoring, and community connections.

4) **Hands Can Help**: Communicate with friends, family, colleagues, counselors, and local organizations to collect information that might help you along your path toward healing.

5) **Learn at Libraries**: Gather resources and materials from the community message boards and helpful staff at your local library.

Here is one single small step I may be able to take in the future:

_____

_____

_____

_____

HEALING STORIES

Doing my homework saved me. When my husband died, I felt lost and alone in this new world. I began scouring my local resources for groups, therapy, grief counselors, and anyone/anything I thought might help. Over the years, I contacted hospices, hospitals, cancer centers, and my health plan for assistance. I also knew of a national database of currently available clinical trials (www.clinicaltrials. gov) and found a complicated grief research study in my hometown! Twenty weeks of interviews and surveys, drug therapy, and behavioral counseling later, I emerged so much better off. If I had continued to hibernate at home, isolated from the world, that is where I'd still be today. Slowly but surely, through all the avenues I discovered, I started to appreciate life again. I still have bad days. But overall, I am on an upward trajectory.
—Lori

My homework was to find resources, reading, talks, groups, videos or movies, counselors, clergy, meditation, somatic work, or whatever it was where I felt I could approach what had happened, both during and after my wife died of cancer. I took those resources in when I could. But unlike homework from school, this grief homework is different:

1) *Homework should not be interpreted as the pressure of an assignment or a syllabus—it should feel like something that interests or helps you.*

2) *You should put it down when you don't feel like doing it. If you want to sleep, sleep.*

3) *You don't have to finish any book.*

4) *You can get other people to do some of it for you.*

5) *It should feel like a refuge, learning, a space where you can breathe and take time to cope by listening to others.*

—Thomas

When my husband died suddenly, I knew I was going to need a lot of help to keep from falling into a state of paralysis and deep depression. One of the things I did that helped me heal was doing my homework. There are so many rich resources out there: local hospices, counselors, support groups, books, inspirational reading materials, and podcasts. I started compiling a long list of podcasts and websites that offered stories, guided meditation, advice, resources, reassurance, and friendship when I needed it. Each time I launched my web browser, it was one small step. A simple search cascaded into a bigger web of resources I built into a library for myself. None of us needs the same exact help, so I was able to tailor my library to my specific needs and beliefs. Not only was it therapeutic to take action, it was empowering to improve my own life at a time when I felt hopeless and helpless.

—Anne

RESOURCES

If you would like to integrate doing your homework into your healing journey, here are some resources that can help you get started.

Books on Grief

How to Go On Living When Someone You Love Dies by Therese Rando

Living with Loss, One Day at a Time by Rachel Blythe Kodanaz

On Grief and Grieving by Elisabeth Kübler-Ross and David Kessler

Permission to Mourn: A New Way to Do Grief by Tom Zuba

Books on Trauma

Healing Trauma: A Pioneering Program for Restoring the Wisdom of Your Body by Peter Levine

Invisible Heroes: Survivors of Trauma and How They Heal by Belleruth Naparstek

Transforming Traumatic Grief: Six Steps to Move from Grief to Peace After the Sudden or Violent Death of a Loved One by Courtney Armstrong

What Doesn't Kill Us: The New Psychology of Posttraumatic Growth by Stephen Joseph

NOTES

Use this section for any notes related to doing your homework.

_____

_____

_____

_____

_____

_____

_____

_____

_____

_____

_____

_____

_____

_____

_____

_____

_____

_____

"It's not one huge step that promotes healing . . .
it's many intentional single small steps."

ENERGY THERAPIES

Energy and persistence conquer all things.

—BENJAMIN FRANKLIN

HEALING POWER

As I stood outside the conference room door waiting to be called in, I wondered what sort of crazy situation I had gotten myself into. But I didn't care. I was already living through the worst pain imaginable, so how bad could this be? "In crisis," I remembered, "you may find yourself experiencing emotions you have never felt before, attempting solutions you have never imagined having to contemplate, and responding with behaviors that seemed fastened together with psychological duct tape" (Daphne Rose Kingma, *The 10 Things to Do When Your Life Falls Apart*). So, yes, my life was in crisis. And, yes, I was attempting to find a solution by volunteering my face for study. Then, yes, I was responding to grief and trauma by sitting in front of fifty student practitioners while Jean Haner, expert in the ancient art of Chinese face reading and author of *The Wisdom of Your Face*, investigated every line, wrinkle, and angle of my face to assist me in personal healing and positive energetic shifts.

"You are the archetype called Warrior," Haner began. "You are linear, logical, commonsense, and action-oriented. You have a large widow's peak (yes, I see the irony here) which indicates that you are highly intuitive in nature. You are a highly spiritual person and have a depth of emotion that others may not know you have. Your forehead indicates that you learn hands-on. The natural arch and fullness of your eyebrows indicate self-confidence, logical thinking processes, strength, and assertiveness. Your eyelids indicate you are really good at stepping up to help others, but not so good at receiving the help yourself. The white underneath your eyes indicates that you are extremely stressed and that needs to be taken very seriously."

But what fascinated me most about Chinese face reading was its capacity to suggest harnessing energy for positive change. Energy? I had never given much thought to energy and how it could help me heal.

"All my work is based on ancient Chinese medicine," Haner continued. "The ancient Chinese culture found that in science, nature, medicine, and business, enormous change comes out of some tiny tipping point, some inconsequential energetic shift. There is energy I want to boost in your life right now, so let's begin with colors. Colors have a frequency. The main color I want to boost for you is yellow. Add more yellow to your wardrobe, your home, your environment, your artwork. Energy of women is also important for you."

After this experience, I started to pay more attention to lifting my own energy and meeting practitioners who used energy to heal. Over the last several years, I have worked with Reiki Master Teachers and Healing Touch practitioners to restore balance to my mind, body, and spirit. I have participated in SomatoEmotional Release sessions where negative energy cysts were cleared from my body. And I have practiced using Emotional Freedom Technique (EFT or Tapping) to harness the healing, centering, and balancing power of my own energy meridians.

I have listed a few general definitions of various energy therapies that have helped me move through grief and trauma healing. This list is not exhaustive. There are many other therapies out there. I invite you to do more research to see what resonates with you and speak with local practitioners about their personal areas of expertise.

Reiki: Reiki is a Japanese word meaning "universal life force energy." During a Reiki session, energy flows through the practitioner to calm, store, and balance the person in need of healing. Reiki sessions are conducted on massage-like tables while fully clothed practitioners gently place their hands in different positions either on or near the recipients' bodies.

Healing Touch: Healing Touch enlists the body's magnetic field to restore balance and harmony to the energy system so that individuals are able to self-heal. Healing Touch sessions are conducted on massage-like tables while fully clothed and practitioners gently place their hands in different positions either on or near the recipients' bodies.

SomatoEmotional Release: SomatoEmotional Release is a therapeutic process that helps rid the mind and body of any remaining effects of past traumas by clearing negative emotions and energy cysts held within the body. SomatoEmotional Release sessions are conducted on massage-like tables while fully clothed and the practitioners gently place their hands in different positions either on or near the recipients' bodies.

Emotional Freedom Technique (EFT): Also known as Tapping, EFT is a healing process that clears disruptions of the mind-body energy system. Individuals can learn EFT to promote their own healing, and sessions can be done anywhere, at any time. EFT is characterized by simultaneously tapping (with fingertips) on certain meridian points of the body while actively calling to mind an emotional challenge, then coupling the emotion with a positive statement or association.

I wonder if energy therapies might assist you on your healing journey.

Why consider energy therapies?

Severe stress from grief and trauma can be stored in the body, disrupting the natural flow of healing energy. Energy therapies such as Reiki, Healing Touch, SomatoEmotional Release, and Emotional Freedom Technique are noninvasive techniques that focus on physically, mentally, emotionally, and spiritually restoring and rebalancing the human energy system. Since the human body is composed of "life force energy," everyone has the capacity to harness self-healing power through energy therapies.

How do energy therapies promote healing?

- By reducing feelings of anxiety, stress, and depression

- By decreasing chronic pain

- By strengthening overall wellness of the immune system

- By promoting integration and balance of the mind, body, and spirit

SINGLE SMALL STEPS

If you would like to integrate energy therapies into your healing journey, here are some single small step suggestions you may be able to use.

Is there one that resonates with you?

1) **Find a Class**: Learn to heal with Emotional Freedom Technique (EFT or "Tapping").

2) **Join a Group**: Find a Reiki Healing circle in your area. Try looking on Meetup.com.

3) **Try a Session**: Locate a Healing Touch practitioner in your community.

4) **Buy a Book**: Discover the ancient practice of Chinese face reading.

5) **Locate a Healer**: Speak to an experienced SomatoEmotional Release practitioner to see if this type of energy healing may be right for you.

Here is one single small step I may be able to take in the future:

_____

_____

_____

_____

_____

_____

_____

HEALING STORIES

It had been three deaths in a row, all sudden, and I was completely in shock. I felt like the rug had been pulled out from beneath me. I landed flat and didn't know where or how to start again. Little things felt stressful and overstimulating to me, and tools that had worked in the past felt like they no longer applied. I decided to branch out beyond my comfort zone and try everything and anything that might help get me level again. I noticed my energy was so low and I felt like the weight of the world was being held in my body. I needed a release. I began researching energy work. I soon found a a Reiki Master that taught courses in my area. I signed up for a course and immediately knew it was right. Learning Reiki and being a part of a monthly Reiki circle has helped me connect with others who are searching for meaning and healing in their life. By connecting to each other's energy, I learned that healing is a process to be shared with others. I learned I wasn't alone and, through helping others to clear their blocked energy, I was unblocking my own.
—Lydia

As a Reiki teacher and practitioner for more than twenty years, I understand energy. As a wife, mother, and grandmother who has lost her husband, oldest son, and grandson to death, I can say I am also familiar with grief. Grief is a physical experience, and anything physical uses energy. When one goes through the trauma of losing a loved one, there are many resulting reactions, and all of them are tied to the physical body. One of the ways to cope, and eventually heal, is through energy work. As one experiences Reiki, for instance, the energy flows into the body, allowing the body to relax, and in that relaxing, it releases some of the grief. Reiki flows into the body, replenishing the store of personal energy that has been drained. It is relaxing and nourishing and, since Reiki is a hands-on modality, it is quite simply comforting to have that connection with someone.
—Serena

My personal life has had ridiculous challenges: divorce, job loss, financial issues, a suicide. One day I found a group that did Tapping, also known as Emotional Freedom Technique, so I attended just out of curiosity. The Tapping group was what got me through. Tapping is a universal healing aid, a form of psychological acupressure based on the same energy meridians used in traditional acupuncture. Simple tapping with the fingertips inputs kinetic energy into specific meridians on the head and chest while you think about your specific problem—whether it is a traumatic event, an addiction, pain, etc.—and voice positive affirmations. This combination of tapping the energy meridians and voicing positive affirmation works to clear the "short circuit" or emotional block from your body's bioenergy system, thus restoring your mind and body's balance. I have a master's in traditional counseling and am now certified in Tapping. I continue to use it myself and as I counsel others.
—Janet

I thought Reiki was a type of massage until after my eighteen-year-old son's death, when I saw a boat in our Alaskan village named Reiki Master. *Soon Kim, the Reiki Master, explained to me that Reiki is energy. It is all about the energy that we all are. The energy that is everything. Eventually I laid on her Reiki table and seriously wondered what I had gotten myself into. She placed her hands lightly on me and told me I was not alone and that I have a few people around me, always, to help me deal with this loss. Their love is holding me up above the drowning waters that I'm wallowing in. Her words. I am so comforted by them, for grief has shown to be a very lonely traveling companion. I left her that day boat feeling much lighter in spirit and a little closer to my boy. Having that Reiki session lightened my heart and gave me a gift of hope.*
—Litzi

RESOURCES

If you would like to integrate energy therapies into your healing journey, here are some resources that can help you get started.

Audio and CD

Self-Healing with Energy Medicine by Dr. Andrew Weil and Dr. Ann Marie Chiasson

Books

Energy Healing: The Essentials for Self-Care by Dr. Ann Marie Chiasson

The Tapping Solution: A Revolutionary System for Stress-Free Living by Nick Ortner
(Also see documentary film of the same name.)

Organizations

International Association of Reiki Professionals
www.iarp.org
General information, articles, research, and locate a practitioner in your area.

Healing Touch Program
www.healingtouchprogram.com
General information, articles, research, and assistance in locating a practitioner in your area.

NOTES

Use this section for any notes related to energy therapies.

_____

_____

_____

_____

_____

_____

_____

_____

_____

_____

_____

_____

_____

_____

_____

_____

_____

_____

_____

"It's not one huge step that promotes healing . . .
it's many intentional single small steps."

F

FLOWERS & FRAGRANCE

Where flowers bloom, so does hope.

—LADY BIRD JOHNSON

HEALING POWER

Going into a sporting goods store with Brent took half the day. He tried on every pair of boxing gloves, swung each brand of baseball bat, lifted dozens of stackable weights, and priced all possible paddles and kayaks. But he also had a thing about candles. And soap. And fragrant lotions. So going into a bath and body shop took half the day too. He unscrewed the tops of all the lotions, stuck his nose in all of the candles, walked our toddler down the aisle of aromatic bath beads, and decided which fragrant soaps he would buy our mothers for Christmas. He had a thing for scent.

And he passed this "scent gene" down to his son.

Six months after Brent died, I was sitting on a comfortable couch in a child therapist's office surrounded by soft teddy bears, familiar board games, baskets of puppets, bright toys, and bottles of scented lotion. Lots of lotion. I watched as my five-year-old son stood on tiptoe near the cupboard above the sink and pulled down bottle after bottle of lotion: eucalyptus, cinnamon, rose, lavender, peppermint. He unscrewed each top, stuck his nose inside each bottle, and took long whiffs. He paused while trying to decide if the scent appealed to him. "Is there a scent that you like? Is there a scent you would like to take home?" asked the therapist. He chose a eucalyptus-spearmint blend. She invited him to put a bit of lotion on his arm at home whenever he was feeling sad, angry, or afraid. There I learned that smelling calming scents is a tangible way for therapists to help clients relax their minds and bodies. Children (adults too) begin to link positive smells with positive feelings and positive experiences in the therapy office. Those positive smells, positive feelings, and positive experiences are then transported home in the lotion bottle to assist in the healing of the child's psyche throughout the days ahead.

I now integrate scent into our daily life.

In addition to using the eucalyptus-spearmint lotion at home, my son chose to put three small scented travel candles on his nightstand: frosted cupcake, coconut leaves, and watermelon lemonade. Numerous times a day he sat on his bed to take huge whiffs of the candles before getting on with whatever he had been doing. But he was calmer. I started burning candles with delicious smells: pumpkin pie, sugar cookie, and chocolate pudding. The house smelled like a bakery and that was comforting for both of us. No wonder my friend, a real estate agent, bakes a batch of chocolate chip cookies in the oven of each home she is trying to sell before she holds an open house. People react to scent.

I also started adding fresh flowers to the house, investigated the world of essential oils (I use Cheering Tangerine and Uplifting Vanilla), and forced myself to stop and smell the roses, quite literally. Each morning as I walk the dog, we pause at bushes and trees with fragrant blossoms like roses, honeysuckles, plumeria, magnolia, and star jasmine. I inhale the scents of healing, hope, and renewal.

I wonder if flowers and fragrance might assist you on your healing journey.

Why consider flowers and fragrance?

Scent can be used to boost overall wellness and provide a simple, natural way to improve emotional and psychological health. Many researchers and medical doctors are now integrating the use of flowers and fragrance into their practices. "Common sense tells us that flowers make us happy. Now, science shows that not only do flowers make us happier than we know, they have strong positive effects on our emotional well-being," notes Julie Chen, doctor of integrative medicine. "Aromatherapy can be utilized in a medicinal fashion with tremendous healing benefits."

How do flowers and fragrance promote healing?
- By reducing levels of stress hormones
- By decreasing levels of anxiety, agitation, and depression
- By promoting feelings of happiness and overall life satisfaction
- By improving the ability to relax and sleep

SINGLE SMALL STEPS

If you would like to integrate flowers and fragrance into your healing journey, here are some single small step suggestions you may be able to use.

Is there one that resonates with you?

1) Flowers

- **Dig in the Dirt:** Spend time with the plants and flowers in your yard.
- **The Weekly Whiff:** Choose one day of the week or month

to bring fresh flowers into your home. You can cut them, grow them, or buy them.

- **Helping Hands:** Ask friends and family to bring fresh flowers when they come to visit.
- **Wander in Wonder**: Take walks at a public garden, local park, or farmer's market.

2) Fragrance

- **Buy a Bottle**: Pick an essential oil that lifts, calms, or relaxes you.
- **Float in Fragrance**: Add drops of essential oil to your bath.
- **Airwaves of Aroma**: Use a diffuser to circulate healing fragrance in your home.
- **Calm with Candles**: Light candles that have comforting scents.

Here is one single small step I may be able to take in the future:

_____

_____

_____

_____

_____

_____

_____

HEALING STORIES

I have always connected scents to people and places. A musty old book reminds me of days in the library as a child with my mom. Lavender reminds me of my freshly bathed babies with their adorable baby rolls. A pot of spaghetti sauce simmering on the stove reminds me of days spent running in and out of my aunt's kitchen with my cousins growing up. When my husband died, I sprayed a bit of his cologne on my pillow as a way of keeping him close to me each night. A couple of years after he died, my sister convinced me to get an essential oil diffuser to help with sinus issues my kids were dealing with. After getting past the sinus issues, I began playing with different oil combinations to help with moods rather than physical issues. A calming blend for nighttime, a refreshing blend for morning, a soothing blend for stressful days. The more I experimented, the more I found that where journaling, meditation, and therapy had fallen flat for me, scents were helping me get through those tough moments as they came up.
—Christina

In the months following my dad's passing, there were many tools I used to take care of myself and support my grieving. One of the best and most effective tools I used was provided by Mother Nature's flowers and plants! Using essential oils as aromatherapy helped put me in a more positive mood, reduced my anxious feelings, and supported more restful sleep. It was amazing to me how quickly the oils I was using helped to take the edge off the severity of my feelings. The flower- and plant-based essential oils provided a healthy coping method for me to move forward and start to heal. Essential oils can have a supportive effect on our energy, emotions, hormones, immune system, stress levels, and more. Essential oils have helped me in so many areas of my well-being, providing me emotional support during one of the most difficult times in my life. In fact, I am so passionate about them that I have now decided to pursue becoming a certified aromatherapist to share essential oil knowledge and guidance for others.

—Maya

Years after my mother's death, I still have her African violet plant that continuously blossoms at all the appropriate times: Mother's Day, family birthdays, Thanksgiving, Christmastime. It is her continuous gift to me. Seeing her violet daily gives me joy. There were so many positive aspects of her life and personality—her complete giving of self. The violet symbolizes her love of flowers, her natural beauty is seen in the flowers, her favorite shade of lipstick is the color of the flowers, and her resilience is like the constant blooming of the flowers. This plant is not a reminder of her death but rather a very positive reminder of her life, of what she was and all that she did for my siblings and me. It is her way of telling us to yes, remember the past, but to enjoy and appreciate the present and also to look forward to the future. She is still with me, smiling down, and perhaps even guiding my hand as I water that African violet she loved.

—Pauline

After my husband's death, my son came over for several weeks, removed more than five thousand pounds of stuff, built new planter boxes, and redesigned the whole yard. This was part of his therapy to deal with his beloved dad's death. He planted some rosebushes in one of the boxes, but one of them was totally empty. So I began visiting garden centers and selecting some flowers that caught my eye. Right now, I have a mix of colorful flowering plants that delight me. I started with some potted plants on my patio and have started growing African violets that bloom inside the house. I regularly tell them how pretty they are and what a great job they're doing. I also buy affordable flowers every other week. When I was buying groceries once, I mentioned grieving to the checker before I realized I forgot my wallet at home. When I returned from my trip home to get my wallet, the checker presented me with a free bouquet. Yay!

—Nancey

RESOURCES

If you would like to integrate flowers and fragrance into your healing journey, here are some resources that can help you get started.

Articles
Rutgers: Flowers Improve Emotional Health by Jeannette Haviland-Jones, Holly Hale Rosario, Patricia Wilson, and Terry McGuire www.aboutflowers.com (Click on "Health Benefits" for both short and long articles.) Research study findings on the positive impact of flowers on overall well-being.

101 Essential Oil Uses & Benefits by Dr. Josh Axe
www.draxe.com/essential-oil-uses-benefits
Guide to using and combining essential oils for spa, relaxation, medicine, and home.

Books
The Home Reference to Holistic Health and Healing: Easy-to-Use Natural Remedies, Herbs, Flower Essences, Essential Oils, Supplements, and Therapeutic Practices for Health, Happiness, and Well-Being by Chrystle Fiedler and Bridgette Mars

The Complete Book of Essential Oils and Aromatherapy by Valerie Ann Worwood

Website
Sierra Essentials
www.sierraessentials.com
Naturally scented body wash, candles, essential oils, lip balms, lotions, and soaps.

NOTES

Use this section for any notes related to flowers and fragrance

_____

_____

_____

_____

_____

_____

_____

_____

_____

_____

_____

_____

_____

_____

_____

_____

_____

_____

_____

"It's not one huge step that promotes healing . . .
it's many intentional single small steps."

G

GROUP SUPPORT

Alone we can do so little;
together we can do so much.

—HELEN KELLER

HEALING POWER

"You definitely marched to the beat of your own drummer when you were a child," my mom often says. While other little girls played with life-sized dolls and flavored lip gloss, I shot a bow and arrow in the backyard. While my friends brought shiny toys and fluffy kittens for classroom show-and-tell, I gathered up the pet snake to share. While other classmates donned tutus and pointe shoes for dance class, I threw on cleats and a baseball hat to play hardball with the neighborhood boys. One year for my birthday, my mom asked me what sort of gift I wanted. She wanted to buy me a pretty outfit or take me out for a fancy dinner celebration. But my response was, "I'll take a two-man tent so I can go camping!" I guess I was never much of a "join the group" person.

Until I was.

Out of pure shock and desperation, I registered for my first group at a local hospice two months after Brent died. The evening of the first meeting,

I arrived early and stopped in the bathroom. Then I made the mistake of looking in the mirror. Gaunt face. Dark circles. Heavy bags. Sunken eyes. Empty eyes. The lights were out and nobody was home. I looked dead. Or was it that I just felt dead? *Is that me in this reflection? Who am I anymore? What is happening to me? What am I doing here? Oh, yeah. I am here because Brent is dead. Brent. Is. Dead.* Brent *is dead? Brent is* dead? *BRENT IS DEAD?* Heart racing. Chest pounding. Mind spinning. Nauseous. I dove back into the stall. After gathering myself enough to enter the grief group room, I knew I had arrived at the right place. These people looked as horrible as I felt. I'm not sure I agree with the adage "misery loves company," but there was one thing I knew for sure: I wasn't alone anymore. I found my people.

The second group I joined while lying on the floor of the local bookstore, tissue box in one hand and grief books in the other. I had stumbled upon a book called *The Grief Recovery Method*, which described a twelve-week program where participants learned new definitions and new ways of being in relation to grief. There was a website on the back of the book, so that day I signed up for a local group. The next week I found myself sitting in a circle with a *Grief Recovery* facilitator and five other participants who were just as grief-stricken and traumatized as I was. The group members gave me support, hope, and community. They gave me a way back to life when I saw none. We completed our twelve-week program and bonded so deeply that we still meet for monthly lunch dates to catch up, reconnect, and share new stories of healing.

The third group I joined was an imagery-based healing group for the bereaved. I was comfortable in groups by this time and knew the therapist running the session, but I sat in our introductory meeting seething with irritation. I was fully engrossed in anger mode. I was furious at Brent for dying in the first place, incensed that he was *still* dead, enraged at society for not preparing me for death, irate at God for letting all of this happen, and silently infuriated when I saw young married couples who still had their spouses next to them. And there was a young married couple sitting in the room that first day of group, so I was completely certain this experience was going to be awful. I was just going to walk out. As we went around introducing ourselves, I sat with my arms across my chest. "I can't stay in this group," I said honestly. "I have an extremely hard time being with young couples right now since my husband is still dead." The therapist sat calmly, as though things were going according to plan. The married couple exchanged worried glances, and I was ready to get up and leave. But, for some reason, we all stayed and somehow surrendered to the discomfort of it all—death, life, purpose, rebuilding, and how-do-we-move-and-breathe-and-live-with-this-hell-on-earth? And in the end, this couple gave me compassion. This couple gave me understanding. This couple gave me wisdom. And years later, now as wonderful friends, our small families gather together on August 6th for burgers, fries, shakes, and plates piled high with fluffy, pink cotton candy as we celebrate and remember my husband and their daughter, who just happen to share the same summer birthday.

I wonder if group support might assist you on your healing journey.

Why consider group support?

Becoming involved in a grief or trauma support group can provide an invaluable network of other community members who have experienced similar life-changing events. In a supportive group environment with others who are traveling the same path, all feelings can be shared and released. Once feelings and experiences are acknowledged and validated by others, positive change can begin to occur. Support groups are offered worldwide for just about every life experience, transition, and challenge.

How does group support promote healing?

- By providing permission to grieve openly and freely in a safe, structured environment
- By allowing the opportunity to receive emotional, social, and spiritual support
- By using the group process to facilitate positive changes in behavior
- By offering support and camaraderie throughout the personal growth and healing journey

SINGLE SMALL STEPS

If you would like to integrate group support into your healing journey, here are some single small step suggestions you may be able to use.

Is there one that resonates with you?

1) **Get Personal**: Link with others in person by attending a local support group.

2) **Build Your Own**: Gather others to form your own support group. People will come!

3) **Type to Heal**: Join a secure online group focused on the same life challenge.

4) **Phone In**: Connect with others on call-in support systems that meet at set times and dates.

5) **Video Call**: Facebook groups now have live streaming options for their communities.

Here is one single small step I may be able to take in the future:

_____

_____

_____

_____

_____

_____

_____

HEALING STORIES

My husband was an elementary school teacher. He was diagnosed with cancer (melanoma) and died eleven months later. Throughout his illness, we had brigades of helpers and visitors to assist with meals, transportation, and occupying our two young sons, ages six and eight. Every seat was filled at this funeral and people were standing in the back, including former students. The support gradually dissolved, and family and friends didn't know how to relate or talk to us. I was a widow at forty, with thirteen years of marriage. My husband's death was the elephant in the room. I eventually found my new support with young widow groups. It was a relief to speak with people that understood what I was going through: fear, anger, resentment, sadness. I wasn't going crazy. I have a supportive group that gets my grief, helps buoy me up when I'm drowning, and celebrates life with me as move forward.
—Arlene

My story started the way so many do—with a phone call that brought me to my knees. Our beautiful, charismatic, talented, brilliant twenty-nine-year-old son had taken a fatal dose of heroin. I was blessedly numb for a month or so, then found myself adrift. I asked my angel son Ryan what I should do in his honor, and I heard his voice in my head say, "Mom, you're really good at making other people feel better." I now had a mission. From that void and the desire to honor my son, the South Denver Metro GRASP (Grief Recovery After Substance Passing) group was formed. We have guest speakers and demonstrations and read excerpts from grief healing books. Through our group, I have absolutely witnessed healing. One mom could do nothing but cry the first meeting, but eighteen months later she has become a strong voice of leadership in the group. Another mom said in her first meeting, "I'm not sure I'm going to survive this," but at our holiday craft meeting, she seemed to come to life. After every meeting, I feel a renewed sense of purpose to reach out and comfort those who are grieving after a substance passing.
—Jeri

When my husband died suddenly, I was left with two teenagers, along with no clue as to how to navigate my way through this immeasurable devastation. But I was willing to do whatever it took to heal so my children would not lose me as well. I eventually came across a three-day grief workshop called *The Grief Recovery Method (TGRM)* offered through the Grief Recovery Institute. It was there I learned the power of group support. I learned the importance of being vulnerable and the value of being open to receive. These were not qualities that came easily to me, but they were the qualities I knew I had to develop if I was going to commit to my own personal healing. I also learned that it takes not only good information about grief but also a community to support the grieving process. Being a part of a group like this also offers you the opportunity to move beyond your own world of grief and help someone else. The value of a group is immeasurable.

—Hanna

I was married to an amazing woman, Judy, for twenty-two years. She died suddenly, not long after we buried our son Alex, who was only nineteen. Three months after my Alex died and six weeks after my Judy died, I met people in a chat room called Widowed Village. They invited me to dinner. I never would've thought that five years later these people would be the reason for and the beginning of my understanding that being around other people who "get it" is so important. I am now in a support group of almost four hundred and sit on the board of directors for an international widow's group called Soaring Spirits International. Choices are what this journey is all about. I choose to fight. I choose to laugh. I choose to cry. I choose to live. I choose to love. My new wife, Beth, encourages me to continue connecting with the widowed community, despite her not being widowed. Group support is that important to both of us.

—Arnie

RESOURCES

If you would like to integrate group support into your healing journey, here are some resources that can help you get started.

Organizations

The Grief Recovery Institute
www.griefrecoverymethod.com
Twelve-week group support program run worldwide. Also see *The Grief Recovery Handbook: The Action Program for Moving Beyond Death, Divorce, and Other Losses including Health, Career, and Faith* by John James and Russell Friedman

GriefShare
www.griefshare.org
Thirteen-week Christian-based grief support group facilitated at churches worldwide.

Soaring Spirits International
www.soaringspirits.org
Support groups for the widowed community: online, regional groups, and conferences.

The Compassionate Friends
www.compassionatefriends.org
Support groups for child-loss community: online, regional groups, and conferences.

The Dougy Center: The National Center for Grieving Children and Families
www.dougy.org
Support groups, programs, and education for children, youth, and families.

NOTES

Use this section for any notes related to group support.

_____

_____

_____

_____

_____

_____

_____

_____

_____

_____

_____

_____

_____

_____

_____

_____

"It's not one huge step that promotes healing . . .
it's many intentional single small steps."

H
HIGHER POWER HELP

*I used to believe that prayer changes things,
but now I know that prayer changes us and
we change things.*

—MOTHER TERESA

HEALING POWER

When Brent died, I was absolutely livid.

I was mad at Brent, yes. But I was absolutely furious with God. My higher power.

I screamed at, yelled at, cursed at God for many, many months. I wrote God hate letters and spoke with priests, pastors, ministers, and rabbis about the extent of my anger toward God. Even after being raised within a church community, participating in youth retreats, volunteering for overseas service missions, and speaking about God at my university's graduation ceremony, I temporarily stopped believing there even *was* a God, One, or higher power. I soon discovered that I felt like many others do when grief or trauma strikes—like my hostile feelings toward my higher power were totally normal. I wasn't irrational or going insane.

Theology professor Jerry Sittser, author of *A Grace Disguised: How the Soul Grows through Loss,* was the first to validate my feelings of uncertainty. After he witnessed the tragic deaths of his mother, wife, and daughter in one horrific family car accident, he reexamined his own relationship with God. He states, "Over time I realized that the trajectory of my grief had set me on a collision course with God and that eventually I would have to wrestle with this most complex of issues. I knew I had to make peace with God's sovereignty, reject God altogether, or settle for a lesser God who lacked the power or desire to prevent the accident."

Clinical psychologist Therese Rando, author of *How To Go On Living When Someone You Love Dies,* also acknowledged my feelings of confusion. She states, "It is quite common to be angry at God, to lose faith in your religion or philosophy of life after the death of someone you love. You may be among the many grievers who have a profound sense of injustice and disillusionment after the death. Values and beliefs that once were comforting to you may now be useless."

Trauma researcher Steven Joseph, author of *What Doesn't Kill Us: The New Psychology of Post-Traumatic Growth,* offered me a reason to revisit any sort of God, church, or higher power at all. He states, "Evidence suggests that religion is often helpful to people. Those who are religious can find a deepening of their faith after trauma. In a study performed after 9/11, religious people reported an intensification of their spiritual growth. One reason for this finding is that religion helps people elicit social support and provides people with rituals they can use to mark events in their lives."

Psychotherapist Belleruth Naparstek, author of *Invisible Heroes: Survivors of Trauma and How They Heal,* suggested that it was indeed beneficial to insert new ways of asking for help. She states, "For those [trauma survivors] who have a more skeptical relationship with matters of the spirit, a well-meaning ritual activity that symbolically invites archetypal assistance from the whole human race, or calls upon benign, fill-in-the-blank, invisible forces to lend their assistance, is all to the good."

These experts were helping me understand the normalcy of my tumultuous spiritual world, but I still felt terrified and disoriented. I had always turned to God for guidance and protection—and now had nothing. Grief and trauma had knocked me to my knees—literally. Several times a day for months and months on end, I made my way into the dark, walk-in closet in my bedroom and found myself on my knees screaming, choking, sobbing, and wailing in misery, defeat, and brokenness. And one day, while on my knees, I finally surrendered. *"Help me. Help me. God? If you are there? I can't do this anymore. I am broken . . . I need help."*

And help came.

Asking for higher power help was just the thing I needed to do.

I surrendered to receiving prayer from strangers: in school parking lots, in home prayer circles, in ministry offices, in beach chairs on the sand.

I surrendered to listening to ministers, rabbis, and priests who shared their philosophies about life and death on the airwaves as I drove around the city in my makeshift "Church of the Car."

I surrendered to attending therapeutic church services where pastors channeled the healing power of God to all those who came to the altar, and I collapsed to the ground in a warm heap of all-encompassing love.

I surrendered to meeting with prayer warriors who held my hands, spoke in tongues, and wrapped my heart with compassion and empathy.

I surrendered to learning from mediums who translated and interpreted what Brent was waiting to communicate, things that only he would know, things that only he would want to tell me.

I surrendered to going on spiritual retreats where I experienced the power of both meditation (my listening) and prayer (my talking) especially in times of crisis.

I surrendered to developing a brand-new way of thinking about and relating to my higher power.

I still don't have the answers. I still wish Brent was physically here. I may never understand the *why* of what happened. But now when I talk to

God I don't scream, yell, cry, and curse. I say, "Thank you for carrying me. Please keep helping me rebuild a life."

I wonder if higher power help might assist you on your healing journey.

Why consider higher power help?

Because symptoms of grief and trauma can be so varied and overwhelming, some form of prayer, meditation, or ritual that calls upon a higher power, a "larger force," or God can aid in healing. Numerous research studies linking prayer and meditation with overall wellness have been conducted, including Dr. Andrew Newberg's *How God Changes Your Brain: Breakthrough Findings from a Leading Neuroscientist*. Newberg's findings conclude that "Spiritual practices, even when stripped of religious beliefs, enhance the neural functioning of the brain in ways that improve physical and emotional health" and "intense, long-term contemplation of God and other spiritual values appears to permanently change the structure of those parts of the brain that control our moods."

How does *higher power help* promote healing?
- By reducing levels of stress
- By decreasing blood pressure and heart rate
- By slowing rate of breath and inducing a sense of calmness
- By strengthening the immune system

SINGLE SMALL STEPS

If you would like to integrate higher power help into your healing journey, here are some single small step suggestions you may be able to use:

Is there one that resonates with you?
1) **Self**: Pray or mediate on your own, asking your higher power for guidance or help.

2) **Other**: Have friends and family members pray for you, over you, or with you.

3) **Community**: Gather with organized prayer partners, worship teams, or spiritual leaders.

4) **Retreat**: Sign up for a retreat emphasizing spirituality, religion, or meditation.

5) **Create**: Design your own ritual for hope and healing. One suggestion: create a "Box of Hope." As author Ann Lamott describes in her book, *Help. Thanks. Wow: The Three Essential Prayers*,

"One modest tool for letting go [in prayer] that I've used for twenty-five years is a God box. I've relied on every imaginable container—from a pillbox, to my car's glove box, to decorative boxes friends have given me. The container has to exist in time and space, so you can physically put a note into it, so you can see yourself let go, in time and space. On a note, I write down the name of the person about whom I am so distressed or angry, or describe the situation that is killing me, with which I am so toxically, crazily obsessed, and I fold the note up, stick it in the box and close it. You might have a brief moment of prayer, and it might come out sounding like this: "Here. You think you're so big? Fine. You deal with it. Although I have a few more excellent ideas on how best to proceed." Then I agree to keep my sticky mitts off the spaceship until I hear back. Maybe after you

put a note in the God box, you'll go a little limp, and in that divine limpness you'll be able to breathe again. Breath is Life. It's oxygen. Breath might get you a little rest. You must be so exhausted."

Here is one single small step I may be able to take in the future:

_____

_____

_____

_____

_____

_____

_____

HEALING STORIES

I was brought up in a French Canadian Catholic family with four siblings. My parents encouraged various ways and times to pray to God. One French Canadian tradition was to be the first child to run downstairs and ask for our father's blessing on New Year's Day. When my father died, we then asked for our mother's blessing. One year after my mother died, I was in church for a New Year's Eve service. As I stood in line to receive Communion, I looked up and there in front of me, above the alter, my mother appeared. She looked beautiful, with her snowy white hair, rosy cheeks, and purple dress. She looked very peaceful as she lovingly smiled down on me. I could not take my eyes off her as I looked in utter amazement. I laughed. I cried. What a gift. I felt so fortunate to see her one more time. When I told my sister what happened in church, she said to me, "Well, you got the blessing!"
—Denise

I've always been a spiritual person with a belief that physical death was just that—physical—and that the spirit and soul remain fully alive. Fully alive in others dear to them; fully alive in the air, the trees, the ocean; fully alive in things they touched, made, enjoyed, saw, heard . . . everything. When my father was close to death, my sister called and told me I needed to fly back to Boston from California because "it was time." It was midday and I left my office in tears. Walking down the sidewalk, I looked down and saw a tiny praying mantis clinging to my pant leg. I found a twig and carefully released his fragile body to a nearby shrub. My father died a few weeks later, a month before Father's Day, and when I woke up on Father's Day, I walked into my living room and there on the sofa was a tiny praying mantis. You see, my father was there with me, both before he died and after, saying, "It's okay. I haven't gone anywhere. I'll always be with you."
—Bill

Over the span of four years I experienced the death of five babies in miscarriage and a journey of grief and loss I never dreamed I'd walk through. I only saw gray, would shake uncontrollably, and became a shell of a person. I had PTSD. Finally, I called out to the Lord and told Him, "You've got to either heal me or take me." What He did was awaken me every night at exactly 2:35 a.m. for a nightly "counseling" or "comforting" time that I can hardly describe with words. The room filled with an amazing peace, presence, and an almost tangible feeling of someone sitting next to me on the bed. In my mind I saw flashbacks, photos from when I was feeling the most desperate, lonely, abandoned, and wanting to die from the pain. He showed that He never left me. I was never alone, not even for a second. And, over time, the "why" question didn't matter to me anymore, and I stopped asking it. God even gave me a vision of my baby Samuel running in a meadow with hundreds of other children, their voices and laughter bubbling. There were the most beautiful colors, butterflies, and flowers. It was a vision of Heaven I can't wait to see.
—Marni

Dealing with cancer was a wakeup call for me; I was paralyzed and diagnosed with spinal cord cancer. Surgery was successful, but I had to relearn how to work the entire left side of my body. Both relatives and my military family were important in my healing, but I knew something was still missing. Once able to walk and drive again, I found myself at daily Mass. Being back at church, I soon discovered Mother Mary and Her Son and found a new family. My faith and the faith community were my salvation. With them, I coped with my struggles and walked my journey when hard times visited me. When I lost my late husband to cancer, my faith allowed me to cope even through my tears. Years later, I remarried a Catholic "convert," and I continue to learn about my faith through him. God has allowed me to continue my journey with someone who believes as I do: that God is Good. Even when struggles are put on the path.
—Jane

RESOURCES

If you would like to integrate higher power help into your healing journey, here are some resources that can help you get started.

Audio and CD

Soul Meditations by Medium Fleur and Derek McCarty
www.mediumfleur.com

Transforming Trauma: A Seven-Step Process for Spiritual Healing by Caroline Myss and James Finley
www.soundstrue.com

Books

A Grace Disguised: How the Soul Grows through Loss by Jerry Sittser

A Grief Workbook for Skeptics: Surviving Loss without Religion by Carole Fiore

After This: When Life Is Over, Where Do We Go? by Claire Bidwell Smith

On Life after Death by Dr. Elisabeth Kübler-Ross

Proof of Heaven: A Neurosurgeon's Journey into the Afterlife by Dr. Eben Alexander

Talking to Heaven: A Medium's Message of Life after Death by James Van Praagh

When Bad Things Happen to Good People by Rabbi Harold Kushner

NOTES

Use this section for any notes related to higher power help.

_____

_____

_____

_____

_____

_____

_____

_____

_____

_____

_____

_____

_____

_____

_____

_____

_____

_____

"It's not one huge step that promotes healing . . .
it's many intentional single small steps."

I

IMAGERY

Logic will get you from A to B.
Imagination will take you everywhere.

—ALBERT EINSTEIN

HEALING POWER

I have always loved words. But not just their meaning, definition, and use.

I love the way certain words *sound*.

Phonaesthetics is the study of the aesthetic properties of speech sound, in particular the study of sound sequences, as in phonaesthesia (Oxford Dictionary).

I guess you could say I was in phonaesthetic heaven when I lived on Oahu and was surrounded by the beautiful singsong melodies of the Hawaiian language: Kamehameha, Manoa, Kailua, Lili'uokalani, Kaimana, Leilani, Manapua, and Pi'ikoi. I loved listening to those words spoken by the island natives.

Now living back on the US mainland, I have a harder time finding those words that strike a similar pleasant chord. But then I found this one—*Belleruth*—and now I use it often and with emphasis to explain one woman's healing effect on my life.

Belleruth Naparstek is a psychotherapist, researcher, and author of numerous books, including *Post-Traumatic Stress Disorder: Reduce and Overcome the Symptoms of PTSD*. She is also one of the world's leading experts in guided imagery. Her supportive publications and vast audio collection have been distributed nationwide by the Red Cross, the Veterans Administration, rape crisis centers, domestic violence shelters, schools, health clinics, and hospitals. Guided imagery has assisted millions of people, including me, in continuing to heal both emotionally, physically, and psychologically.

"Guided imagery is a form of deliberate, directed daydreaming—a purposeful use of the imagination, using words and phrases designed to evoke rich, multisensory fantasy and memory, in order to create a deeply immersive, receptive mind-state that is ideal for catalyzing desired changes in mind, body, psyche, and spirit . . . imagery is fast, powerful, costs little or nothing, and gets more and more effective with continued use . . . users can be bone-tired, disgusted, depressed, disbelieving, listless, resistant, distracted, mentally disabled, physically unfit, or at death's door, and imagery will still be something they can use, because it requires so little of them."
—Belleruth Naparstek,
Invisible Heroes: Survivors of Trauma and How They Heal

Every night for two years straight, I put my son to bed before soaking in a bathtub full of lavender Epsom salts, alternatively crying and listening to the soothing voice of Belleruth Naparstek and her audio series *Guided Imagery for the Three Stages of Healing Trauma*. I had no idea if using guided imagery would help relieve any of my symptoms of grief, trauma, and overall sense of horrified bewilderment after Brent's death, but I was willing to try anything. So I would slide beneath the water, rest my head against the back of the tub, close my eyes, and intentionally drift off into an imaginary world that somehow helped me to heal.

I wonder if imagery might assist you on your healing journey.

Why consider imagery?

Imagery is a powerful practice for reducing the often-paralyzing effects of trauma, including anxiety, sleeplessness, nightmares, abrupt mood swings, hypervigilance, and intrusive flashbacks. Both self-created imagery and guided imagery have been found to promote overall wellness for individuals moving through various types of challenges, including addiction, cancer treatments, cardiovascular issues, depression, fatigue, grief, hospice care, migraines, post-traumatic stress disorder, rehabilitation, and surgery.

How does imagery promote healing?

- By reducing anxiety and depression
- By restoring a sense of mastery and control
- By rebalancing the nervous system
- By assisting in the ability to fall asleep and stay asleep

SINGLE SMALL STEPS

If you would like to integrate imagery into your healing journey, here are some single small step suggestions you may be able to use:

Is there one that resonates with you?

1) **Grab a Book**: Read a short guided imagery script, then focus on the imagery it provides.

2) **Partner Up**: Find a friend to take turns reading and visualizing restorative imagery.

3) Try It: Find guided imagery that is right for you by sampling audio snippets on websites.

4) Buy It: Browse the guided imagery collection offered by Belleruth Naparstek's Health Journeys.

5) Opt for Others: Find a guided imagery class, drop-in session, or group in your community.

Here is one single small step I may be able to take in the future:

_____

_____

_____

_____

_____

_____

HEALING STORIES

Symbolic imagery—mindfully refocusing my personal camera—was a tool that effectively eased my pain of traumatic images after my parents died on the same day. When my mind fixates on an image, I imagine that my mind's eye is a camera pointed at that image. I take a deep breath. Then, very slowly, I move the camera back or forward and look at a different scene. Here's an example: My mom died in her bathroom. I was haunted by the image of her body in the bathroom while my dad watched and died at the same time. I catch myself consumed with the feelings the image evokes. I take a deep breath and slowly move the lens of my camera to a different scene. Now, I see my mom sitting in her lovely bathroom on her vanity chair. She is putting on makeup to "go out for a bite" with my dad. She is in her normal routine of putting on her face. I see her manicured hands, her beautiful face in the mirror, and her collection of fancy perfume bottles on the shelf behind her. When I look at this scene, I am able refocus on my own day-to-day life and feel a greater sense of peace.
—Gail

Although we were divorced when she died, I grieved deeply for my former wife and for our young son, who was left in my care but without his mother. Fortunately, I'd been going through counseling (group and one-on-one) for several years before she died and had collected techniques that worked well, both for me and for my grieving son. One counselor gave me this imagery-based example: She asked me to simply stop and breathe and then describe everything I could hear, see, smell, or touch. I described birds singing, sunlight in the window, a car going by, my hands touching the table, an airplane flying above—anything my senses were aware of. I reported these and she'd prompt me for more. In only minutes, I felt grounded and back in touch with life, literally with the reality all around me. I also used this technique with my son when needed. Grounding through sensual imagery is a wonderfully easy way to get through a momentary crisis.
—Morton

I couldn't focus, breathe, or sleep after my partner died, so I used different types of imagery to help my system calm down. At first, someone else (a therapist or a friend or an audio CD) would have to guide my mind to a more relaxed place. But as time went on, I could use my own imagination to visualize and feel peace, clarity, and calm. Sometimes I closed my eyes and pictured the most relaxing place I could envision. For me, it was always a beautiful, grassy meadow. Once my mind was transported to that place and I could feel what it was like to be there, my mind and body could be still. The grasses in the meadow blew in a gentle breeze, a soft hammock was resting between two welcoming oak trees, and the brilliant blue skies were filled with colorful birds and butterflies. In my mind, I would rest in the hammock and continue to heal.

—Elizabeth

RESOURCES

If you would like to integrate imagery into your healing journey, here are some resources that can help you get started.

Audio and CD

Guided Imagery for the Three Stages of Healing Trauma: Nine Meditations for Posttraumatic Stress by Belleruth Naparstek

Magic Island: Relaxation for Kids by Betty Mehling

Books

Guided Imagery for Self-Healing: An Essential Resource for Anyone Seeking Wellness by Martin Rossman

Healing Trauma: A Pioneering Program for Restoring the Wisdom of Your Body by Peter Levine

Invisible Heroes: Survivors of Trauma and How They Heal by Belleruth Naparstek

Organizations

Health Journeys
www.healthjourneys.com
Education, products, and guided imagery CDs, sample clips, and large audio library.

Sounds True
www.soundstrue.com
Various guided imagery CDs, books, and interactive audio learning kits.

NOTES

Use this section for any notes related to imagery.

_____

_____

_____

_____

_____

_____

_____

_____

_____

_____

_____

_____

_____

_____

_____

_____

*"It's not one huge step that promotes healing . . .
it's many intentional single small steps."*

JOURNALING

Start writing, no matter what. The water
does not flow until the faucet is turned on.

—LOUIS L'AMOUR

HEALING POWER

The summer following my graduation from college, my best friend and I bought train passes and traveled by rail through Europe for six weeks. I wanted to remember everything about the experience, so I bought a journal and recorded my trip. I wrote about stuffing items into my new backpack because I needed them; then I wrote about taking half of the items out of the backpack to make it lighter. I recorded new sights I saw (Big Ben) while sitting on a red double-decker bus near the Houses of Parliament; then I recorded new phrases I learned ("mind the gap!") while sitting on trains in the London Underground. I took notes after attending a cow auction in rural Ireland; then I took notes after hearing cowbells in mountainous Switzerland. I scribbled about the unbelievable creativity at the World's Fair in Spain; then I scribbled about the delicious gelato near the Colosseum in Italy. I journaled about the talented woman spinning lace at the tree-lined park in Belgium; then I journaled about our unbelievable decision to jump off a moving train in the middle of the night to visit a scenic hillside town in France.

After that trip, I continued to write religiously for the next twenty years. I journaled about work, school, relationships, moving, traveling, marriage, and parenting. Journaling helped me sort, process, and grow in every aspect of my life.

Until Brent died.

Then I was left speechless. Wordless. Lifeless.

While peers in the community wrote their way through grief with much progress and success, I only stared at blank pages. While counselors in the community prescribed journaling as a therapeutic tool, I only chewed on my pencil. I was completely frustrated that a tool that once came so naturally to me had become so aggravating and senseless. So, in lieu of traditional journaling, a trauma therapist recommended nontraditional journaling using pictures. An Illustrated Discovery Journal, a pictorial journal, has been an effective, therapeutic way for me to record and process what was, examine and explore what is, and wonder and hope for what could possibly be.

I began my Illustrated Discovery Journal by sitting down with stacks of old magazines. I ripped out pages that appealed to me in some way, cut around the images, then glued the pictures into a blank artist's sketchbook. I didn't think about *why* I was drawn to an image. I just ripped, cut, and glued. And months later, interesting patterns emerged.

There were many pages of nature things (pine trees, palm trees, beaches, caves, mountains, flowers); many pages of exercise things (paddleboarders, kayakers, bikers, surfers, yogis); and many pages of animal things (dogs, goats, horses, a koi fish, a moose). *Huh. Nature, exercise, and animals were all things I loved before Brent died.* So, without using words at all, I discovered parts of my core self were still there—buried under lots of sorrow, anger, and confusion—but there nonetheless. The process of keeping an Illustrated Discovery Journal allowed me to rediscover the parts of the "old me" that were still intact, and I began inserting more nature, exercise, and animals into my healing process.

There were also pages of random, unexpected things: an athletic young man in a lime-green puffy jacket, two little boys coloring on their closet door, a pair of dusty brown cowboy boots, a sneaker with a scoop of ice cream sitting on top. Initially I had no idea what these images related to, but they were wonderful starting points for digging deeper in counseling sessions.

If you'd like to start your own Illustrated Discovery Journal, all you need is:
1) a blank notepad, artist's sketch pad, or spiral notebook

2) images from magazines, catalogs, calendars, or brochures

3) scissors

4) glue or tape

I wonder if journaling might assist you on your healing journey.

Why consider journaling?
Journaling, writing, composing letters, or collecting images can be a helpful practice for those living with grief and trauma. Nowadays various workshops, retreats, and online classes serve as effective tools to assist people in writing their way through the darkness. The act of transferring conscious or subconscious words, feelings, and images from mind to paper may help to release internal feelings of despair, promote a sense of self-compassion, and provide a stepping stone to realize future hopes, goals, and dreams.

How does journaling promote healing?
• By reducing emotional stress
• By lowering blood pressure

- By improving heart health
- By tapping into the subconscious
- By aiding in the therapeutic growth process

SINGLE SMALL STEPS

If you would like to integrate journaling into your healing journey, here are some single small step suggestions you may be able to use.

Is there one that resonates with you?

1) **Stream of Consciousness**: Start the flow of writing with whatever words come to mind.

2) **Illustrated Discovery**: Use pictures instead of words to express thoughts and emotions.

3) **Connect with a Class**: Join a local or online group and write your way through adversity.

4) **Sentences Starters**: Use a sentence starter or writing prompt for daily focus.

Here are some examples of sentence starters:

- Today I feel . . .
- Tomorrow I hope . . .
- I will always remember . . .
- I will allow myself . . . because . . .
- I will take care of myself because . . .

- Once upon a time . . .
- I really wish they knew . . .
- The other day I wanted to . . .
- This person has been so helpful . . .
- I am so thankful for . . .

Here is one single small step I may be able to take in the future:

_____

_____

_____

_____

_____

_____

HEALING STORIES

I have been journaling since my wife died a few years ago. I prefer to journal in a little notebook, but I also write on my iPhone or iPad whenever emotions and thoughts are overwhelming. Journaling is a means to express myself, to express deep feelings and thoughts. Maybe I share them with others or maybe they're for my eyes only. But regardless, writing them down separates the more poignant from the continuous flow of things that cross my mind. We yearn to find meaning in the grief, as well as within the forward footsteps of this new life. The act of writing these thoughts and feelings allows me to bring some order and gain perspective. It is a written record of my depths and my ascents. Journaling has also stopped or at least reduced the time I spend ruminating over certain issues. Journaling also helps me to share tales from this journey with others.
—Paul

I wrote a poem about my favorite painting. It was painted by my grandma and it is called Gone. *The painting was about my dad, who was not doing so well and then died. He was walking into a fog. It was my grandma's thoughts about how she thought my dad was feeling.*

Poem

Oh, it was a painting about my dad,
who was feeling so sad.

He was lost in life,
and couldn't find his wife.

But now I think he is glad.

—Cole

When I faced a critical personal trauma, I knew I needed to be alone to work out my thoughts and feelings and hopefully figure out what to do. I ended up in a forest at 10,500 feet along a river that felt so peaceful and perfect for getting in touch with myself. In this setting, I pulled out the paper I brought and started my journaling exploration. I asked myself a series of questions and wrote until I felt finished. 1) What am I afraid of? 2) What should I do? 3) What if I don't do that? After several pages of writing responses to these questions, I sensed I was ready to go deeper, so I finished with another question: 4) What am I really afraid of? I had to sit with my understanding for two days to get the full force of what I had learned. My perceptions shifted and healing began. I believe the calming internalization of journaling can lead us to our own inner knowing, which is wiser and purer than what our churning minds and emotions tend to spit out without reflection.

—Jean

RESOURCES

If you would like to integrate journaling into your healing journey, here are some resources that can help you get started.

Books

Grief Quest: A Workbook & Journal to Heal the Grieving Heart by I. J. Weinstock

On Coming Alive: Journaling Through Grief: 100 Prompts to Guide You from Darkness to Light by Lexi Behrndt

The Unedited Heart: Letters on Loss by Monique Minahan

Handy to Have at Home

Blank journals
Colored pens
Illustrated Discovery Journal Materials (blank notebook, glue, magazines, scissors)
Journal prompts (Google "Grief Journal Prompts" or "Grief Writing Starters")

Organizations

Center for Journal Therapy: Life-based Writing for Healing, Growth, and Change
www.journaltherapy.com
Beginning techniques, classes, conferences, resources, and links.

Refuge in Grief: Emotionally Intelligent Grief Support
www.refugeingrief.com
Offers a thirty-day creative writing e-course called "Writing Your Grief."

NOTES

Use this section for any notes related to journaling.

_____

_____

_____

_____

_____

_____

_____

_____

_____

_____

_____

_____

_____

_____

_____

_____

_____

_____

"It's not one huge step that promotes healing . . .
it's many intentional single small steps."

KNOWING YOUR NEW ENVIRONMENT

*What do you need? Who do you need? As
you're going through this extremely difficult
time, walk or hopscotch, take a train, a
plane, or a bus, to the places and people who
can give you some love.*

—DAPHNE ROSE KINGMA

HEALING POWER

I once knew a lot about certain environments—traveling, working, living
overseas, maintaining friendships, being in a marriage, raising a small child,
dual parenting. But when grief and trauma blew up the life I knew, I felt as
if I knew nothing. In an instant, I had been completely altered and nothing
would ever be the same. It was as if a spaceship had landed, scooped me
up, and dropped me off on an alien planet. And I knew nothing about this
planet; it was full of shock, numbness, disorientation, confusion, sobbing,
wailing, isolation, rage, helplessness, irritability, flashbacks, nightmares,
anxiety, nausea, cold sweats, and extreme fatigue.

Where was I?

Oh, yeah. This must be Griefland. The United States of Traumaville.

Where nothing makes sense. Nothing seems familiar. Nothing feels right.

Where nobody understands. Nobody can fix things. Nobody has instructions.

Where everything is uncomfortable. Everything is off-kilter. Everything is surreal.

Even the gym.

The gym had always been a second home to me. It's where I worked as a summer camp counselor, where I learned to lift weights, where I relaxed by the pool, where I met my husband.

The gym was always a place of rest and safety. Until it wasn't.

A few months after Brent died, I managed to numbly make my way into the fitness center one morning. I was in search of respite. I pushed and pulled the weight machines on autopilot, feeling the silent stares of pity flying at me from every corner of the room. I moved the StairMaster in a trance, noticing the people who whispered while looking in my direction. I went into the locker room and stood in line to take a shower. And as I stood there—in all my vulnerability and half-nakedness, shower bag in hand—a woman approached me from behind. She peppered me with questions.

"What happened?! How did the accident happen? Were you there? Or did you get a phone call? What did they say? What did your family say? Where is the car? The roads are so dangerous there! What are you going to do now? What about your son? He's so young!" And as I stood there in all my raw pain, I had three simultaneous thoughts:

1) I am going to punch her.

2) I can't stand this place for one more second.

3) I need to find a new gym.

And a new hairdresser. And a new grocery store. And a new set of friends. And a new job. And a new community. And a whole new life.

Dumbfounded and stunned, I stared blankly at the woman at the gym. I backed away from her without response, walked into a newly vacant shower stall, and allowed my stinging tears to mix with the running water. Then I got dressed in the locker room, packed up my duffel bag for the last time, and canceled my gym membership on the way out the front door.

But wait. There were also places, people, and things that somehow felt okay, that gave me some comfort, that helped in some way. Did I need to get rid of everything and everyone from my old life?

I remained stuck in indecision for quite a while, trying to determine who and what from my old environment (before death) fit into my new environment (after death).

Eventually I busted out an ecomap to help me sort things out. As a social worker, I had drawn ecomaps for others countless times. Now it was time to complete one for myself.

So I did.

Here is an example of my ecomap. In just a few pages, you will have the opportunity to draw your own ecomap if you would like to do so.

Susan's Ecomap Example

1) In the center square, I wrote my name.

2) I thought about my typical day or typical week. Where did I go? Who did I interact with? In the outer circles, I wrote the names of the people, places, or things that were part of my current life (e.g., home, school, work, gym, family, friends, church).

3) I drew lines connecting myself to each circle.
   Solid lines (———) signified positive relationships.
   Dotted lines (------) signified neutral relationships.
   Crisscross lines (#####) signified stressful relationships.

4) I noticed the current sources of support and stress in my new environment.

5) I jotted down ways to strengthen, alter, or change various relationships.

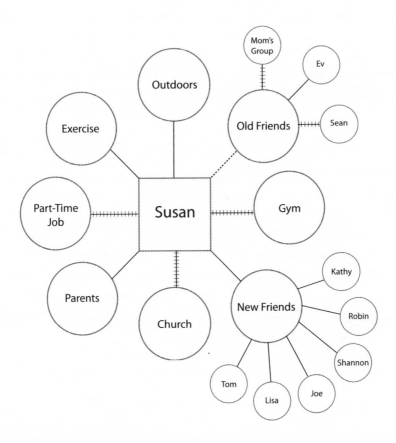

When I was done drawing my ecomap, I knew which community relationships I eventually needed to change (crisscross lines) because they were negative for my new life, which ones I needed to strengthen (solid lines) because they were positive and supportive of my new life, and which ones I needed to revisit (dotted lines) because, although I didn't love these components of my life, I couldn't change them or didn't know how to change them right away.

Over time I changed my gym, my hairdresser, a grocery store, my church, certain old friends, and my job. I strengthened relationships with my parents, certain old friends, two cousins, an aunt, new peers in the grief community, volunteer organizations, nature, outdoor activities, and healing mentors. I chose to revisit my child's school and our city of residence.

I wonder if knowing your new environment might assist you on your healing journey.

Why consider knowing your new environment?

In so many areas, life before grief and trauma looks very different than life after grief and trauma. Not all the same relationships work. For a life that has been altered, an ecomap can help provide clarity about your new environment. An ecomap is a written diagram ("map") of an individual's environment ("eco") that provides a visual picture of clarity. Social workers have used ecomaps for decades as simple tools to chart and assess both positive and negative relationships within social environments, families, and groups. But everyone can ecomap their lives—no need to be a social worker! Through an ecomap, plans can be made to change, modify, or strengthen relationships in a "new life" environment.

How does knowing your new environment promote healing?

- By determining positive social supports and assisting in strengthening those relationships

- By determining negative social supports and assisting in modifying those relationships

- By providing clarity and focus about social, emotional, and behavioral relationships

- By decreasing anxiety, stress, and pressure in relation to social situations

SINGLE SMALL STEPS

If you would like to integrate knowing your new environment into your healing journey, here are some single small step suggestions you may be able to use.

Is there one that resonates with you?

1) **The Lift Up**: Write the name of one person who lifts you up. Spend more time with them.

2) **The Pull Down**: Write the name of one person who pulls you down. Spend less time with them.

3) **The Lift Up**: Think of one place that lifts you up. Spend more time there.

4) **The Pull Down**: Think of one place that pulls you down. Spend less time there.

5) **Map It**: Try completing the full ecomap exercise on the following page.

Here is one single small step I may be able to take in the future:

_____

_____

_____

_____

_____

_____

Ecomap Exercise
KNOWING YOUR NEW ENVIRONMENT

This exercise will take 10–20 minutes. Grab a pencil and find a calm space.

1) In the center square, write YOUR NAME.

2) Think about your typical day or typical week. Where do you go? Who do you interact with? In the **outer circles**, write the names of the people, places, or things that are part of your current life (example: home, school, work, cafe, gym, family, friends, church). Add more circles, if needed. Be specific.

3) Draw lines between YOU and each circle. **Solid lines** _____ signify positive relationships. **Dotted lines** - - - - signify neutral relationships. **Crisscross lines** ### signify stressful relationships.

4) Notice the current sources of support and stress in your environment.

5) Jot down ways to strengthen, alter, or change the relationships that are currently stressful.

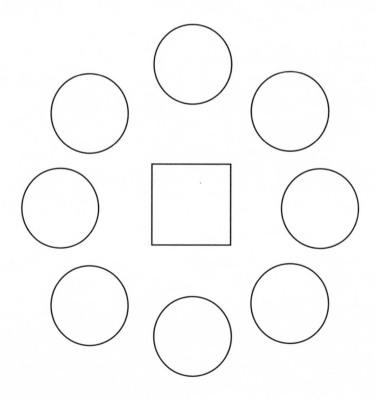

HEALING STORIES

We are a husband and wife who both had our sisters die suddenly, within a few years of our marriage. Our sisters were the best. Michele was a great mom of four children who was into playing and watching sports. She was especially witty and loved to joke around. Sabrina was beautiful and gracefully shy. She was a social butterfly and could talk anyone into doing anything for her. We felt sadness, tremendous loss, and huge voids. As we learned we were pregnant with our second child, we knew her name would be Sabrina Michele. "SAM" became the acronym that solidified and we call our daughter by both names: Sabrina and Michele. Sam has a little bit of both aunt's characteristics. She is sporty, fearless, and witty like her Aunt Michele; she is beautiful and social like her Aunt Sabrina. Naming our daughter after our two sisters has helped us integrate our losses and helped us to get to know our new life in a healthy way.
—Shannon and Teresa

My husband and I had five children (ages ten to seventeen) when we filed for divorce. Less than two years later, he suicided and I was left a single mother of five with no child support or death benefits. One thing I do know is we can't tell anybody how to feel because we ourselves cannot control the emotions we are processing in tragic situations. For me, emotional release and healing have always happened through creation, so I started using painting and woodwork to rise above the challenges I have been dealt. Over time, I have learned to chuck the safe route of a traditional job that did not support my family, and now I create and express something that I love. I have started a business painting furniture and refinishing bathroom and kitchen cabinets. I'm beginning to establish a notable reputation with my talent while creating enough business to support the family expenses. Best yet, now I am an almost-stay-at-home single mom.
—Mindy

About a month after my boyfriend passed, I ended up losing my job. I was in a really low place. I needed a change and needed a way to get myself into more than just a job so I had some security. I decided to go back to school to earn my degree at forty years old. I had always felt I missed out on the "college experience" since I only went to a one-year secretarial school after high school before having my son. I didn't have time to go to school then, but now that my son is older, he doesn't need 24-7 babysitting. When I learned I could earn my degree by taking courses online around my schedule, I decided to go for it. I'm now finishing up on what will be my associate degree in health information management. It's been quite a journey, but I've enjoyed it and hope to find employment in my new career.

—Jen

How do you say "goodbye" to a child that is gone in an instant? Nothing in life prepared us for this moment. A falling boulder struck our son during a climbing outing with friends. We grasped for reality and security, but they could not be found. Eventually, our path forward came in the form of a novel our son had finished about six weeks before his accident. Publishing our son's novel became our healing pathway. Each step gave us the opportunity to "listen" to our son through his writing. Today we are pleased to say that our son's novel, The Road of the Innocents, *has been published and all book donations go to the San Diego Library Foundation in his memory. Clearly our path to saying "goodbye" was unique to our circumstances. However, we believe there is a universal lesson applicable to the healing process: involve yourself in something that was important to your loved one. Whatever that might be—a place, an activity, a hobby—spend time with it. By absorbing that experience, you will have a prolonged connection to your loved one that, over time, will soften the shock of their abrupt departure.*

—Cheryl and Stephen

RESOURCES

If you would like to integrate knowing your new environment into your healing journey, here are some resources that can help you get started.

Books

It's OK That You're Not OK: Meeting Grief and Loss in a Culture that Doesn't Understand by Megan Devine

On Grief and Grieving by Elisabeth Kübler-Ross and David Kessler

Permission to Mourn: A New Way to Do Grief by Tom Zuba

The Ten Things to Do When Your Life Falls Apart by Daphne Rose Kingma

Websites

Smart Draw
www.smartdraw.com/ecomap
Explanation of Ecomaps and sample Ecomaps.

NOTES

Use this section for any notes related to knowing your new environment.

_____

_____

_____

_____

_____

_____

_____

_____

_____

_____

_____

_____

_____

_____

_____

_____

"It's not one huge step that promotes healing . . .
it's many intentional single small steps."

138 | A to Z HEALING TOOLBOX

L

LAUGHTER

A good laugh is sunshine in a house.

—WILLIAM MAKEPEACE THACKERAY

HEALING POWER

Brent had a great sense of humor. Once, I bashed my head on the sliding door of our old Volkswagen camper van and he called me "Lumpy" for the next week. Once, he mixed protein powder into the cat's food just to see if the feline would get bigger. Once, he gelled our four-month-old son's hair into a Mohawk for a party. Once, he strapped on a miner's headlamp and crawled into the garden at night to capture the bug that was chomping on his bean plants. Once, he gave some rowdy-and-rude-at-night college students an early morning "lesson" by practicing his bagpipes on their doorstep at the crack of dawn. Once, when our mailman came up the path, he lifted me up to our large picture window and belted out the Beatles' "Please Mister Postman" at full volume.

After Brent died, I waited a long, long time before I heard my own laughter again. How could there be any room for laughter with such all-encompassing pain?

I thought I would never laugh again.

But I did, many months later, when I met Laffy.

Laffy Laffalot is a bright orange plastic toy that was created by a professional firefighter who understood firsthand the stress families experience when faced with grief and trauma. Laffy was created with the sole purpose of making children laugh, a unique way to distract them while they suffered. But it turns out Laffy promotes laughter in adults too because as soon as my son turned that thing on, we were both in stitches. Laffy entertains with twenty recorded laughs (think "sleepy," "goofy," and "snort") and the ability to create four other custom laughs or audios. When a girlfriend gifted us this toy, she brought a little life, energy, and hope back into our sad, heavy home. Laffy was the beginning of inserting more laugher into our lives.

Here are five other laugh-inducing things that we now do:

1) Subscribe to Sirius XM radio so we can access comedy channels while driving in the car.

2) Listen to YouTube videos of comedians before going to bed (Jim Gaffigan, Brian Regan, and Sinbad work for us).

3) Watch reruns of laugh-inducing sitcoms (*Seinfeld* and *Big Bang Theory* are our favorites).

4) Read *Would You Rather* books (by Justin Heimberg and David Gomberg) and hoot over their absurd questions. ("Would you rather not be able to eat again until you see a bald eagle in the wild OR until you can find a four-leaf clover?" or "Would you rather have a small butt on your chin OR two little feet dangling from your nose?" or "Would you rather sleep upside down like a bat OR standing up like a cow?")

5) Spend more time with our funny friend, Miss Laff. (Yes, that really is her name!)

I also make a point to be entertained by young children. When our son was about six years old, I once peeked around the corner to see what he was doing in the playroom. He was holding a harmonica in one hand and an ink pad in the other, playing a tune while stamping pink butterflies all over his naked butt. I completely lost it. I wound up doubled over in the hallway, enjoying the first belly laugh I'd had in ages.

I wonder if laughter might assist you on your healing journey.

Why consider laughter?

Nothing seems funny when grief and trauma barrel into life. Yet the psychological and physiological benefits of laughter have been researched and documented. It's no wonder why comedian Bob Hope traveled to entertain the troops throughout World War II; it's no wonder that physician Patch Adams continues to bring his clown-like antics to children in hospitals around the world; it's no wonder that laughter yoga has become popular with groups of all ages. Whether forced or spontaneous, laughter can help heal life.

How does laughter promote healing?

- By reducing feelings of anxiety and depression
- By strengthening the immune system
- By reducing levels of physical pain
- By lowering blood pressure

SINGLE SMALL STEPS

If you would like to integrate laughter into your healing journey, here are some single small step suggestions you may be able to use.

Is there one that resonates with you?

1) **Morning**: Chuckle during your commute by tuning into comedy channels on your radio or phone.

2) **Noon**: Laugh on your lunch break by downloading audiobook excerpts from your favorite humorous author, or eat your meal with a friend or coworker who makes you laugh.

3) **Work Break**: Stick a pen or pencil between your teeth (the long way). It forces a smile and gives you a quick surge of happy.

4) **Night**: Unwind in the evening by smiling at silly sitcoms or a favorite funny film.

5) **Before Bed**: Relax a ruminating mind by reading funny books and magazine articles.

Here is one single small step I may be able to take in the future:

_____

_____

_____

_____

_____

_____

_____

HEALING STORIES

Truly, laughter is the best medicine. That's what comes to mind when I think of my sister. My sister was always a ton of fun to spend time with. She had a tongue that was quick and witty. Not a moment passed that she didn't have you in stitches. When she passed suddenly, it was difficult at first to exchange the tears for the laughter. As time healed me, I couldn't help but think of the things my sister would tell me that put a smile on my face. There are times that I burst out laughing just thinking of her words or jokes. To this day, when our family gets together we still think of our sister, what she might say in that moment, and we all start laughing. I feel her presence in my life just by remembering how special her gift of laughter was to all of us.
—Teri

So what could possibly be funny about being a widow? Everything, if you choose to see it that way. For me, it was never a choice to "find the funny inside of the pain." It was survival. Friends flew into action and organized a comedy benefit to honor my husband's life. Elayne Boosler headlined and Jim Gaffigan gave a surprise performance. Then I got up onstage. I joked about all the stupid things people say to you when someone dies. I reenacted a phone call I had with the phone company, where the customer service representative insisted over and over again she speak directly with the account holder—my dead husband. I talked about the giant box of my six-foot-three husband's cremains that his EMS brothers handed over to me and said: "Brace yourself. There's a lot of him." I laughed and cried all in the same breath up on that stage. And it resonated with people in ways I never imagined.
—Kelley Lynn Shepherd, author of *My Husband Is Not a Rainbow: The Brutally Awful, Hilarious Truth about Life, Love, Grief, and Loss*

I grew up in a large family; I'm number nine of ten children. We didn't have a lot financially, but our home was filled with happiness, laughter, and lots of one liners from my parents. When my father died, I was asked by my siblings to do the eulogy. I knew my dad would not want tears, so I started by saying one of his many one liners. The laughter was amazing and made the serious part of the eulogy easy. What a celebration of his life. My parents are both gone now, but when I think of them, it almost always makes me smile and laugh out loud. I have been blessed with four children, two stepchildren, and—at last count—twelve grandchildren, and all of them have heard many of my parent's one liners. The result has been lots of laughter. I have experienced plenty of loss in addition to my parents, including my second son, my sister, my first wife, close neighbors, and friends. I miss everyone greatly, but I choose to celebrate life with positive memories, lots of smiles, and of course laughter. I find that laughter brings me peace and allows me to not dwell on negative things in my life.

—Brian

RESOURCES

If you would like to integrate laughter into your healing journey, here are some resources that can help you get started.

Books

My Husband Is Not a Rainbow: The Brutally Awful, Hilarious Truth about Life, Love, Grief, and Loss by Kelley Lynn

The Laughing Cure: Emotional and Physical Healing—A Comedian Reveals Why Laughter Really Is the Best Medicine by Brian King

Would You Rather...? Over 200 Absolutely Absurd Dilemmas to Ponder by Justin Heimberg and David Gomberg

Games and Toys

Laffy Laffalot by Steve Islava (toy for children and adults)

Would You Rather...? The Game of Mind-Boggling Questions by Zobmondo!! (board game for kids and adults twelve and up)

Organizations

American School of Laughter Yoga
www.laughteryogaamerica.com
Laughter clubs, conferences, and professional trainings.

Laughter Yoga International
www.laughteryoga.org
Laughter articles, blogs, books, CDs, DVDS, and videos.

NOTES

Use this section for any notes related to laughter.

_____

_____

_____

_____

_____

_____

_____

_____

_____

_____

_____

_____

_____

_____

_____

_____

_____

_____

"It's not one huge step that promotes healing . . .
it's many intentional single small steps."

MEDITATION

In meditation, healing can happen.
When the mind is calm, alert and totally
contented, then it is like a laser beam—it is
very powerful and healing can happen.

—SRI SRI RAVI SHANKAR

HEALING POWER

"So there will also be another retreat option this year," our program coordinator explained. "The three-day silent retreat, which will be offered in the springtime."

It was right then that all six pairs of eyes opened wide and all six mouths dropped to the floor. We all gasped. *You want us to be* silent*? For three days?! Why on earth would we ever want to do* that*?*

The six of us had just graduated from various colleges and signed up to be housemates for a year through a domestic volunteer program called the Jesuit Volunteer Corps (JVC). We all knew the foundation of JVC was constructed upon four core values: spirituality, simple living, community, and social justice. But as we sat there on the living room floor in our ripped-up jeans, disheveled T-shirts, and Birkenstocks, no one had any idea which core value a three-day silent retreat fell under. We were too busy talking about our deep spiritual selves, chatting about what to buy with our monthly forty-dollar volunteer stipend, discussing the challenges of living in community with five strangers, and debating the social injustices of our society. Needless to say, not one of us signed up for that silent retreat. We all arrived later in life to the silent inner party known as meditation.

> *"Meditation is really a non-doing. It is the only human endeavor I know of that does not involve trying to get somewhere else but, rather, emphasizes being where you already are. Much of the time we are so carried away by all the doing, the striving, the planning, the reacting, the busyness, that when we stop just to feel where we are, it can seem a little peculiar at first . . . It takes a while to get comfortable with the richness of allowing yourself to just be with your own mind. It's a little like meeting an old friend for the first time in years. There may be some awkwardness in the beginning..."*
> —Jon Kabat-Zinn, *Full Catastrophe Living: Using the Wisdom of Your Body and Mind to Face Stress, Pain, and Illness*

Meditation was *very* awkward for me at the beginning of my healing journey. So awkward, in fact, that I avoided it all together. I didn't want to feel where I was (it was way too painful), I didn't want to be with my own mind (it was upside down with anxiety and fear), and I didn't want to meet any old friends (they couldn't bear the anguish I held inside).

It wasn't until these words sunk into my head that I finally acquiesced to giving meditation a try:

1) *"Your life provides the perfect conditions for awakening freedom. To find this freedom you must learn how to quiet the mind and open the heart. This is the purpose of meditation."* —Jack Kornfield, Buddhist teacher and author of *Bringing Home the Dharma: Awakening Right Where You Are*

2) *"Lean into the sharp points and fully experience them."*
   —Pema Chödrön, Buddhist nun and author of *When Things Fall Apart: Heart Advice for Difficult Times*

3) *"Lean into the discomfort."*
   —Brené Brown, research professor and author of *The Power of Vulnerability: Teachings on Authenticity, Connection, and Courage*

I wanted freedom from my all-encompassing pain, so I chose to lean into the discomfort of the million sharp points in my body, mind, and spirit to get some relief.

The first time I tried integrating mediation into my life was attempting "moving meditation" while I walked and swam.

The second time I tried integrating meditation into my life was trying three different guided meditation CDs: *Guided Meditations for Difficult Times* by Jack Kornfield, *The Grief Process: Meditations for Healing* by Stephen and Ondrea Levine, and *A Meditation to Ease Grief* by Belleruth Naparstek.

The third time I tried integrating meditation into my life was attending a weekend grief-healing retreat led by two marriage and family therapists, one of whom was a yoga-meditation instructor.

The last time I tried integrating meditation into my life was signing up for an eight-week program called MBSR—Mindfulness-Based Stress Reduction. MBSR classes, developed by author, scientist, and meditation teacher Jon Kabat-Zinn, are offered at hundreds of medical centers around the world and combine mindfulness, meditation, education, yoga, and breathing techniques to alleviate symptoms of stress.

I wonder if meditation might assist you on your healing journey.

Why consider meditation?

Participating in some form of meditation practice to calm a stressed and ruminating mind promotes overall health and well-being. And since meditation practices are so varied, anyone can reap the benefits. Meditation can be done alone or in a group setting, and practice can be self-led or teacher guided. There are hundreds of types of meditations to choose from, including practices that focus on mindfulness, compassion, healing grief, healing trauma, and restful sleep as well as traditional teachings from Hindu, Chinese, Buddhist, and Christian cultures.

How does meditation promote healing?

- By relieving emotional and physical stress
- By improving brain functioning
- By reducing pain and anxiety
- By strengthening the immune system

SINGLE SMALL STEPS

If you would like to integrate meditation into your healing journey, here are some single small step suggestions you may be able to use:

Is there one that resonates with you?

1) **Make a Move**: Move your body but relax your mind by trying a moving meditation.

2) **Listen and Learn**: Try sampling a guided meditation audio or CD.

3) **Try a Teacher**: Sign up for an instructor-led meditation group, class, or retreat.

4) **Go for Guidance**: Look for a Mindfulness-Based Stress Reduction program in your area.

5) **Buy a Book**: Pick up a meditation book for beginners at your local library or bookstore.

Here is one single small step I may be able to take in the future:

_____

_____

_____

_____

_____

_____

HEALING STORIES

After losing my husband in my twenties, I finally experienced the first peace of mind four or five years after his death while listening to a guided body scan by Jon Kabat-Zinn. It was a CD included with his book Full Catastrophe Living. *I felt as if I had landed in my own body for the first time. I realized then that no one had told me grief wasn't just in my mind. It was also in my body. Before this moment I had been grieving the loss of my partner, but I had never turned my attention inward to my own fragility and vulnerability. I had never grieved the parts of myself I lost when he died because I was so focused on grieving him. Becoming truly present for maybe the first time in my life allowed me to meet myself where I actually was, to see my grief clearly, and to finally get out of my own way and allow my body and mind to heal as they had been trying to do for years.*
—Mo

My dad's health had been declining for some time, but his actual passing was much quicker than any of us expected. After he passed, I soon realized this loss was far bigger and more intense than anything I'd experienced before. It scared me. I really wanted to run from it, but somehow felt that doing so would dishonor his memory and the impact he'd made on my life. At the time, I'd been doing a morning meditation and found this practice served a new purpose in grief; it provided a space to just let the sadness and loss wash over me and to connect with memories and reflections. When I didn't meditate for a few days, I found myself inexplicably angry and frustrated because I had no other outlet for these emotions and thoughts. In retrospect, the most important gift that meditation gave me was being less afraid of grief. By being still and sitting with the sadness, I saw that grief comes in waves and that I could either fight the wave or flow with it. And ultimately, flowing with it was the only thing that would ever bring relief.
—Lydia

Two years after my husband died, I hit a new low. I was dealing with depression and started to drink more. I started working with a healer who suggested I meditate twice a day for twenty minutes each time. At first I thought it was too much! How could I fit in forty minutes of meditation a day? My morning mediation was easier to do than the midday one, but both were very hard at first. I felt like I was doing it all wrong because I couldn't empty my mind. Then I stopped judging myself. I didn't realize how much these sessions were helping me until one day when I missed meditation and my kids said, "Mom, did you meditate yet? Cause it doesn't seem like it." They noticed. Now, whenever I am short with them or I seem distant, my kids assume I have not meditated and will tell me to go meditate! It's pretty funny. I never thought I would meditate forty minutes a day. Never. But now it's as important to me as brushing my teeth.
—Kim Hamer, author of *100 Acts of Love: A Girlfriend's Guide to Loving Your Friend Through Cancer or Loss*

My brother died when I was seventeen, and it was an earth-shattering, knee-buckling blow to my heart and soul; everything hurt. I was mad, devastated, and everything in between. Then a few years later, my mother almost died on the operating table. I had never felt such panic in my life and didn't know up from down. Meditation practice is one tool that helped me mend. My first time meditating was in a classroom of about thirteen other students, with the lights dimmed, listening to a guided meditation CD. It was hard. *Meditation did not come easy. Over time I found what worked for me; I began with guided meditations but eventually branched off into walking and solitary meditations. I have a small "altar" in my room that holds items that aid in re-centering myself. From meditation, I found the greatest lesson I learned was that what I needed to care for and soothe myself was inside me all along.*
—Honor

RESOURCES

If you would like to integrate meditation into your healing journey, here are some resources that can help you get started.

Audio and CD
A Meditation to Ease Grief by Belleruth Naparstek

Guided Meditations for Difficult Times: A Lamp in the Darkness by Jack Kornfield

Mindfulness Meditations for Teens by Bodhipaksa

The Grief Process: Meditations for Healing by Stephen and Ondrea Levine

Books
Bringing Home the Dharma: Awakening Right Where You Are by Jack Kornfield

Full Catastrophe Living: Using the Wisdom of Your Body and Mind to Face Stress, Pain, and Illness by Jon Kabat-Zinn

When Things Fall Apart: Heart Advice for Difficult Times by Pema Chodron

Organization
Center for Mindfulness in Medicine, Health Care, and Society at University of Massachusetts
www.umassmed.edu/cfm/mindfulness-based-programs
History of and classes for Mindfulness-Based Stress Reduction (MBSR).

NOTES

Use this section for any notes related to meditation.

_____

_____

_____

_____

_____

_____

_____

_____

_____

_____

_____

_____

_____

_____

_____

_____

*"It's not one huge step that promotes healing . . .
it's many intentional single small steps."*

N

NUTRITION

*Let food be thy medicine and medicine
be thy food.*

—HIPPOCRATES

HEALING POWER

When I was a child, my father was a pilot in the United States Navy. This enabled my brother and me to hang out on aircraft carriers, test our aviation skills in flight simulators, and get incredible seats to watch the Blue Angels Air Show. Another perk of my dad's job was having access to the Navy Commissary, a massive grocery store that sat on the military base. Once a month my mom made the trek to the Commissary to load up on food for the upcoming weeks. When my brother and I heard our old Buick station wagon roll into the driveway, we would hustle out to help unload the bags of food. We rooted through pasta, chicken, fish, fruits, and vegetables in search of the "fun food." The fun food was always the same: two Hostess pies (cherry for my brother and lemon for me), one box of Little Debbie oatmeal cream sandwich cookies, and two large tin cans of a Hi-C fruit punch. Twenty-five heaping bags of groceries and only three fun food items to last the whole month. A kid's worst nightmare! But our mom was a family nurse practitioner, so it seemed she had a heads-up on nutrition before the rest of society. To this day, she still ends many conversations with her children and grandchildren by saying, " . . . And don't forget to eat nutritiously!"

Thanks to my mom, I started out life with pretty healthy eating habits.

But all of that went out the window when grief and trauma snuck into my kitchen and took up residence.

The first year of healing, I only ate because people reminded me. I was in shock and nauseous most of the time, so food was the last thing on my mind. Even so, random casseroles came in from a local church. A mother's group started a meal chain. My mom fed us on the weekends. On Mondays and Fridays, I had friends who brought over dinner. I had no weight to lose and I lost ten pounds.

During my second year of healing, my appetite came back somewhat, but I could not muster up the energy to make meals. I was too exhausted trying to survive. Cooking had been Brent's thing, not mine. So when people asked, "How can we help you?" I replied, "Restaurant gift cards." We ate out a lot and signed up for an in-home meal delivery service. I ate because I knew I was supposed to, but my taste buds had gone dormant.

In the third year of healing, I began eating lots of carbs and sugars—crackers, cookies, cereal, bagels, candy, chips, pretzels, pepperoni pizza, macaroni and cheese, burgers, and fries. I didn't have to cook, didn't have to spend much money, and didn't have any complaints from my son. It was perfect, except that I felt tired and lethargic and was gaining weight.

The fourth year of healing, I enlisted the help of a nutritionist friend. I have slowly started to make small changes toward eating for health. Now I log what I eat in a food journal, drink water all day long, buy prewashed lettuce for salads, make multiple meals in advance, and snack on protein shakes, cheese sticks, nuts, and Greek yogurt. I still eat the occasional fast-food meal. I still prefer dish duty over cooking. I still struggle with eating vegetables. I still live with a massive sweet tooth. But I am making healthier strides forward.

I wonder if nutrition might assist you on your healing journey.

Why consider nutrition?
In times of emotional distress, our relationship with food changes. With a stomach in knots from grief, pain, and anxiety, some forget to eat entirely. Others survive by reaching for foods that provide comfort—sugar, processed foods, caffeine, and alcohol—and emotional eating may continue for years after the initial grief or trauma. Enlisting help from community resources is an effective tool for getting eating habits back on track. Nutritional tools and information are widespread, from television chef shows and specialty cookbooks to nutritional counseling centers and online health communities.

How does nutrition promote healing?
- By aiding in digestion
- By fighting depression
- By boosting vitamins that increase energy levels
- By reducing nausea and constipation

SINGLE SMALL STEPS

If you would like to integrate nutrition into your healing journey, here are some single small step suggestions you may be able to use:

Is there one that resonates with you?

1) **Drink Up**: Stay hydrated for healing by keeping a water bottle at your bedside table, in your car, at your desk, in your backpack, and ready to go in the fridge.

2) **Shop Smart**: Print out a copy of a "healing foods list" and bring it with you when you shop at the grocery store.

3) **Jot and Journal**: Write down everything you eat because daily food journals can help you stay focused on what's going into (or missing from) your body.

4) **Fix the Fridge**: Take the healthy stuff out of the drawers! Put fruit and veggies and lean proteins front and center where you can see them.

5) **Magic Meals**: Friends, family, and colleagues can assist with homemade meals, restaurant gift cards, meal delivery service, and stocking the freezer.

6) **Expert Eats**: Nutritionists can give you tips, tricks, and ideas for keeping emotional eating at bay and bumping up healthy food choices.

Here is one single small step I may be able to take in the future:

_____

_____

_____

_____

_____

_____

HEALING STORIES

When my husband died, my only concern was to help my kids get through the loss. I put my grief on a closet shelf, slammed the door, and cried into my chocolate chip ice cream. Thirty pounds later, I hit rock bottom. Unrecognizable on so many levels, I was embarrassed by the physical and emotional damage I caused myself. I hated how I looked and felt. I didn't want my photo taken. And worst of all, my kids unfairly bore the brunt of how unhappy I was with myself. Desperate, angry, depressed, and frightened of something happening to me, which would leave my kids orphaned, I knew sweeping changes were needed. One day I stumbled upon a Facebook page written by a young widow with two small children who, at one point, had been overweight. Everything about her resonated with me. I joined her private virtual training community and finally learned about nutrition and eating clean.
—Robin

At the age of thirteen, real life hit me out of nowhere. My parents sat the family down and told us they were filing for divorce. Little did I know, this announcement was the family's tipping point. My father suicided the night I graduated from the eighth grade. Before he died, I made a promise to him that I would lose weight and earn the grades required to enter and finish college with a degree in business and finance. But I discovered that having a goal was not enough. I needed a plan, initiative, and commitment to demonstrate action. After months of trying and saying I would lose the weight for my dad, I was unsuccessful. So I told myself I could lose the weight for myself and my own health. As I became educated on nutrition and changed my mindset toward food, the weight came off. My grades also improved. I got a better job and I started realizing I could accomplish my dreams.
—Chad, age seventeen

My happy life as I knew it completely shattered with the sudden loss of my dear husband. In the blink of an eye, I was a grieving widow, not something one expects to be on a lazy Sunday evening with two teenagers. The last thing I wanted to think about was food and eating right, but it was then I needed to do that the most. At first, I had no appetite and I lost quite a bit of weight, energy, and focus. So the healing process for me involved finding ways to regain an appetite for food. Getting back into the meal-making saddle was a gradual process. One of the things I did was to get the children involved. We planned meals, shopped for nutritious ingredients, cooked the food, dined together, and shared memories of their father. I now realize that feeding the body is feeding the heart and soul. Finding a way to make nutrition work as a family has been so rewarding and healing.

—Sade

RESOURCES

If you would like to integrate nutrition into your healing journey, here are some resources that can help you get started.

Books

5 Ingredient 15 Minute Cookbook by Weight Watchers

Fix-It and Enjoy-It! 5-Ingredient Recipes by Phyllis Pellman Good

Meal Assistance

Blue Apron
www.blueapron.com
Meal ingredients and recipes delivered to your home. Follow the recipe and make the meal.

Freshly
www.freshly.com
Healthy meals prepared and delivered to your home. Reheat the meal if needed.

Dream Dinners
www.dreamdinners.com
Make meals in store kitchen and take home and freeze. Thaw and cook meal when ready to eat.

Websites

Dr. Axe
www.draxe.com
Provides tips on nutrition, natural medicine, fitness, and healthy recipes.

NOTES

Use this section for any notes related to nutrition.

_____

_____

_____

_____

_____

_____

_____

_____

_____

_____

_____

_____

_____

_____

_____

_____

_____

*"It's not one huge step that promotes healing . . .
it's many intentional single small steps."*

O

ORGANIZING YOUR SUPPORTS

When everything goes to hell, the people
who stand by you without flinching—they
are your family.

—JAMES BUTCHER

HEALING POWER

It's funny how one little thing someone says can be the catalyst for huge change.

As I sat on my couch a few weeks after Brent's death, she said it.

And something clicked.

"Susan," the kind stranger began, "I believe that in life there are those who *be* and there are those who *do*. I am a BE-er. My job here is to be with you. I will hold the space for whatever feelings, emotions, and challenges come up for you while going through this massive life transition. I will sit with you. I will listen to you. I will not judge you. I will hold your hand and hug you, if that is okay." She continued, "Other people will *do* things for you: wash your dishes, help with your son, buy your groceries, cook your meals. But I am here to *be* with you."

Instantly, in my head, I saw a large blank sheet of paper with a line drawn down the middle. On one side were the BE-ers. On the other side were the DO-ers. The names of people in my new life started jumping onto the page, filing into order. Some names even sat right on the center line because they were both. This made total sense to me! We needed massive amounts of help and now I could rely on people's strength areas to help us. I could stop being so frustrated that the DO-ers weren't being what I needed them to be; I could stop wishing for the BE-ers to start doing things to help me. This categorization would make life a little easier and release all of us from any unrealistic expectations.

One DO-er who showed up in my new life was a woman from the community. I did not know her at all. Yet she showed up at my door to help us because she knew what it was like. She was the gal who picked up the pieces of her own shattered life when her husband died suddenly, years earlier. She was the gal who brought a huge Styrofoam cooler to my house, full of gourmet meals that she cooked, vacuum packed, and froze so my son and I would have healthy meals to eat in the upcoming weeks. She was the gal who organized us to participate in a local 5K mud run, where we slipped and slid our way to "having a little life again." She was the gal who knew our immune systems were weak, reminded us to get our flu shots, then gave them to us herself because she happened to be a nurse. She was the gal who baked dozens of cake pops for my son's Thomas the Train birthday party, earning her the household title "Cake Pop Kathy." She was there to do so many things to support our new life.

One BE-er who showed up in my new life was a former work colleague. I had only known him a few months. Yet he showed up at my door one day to help us because he knew what it was like. He was the guy who survived war in the Middle East and gently swapped battle stories with me to let me know I wasn't alone in my trauma, healing, and life rebuilding. He was the guy who came over countless times to sit with me on the patio while I struggled to believe my husband was actually dead. He was the guy who accompanied me on endless hikes and kayak trips while I tried to make sense of my new shattered-in-a-million-pieces world. He was the guy who launched my small son out of the pool water over and over again, giving him the same feeling of flying that his dad used to give him. He was there to be with it all, no matter how messy it looked or how horrible it felt.

One BE-er/DO-er who showed up in my new life was already a good friend. I had known her for fifteen years. And she showed up at my door one day to help us because she had no idea what it was like. She was the friend who committed to come over to our house every Friday night for a year because she wanted to both do something to assist and be in our transforming world. She was the friend who drove forty-five minutes through rush hour traffic to bring us a warm dinner after work. She was the friend who made sure my five-year-old son stuck with his nighttime routine of "bath-brush-books-bed" by getting him in the tub and washing his hair "at the famous salon" while speaking with a fake French accent. She was the friend who squirted toothpaste on his tiny toothbrush, read a million nighttime stories, and got on her knees with us to pray that Daddy was doing okay in Heaven. Then, after all that DO-ing, she would succumb to the BE-ing and we would sit on the couch and cry for hours. She was there to pick up the pieces, to both do and be.

Numerous other friends, colleagues, and family members rushed to our side after the medical examiner left the house and the death announcement went out. They cried with me, stood in pain with me, and brought books, meals, prayers, and childcare. But their own anxiety, fear, shock, and dread coupled with my own anxiety, fear, shock, and dread became too much for me to handle. I became exhausted trying to navigate these relationships while I was juggling the myriad of complex reactions to my own grief, trauma, and suddenly solo parenting. I didn't want to hear any advice, couldn't bear answering any questions, and pushed away any and all judgment. I needed room to breathe. I needed a break. I had to set some people "on the shelf" so I could cope. They became SHELF-ers.

I wonder if organizing your supports might assist you on your healing journey.

Why consider organizing your supports?

Just as lives are forever altered by grief and trauma, many once-stable relationships are at least temporarily changed. Relationships with friends, family, colleagues, and other community members can strengthen, weaken, or be suddenly conflicted. In addition, new people may appear in your life to support, guide, or mentor. By determining who can provide support, where their strength areas lie (Can they *be*? Can they *do*?), and if the relationship can be supportive at all (SHELF?), it is possible to rest at ease in the healing power of those who seek to assist with a newly transforming life.

How does organizing your supports promote healing?

- By releasing any unrealistic expectations you may have of family, friends, and colleagues

- By assisting other people in supporting you with their BE-ing or DO-ing

- By taking a break from people who may release negative energy in your direction

SINGLE SMALL STEPS

If you would like to integrate organizing your supports into your healing journey, here are some single small step suggestions you may be able to use.

Is there one that resonates with you?

1) **Be**: Determine who the BE-ers are in your new life and ask them to be with you. These are the people who can sit, cry, listen, hug, and hold nonjudgmental space for your feelings.

2) **Do**: Determine who the DO-ers are in your new life and ask them to do things for you. These are the people who can make meals, do chores, shuttle kids, run errands, organize events, and feed the pets.

3) **Shelf**: Determine who the SHELF-ers are in your new life and let them know you need a break. These are the people who advise you, question you, judge you, hurry you, or leave you feeling drained and depleted.

4) **Try**: Complete the full exercise on the following page.

Here is one single small step I may be able to take in the future:

_____

_____

_____

_____

_____

_____

Exercise:
WHO'S IN YOUR LIFE?

This exercise will take 10–20 minutes. Grab a pencil and find a calm space.

BEers	DOers	SHELFers
These people will be there to: • sit with you • cry with you • listen without judgment • sleep next to you and your children • hold you and hug you without words	These people do things for you like: • making your meals • shuffling your kids to their activities • completing household chores • helping you reorganize your finances • dragging you outside for a walk or run	These people may need to sit on your shelf due to negative or toxic habits, such as: • constantly judging you • consistently giving unsolicited advice • leaving you feeling even more drained
Your BEers	**Your DOers**	**Your SHELFers**

HEALING STORIES

I was the principal of a small elementary school when I got the call a little after midnight. "I'm sorry, there were no survivors." I just learned that my two sons and my husband died in a small airplane crash. Eventually the food, the cards, and the calls stopped, but the grief did not. I had to find support on my own. I made myself say yes more often than not when friends asked me to go to dinner or for hikes, a movie, or shopping. I saw a therapist. I cried. I spoke of my husband and sons often. I learned to continually put things in perspective by visiting others who had experienced loss and knowing that "things could always be worse." I looked for joy everywhere. My tools may not suit others. My lessons may be different. But here's the secret: the simple act of reaching out to be with someone, to hold a broken heart with care and love, is the most powerful help and comfort anyone can ever offer. And that's something every single one of us can do.

—Dr. Nancy Saltzman, author of *Radical Survivor*

When our dad died, we were seven and nine years old. We were devastated. We missed our dad. So our mom signed us up for the Big Brothers Big Sisters Program. Now we both have a volunteer who spends time with us every few weeks. We like our Bigs because we can easily talk to them, they understand us, and we like to do the same things. We do things that our father would likely do with us. We do things with our Big Brothers like rock climbing, ceramic painting, playing tennis, going to the movies, and visiting the arcade. We also just hang out. We like our Big Brothers because they help us feel better. We would have been much more doleful without our Bigs.

—Casey and Aiden

Several months after the sudden death of my thirty-two-year-old husband, the subtle hints from my friends, family, and coworkers appeared—suggesting "the time has come for me to move on." Move on from what—the dissolving of my family, the loss of my true love, the death of the father of my daughter?

In retrospect, I know they wanted to see me happy and remove the pain, but mostly they wanted to have the old Rachel back. Really? Would I ever be back? I suggest: create an elevator speech for those around you who are trying to fix you—a simple message that the situation is emotionally all-encompassing but you are doing better than yesterday and truly appreciate their support. The true message is, "Please let me be for now, I am trying the best I can!" Without a canned response, they will push harder and you will push back more. Stay in your refuge for as long as you need and enter the battlefield when you are ready and able.

—Rachel Kodanaz, author of *Living with Loss: One Day at a Time*

I have always been a "giver." I was the friend, daughter, sibling, leader who gave 150 percent of myself (often resulting in my own lack of sleep, mental capacity, money, etc.). Needless to say, when my husband died, I went into a mental place I had never been in before and immediately started to pull in my capacity net. I had a full-time job, two young sons with special needs, and a house to support. I just did not have the tolerance to deal with other people's issues or unacceptable behaviors anymore. I took a long look at the people and situations that were draining me, took actions to "put those people on the shelf," and changed my life for the better. Here are a few examples: 1) Family: I was no longer going to accept anything less than civil behavior from my mother-in-law. 2) Friends: I stopped calling some people—and actually felt okay with it. 3) Work: I approached my boss and was finally transitioned to a new position. I was able to shelve those people in my life whom I did not have the capacity to deal with and change situations in my life that I could no longer tolerate. Now, I am a better mother, friend, daughter, sibling, and leader.

—Catherine

RESOURCES

If you would like to integrate organizing your supports into your healing journey, here are some resources that can help you get started.

Books

100 Acts of Love: The Girlfriend's Guide to Loving Your Friend Through Cancer or Loss by Kim Hamer

Effective Grief and Bereavement Support: The Role of Family, Friends, Colleagues, School, and Support Professionals by Atle and Kari Dyregrov

How to Help a Grieving Friend: A Candid Guide for Those Who Care by Stephanie Whitson

Websites

100 Acts of Love
www.100actsoflove.com
Provides practical podcasts, videos, and teleseminars for helping those who grieve.

NOTES

Use this section for any notes related to organizing your supports.

_____

_____

_____

_____

_____

_____

_____

_____

_____

_____

_____

_____

_____

_____

_____

_____

_____

_____

*"It's not one huge step that promotes healing . . .
it's many intentional single small steps."*

P

PEER MENTORS

*Friendship is born at that moment when
one person says to another:
"What? You too? I thought I
was the only one."*

—C. S. LEWIS

HEALING POWER

My friend Robin started dragging me along the road of my new life several years ago, after I met her in a class at our local gym. It was right after my husband died in the car accident and four years after her husband died of pancreatic cancer. We lifted weights together and did hundreds of squats, crunches, and push-ups, all the while speaking about life and death, school-aged children, a love for exercise, and a will to survive. Over time, Robin became my unofficial peer mentor, and she has continued to encourage me, support me, and lift me through the myriad of complex feelings, emotions, and life struggles as I learn to live in a world without my life partner.

Recently we went dress shopping together. Robin loves to shop! I don't. Robin loves dresses! I don't. But I needed a dress for a semiformal fundraising event I was attending, and so, once again, Robin dragged me to do something I didn't want to do.

Because that's what peer mentors do.

Sometimes they must drag us along.

Through the grief.

Through the trauma.

Especially when we don't want to get out of bed ("You are going to get up because your son needs a functional parent"); when we don't want to live another second without our person ("I am living proof you will survive this all-encompassing pain"); when we can't fathom living in a world without the familiar life we once knew ("It won't look the same; it will be different, but still be good—and I will help you rebuild"); when we want to smack people for saying stupid things to us ("Death makes people nuts. They didn't say that to hurt you intentionally").

Robin has dragged me out of bed, dragged me to eat, dragged me to the gym, dragged me to spiritual healing retreats, dragged me to weekend widow conferences, dragged me into the world of social media, dragged me through family school events, dragged me to new hairdressers, dragged me to massage therapists, dragged me to see most everything in a new way.

So Robin did drag me out again, only this time it was to shop for a dress. But this time the dress wasn't black and I wasn't in mourning. Because the dress shopping wasn't about death—it was about life. And that's the power of peer mentors. They invite us back to life.

But we help them, too, I realized. Peer mentoring is a win-win situation.

Here is Robin's recount of me, the peer mentee, helping her, the peer mentor:

Well, it's interesting how life works.

Some people believe in fate and say everything happens for a reason. Others think people come into our lives to help us with a life lesson. I truly don't know what the answer is. But during one of our gym training sessions, it came up that I was widowed for four years and raising two young kids all on my own. As fate, circumstance, or really bad luck would have it, Susan's husband died in a car accident less than a week after me revealing my widowhood. The sudden, shocking, numbing news was surreal. Susan immediately reached out for support (I had plenty to give), a magic wand to bring back Brent (how I wished I had one of those), and guidance. And so a new friendship was birthed. It was a friendship built on trust, death, life, fear, moving forward then sliding back, get-your-butt-to-the-gym-and-take-care-of-yourself-so-you-can-take-care-of-your-son, grief, laughter through tears, more grief, more tears, loss, oh-my-god-our-husbands-are-dead-how-the-hell-do-we-do-this, healing, more healing, and yes we are still healing.

Through all of this, it never occurred to me I was mentoring her. I simply saw a beautiful new friend who was hurting down to her soul. I recognized the pain and vertigo which comes when your world is upended and the one person you would instinctively turn to for support is the very person who is no longer here to help. So while I was busy mentoring Susan, I discovered how much she was helping me. I watched her go through the agonizingly raw early grief stages and realized how far I had journeyed through my own grief. Somehow I had forgotten how dark and suffocating those early post-loss days were, but being her sounding board allowed me to remember (Did I want to remember?) what my kids and I had survived. When she asked me to co-lead a new regional peer support group I immediately, yet reluctantly, said yes. I knew it would be added responsibility. I knew it would put one more thing on my plate. I also knew how much support and hope peer support provided, so how could I not help her, and others?

Years later, Susan and I still talk regularly. We text, email, hike, cry, laugh through tears, paddleboard, lift weights, eat frozen yogurt, take our dogs to the beach, and curse our heads off while pondering widowhood and how one finds a new normal while rebuilding a life.
—*Robin, peer mentor*

I wonder if establishing peer mentors might assist you on your healing journey.

Why consider finding peer mentors?

Peer mentors are invaluable resources for healing. They offer perspective about living with grief and trauma, provide a safe space to discuss deeply personal experiences, and normalize feelings and reactions to the life-rebuilding process. Those who have "walked the road before" have tools, resources, ideas, understanding, and support to share. Mentors can provide a sense of normalcy when the new world view looks upside down.

How does having peer mentors promote healing?

- By promoting social inclusion, support, and connection in a unique community
- By building resilience and instilling a sense of hope
- By enhancing overall social and emotional wellness
- By empowering individuals with a sense of "normalcy"

SINGLE SMALL STEPS

If you would like to integrate peer mentors into your healing journey, here are some single small step suggestions you may be able to use.

Is there one that resonates with you?

1) **Reach Out**: If you hear of someone in your current situation, contact them. Ask them to mentor you or ask them for a list of helpful tools and resources they have used.

2) **Referral**: Ask friends, family, colleagues, and health providers for peer mentor recommendations, referrals, and resources.

3) **Research**: Scan the internet to help you locate a supportive in person, online, or in a group peer-mentoring community.

Here is one single small step I may be able to take in the future:

_____

_____

_____

_____

_____

_____

HEALING STORIES

Peer mentors: It's not an oxymoron. The words are neither incompatible nor mutually exclusive. A mentor can be someone who has been on the road of profound loss longer than you, is a leader of a group, or has more specialization or education. But mentors quickly become peers when eyes lock and knowing is shared. We know pain that can't be explained. We are peer mentors, slingshotting each other from depths to solid ground, over and over again. Barb, who runs a group called Hope for Hurting Moms, was my first peer mentor in my life after—after my son, Kade, died at the age of nineteen. Then came so many others: Jim and Ann from my Compassionate Friends chapter meetings; Dr. Joanne Cacciatore of the MISS Foundation Retreat for Traumatic Bereavement; Paula Stephens of Crazy Good Grief. I am now in graduate school studying to become a grief counselor. I couldn't pursue something like this if I didn't have these peer mentors, and countless more, to look up to.
—Jenny Gibson Robbins, author of www.HeWoreFlannel.com

At the age of thirty-one, the unimaginable happened. It was a normal day—until it wasn't. My boyfriend of four years, the man with whom I was building a future, died in a work-related accident. I was alone. Sure, I had the support of friends and family, but not a single one of them could relate to this experience. I knew if I was going to survive, I had to find someone that understood. Hesitantly, I searched the internet for the words "young widow" and found Soaring Spirits International, a nonprofit that provides peer support and mentoring for widows of all ages and marital statuses. I was connected to several different unofficial peer mentors. People I could call at all hours of the night, people I could ask about their experiences, people who told me I wasn't going crazy when I couldn't remember where I put my toothbrush. I will always be grateful for the time, wisdom, and kindness they shared with me. Finding support from people that understand your loss . . . it can be lifesaving, even when you don't feel strong enough to live.
—Jenny

My son Trent passed away five days after he turned twenty. It sent me on a search for natural ways to help me heal. I saw a grief counselor, I found a medium, and I rebalanced my chakras through Reiki. I soon found Crazy Good Grief on Facebook and began talking to other grieving parents. I must say, this still gives me the most healing—connecting with peers, others who know the feeling of a broken heart, spirit, and life. Sharing my story over and over and listening to other stories showed me I wasn't alone. I still keep in touch with several of our original "warrior moms and dads" (what we call each other). I am now living my life and able to be a mom to my older son and a mema to my beautiful grandchildren. I believe we get better or we get bitter. And I want to be better.

—Kerri

RESOURCES

If you would like to integrate peer mentors into your healing journey, here are some resources that can help you get started.

Books

From Grief to Growth: 5 Essential Elements of Action to Give Your Grief Purpose & Grow From Your Experience by Paula Stephens

Radical Survivor: One Woman's Path Through Life, Love, and Uncharted Tragedy by Dr. Nancy Saltzman

The Rules of Inheritance: A Memoir by Claire Bidwell Smith

Permission to Mourn: A New Way to do Grief by Tom Zuba

Organizations

American Widow Project
www.americanwidowproject.org
Peer mentoring for military widows.

The Compassionate Friends
www.compassionatefriends.org
Peer mentoring for child-loss community.

Soaring Spirits International
www.soaringspirits.org
Peer mentoring for worldwide widowed community.

NOTES

Use this section for any notes related to peer mentors.

_____

_____

_____

_____

_____

_____

_____

_____

_____

_____

_____

_____

_____

_____

_____

_____

_____

_____

"It's not one huge step that promotes healing . . .
it's many intentional single small steps."

QUOTES THAT INSPIRE HOPE

Hope is being able to see that there is light
despite all of the darkness.

—DESMOND TUTU

HEALING POWER

My current therapist is one part brilliant counselor and one part inspired artist. Walking into her office feels almost like stepping into a child's playhouse. You know you are there to do adult work, but along the way there is comfort, color, and ease. Huge cheerful pillows sit on her fluffy couch, shelves of enticing trinkets wait to be used in therapeutic sand trays, weekend retreat schedules hang from beautifully beaded bracelets, two friendly dogs provide animal assisted therapy, and handmade bookmarks gleam with streaming ribbons and inspirational quotes. I am always drawn to the bookmarks while I sit in the waiting room. "At any given moment you have the power to say: this is NOT how my story is going to end," one reads. Another says, "Dear Child of Mine, I do not need your help today. Love, God." And, "Hope is the feeling that the feeling you have isn't permanent." Those quotes resonated with me the first day I entered the office. They gave me hope.

One day, after flipping through the bookmarks and realizing I needed to take home some hopeful quotes of my own, the therapist handed me a stack of twenty-five small cards. The colorful cards were hooked together by a shiny silver ring. And each card, written by hand and beaded with tiny stick-on jewels, contained a quote. They were beautiful! But I didn't like them. Most of them were untrue.

I am at ease with others. I relate with comfort and joy. (Nope! I can't relate to most people anymore and feel like an alien.)

I am human and accept mortality as a natural part of life and my human experience. (Ugh! Brent was supposed to live until he was ninety-nine and I am sick to death of dealing with death.)

I wake each day refreshed and with vitality. I have energy for myself and family. (Ha! I'm not sleeping at all, I'm too exhausted to brush my teeth, and my son is lucky if he gets breakfast.)

Then I learned about the power of affirmations—words, quotes, and phrases that, when read and said, can effect positive change in our conscious and subconscious mind. Affirmations can help to inspire, motivate, heal, and provide hope that we can survive (and eventually thrive). Once I learned about the power of affirmations, I began listening to audio affirmations, reading aloud affirming quotes that friends sent, and wandering into my bedroom multiple times a day to stare and recite from the large bulletin board I nailed to my bedroom wall. The bulletin board is full of quotes, images, photos, buttons, and symbols that inspire hope. My simple, all-time favorite is by Winston Churchill: "Never, never, never give up."

I wonder if quotes that inspire hope might assist you on your healing journey.

Why consider quotes that inspire hope?

Reading and verbalizing positive quotes, statements of affirmation, and hope-filled pieces of writing has a direct connection to overall health and well-being. Since positive and negative thoughts produce corresponding reactions in the body, happier thoughts produce happier hormones, such as dopamine and serotonin. Reviewing quotes that inspire hope interrupts the negative thinking and negative feeling brain pathways that are associated with symptoms of grief and trauma.

How do quotes that inspire hope promote healing?
- By reducing the occurrence of negative, anxious, or fearful thoughts
- By rewiring the brain to strengthen positive neural pathways
- By increasing feelings of hope, control, independence, coping, and calmness

SINGLE SMALL STEPS

If you would like to integrate quotes that inspire hope into your healing journey, here are some single small step suggestions you may be able to use.

Is there one that resonates with you?

1) **Print**: Search books, magazines, articles, and the internet for quotes that instill hope in you. Tape printed copies to your mirrors, doors, dashboard, and desk.

2) **Stick**: Use sticky notes to jot down hopeful quotes. Stick the quotes on your refrigerator or bathroom mirror. Read the quotes aloud as you spend time in that room.

3) **Carry**: Keep a notebook or journal full of hopeful quotes. Carry the notebook with you and review it in the car, on the bus, while eating meals, and before you fall asleep.

4) Listen: Download guided affirmations onto your device, listen to affirmation videos on YouTube, or find guided affirmation CDs at the store.

5) Review: Identify passages, poems, letters, stories, or cards that resonate with you and provide a sense of hope. Put them in a place where you can review them often.

Here is one single small step I may be able to take in the future:

_____

_____

_____

_____

_____

_____

_____

HEALING STORIES

My dad died in a car crash when I was five. I am ten now and I don't remember too much about that time, but I do remember my mom and her friends reading me lots of kid's books about life and death. I recommend The Fall of Freddie the Leaf *to other people. It's about a leaf who goes through his lifetime hanging on a tree with his leaf friends. There is a wise leaf named Daniel who talks about life and death. The quotes I liked best from Daniel are: "It's time for the leaves to change their home. Some people call it to die," and "We all fear what we don't know, Freddie. It's natural. Yet you were not afraid when Spring became Summer. You were not afraid when Summer became Fall. They were natural changes. Why should you be afraid of the season of death?"*
—Jacob, age ten

A few years before Dad's gradual decline (both physical and mental) became evident, I had already begun my own path of spiritual renewal and rebirth, and I was able to spend a significant amount of time with Dad—more concentrated and quality time than we had ever had together. Dad was always more faith-filled than I, but he didn't push his beliefs or let his discontent in my choices openly affect our relationship. In one of our conversations, he shared a letter he had sent (as chairman of a capital campaign) to his fellow church parishioners. His sentiments have stayed with me, and strengthened me, through his passing and the deaths of my son-in-law and my sister. I was taken by the strength and message in Dad's words when I read them, and I've kept a copy of this letter on my desk for years.
—Steve

Our beloved firstborn daughter, Eunice, collapsed at work, and in a couple of hours we lost her. As I've walked this journey, I have become fascinated with the writings of poets from various times and cultures. Some of their poems transcend time, some are ancient, and some are more recent, but I feel accompanied in the sense of knowing that grief—and longing for what we love—is as inherent to the human soul as the stars are to the sky. These poems have given me inspiration and hope:

1) *"There is a sacredness in tears.*
They are not the mark of weakness, but of power.
They speak more eloquently than ten thousand tongues.
They are messengers of overwhelming grief . . .
and unspeakable love."
—Washington Irving

2) *"When you go through a hard period,*
When everything seems to oppose you,
When you feel you cannot even bear one more minute,
NEVER GIVE UP!
Because it is the time and place that the course will divert!"
—Jalaluddin Rumi

—Claudia

RESOURCES

If you would like to integrate quotes that inspire hope into your healing journey, here are some resources that can help you get started.

Audio and CD
Affirmations for Mind, Body and Spirit by Belleruth Naparstek

Feeling Fine Affirmations by Louise Hay

Books
365 Days of Wonder: A Quote for Every Day of the Year About Courage, Friendship, Love, and Kindness by R. J. Palacio

Greatest Inspirational Quotes: 365 Days to More Happiness Success Motivation by Dr. Joe Tichio

Positive Affirmations: Daily Affirmations for Attracting Health, Healing, and Happiness Into Your Life by Rachel Robins

You Can Heal Your Heart by Louise Hay and David Kessler

Cards
My Daily Affirmation Cards by Cheryl Richardson
(deck of fifty affirmation cards)

Power Thought Cards by Louise Hay (deck of sixty-four affirmation cards)

NOTES

Use this section for any notes related to quotes that inspire hope.

_____

_____

_____

_____

_____

_____

_____

_____

_____

_____

_____

_____

_____

_____

_____

_____

_____

_____

"It's not one huge step that promotes healing . . .
it's many intentional single small steps."

R

RIGHT-BRAIN RELEASE

*Creativity healed me. I don't know that
I could think of any word that I get more
inspired by than the word healing.*

—SARK

HEALING POWER

When I was a social work intern, I accrued some of my supervised counseling hours by working at a community center for survivors of domestic violence and sexual assault. It was a wonderfully supportive, comprehensive organization for the clients. It was also an incredible training facility for those of us studying to be social workers, marriage and family therapists, and psychologists. At one staff meeting, fifteen of us sat around a large tray of sand while our supervisor introduced the guest speaker, a Sandtray therapist. *A what?* I wondered.

The therapist explained to us that when people are in traumatizing, terrifying situations (such as our clients), the left side of the brain often shuts down, leaving them temporarily unable to apply verbal expression, logic, reason, or order. She told us one of the best ways to assist traumatized people in their healing is to give them ways to use the nonverbal side of their brain (the right hemisphere) where color, sound, music, art, imagery, light, smell, intuition, and imagery are stored.

She opened a large suitcase full of small trinkets, symbols, and statues—mini balls, tiny people, pyramids, airplanes, cars, trash cans, feathers, necklaces, army men, angels, pinwheels, monsters, butterflies, coffins, dogs, mermaids—and asked for a volunteer so she could demonstrate how this therapy session might look with a client. She wanted an intern to choose five to six items from the suitcase before returning to the Sandtray. Seemed simple enough.

So I raised my hand.

Little did I know that, fifteen years later, I would need to use this type of right-brain release for my own too-traumatized-to-speak, I-have-no-words, this-horrific-situation-is-beyond-the-enormity-of-anything-I-can-comprehend, how-did-my-husband-go-missing-for-two-weeks-and-then-die, this-must-be-happening-to-someone-else life. I snooped around the community and eventually got a referral to a Sand-play therapist (just slightly different from Sandtray therapy) in my area who works with veterans, widows, parents whose children have died, and victims of sexual assault. As mentioned in the chapter on counseling, I have done much right-brain grief and trauma healing by working in a sandbox with hundreds of tiny figures.

SoulCollage is another powerful right-brain process, but one that was very new to me. Participants are invited to discover their own inner wisdom, direction, and healing by making a deck of collaged cards, a single card at a time. In one SoulCollage session, my workshop group was given scissors, glue, one small cardstock board, and an invitation to quietly browse through images from various magazines. We were instructed to paste any three images "that call to you" onto our card—one background (any scene), one subject (person or animal), and one embellishment (any thing). The background I chose was a forest of trees with bright sunlight filtering through the dark canopy. The subject I chose was a young woman who sat casually in an aqua-blue chair and focused intently on her hand of playing cards. The embellishment I chose was of red-hot, swirling lava. So I had just put together my first SoulCollage card, but I had no idea what it meant. The facilitator then gave us a sheet of paper with five prompts, which we were to answer in a quick two minutes. "No thinking, just go with your gut," she instructed.

Here are the prompts and my answers:

#	Prompt	Answer
1	*I am the one who:*	is angry and confused but dressed and ready nonetheless to figure out this new deck of cards.
2	*I am appearing for you now because:*	there is light and new lava land amidst the anger.
3	*I am here to remind you:*	you will feel and see light again, have a seat and no need to rush.
4	*Please notice:*	the sunrays still make their way into the dark forest and volcano anger does make new land.
5	*I am named:*	DETERMINATION.

I burst into tears when I started sharing my answers with the SoulCollage group. Until that moment, I had no idea the young woman in the picture represented me. The dark forest represented my grief and trauma; the lava represented my anger; and the sunrays and volcano represented hope, healing, and growth. This right-brained activity—utilizing symbolic color, imagery, light, creativity, and intuition—enabled me to learn so much about my internal rebuilding process. To this day, my SoulCollage card sits in clear view on my bathroom countertop, reminding me to be determined, intentional, and optimistic while playing the new hand of cards I have been dealt.

I wonder if right-brain release might assist you on your healing journey.

Why consider right-brain release?

Traumatic experiences are sometimes impossible to talk about, and talking is a left-brained activity. When there are "no words" to express life-altering situations, the right side of the brain must be accessed and utilized. This is where images, emotions, and body sensations are stored. The right hemisphere tends to be creative, nonlinear, irrational, intuitive, relational, and holistic, and this is often where grief and trauma healing can begin. Music, art, movement, sand, symbol, and imagery can be highly effective in accessing the right side of the brain, which in turn leads to more comprehensive healing.

How does right-brain release promote healing?
- By providing access to psychological healing through nonverbal means
- By increasing awareness of innate internal coping mechanisms
- By allowing the subconscious mind to unlock the door to expression
- By enabling trauma resolution in connecting right and left side of the brain

SINGLE SMALL STEPS

If you would like to integrate right-brain release into your healing journey, here are some single small step suggestions you may be able to use.

Is there one that resonates with you?

1) **Play in the Sand**: Work with a Sandplay or Sandtray therapist in your area.

2) **See Your Soul**: Find a SoulCollage workshop, retreat, or training program in your community.

3) **Imagine the Possibilities**: Start browsing, cutting, and pasting images of your own.

4) **Unlock Your Mind**: Look for classes and workshops that focus on healing through music, art, symbolic imagery, or movement.

5) **Get Creative**: Ease the mind with meditative coloring books, clay, paint, or kinetic sand.

Here is one single small step I may be able to take in the future:

_____

_____

_____

_____

_____

_____

_____

HEALING STORIES

Art found me during the darkest period of my life. I had recently lost my father, was newly divorced, and had just gotten sober. Grief about my father and my old life coupled with shame about my drinking nearly overwhelmed me. That's when a friend asked me to take an art class with her. I had nothing to lose. That first class changed my life. Swirling paint across a canvas felt free and limitless. Finding images to collage offered me expression of feelings I was unaware I had. Gluing broken tiles into a cohesive mosaic taught me that there is a perfect fit for every piece no matter how broken. Art became my voice. Today, I never know what to expect when I sit down to paint, but I know that it will be authentic and healing. Art is very meditative. Art delivers me to a place free of time and space where I am one with my creative energy and its source and at peace with myself and the world. That is true healing.
—Ann

I have always played classical music on the flute, and my husband was always so supportive of my passion to make beauty in the world. When he died suddenly in an accident, we had been married for twenty-five years, with four children ages ten, twelve, fifteen, and seventeen. In utter shock, I played at his funeral service. It was the only way to express myself. In the long and lonely days of early grief, I took out my old music from childhood—Irish music with its songs of loss, Bach sonatas, Telemann—to retreat and try to find myself again. Slowly, I came out of my solitude and rejoined my community orchestra. Then a few friends asked if we could finally start a woodwind quintet: the Janus Quintet, named for the Roman god of doorways and transitions.
—Monika

A few years after my father's too-early death, my family made our way to the Adirondack Mountains, visiting for the first time the famous "Slanty Shanty" ramshackle cabin of my father's childhood stories. It was still standing in the woods, despite its pronounced slantiness. The nearby rustic resort where we stayed had a woodshop and a kind woodworker. Together, we found a branch of birchwood, and he helped me craft a small, simple sculpture of a stand of three birch trees, leaning over and across each other as the trees had done in the woods. That trip to the Adirondacks and the process of creating that sculpture was a healing one for me, physically connecting me to that place my father had loved and to the particular spot that was now his final resting place. Back at my home in Seattle, the sculpture (as well as a painting of birch trees I later purchased) helps me to continue to feel connected to him.

—Kathy

RESOURCES

If you would like to integrate right-brain release into your healing journey, here are some resources that can help you get started.

Audio and CD
Vibrational Sound Healing by Andrew Weil

Handy to Have at Home
Art supplies (blank sketchbooks, clay, colored pencils, crayons, paint)
Coloring books (doodle books, inspirational words, mandala designs, meditative shapes)
Illustrated Discovery Journal (blank notebooks, glue, magazines, scissors)
Kinetic sand

Organizations
American Art Therapy Association
www.arttherapy.org
Facts, frequently asked questions, and tools to find an art therapist near you.

American Music Therapy Association
www.musictherapy.org
Facts, frequently asked questions, and tools to find a music therapist near you.

Sandplay Therapists of America
www.sandplay.org
Events, trainings, and tools to find a Sandplay therapist near you.

SoulCollage®
www.soulcollage.com
www.kaleidosoul.com
Blog, newsletter, resources, retreats, trainings, and SoulCollage workshops near you.

NOTES

Use this section for any notes related to right-brain release.

_____

_____

_____

_____

_____

_____

_____

_____

_____

_____

_____

_____

_____

_____

_____

_____

_____

_____

_____

*"It's not one huge step that promotes healing . . .
it's many intentional single small steps."*

S

SLIDING INTO EXERCISE

*It does not matter how slowly you go as
long as you do not stop.*

—CONFUCIUS

HEALING POWER

My childhood home was situated in a small residential community at the top of a hilly street, joined by two cul-de-sacs full of rowdy kids. After school, on weekends, and throughout summertime, the neighborhood boys flew down the street on anything with wheels—bikes, skateboards, roller skates, and wagons—launching themselves into the air with homemade ramps. I was a typical tomboy and loved this kind of fun. One day, six of us decided to make a catamaran with our skateboards. We lined up our boards facing each other—three in one line and three in another—then sat down with legs outstretched onto the person sitting across from us. Once lined up, we released our hands from the ground and started moving straight down the hill. Fast. To steer the catamaran, one side of us kids leaned in while the other side leaned out. Somehow we always made it to the bottom of the hill without crashing. How fun was this?! So five boys and one girl ran up and rolled down the hill about seventy-five times that day. Huffing and puffing, hearts pounding and lungs bursting. This was my introduction to hours of exercise. And I loved it.

All the "accidental exercise" I did as child continued intentionally in my adulthood. I enjoyed soccer, baseball, softball, rollerblading, swimming, hiking, biking, rowing, paddling, surfing, running, and weight lifting. After Brent's death, when absolutely nothing made sense to me, exercise was the only thing that did. Exercise helped me to feel "normal" in my completely new, upside-down world. Even though I felt immobilized, even though I couldn't breathe, I somehow knew I had to *move*. I reached for anything that helped me feel better. I needed endorphins.

At first, sick with despair, I aimlessly walked the hills of the neighborhood.

After that, I got into the pool and swam as I cried. I went to the mountains and hiked as I cried. I dragged myself to a local lake and rollerbladed as I cried. I headed to nearby shorelines and kayaked as I cried. I stood up in the lagoon and paddleboarded as I cried. I reentered the gym and lifted weights as I cried.

But when I joined the gym's small group training class for women, I stopped crying. I looked around. The fitness trainer was a beautiful, motivated, solid-muscled leader whose mother had died of an autoimmune disease when the trainer was pregnant with her first child. The blond next to me was a healthy, hopeful, determined woman whose husband had died of cancer, leaving her with two young children to raise. The brunette was a graceful, soulful, kind woman, and her two grown children died at two different times in two different accidents. And here they were. Exercising. These women showed me how to stretch, lift, pull, push, jump, squat, sweat, swing, and move my way back to life.

I wonder if sliding into exercise might assist you on your healing journey.

Why consider sliding into exercise?

Exercise has long been prescribed by doctors to ease the negative effects of stress and depression. Body-based movement also helps alleviate a myriad of grief and trauma symptoms, such as sleep disruption, appetite change, muscle tension, and fatigue. There are so many exercise options to choose from to keep moving, and they can be done solo (walking, swimming, yoga), with a partner (dancing, hiking, kayaking), or in a group (soccer, cycling, fitness class).

How does sliding into exercise promote healing?
- By releasing "feel-good" endorphins into the body's system
- By decreasing isolation (through joining a league, taking a class, or working out with a buddy)
- By reducing symptoms of anxiety and depression
- By stimulating the growth of new brain cells that sharpen concentration and memory skills

SINGLE SMALL STEPS

If you would like to integrate sliding into exercise into your healing journey, here are some single small step suggestions you may be able to use.

Is there one that resonates with you?

1) **Stay In**: If you can't get out of the house, find an exercise video, YouTube channel, or piece of stationary exercise equipment that motivates you to move.

2) **Go Out**: Lace up your sneakers and walk a local path, trail, hill, sidewalk, or track.

3) **Pick a Partner**: Enlist a friend or colleague to be your exercise buddy. Choose days and times that work for you, keep your scheduled appointments, and motivate each other.

4) **Join a Team**: Join a community league or exercise with a "fundraise for a cure" group.

5) **Meet Up**: Check out Meetup.com for hundreds of exercise groups worldwide.

Here is one single small step I may be able to take in the future:

_____

_____

_____

_____

_____

_____

_____

HEALING STORIES

My husband, and best friend, was a marathon runner who also loved rock climbing and hiking. He had a way of pulling you into his enthusiasm, which is why I started running half marathons. On days when I don't run or exercise, I find myself crying a lot more as those days seems long, lonely, and full of obstacles. Once I push myself out and get my blood pumping, it almost feels like my husband is right there with me. He's the wind blowing into my face to cool me off, and he's the wind from behind that makes me go faster. No more whining, either! I'm just happy to be out there. After my run, my head is clear, and I'm confident that I can get through the day. Running has given me a positive attitude; running is my best friend.
—Heidi

My twin sons, Mark and Eric, were born medically fragile and lived with cerebral palsy, complete with two feeding tubes, two wheelchairs, oxygen, and speech computers. Mark passed away at age twenty-one and Eric died seventeen months later. As a strategy to make sense of my life and figure out how to recover from grief, I took yoga teacher training (YTT). While never intending to teach, I knew I had to move and that it would be a safe place for peace and growth. Much to my surprise, my recovery tool has grown into so much more. I describe YTT as exercise, wisdom, spirituality, anatomy, and quantum physics! It's been a place to rebuild my broken heart and exhausted body; to learn to rethink when my grief brain has short-circuited; and to feel the energy of pranayama, *which can be interpreted as a life force or the Holy Spirit. Movement through YTT lets me know that my sons are in a good place and that I can find happiness again.*
—Kelly

When I was fifty-six, one earthquake after another began to shake my life. My mother was diagnosed with Alzheimer's disease; my father and brother both died from cancer; my children moved cross-country, leaving me with an empty nest; my sister and her daughter became estranged from me; and I experienced a crisis of faith. I knew the first key to moving through my grieving process was to stay engaged. For me, it was continuing to exercise. I played tennis socially and competitively, took regular Pilates classes, paddleboarded, and walked with friends. When exercising outdoors, I more intensely noticed the colors of nature, the heat of the sun and the chill of the ocean, the sound of the birds, and the frolicking of seals and dolphins. Slowly things began returning to normal and my grief was not as painful. My appreciation of exercise, loved ones, and the natural world is now greater than ever—I seem to savor each moment a little more than before.

—Mary

RESOURCES

If you would like to integrate sliding into exercise into your healing journey, here are some resources that can help you get started.

Books

You Are Your Own Gym: The Bible of Bodyweight Exercises
by Mark Lauren and Joshua Clark

Spark: The Revolutionary New Science of Exercise and the Brain
by John Ratey

Cards

Yoga Cards by WorkoutLabs
A deck of over 50 flashcards incorporating yoga poses, breathing exercises, and meditation forms.

Yoga Pretzels by Tara Guber and Leah Kalish
A deck of 50 jumbo illustrated flashcards with yoga activities for children and adults.

Handy to Have at Home

BOSU® Balance Trainer
www.bosu.com
Exercise clips, equipment, and DVDs about training with the BOSU® ("Both Sides Up") ball.

Foam Roller
www.foam-roller.com
Products, educational tools, and information on the benefits of using foam rollers for exercise and muscle massage.

Stability Exercise Ball
www.ball-exercises.com
Equipment, exercises, and various workouts using a stability ball.

TRX Suspension Training Band
www.trxtraining.com
Articles, equipment, and videos about exercising with the TRX band.

<u>Organizations</u>
Brilliant Body and Mind
by Tori Brillantes
www.facebook.com/brilliantbodyandmind
Inspiration, motivation, and videos about solo and group exercise at any age.

Meetup
www.meetup.com
Find fun indoor and outdoor exercise groups in your area.

One Fit Widow
www.onefitwidow.com
Blog, exercise coaching, nutrition, and fitness tips.

Team in Training
www.teamintraining.org
Train to walk, run, or cycle while raising funds with the Leukemia & Lymphoma Society.

NOTES

Use this section for any notes related to sliding into exercise.

_____

_____

_____

_____

_____

_____

_____

_____

_____

_____

_____

_____

_____

_____

_____

_____

_____

"It's not one huge step that promotes healing . . .
it's many intentional single small steps."

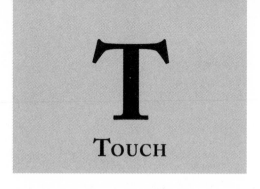

TOUCH

To touch is to give life.

—MICHELANGELO

HEALING POWER

Several times a year in San Diego, the warm Santa Ana winds blow in from the desert and render the city unseasonably hot. People flock to the beaches in droves for relief from the high temperatures, and I am usually part of the crowd. A few years ago, I was meeting a friend there whom I hadn't seen in months, and was looking forward to standing in the cool water. Since childhood, the beach had always been a calming, centering spot for me, and in the eighteen months that Brent had been gone, I was spending more and more time there. I felt as if the ocean were the only place vast enough to hold my tears, heartbreak, emptiness, confusion, rage, anxiety, fear, and overall state of not-caring-about-anything-at-all-because-I-died-inside-when-Brent-died-so-what-was-the-point. I was a walking, talking, semifunctioning shell of a person.

As I poked a toe into the water, my friend came strolling along the sand. As he approached me, he smiled, said *"Hey! How are you?"* and then picked me up off the ground to give me a huge bear hug. At five foot nine, I am not a tiny female. But my friend is six foot six, weighs about 280 pounds, and used to play football, so I guess he can pick up just about anybody. We spent the next few hours in the ocean with hordes of other people. We talked about life, I dove under the waves, and he played "toss Susan around in the water like a football." Being thrown around in the ocean reminded me of fun-loving times spent roughhousing with my older brother, playing full-contact sports with college buddies, piggybacking through rivers with strong husband transport, and wrestling on the bed with an energetic young son. "Play" for me had always included lots of physical touch.

Physical. Touch. Brent had taken my daily dose of physical touch with him when he departed. The morning hug, the evening kiss, the hand hold, the foot massage, the hair comb, the playful carry, the sexual intimacy, the hundreds of casual touches received without a thought—all of that had been yanked away.

So that day at the beach, after my huge friend threw me around for the last time and sauntered away, I felt like I had been stunned with a Taser. I sat down in my beach chair and unpacked my lunch while my body steadily hummed in a comforting but slightly unfamiliar way. I was confused. *What is happening to me?* Eventually I realized what was going on: my five senses were kicking back in. I was slowly seeing the beauty of the Pacific Ocean, slowly hearing the waves crashing onto the shore, slowly smelling the salty ocean air, slowly tasting the sandwich I brought to eat, slowly feeling the warm sand between my toes.

I was returning to the land of the living.

I wouldn't just exist anymore.

Touch brought me back to life.

I wonder if incorporating touch might assist you on your healing journey.

Why consider adding touch?

Touch is a basic human need that can lessen or change when a loved one dies. Studies have shown that touch-deprived infants have a variety of health issues stemming from their lack of tactile attention, which is why many hospital programs enlist volunteers to simply hold babies. While on the grief and trauma healing journey, the touch factor can be increased by the help of friends, family, pets, licensed body workers, and certified massage therapists.

How does touch promote healing?

- By inducing oxytocin, the "bonding hormone" that is known for reducing stress
- By lowering stress level, heart rate, and blood pressure
- By strengthening the immune system
- By easing symptoms of depression and anxiety

SINGLE SMALL STEPS

If you would like to integrate touch into your healing journey, here are some single small step suggestions you may be able to use.

Is there one that resonates with you?

1) **Hug**: Hug friends and family more. (The hug will always come back to you!)

2) **Hold**: Hold babies, children, family members, friends, and animals more.

3) Hands: Enjoy touch on hands, feet, and hair by seeing a professional hairdresser, barber, manicurist, pedicurist, or reflexologist.

4) Harness: Harness the healing power of touch by treating yourself to a massage.

5) Help: Help yourself and others by volunteering to connect with hands and hearts at hospitals, daycare centers, animal shelters, or retirement homes.

Here is one single small step I may be able to take in the future:

_____

_____

_____

_____

_____

_____

_____

HEALING STORIES

I read some years ago that in some primitive tribes, when someone committed an unforgivable crime, no one spoke to that individual ever again and the person eventually died from lack of human contact. Becoming an instant widow or widower is akin to that. The person who was the complement and responder to your daily communication is no longer there; all the touch you received from them is absent. It's like you're floating. When Larry died, I was given a massage as a present. I used to regard massage as an unaffordable luxury, but the physicality of it helped bring me back to humanity. Also, any clothing I buy now must provide comfort; a soft jacket or sweater can feel like an arm around me. Oh, and sheets! Having cuddly fleece sheets is very soothing—the tactile effect makes sleeping alone much more bearable. I know touch has always been important to me. I now use anything that soothes me.
—Nancy

I lost my mother to cancer when I was eighteen. My grandfather died a month later. My father died in my early twenties. I've learned that as we move through the seasons of our lives, we mourn and grieve the loss of loved ones, our past selves, and the feeling of security knowing we are safe and loved. I am now in my fifties and a holistic health practitioner, using healing arts like massage to work with people who know grief and loss intimately. Massage is a physical act of kindness, a connection that is instinctual, surpassing language. It silently works, calming fears and soothing worries layer by layer, as you drift deeply into an alpha state while lifting tension. When clarity begins, you see a way to do something better, you resolve a problem, and you know there is hope after all.
—Kathleen

Our girls were born premature. Elina was stillborn, Signe died after eight days, and Ines died after seven weeks. When we were at the hospital with Ines, my husband and I did "kangaroo-care." We held her skin to skin; the nurses lifted her from the incubator to us, we took turns holding her for up to eight to ten hours

per day. That's one thing I like to get lost in, the memory of how it felt to hold Ines, the memory of her body, skin to skin with my body. When our girls died, the hospital staff made plaster casts of the girls' hands and feet. For a long, long time, when I went to bed at night, I touched the plaster casts hung beside my bed. I touched the hands and feet of my children, sort of. I touched the last thing they had touched. I believe the memory of touch stays on for a long, long time. I hope forever.
—Camilla

RESOURCES

If you would like to integrate touch into your healing journey, here are some resources that can help you get started.

Articles
25 Reasons to Get a Massage by American Massage Therapy Association

The Health Benefits of Hugging by Stacy Colino in *U.S. News & World Report*

Books
Touch: The Power of Human Connection by Samantha Hess

Touch: The Science of the Hand, Heart, and Mind by David Linden

Handy to Have at Home
Hand-Held Massage Stick
www.thestick.com
Instruction and video on how and why to use The Stick as "a toothbrush for muscles."

Organizations
American Massage Therapy Association
www.amtamassage.org
Research links and tools to find a massage therapist in your area.

Healing Touch Program
www.healingtouchprogam.com
Classes, resources, and tools to find a Healing Touch practitioner in your area.

NOTES

Use this section for any notes related to touch.

_____

_____

_____

_____

_____

_____

_____

_____

_____

_____

_____

_____

_____

_____

_____

_____

_____

_____

_____

_____

*"It's not one huge step that promotes healing . . .
it's many intentional single small steps."*

U

UTILIZING NATURE

*In every walk with nature one receives far
more than he seeks.*

—JOHN MUIR

HEALING POWER

Birthdays were always a big deal in my family of origin. And since my birthday fell during summer vacation, we celebrated all day long. In the morning, my mom piled my friends into the station wagon and headed to the beach for the day. At the shore, we spilled out of the car like dozens of little clowns with too much gear: snorkels and masks, boogie boards and buckets, sunscreen and shovels, towels and Tonka Trucks, coolers and chairs. At lunchtime, the birthday party brigade barely stopped to eat because we were too busy riding the waves, having relay races on the sand, jump roping with thick strands of kelp, decorating sand castles with seaweed and rocks, and collecting sand crabs. In late afternoon, when it was time to pack up and head home for cake and ice cream, my mom stood on the shoreline motioning us to get out of the water. More times than not, my brother and I lay flat on our boogie boards, ducking behind the waves, pretending not to see her. We wanted to stay! We loved the water. We loved the sunshine. We loved nature.

It's no surprise, then, that I married another nature nut. Brent grew up hiking, skiing, and fishing in the mountains of the Pacific Northwest and integrated surfing, sailing, and kayaking after moving to California as a young adult. Much of my past worldly relationship with him was nurtured outdoors (our first daylong date was composed of an eight-mile hike in the mountains followed by a sunset walk on the beach) and much of my current spiritual relationship with him is still being nurtured outdoors. Being outdoors always calmed us, centered us, and allowed us to listen to each other.

The first year of missing him, I walked a local trail. A warm wind came across the hills and I felt his presence. "Babe, I'm still with you," he expressed. But I was too grief-stricken to agree.

The second year of missing him, I kayaked on the ocean. A pod of dolphins appeared and I felt his presence. "Sue, I'm always with you in the things we love," he reminded. But I was too angry to believe.

The third year of missing him, I paddleboarded in the lagoon. The water was calm and I felt his presence. "Hey, maybe it's time to go get my surfboard from your mom's garage? I think your new paddleboard needs a partner," he suggested. But I was too lonely to comply.

The fourth year of missing him, I hiked a rocky mountain. Out of nowhere, amidst the brown desert landscape, a bright-blue bird landed on a tree branch in front of me and chirped loudly. I felt his presence. "Hellooo! I'm stiiiiiiiill here!" he joked.

I finally acquiesced.

"Ok. Fine," I said to the bird. "You're here. I get it now. Well, please stay with me, mister, because I have a lot of things I'm going to need help with!"

I wonder if utilizing nature might assist you on your healing journey.

Why consider utilizing nature?

Studies show that people who spend more time outside in nature have a more positive outlook on life. Interacting with trees, sun, sand, water, and fresh air is especially important for those living with grief and trauma. New studies in "grounding" or "earthing" show that by taking off shoes and reconnecting with nature, there is a significant reduction of pain, stress, and inflammation in the body. Grounding mats are becoming popular to sleep on because the body soaks up the earth's natural healing electrons while dozing at night.

How does utilizing nature promote healing?

- By reducing symptoms of stress, anxiety, and depression
- By increasing production and absorption of natural vitamin D
- By enhancing brain functioning and cognitive ability
- By improving overall health, energy levels, and ability to sleep

SINGLE SMALL STEPS

If you would like to integrate utilizing nature into your healing journey, here are some single small step suggestions you may be able to use.

Is there one that resonates with you?

1) **Earth**: Get grounded. Go barefoot whenever possible on the grass, sand, or soil.

2) **Air**: Head for the hills. Walk, hike, or run near the trees for a dose of fresh oxygen.

3) **Fire**: Use the sun. Head outdoors with your book, meal, hammock, work, or sunscreen.

4) **Water**: Stay wet. Spend time in, on, or near a local pool, pond, river, lake, or ocean.

Here is one single small step I may be able to take in the future:

_____

_____

_____

_____

_____

_____

_____

HEALING STORIES

After the numbness and sadness started to subside, I needed to redefine who I was and what I enjoyed doing (instead of being the spouse and caregiver of my husband). It was a time of reflection. I remembered how much I loved sailing and searched out a Meetup group. I've made some wonderful connections through this venue, and I find peace when we turn off the motor, the wind powers us through the water, the swells rock me, and the water slaps on the boat sides. It's my happy place.
—Lori

A few years ago, I experienced a trauma that reopened wounds I thought had long since healed. My repetitive, obsessive thought was: "I'll never be truly joyful or free from fear—so what's the use of pretending?" I stopped eating except for just enough to sustain energy, and I passively withdrew from family and friends. After a few weeks of this, I found myself in my backyard at sunset, leaning against a huge Monterey pine tree. I stayed there, almost in a trance, for a long time. Strength flowed into me. Something whispered, "Look to the light" and I saw, through a crack in my neighbor's fence, the sparkle of the last sunrays of the day, caught by his small garden fountain. I went to the tree the next day, and the next, and have gone almost every day since—finding light, guidance, and compassion for myself. And deep joy.
—Leigh

When my husband died, we had three children. I was in shock and completely unprepared for what was to follow. I don't really remember the first six months after he died, but later I knew I needed to find something that allowed me a space to clear my head and let my heart feel the loss so I could begin to heal. I have always loved being in and on the water, and one day I saw some people stand-up paddleboarding (SUPing) in the ocean and bay. I knew it was my answer!

It is my place to allow myself to put my stress, troubles, anxieties, pain, and sadness on the paddleboard. Sometimes it's windy and the water is choppy and rough, just like my new normal. And yet if I just persevere, the wind calms, the water becomes smooth, and I can just listen. I leave the water with a sense of peace and a stronger heart.

—Jean

RESOURCES

If you would like to integrate utilizing nature into your healing journey, here are some resources that can help you get started.

Books

Vitamin N: The Essential Guide to a Nature-Rich Life by Richard Louv

Earthing: The Most Important Health Discovery Ever? by Clinton Ober, Stephen Sinatra, and Martin Zucker

Handy to Have at Home

Bare feet
Bird house
Hammock
Plants
Sandbox
Seeds and soil
Walking shoes

Organizations

Meetup
www.meetup.com
Search for nature-based groups, outings, and gatherings in your area. Key words: Bird, Boating, Camping, Flower, Gardening, Hiking, Lake, Ocean, Outdoor, Park, Plant, Picnic, Pond, River, Trail, Walking

National Park Service
www.nps.gov
Plan a park visit, find nature-based events, buy a park pass, get the kids outdoors, and volunteer in the fresh air.

NOTES

Use this section for any notes related to utilizing nature.

_____

_____

_____

_____

_____

_____

_____

_____

_____

_____

_____

_____

_____

_____

_____

_____

_____

_____

_____

"It's not one huge step that promotes healing . . .
it's many intentional single small steps."

VOLUNTEERING

*The best way to find yourself is to lose
yourself in the service of others.*

—MAHATMA GANDHI

HEALING POWER

When I was in my early twenties, I spent quite a bit of time caught up in the angst of what I used to think were life's big questions: *Who am I supposed to be? What is my career path? Where should I live? When will I ever get married? Why is there so much talk about having children? If I have them, how many will I have?* A good friend and mentor—who was much older and wiser than me—sensed my possible slow slide into a state of anxiety. She quickly suggested I come back to volunteer in her kindergarten classroom, where we had taught together years before. The classroom was in a unique school for abused, neglected, and homeless children, and since I knew these kids needed tons of love and support, I acquiesced. I spent two days per week in that classroom for months on end, and as it turned out, the kids were the ones who gave *me* tons of love and support. They guided me back to meaning, wonder, gratitude, and fulfillment.

My mentor knew what I didn't at the time: by helping others, we help ourselves.

Fast-forward nearly twenty years, and I was entering my own child's kindergarten classroom. Two weeks before the start of his school career, we learned his father was dead. I was barely functioning when we went into the classroom for new student orientation. Part of me wanted to run screaming from the room because I couldn't imagine a lifetime of solo parenting through grades K–12. The rest of me wanted to curl up with the kids, books, and beanbags in the Reading Corner and never have to function as a human being again. Instead of living full time in the classroom, however, I started volunteering.

I have been volunteering in my son's classrooms for years now, facilitating reading groups, giving spelling tests, correcting math homework, helping with holiday parties, organizing items in the class store, and boarding buses to chaperone field trips. It's been the perfect deal: I help the teachers; the kids help me. They help me laugh. They help me loosen up. They help me feel better about life, better about living, better about the future, and better about the human capacity for resilience and healing, hope, and love.

One day, while I was sorting through the bookshelf in my son's first-grade classroom, a student came up to me. Her hair was in pigtails, she was missing her two front teeth, and she was wearing a bright pink T-shirt with sparkles. She was very cute. Yet she looked concerned.

"Excuse me, Jacob's Mommy?"

"Hi, Erica," I said. "What's up?"

"Is it true that Jacob's daddy is in Heaven?" she asked boldly.

My stomach lurched. Where was this conversation going? I could barely say Brent's name without completely falling apart, much less have a lengthy conversation about life and death with an innocent child on the floor of her classroom. I braced myself for a million questions for which I had no answers.

"Yes, Erica. That's true. Jacob's dad died," I responded.

"Did he have white hair?" she asked me.

"White hair?" I shook my head. "No. His hair was brown."

"Did he have a wheelchair?" she asked me.

"Wheelchair?" I shook my head again. "No, he didn't have a wheelchair." I must have looked confused.

"So he died, but he wasn't old?" she asked with a furrowed brow.

"Yes," I said. "He died but he wasn't old. He was in a car accident."

"Huh," she said. "Well, that's confusing! I've never heard of *that* before!"

Then she turned on her heel and skipped happily back to her seat.

I almost laughed out loud. So much for the lengthy conversation about life and death!

And then it hit me.

She is confused. She is pondering. She is wondering.

Yet she is happy. Yet she is smiling. Yet she is living.

And that day, while volunteering, I became hopeful that someday I could get to that point too.

Where I may be confused, yet happy.

Where I may be pondering, yet smiling.

Where I may be wondering, yet living.

I wonder if volunteering might assist you on your healing journey.

Why consider volunteering?

There is a growing body of research that indicates volunteering provides mental, physical, and social benefits to all individuals. Those whose lives are being transformed by grief and trauma may choose to channel their pain and struggle into a process of helping others who are on the same journey; take a break from their own pain by assisting with people with a completely different set of life circumstances; or organize a group, class, foundation, or nonprofit organization geared toward bettering the world in some way. Volunteering time, energy, resources, knowledge, and life experience help both the giver and receiver.

How does volunteering promote healing?

- By providing a sense of purpose when life seems out of control
- By increasing community connections and social interactions
- By boosting self-confidence, self-esteem, and life satisfaction
- By promoting physical and emotional health and well-being

SINGLE SMALL STEPS

If you would like to integrate volunteering into your healing journey, here are some single small step suggestions you may be able to use.

Is there one that resonates with you?

1) **In Your Home**: Babysit for a single parent. Watch a friend's pet. Stuff envelopes for a nonprofit organization. Cook a meal for a family in need.

2) **In Your Community**: Visit an elderly neighbor. Sort books at the library. Spend time at an animal shelter. Help elementary school kids learn to read. Help an adult learn to read. Assist in church outreach.

3) **In Your City**: Deliver Meals on Wheels. Fundraise for a cause. Walk a charity 5K. Be a Big Brother or Big Sister. Help kids at Boys and Girls Clubs.

4) **In Your State**: Be a court-appointed advocate for a child in need. Be a campground or park host for a state park. Join an organized crew to maintain state trails, roads, highways, lakes, and riverbeds.

5) **It's Your Choice:** The volunteer list is endless! Start with what brings you a little joy.

Here is one single small step I may be able to take in the future:

_____

_____

_____

_____

_____

_____

_____

HEALING STORIES

Volunteer for a day at school full of first and second graders; it's a guaranteed temporary relief from grief for at least that amount of time. After my wife died, I joined a local elementary school's Watch DOGS program (Dads of Great Students). Watch DOGS is a national program that recruits dads, granddads, uncles, and male role models to work with young kids. I start the day helping the principal direct the incoming student drop-off traffic. Then I work in the classroom with small groups of children on their spelling, math, or reading assignments. The best part is that I was assigned to work in the classroom with my grandkids. I also have lunch with the students and play basketball with them at recess. I end the day by getting my picture taken with the class and it goes up on the Watch DOGS bulletin board. These kids give me both grief relief and faith in the younger generation.
—Mark

At age nineteen, our son Raymond died from an overdose of over-the-counter medicine. Sometime shortly after his death, our family and friends came together and formed the WOLFpack. WOLF stands for Warriors of Life and Family. As a large volunteer group, we work together in memory of RAYMOND to: Raise Awareness for our Youth Making Options and New Decisions. We now volunteer to deal with our own grief while educating the community about the dangers of illicit street drugs and prescription drugs that are found within every home's medicine cabinets. We participated in the Brandywine Out of the Darkness Walk; the national Fed Up! Rally in Washington, DC; Walden Sierra's Labyrinth Walk; Naval Air Station Patuxent River's "First Light" seminar; and a Suicide Prevention Month walk. Forming the WOLFpack has helped in our healing and has allowed us to become more involved in educating and volunteering in the community.
—Ted and Ann

After my wife passed away, I was grasping for something, anything, to help me float. Surfing has always been my "at peace" activity, but surfing alone gave me too much time in between waves to dwell. So, a couple of months after my wife's passing, I decided to volunteer as a surf instructor for veterans recovering from amputations, PTSD, TBI, and other severe injuries. The veterans' willingness to push through their trauma to seek joy in life is the reason why I volunteer as a surf instructor. This surf clinic volunteering works for me because it puts things into perspective, allows me to regain some of my self-esteem, and allows my body and mind to recover by helping these vets in the greatest office in the world: a California beach! When the guys thank me for surf coaching, I respond, "You have no idea what you do for me."

—John

My son, Joshua, died in a car accident at age twenty-two and left his eighteen-month-old son, Gabriel, with my husband and me. We adopted Gabriel and took on the blessing of raising him. Our new life circumstances no longer allow us to go out with friends—we have homework, baths, dinner, stories, and bedtime—so eventually, my husband and I volunteered to be coach and team mom for Gabriel's football team. I soon realized there were three other grandparents on our team that were raising their grandchildren. I started a Facebook page called Grandparents Raising Grandchildren, began a local support group, and am currently writing grants for financial support for Grandfamilies. The grandparents love the constant Facebook support, and the kids have a blast getting together each month. Volunteering is something I do for Josh. It helps others while helping our family.

—Martina

RESOURCES

If you would like to integrate volunteering into your healing journey, here are some resources that can help you get started.

Books

The Lemonade Stand: How to Make a Difference 101 by David Justus

Volunteering: 101 Ways You Can Improve the World and Your Life by Douglas Lawson

Organizations

American Red Cross
www.redcross.org
Search for a wide range of volunteer opportunities in your community.

Big Brothers Big Sisters of America
www.bbbs.org
Become a "Big" for youth in your area who need extra support.

Meals on Wheels America
www.mealsonwheelsamerica.org
Deliver food to seniors who can no longer go to the store or cook for themselves.

Modern Widows Club
www.modernwidowsclub.com
Join a local service chapter to make a global impact.

National Park Service
www.nps.gov
Clear a trail, clean the beach, plant new trees, or restore the dunes in a national park.

NOTES

Use this section for any notes related to volunteering.

_____

_____

_____

_____

_____

_____

_____

_____

_____

_____

_____

_____

_____

_____

_____

_____

_____

_____

*"It's not one huge step that promotes healing . . .
it's many intentional single small steps."*

WESTERN & EASTERN MEDICINE

He who has health has hope; and he who has hope has everything.

—THOMAS CARLYLE

HEALING POWER

When I entered graduate school to study social work, one of the many books I was required to buy was the *Diagnostic and Statistical Manual of Mental Disorders*, otherwise known as the *DSM*. The *DSM* is a handbook published by the American Psychiatric Association, and it is filled with guidelines, descriptions, and symptoms that health care professionals reference when diagnosing patients. I had referred to the *DSM* many times while working with clients as a social worker, but I never had to use this book to investigate my own well-being. One night, sweaty and shaking after being jolted awake from another intense nightmare, I scanned the *DSM* pages marked Post-Traumatic Stress Disorder. I had all the persistent symptoms of PTSD. I needed help.

A week later I found myself sitting in an exam room at the Center for Integrative Medicine, a medical facility where Eastern practitioners meet Western doctors to provide comprehensive care to patients with a wide array of health issues. When the doctor entered the room, I was somewhat taken aback. He had an uncanny resemblance to Dr. Derek Shepherd from *Grey's Anatomy*. But this doctor was not Patrick Dempsey, and this was not prime-time television—although I did feel like I had been thrust into the starring role on a tragic reality show.

The doctor sat down.

"So what brings you in today?"

I sighed. "Well, would you like the long version or the short version?"

"Whichever version you would like to give me," he answered, glancing curiously at the *DSM* held in my hands.

"Ok," I started. "The short version. My husband died in a car accident seven months ago. He was missing for weeks before they found his body. We have a five-year-old son. I am a social worker. I have PTSD. I have insomnia, nightmares, and flashbacks, and I wake up nightly in a cold sweat with my heart pounding. My neck hurts. My back hurts. My jaw hurts. My head hurts. I have a constant eye twitch. I can't breathe. I've been constipated for seven months. I have no appetite. I am agitated, jumpy, irritable, and unfocused, and my startle response is through the roof. I cannot get into a car or look at mountains without wanting to vomit, and I am prone to anxiety attacks, which I've never had before. So. Here is a highlighted photocopy of my PTSD symptoms from the *DSM*. I've printed a list of the medical services offered at your center. I would like to sign up for all of them."

The doctor stayed silent for what seemed a long time. He finally scanned my *DSM* photocopy, then sighed empathetically.

"I'm just so sorry," he said. "Let's see what we can do for you."

We spoke for another forty-five minutes—about the nervous system, about sleep aids, about options at the Center for Integrative Medicine—and came up with both short-term and long-term game plans.

Over the past four years, I have received care from numerous talented professionals in both Western and Eastern medicine, all in the name of healing my mind, body, and spirit. Appointments and sessions have included acupressure, acupuncture, biofeedback, chiropractic, medication, meditation, and physical therapy (including cupping therapy, electrical stimulation, Gua sha, kinesiology taping, low-level laser therapy, and soft tissue massage).

I wonder if using Western and Eastern medicine might assist you on your healing journey.

Why consider Western and Eastern medicine?

Certain Western practices and medications can help alleviate severe grief and post-traumatic symptoms such as anxiety, depression, panic attacks, sleep disturbances, intrusive thoughts, and flashbacks. Eastern medicine modalities and practitioners also assist in transformative healing by balancing the body's qi ("chee") and restoring the mind, body, and spirit. Many cities now have integrative medical centers that have both Western and Eastern doctors, allowing for comprehensive treatment options.

How does incorporating Western and Eastern medicine promote healing?

- By calming and regulating the nervous system
- By increasing "feel good" hormones such as serotonin and dopamine
- By improving the ability to fall asleep and stay asleep
- By increasing overall mental and physical well-being

SINGLE SMALL STEPS

If you would like to integrate Western and Eastern medicine into your healing journey, here are some single small step suggestions you may be able to use.

Is there one that resonates with you?

1) **Gather**: Find information about both Western and Eastern practices in your area. As with many things in life, a variety and combination of tools may give you the best result.

2) **Get**: Ask for referrals from family, friends, neighbors, and coworkers. Who sees an experienced Western doctor? Who receives Eastern acupuncture or reflexology?

3) **Grab**: Seek out reputable online resources, websites, books, videos, and recommendations.

4) **Gab**: Consult with the practitioners themselves. Make an appointment. Tell them your struggles. Ask about options, treatments, services, plans, and any insurance coverage.

5) **Go**: Be your own health advocate. Your mind, body, and spirit depend upon it!

Here is one single small step I may be able to take in the future:

_____

_____

_____

_____

_____

_____

HEALING STORIES

Following the sudden loss of my mother, I experienced a severing of my deepest connection. I lamented the feeling of safety I once had. My processing of death and the physical upheaval brought on by grief were softened by some antianxiety medication. The pain was not muted, but the loud nerves associated with shock, adjustment, and reentry into the world could be silenced to a degree. Mourning is much more complex than feeling sad. Being able to relieve myself of some of the physical tension and mental hypervigilance that accompany sorrow was a welcome and critical part of occasionally letting my mind and body stop bracing so tightly.
—Miranda

When I was young, I was very sporty. I enjoyed running, field hockey, and soccer. Then I had a sudden stroke and couldn't move half my body. A new chapter of my life began. My family and I looked into all possibilities that might help me. My cousins came to visit and left me some money to find a certified reflexologist, saying reflexology had to do with using pressure points on the body to heal. I found a certified reflexologist and climbed the stairs to my first two appointments by using a modified walker. By my third appointment, I attempted the stair-climbing feat on my own, just using my cane. When I made it to the top, it felt like I had made it to the top of Half Dome! My balance was coming back! This was liberating. My independence was slowly coming back with just a few reflexology treatments. There is always a light at the end of the tunnel.
—Jean

When my husband died, our son was in preschool. The anxiety and fear inside his little body manifested into something called "tactile defensiveness," which is a type of sensory integration disorder. He couldn't stand wearing socks or underwear; couldn't stand getting his nails clipped or his hair cut; couldn't stand lotion, sunscreen, hats, helmets, sweat, sand, or water. A pediatrician recommended an occupational therapy center for children. The occupational therapists started giving my son "tiny touch steps" to master, like "Let's try keeping socks on your hands for twenty seconds." Then they pushed him in large, colorful swings that hugged his body; had him walk barefoot on various types of textured mats like grass, wood, and fluffy cotton; and sent us home with a soft body brush, which we used on his arms so he could get used to the feeling of touch again. Now, years later, my son happily puts on sunscreen, a helmet, and socks to bike through the neighborhood. It's a beautiful sight to see!

—Sue

RESOURCES

If you would like to integrate Western and Eastern medicine into your healing journey, here are some resources that can help you get started.

Books

Kitchen Table Wisdom: Stories That Heal by Dr. Rachel Naomi Remen

Mind Over Meds: Know When Drugs are Necessary, When Alternatives are Better - and When to Let Your Body Heal on Its Own by Dr. Andrew Weil

Stop Panic Attacks in 10 Easy Steps: Using Functional Medicine to Calm Your Mind and Body with Drug-Free Techniques by Dr. Sandra Scheinbaum

The Wisdom of Your Face by Jean Haner

Why Zebras Don't Get Ulcers by Dr. Robert Sapolsky

Organizations

Dr. Andrew Weil
www.drweil.com
Health and wellness, diet and nutrition, health A-Z, research, and videos.

The Center for Mind-Body Medicine
www.cmbm.org
Global trauma relief, mind-body medicine, PTSD research, and self-care.

NOTES

Use this section for any notes related to Western and Eastern medicine.

_____

_____

_____

_____

_____

_____

_____

_____

_____

_____

_____

_____

_____

_____

_____

_____

_____

_____

_____

*"It's not one huge step that promotes healing . . .
it's many intentional single small steps."*

eXamining Your Positives

The power, the wisdom,
the creativity of the universe . . .
you open the door through gratitude.

—Deepak Chopra

HEALING POWER

"What am I supposed to do with all of his stuff?"

I agonized over this question for months after Brent died. The question itself was debilitating. It was a constant reminder that he was actually dead. And, like most things grief-related, there was no definitive how-to manual. I had no idea what I was going to do with the surfboards, musical instruments, artwork, professional books, framed diplomas, business suits, Hawaiian shirts, and favorite sunglasses. Then one day, a partial answer came. I was going to donate his clothes to people who lived over the border in Mexico. Brent was a professor of international business, after all, so I knew he would love some of his things to be used in another country. The next week I packed up boxes of clothes, grabbed my child and our passports, and joined a local mission trip to Tijuana, Mexico. Once over the border, we boarded a bus that took us to an impoverished neighborhood where we spent the day surrounded by teenage boys playing soccer in Brent's clothes; helping build the foundation for small homes by mixing and pouring cement with old buckets; walking through narrow streets full of mud and broken vehicles; and interacting with local families living in the community. We sat in one home owned by a family of four who lived in a single room with dirt floors, a leaky tin roof, no toilet, and walls fashioned from four old, nailed-together garage doors that had been shipped down from landfills in America.

That was the first time in a year I stopped to examine my own positives.

Yes, my husband is dead, but my son and I are still alive. Yes, my husband is dead, but we have enough food to eat. Yes, my husband is dead, but we have a home with comfortable beds, carpeted floors, and sturdy walls. Yes, my husband is dead, but we have paved streets, a reliable vehicle, and warm water in our house.

After that trip to Mexico, I started pondering the idea of being thankful.

By connecting with the Greater Good Science Center at the University of California–Berkeley, I learned about the neurobiology of gratitude.

By attending seminars given by researchers from the Institute for Brain Potential, I realized gratitude is one of the primary habits of happy people.

By watching the Dalai Lama speak at the University of San Diego, I took to heart his words, "We can let the circumstances of our lives harden us so that we become increasingly resentful and afraid, or we can let them soften us and make us kinder. We always have the choice. Happiness is not something ready-made. It comes from your own actions."

By writing texts, emails, and letters to people I truly appreciated, I made others feel better, but so did I.

I wonder if examining your positives might assist you on your healing journey.

Why consider examining your positives?

Research has shown that people who consciously focus on gratitude experience greater emotional well-being and physical health than those who don't. For those grieving, practicing thankfulness can be a challenge because there is an understandable focus on what is missing, instead of what is still present. Examining the positives by focusing on what is still good can strengthen the brain's positive neural pathways and contribute to overall mental wellness.

How does examining your positives promote healing?

- By rewiring the brain for positive emotions

- By lifting mood, optimism, and resilience

- By counteracting the effects of painful experiences

- By increasing levels of energy, determination, persistence, and focus

SINGLE SMALL STEPS

If you would like to integrate examining your positives into your healing journey, here are some single small step suggestions you may be able to use.

Is there one that resonates with you?

1) **Journal**: Keep a journal, notepad, or list on your bedside table. As you wake up or before you go to sleep (or both), write down three things for which you are grateful.

2) **Jar**: Keep a jar, small sticky notes, and a pen on the kitchen table. As you pass the jar, write down one thing for which you are grateful. (If others live in the house, they can do this too.) Fold up the note and place it in the jar. At the end of the month, open the jar and review all for which you are thankful.

3) **Text**: When you think of someone for whom you are grateful, send them a text, email, or letter to let them know.

4) **Tell**: When you are interacting with family, friends, colleagues, and neighbors throughout the day, tell them why you are grateful for them.

5) **Bust**: When feeling overwhelmed, take a moment to bust the stress by switching your thought process. List five to ten things for which you are grateful.

Here is one single small step I may be able to take in the future:

_____

_____

_____

_____

_____

_____

_____

HEALING STORIES

Feeling grateful was an important lesson my mom taught me at a very young age. Through her actions, I realized the importance of giving and receiving; making the most of what you have and showing appreciation create a healthy and balanced life. I was a teenager when she died of aggressive cancer. During the days, months, and years after her death, I found comfort in giving to others and decided to dedicate my life to helping those in need. Twenty years later, when I was faced with my husband's death (from the same type of aggressive cancer) and left raising our five-year-old son, I forced myself to be grateful during my darkest moments. My son and I started delivering monthly meals with Volunteers of America's Meals on Wheels program and shoveling snow through their Snow Buddy program. I feel so grateful we can brighten someone's day just as others did for us in our time of need. Gratitude truly helped me find hope during my most hopeless moments.
—Lisa

I woke up, pushed through the pain and sadness, and honored my wife in a unique but rewarding way. Sipping on my morning coffee, I wrote a thank-you letter to the hospice staff, wrote a small donation check to the amazing facility that did so much for my wife, and drove thirty-five minutes to the donut shop. I walked into hospice—donuts, thank-you letter, and donation check in hand—and asked the receptionist if I could head to the back. From the moment I put that pen to paper to write that thank-you letter until the moment I left the building after delivering two dozen donuts, I had hope. A sense of purpose. It wasn't just about a couple of boxes of donuts. Whether it is through my blog, my Facebook page, my upcoming book, or a couple boxes of donuts, nobody is going to forget Michelle.
—John Polo, author of *Widowed: Rants, Raves, and Randoms*

I had two strokes at the age of twenty-nine, resulting from two tears in my vertebral artery. I was in three different hospitals over a four-month period. Before my strokes, I was a very pessimistic person. I was always pointing out the bad things that happened. This continued until after my strokes. It is amazing how almost dying twice has changed my entire perspective. I am very positive now and always try to look on the bright side. I have found that by having this positive outlook, I help my other friends with brain injuries when they get in a deep depression. Even something as traumatic as my strokes has turned out to be a semi-positive experience. Now, when I get down, I think that there are a lot of people going through something worse than I am.
—Kelley

I am thankful for what I don't have
For what would there be to look forward to?

Be thankful when you don't know something
For this gives you an opportunity to learn.

Be thankful for the difficult times
In these times you grow.

Be thankful for your mistakes
For these teach you valuable lessons.

It is easy to be thankful for the good things,
But be thankful for your troubles
For they can become your blessings.
—Brook, age twelve

RESOURCES

If you would like to integrate examining your positives into your healing journey, here are some resources that can help you get started.

Books

Buddha's Brain: The Practical Neuroscience of Happiness, Love & Wisdom by Rick Hanson and Richard Mendius

Hardwiring Happiness: The New Brain Science of Contentment, Calm, and Confidence by Dr. Rick Hanson

Learned Optimism: How to Change Your Mind and Your Life by Martin Seligman

Second Firsts by Christina Rasmussen

Organizations

Awakening Joy
www.awakeningjoy.info
App, blog, book, classes, events, free audio talks, retreats, and workshops focused on joy.

Greater Good Science Center at UC Berkeley
www.greatergood.berkeley.edu
Researched-based tools and practical resources to build happiness, resilience, and connection.

Live Happy
www.livehappy.com
Articles, clothing, gifts, *Live Happy* magazine, and podcast centered on positive psychology.

NOTES

Use this section for any notes related to examining your positives.

_____

_____

_____

_____

_____

_____

_____

_____

_____

_____

_____

_____

_____

_____

_____

_____

_____

_____

_____

_____

"It's not one huge step that promotes healing . . .
it's many intentional single small steps."

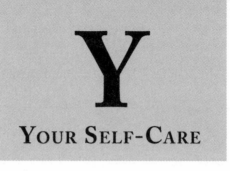

Y

YOUR SELF-CARE

*I have come to believe that caring for myself
is not self-indulgent.
Caring for myself is an act of survival.*

—AUDRE LORDE

HEALING POWER

When I was eight years old, one of my favorite tricks was to put a fat stick of chewing gum through the massive space between my two front teeth. The stick of gum would move through, with room to spare on either side, and my friends would laugh. The laughing was over for my parents, however, when they realized how much orthodontic work I was going to need throughout my childhood to align my teeth, bite, and jaw. They like to say that they bought my orthodontist a condominium in Hawaii with the money spent reconstructing my mouth. First there was the extraction of six baby teeth to make room for the permanent teeth that would soon come in. Next there was the palette expander cemented to the roof of my mouth, which my mother would have to cock with a key every night. Then came full braces with rubber bands that crisscrossed throughout my mouth. Headgear was on the orthodontic agenda too. The metal contraption locked into the braces and strapped oh-so-comfortably around the back of my neck. I even went to myofunctional therapy, where therapists tried to reteach my tongue to swallow correctly by using large buttons and fancy string. Last, but not least, were retainers to keep my teeth in place, oral surgeries for extracting four impacted wisdom teeth, a frenectomy to reposition the tissue connecting my lower lip and gum line, and a periodontal graft that I won't even get into. Whew! At least that work was over and done with.

Or so I thought.

One evening when I was an adult, Brent and I were at the bathroom sink, toothbrushes in hand.

"Huh. That's odd," I said. "My front teeth aren't even on the same plane anymore." I leaned in toward the mirror and looked closer.

"Wait. One is really sticking out! Why didn't you tell me I was starting to look like a beaver? And come to think of it, my jaw has been popping! No wonder it's hard to chew—look at this! My teeth don't even meet anymore! Are you kidding me?" I slumped down on the toilet seat, dejected.

Brent knew the litany of my childhood orthodontic treatments. He smiled mischievously and gave me a hug. "Well, Miss Beaver, let's take care of it. You are worth it. Besides, we don't need any wood gnawed or dams built."

You are worth it. You are worth it. That phrase became engrained in my mind. And although Brent hasn't been here to remind me of that anymore, others have.

Peer mentors remind me: "Go get a massage this week. Take care of you." *You are worth it.*

Gym trainers reminded me: "Exercise for you today. I am here to motivate you." *You are worth it.*

Therapists reminded me: "Lie down and put your feet up daily. You need to rest." *You are worth it.*

Medical professionals reminded me: "You need to sleep. You need to breathe. Let's reteach you how." *You are worth it.*

Parents reminded me: "We are going to pick up your son from school, help him with homework, take him to get a haircut, and give him dinner. You can have some time to do what you need." *You are worth it.*

A while ago a friend suggested I visit a local day spa called All About Me. I thought, *I'm a social worker. It's never been all about me! I'm a solo parent. It's never been all about me!* She knew what I was thinking. She looked at me and said, "Brent is not here anymore to remind you to take care of yourself. So I'm going to do it. Self-care is *not* frivolous. You need to stay well for both you and your child. Go do something for yourself."

So I went.

And for that perfect hour, it was all about me.

I wonder if incorporating your self-care might assist you on your healing journey.

Why consider your self-care?

Grief and trauma are experienced in a variety of ways: emotionally, physically, mentally, socially, psychologically, behaviorally, and spiritually. Our minds and bodies can react with shock, rage, fatigue, sleep disturbances, appetite changes, mood fluctuations, isolation, forgetfulness, and loss of concentration. Making time for extreme self-care is one healthy way to *cope with the myriad of life-transforming changes.* Many cognitive behavioral therapists recommend getting a daily dose of the acronym "GRAPES" for optimum mental health. (See the following Single Small Steps section.) *Since the healing process is a marathon, not a sprint, it is imperative to stop at self-care rest stations along the way.*

How does your self-care promote healing?

- By reducing feelings of stress and anxiety
- By boosting physical energy levels
- By assisting the mind with clarity, focus, and concentration
- By increasing self-esteem and feelings of self-worth

SINGLE SMALL STEPS

If you would like to integrate your self-care into your healing journey, here are some single small step suggestions you may be able to use.

Is there one that resonates with you?

1) **G – Gentle with Self**: Can you eat a healthy meal, sleep more, only do what you want?

2) **R – Relaxation**: Can you soak in the tub, get a massage, rest under a tree, breathe deeply?

3) **A – Accomplishment**: Can you pay a bill, wash a dish, vacuum a floor, make the bed?

4) **P – Pleasure**: Can you watch a movie, read a book, watch the sunset, play with a pet?

5) **E – Exercise**: Can you walk, bike, swim, surf, dance, stretch, hike, run, play a team sport?

6) **S – Social**: Can you sign up for a class, meet a friend, stay with family, join a group?

Here is one single small step I may be able to take in the future:

_____

_____

_____

_____

_____

_____

_____

HEALING STORIES

After my life suddenly fell apart, I felt an almost constant tightening in my stomach from panic and anxiety. To survive, I had to force the self-care. Self-care is like a never-used muscle for me. I often felt conflicted about using it, but intellectually I knew I needed me *to take care of my two little girls. Self-care for me means acupuncture, a mindfulness app on my phone, weeping, finding strength in music, going to church, and trying to not beat myself up when I don't make it to my body flow class. It means walking the dog and coping and surviving through the holidays. It means learning how to be still. Self-care is a little like playing the violin, which I have no idea how to play. I have to use my muscles to hold up the violin, use the bow, use the brain, keep time, read the music. I know that like any other muscle, the self-care muscle will get stronger the more I use it.*
—Darlene

After my daughter died in her twenties, I ran for what came naturally, and that was and still is self-love and self-care. I have always been a big believer of self-care. I knew I needed to put myself first and totally embrace someone else taking care of me. I got massages, facials, pedicures, and manicures regularly, but knew I needed to bump it up a notch. I was unsure what was going to help my broken heart, but I knew if I was going to be a mom to my son, be a wife to my husband, and honor my daughter, I needed to double up on self-love. I needed and owed it to my grief to give myself the best care I could and as often as I could. Self-care was the main tool that helped me on my journey. My new motto is "Have you given yourself some love today?"
—Trish

After years of grief and trauma, I had finally reached my proverbial bottom. I knew there must be a better way to cope than through self-destructive behaviors such as substance use, perfectionism, and codependency. Self-care became my go-to tool after learning what it was. Every day, I choose to support myself through engaging activities that promote well-being on the mental, emotional, physical, and spiritual levels. I pull affirmations from a deck of cards and using Emotional Freedom Technique (EFT or Tapping); I love diffusing essential oils and visualizing sending compassion to myself. I enjoy 5-5-7 breathwork and practicing yoga. I light naturally scented candles and practice a light-sourcing meditation. I consider self-care to be foundational to dealing with grief and trauma work. And self-care is fun!

—Beverly

One of the jobs all parents have is to guide their children to process feelings and information for their own self-care. One particular incident taught me this. It was just a few months after my son's mom died in a sudden accident. We were in the backyard playing catch. My son turned and gazed intently at some trees at the side of the yard. "I saw Mom," he said. I knelt by him and looked. "Where was she?" I asked. "Next to that big tree," he pointed. He was so matter-of-fact that I had no doubt he saw her. From that point on, I never took anything he felt or saw lightly, always kept our conversations real and grounded, and drilled into him that whatever happened in life, he always had choices. My son grew to be very capable of managing his thoughts, feelings, and connections rather than being overwhelmed or puzzled by them. He takes care of himself by maintaining close friendships, traveling to see family members, integrating sports and recreation, and exploring the world as his mother would have.

—GC

RESOURCES

If you would like to integrate your self-care into your healing journey, here are some resources that can help you get started.

Books

An Invitation to Self-Care: Why Learning to Nurture Yourself in the Key to the Life You've Always Wanted, 7 Principles for Abundant Living by Tracey Cleantis

Self-Care for Life: Find Joy, Peace, Serenity, Vitality, Sensuality, Abundance, and Enlightenment - Each and Every Day by Alexander Skye

The Art of Extreme Self-Care: Transform Your Life One Month at a Time by Cheryl Richardson

Cards and Journals

Self-Care Cards by Cheryl Richardson

Start Where You Are: A Journal for Self-Exploration by Meera Lee Patel

Wisdom Cards by Louise Hay

Handy to Have at Home

Bath salts
Candles
Essential oils
Eye pillow
Healthy snacks
Journal
Self-massage roller

NOTES

Use this section for any notes related to your self-care.

_____

_____

_____

_____

_____

_____

_____

_____

_____

_____

_____

_____

_____

_____

_____

_____

_____

_____

*"It's not one huge step that promotes healing . . .
it's many intentional single small steps."*

Z
ZZZZZs

A good laugh and a long sleep are the best cures in the doctor's book.

—Irish Proverb

HEALING POWER

Snoozin' Susan. That was the nickname my brother gave me when we were kids because I could catch z's anywhere, anytime, in any circumstance. He would peek into my bedroom on Saturday mornings, hoping to find a cartoon-watching buddy but instead finding a sister sleeping soundly, sunrays streaming onto the bed, birds chirping loudly from outside the window, stuffed animals crammed around her, and a dog passed out at her feet. In a hot car? Susan is asleep. On a noisy plane? Susan is asleep. In the middle of a July 4th fireworks show? Susan is asleep. In a tent on lumpy, bumpy ground? Susan is asleep. To my brother, my ease of sleep was comical. Maybe it reminded him of the Dr. Seuss book *Green Eggs and Ham. Yes, she could sleep in a boat. And she could sleep with a goat. And she would sleep in the rain. And in the dark. And on a train. And in a car. And in a tree. Sleep is so good, so good, you see! So she will sleep in a box. And she will sleep with a fox. And she will sleep here and there. Say! She will sleep anywhere!*

I *loved* sleep.

Until I didn't. Until I couldn't. Until my mind and body wouldn't.

Restful sleep became impossible when grief and trauma slammed into my life. There was the obvious issue of the missing person in my bed. But there were also shock, fear, anxiety, restlessness, flashbacks, nightmares, and cold sweats. My nervous system was completely derailed.

Over the past few years, I have tried a multitude of things to assist me in getting restful, regular sleep. These are the same things, in fact, that have helped me to restore, renew, and rebuild a new life altogether: the A to Z tools. I will list the tools here, in relation to their assistance with my sleep, in the hope that one or two or five of them may help you get restful nights of your own.

A: I sleep in the same room with my dog and fish, since animals help me relax.

B: I do a five-minute bed breathing exercise to slow my rate of breath and calm my body.

C: I revisit counseling sessions in my head to rest assured my healing is progressing.

D: I review recommendations by sleep researchers and medical professionals.

E: I envision giving myself positive energy by resting my hand on my heart.

F: I diffuse the relaxing fragrance of essential oils before bedtime.

G: I use the phone to connect with support group members if I can't fall asleep.

H: I pray nightly for health, wellness, and restful sleep.

I: I listen to guided imagery CDs for relaxation.

J: I journal pre-nighttime worries with words or pictures.

K: I know that my new environment is different now, and I reassure myself that I will be okay.

L: I listen to comedians on YouTube as I brush my teeth and get ready for bed.

M: I tune into guided meditations before turning out the light.

N: I cut back on caffeine and sugar consumption, especially in the evening.

O: I write down the names of people I would like to spend time with that week.

P: I talk to peer mentors about sleep remedies they have used.

Q: I repeat affirming quotes about my overall intention to heal and sleep soundly.

R: I keep a meditative coloring book and colored pencils on my bedside table.

S: I save exercise for daytime hours only.

T: I give my child and dog lots of hugs at night.

U: I download sounds of steady rainfall, mountain streams, and waves lapping on the shore.

V: I remember positive interactions at volunteer placements before I fall asleep.

W: I listen to my physical therapist and switch to a supportive pillow for my aching neck.

X: I jot down three things that I am grateful for each day.

Y: I relax before bedtime in a warm tub full of lavender Epsom salts.

Z: I choose one, two, or three items on this A to Z list.

I wonder if incorporating more z's might assist you on your healing journey.

Why consider z's?
The health benefits of sleep have been documented for decades. Sleep is crucial to our mental, physical, and emotional well-being. Sleep improves memory, repairs body systems, controls weight, reduces stress, maintains heart health, and improves memory function. Those grieving and living with trauma, however, find they sleep very little or not at all for reasons such as intrusive thoughts, panic and anxiety, a racing mind, heightened startle response, nightmares, or difficulty sleeping without loved ones nearby or in bed. Sleep studies, sleep schools, and specialized sleep doctors can all provide extensive suggestions for getting some much-needed z's while on your healing journey.

How do z's promote healing?
- By improving memory, concentration, and focus
- By promoting heart health and weight consistency
- By increasing self-esteem and productivity
- By lowering risk of anxiety and depression

SINGLE SMALL STEPS

If you would like to integrate z's into your healing journey, here are some single small step suggestions you may be able to use.

Is there one that resonates with you?
1) **Pets & Pillows**: Buy a body pillow or grab your pet and lay them next to you on the side where your loved one slept.

2) **Nature & Noise**: Download calming sounds of nature to your device, or buy a white noise machine to help you sleep.

3) **Jot & Journal**: Grab a notebook to write about pre-bedtime worries, fears, and anxieties.

4) **Move & Meditate**: Exercise during the daytime, but try meditating at night.

5) **Pause & Play**: Read a book or magazine, use aromatherapy or essential oils, or play with kinetic sand or calming coloring books.

6) **Scrap the Screens**: Avoid computer, phone, and TV screens before bedtime.

Here is one single small step I may be able to take in the future:

_____

_____

_____

_____

_____

_____

_____

HEALING STORIES

My boyfriend of fifteen years had an unexpected seizure and died in his sleep. As a single mom of a twenty-one-year-old autistic adult, I work full time and go to school part time. Sleep is something I'm often deprived of. Over the past month or so, I have taken some extra steps to nap during the day and to sleep at least six hours at night. I often grab my Cavalier King Charles Spaniel to cuddle with at night, and I am adamant about no screens of any kind in the bedroom—I don't even have a TV in there. I need darkness and silence to fall asleep. Before bedtime, the one TV show that always helps me relax and makes me laugh is TruTV's Impractical Jokers. *My boyfriend and I watched it before bedtime together. Sometimes I feel as if he's right beside me and can almost hear him laughing.*
—Jennifer

My six-year-old son started having nightmares after his mother died. Somehow I knew what to do when he came to my bed and said he'd had a bad dream. I invited him into my bed and asked about the dream, and he described it in as much detail as he could. If it was a monster chasing him, I asked him to describe the monster and then asked what it was doing when he woke up. After he told me, I asked him to close his eyes and go back to that point in the dream. "What would you like to happen in this dream?" I asked. He might answer, "I want to chase him away." So I'd direct him to keep his eyes closed and find his power to chase the monster off. Once the monster was gone, I pointed out to him that he had a lot of power and could always make his dreams turn out the way he wanted. This was an effective technique to get him back to bed and back to sound sleep, but it also reinforced his own intelligence and power to influence his own life.
—Gary

Grief and restful sleep do not always go together. When I was newly widowed, sleep often eluded me. I have been a grief therapist for the past twenty-five years, and a majority of my clients have struggled with sleep issues. Sleep is such an important component for healing and yet it is often so difficult to achieve, especially in the early days. A few natural sleep aids I suggest include: 1) Rescue Remedy, an over-the-counter Bach flower remedy; 2) Relaxation CDs, nature sounds, or a white noise machine; 3) Body pillows, stuffed animals, or items of clothing from the person who has died; 4) Self-soothing techniques like Emotional Freedom Technique (EFT or Tapping) or self-hypnosis; 5) Avoiding alcohol, especially right before bed. Be gentle with yourself. You are doing the best that you can. Eventually sleep will return.

—Kath

RESOURCES

If you would like to integrate z's into your healing journey, here are some resources that can help you get started.

Books

The Sleep Book: How to Sleep Well Every Night by Dr. Guy Meadows of The Sleep School

The Post-Traumatic Insomnia Workbook: A Step-by-Step Program for Overcoming Sleep Problems After Trauma by Karin Thompson and C. Laurel Franklin

Sleep Apps (free)

www.sleepgenius.com
www.relaxandsleepwell.com
www.hypnosisappstore.com

Sleep CDs

A Meditation to Help You with Healthful Sleep by Belleruth Naparstek
Sleep: Fall Asleep Easily and Naturally by David Ison

Sleep Tools

Body pillow
Candles
Coloring book
Earplugs
Essential oils
Eye mask
Journal
White noise machine

NOTES

Use this section for any notes related to z's.

_____

_____

_____

_____

_____

_____

_____

_____

_____

_____

_____

_____

_____

_____

_____

_____

_____

_____

"It's not one huge step that promotes healing . . .
it's many intentional single small steps."

Conclusion

There will come a time when you believe
everything is finished.
That will be the beginning.

—Louis L'Amour

As I wheeled my overstuffed black office cart down the corridor of conference rooms, I turned the corner and bumped into the wall, and my presentation supplies tumbled to the floor in disarray—yellow folders, hand-painted rocks, boxes of art supplies, bags of bendable drinking straws, brightly colored candies, and two large buckets labeled "Grief" and "Trauma." As I knelt down to scoop everything up, a pair of shoes stopped in front of me.

The voice attached to the shoes spoke. "Excuse me? Do you know which room I go to for the A2Z workshop on tools for grief and trauma?" *Huh. That voice sounds familiar. Wait a minute. I have seen these shoes before!* I looked up, smiled, and gave my friend a big hug.

Her name was Faith.

Such a perfect name to have while traveling the grief and trauma healing journey.

Faith and I initially met because our sons were attending the same elementary school when her husband died suddenly. We became fast friends, I became her unofficial peer mentor (P – Peer Mentors), she joined the local chapter of our widows and widowers support group (G – Group Support), and now she was here at the conference attending my workshop "A2Z Healing Toolbox: Powerful Tools & Resources to Accompany and Accelerate the Healing Journey of Those Living with Grief and Trauma" (D – Doing Your Homework).

Faith and I live in the same community, so I have witnessed her intention—one small step at time—to move toward the restoration, renewal, and rebuilding of her life. She chose active healing, rather than the "waiting for time to heal all wounds" approach, in order to bring accelerated healing to her mind, body, and spirit. Faith chose to integrate many of the A to Z tools and resources on her new path, and her continued growth is exemplified in the letter she recently wrote to her deceased husband (J – Journaling).

Dear John,

So, while I am not happy about your death, and I did not ask nor plan for this, I thank you for dying.
(X – eXamining Your Positives)

Since your death . . .

- *I get hugged a lot (really . . . I have noticed that a lot of people hug me . . . and I like it)*

  (T – Touch)

- *I finally went out and purchased all new, fancy, lacy bras at Victoria's*

Secret (You were right, I do feel extra sexy even though no one knows about the hot pink, lacy bra under my sweater at work)

(Y – Your Self-Care)

- *I've laughed more this past year (mostly laughing off things that I now realize are insignificant in the whole picture)*

  (L – Laughter)

- *I hug everyone like it's the last time I'll see them*

  (T – Touch)

- *I have learned . . .*

  - *Perseverance (K – Knowing Your New Environment)*

  - *How to fix drywall, work power tools, hang light fixtures, fix plumbing, install a water heater, tile, and grout (D – Doing Your Homework)*

  - *To ask for help (O – Organizing Your Supports)*

  - *To accept help (O – Organizing Your Supports)*

  - *To stop what I am doing to:*

    - *Hug the boys (T – Touch)*

    - *Pick up the cats for love (A – Animals)*

    - *Compliment family, friends, and strangers (X – eXamining Your Positives)*

    - *Rest (Y – Your Self-Care and Z – Zzzzzs)*

- *I have...*

  - *Forgiven you*

  - *Painted and redecorated (R – Right-Brain Release)*

  - *Purged lots of stuff we'd been dragging around for two decades*

  - *Laughed (L – Laughter)*

- *Listened*
- *Cried*
- *Hugged (T – Touch)*
- *I am a better . . .*
  - *Person*
  - *Mother*
  - *Friend*
  - *Daughter*
  - *Sister*
  - *Leader*

So, while I am not happy about your death, and I did not ask nor plan for this, I thank you for dying.

Love, your wife,

Faith

The details of our grief healing journey or trauma healing journey may differ. For example, I learned to manage a massive amount of trauma while Faith was beginning to navigate an enormous amount of grief.

The tools and resources that we choose to gather and integrate may vary. I initially chose tools of comfort and familiarity like counseling, nature, sliding into exercise, and Western and Eastern medicine, while Faith navigated toward integrating laughter, touch, examining her positives, and her self-care.

But we all belong to the same community of intentional healers. In conclusion, I would like to offer you:

1) An Invitation: Stay connected to the A2Z Healing Toolbox community by joining us at conferences, workshops, and retreats. Find out more by simply visiting the A2Z Healing Toolbox website at www.a2zhealingtoolbox.com.

2) An Assignment. Take a few moments to recognize all the hard work you have done so far. Commend yourself on making the decision to heal with action and intention. Healing grief and trauma is no easy task, but you are doing it! You are on your way to a life of thriving, not just surviving.

3) An Acknowledgment: You are (still) most definitely not alone. Please know there are thousands of us walking alongside you on your journey . . . sending support and encouragement (and tools!) along the way.

With much love in the days to come,

Susan ☺

REFERENCES

GRIEF

Bryant, Clifton D. and Dennis L. Peck. *Encyclopedia of Death and the Human Experience*. Thousand Oaks, CA: SAGE Publications, 2009.

Didion, Joan. *The Year of Magical Thinking*. New York: Random House, 2005.

Doka, Kenneth and Terry J. Martin. *Grieving Beyond Gender: Understanding the Differences Between the Way Men and Women Mourn*. New York: Taylor and Francis Group, 2010.

James, John W. and Russell Friedman. *The Grief Recovery Handbook, 20th Anniversary Expanded Edition: The Action Program for Moving Beyond Death, Divorce, and Other Losses Including Health, Career, and Faith*. New York: HarperCollins, 2017.

Kodanaz, Rachel Blythe. *Living with Loss: One Day at a Time*. Golden, CO: Fulcrum Publishing, 2013.

Kübler-Ross, Elisabeth and David Kessler. *On Grief and Grieving: Finding the Meaning of Grief Through the Five Stages of Loss*. New York: Scribner, 2014.

Lewis, C. S. *A Grief Observed*. New York: Harper Collins, 1996.

McCoyd, Judith L. M. and Carolyn A. Walter. *Grief and Loss Across the Lifespan, Second Edition: A Biopsychosocial Perspective*. 2nd ed. New York: Springer Publishing Company, 2015.

Neeld, Elizabeth Harper. *Seven Choices: Finding Daylight after Loss Shatters Your World*. Austin: Grand Central Publishing, 2003.

Noel, Brook and Pamela Blair. *I Wasn't Ready to Say Goodbye: Surviving, Coping and Healing After the Sudden Death of a Loved One*. Naperville, IL: Sourcebooks, 2008.

Rando, Therese. *How to Go On Living When Someone You Love Dies*. Lexington: Bantam Books, 1991.

Rasmussen, Christina. *Second Firsts: Live, Laugh, and Love Again*. Carlsbad, CA: Hay House, 2013.

Silverman, Phyllis R. and Madelyn Kelly. *A Parent's Guide to Raising Grieving Children: Rebuilding Your Family after the Death of a Loved One*. New York: Oxford University Press, 2009.

Stephens, Paula. *From Grief to Growth: 5 Essential Elements of Action to Give Your Grief Purpose and Grow From Your Experience*. Colorado: printed by author, 2016.

Zuba, Tom. *Permission to Mourn: A New Way to Do Grief*. Rockford, IL: Bish Press, 2014.

TRAUMA

American Psychiatric Association. *Diagnostic and Statistical Manual of Mental Disorders: DSM-IV-TR*. Washington, DC: American Psychiatric Association, 2000.

Calhoun, Lawrence, Richard Tedeschi, Arnie Cann, and Emily Hanks. "Positive Outcomes Following Bereavement: Paths to Posttraumatic Growth." *Psychologica Belgica* 50.1-2 (2010): 125-143.

Dubi, Michael, Eric Gentry, and Patrick Powell. *Trauma, PTSD, Grief & Loss: The 10 Core Competencies for Evidence-Based Treatment*. Eau Claire, WI: PESI Publishing, 2017.

Figley, Charles R. *Encyclopedia of Trauma: An Interdisciplinary Guide*. Los Angeles: SAGE Publications, 2012.

Janoff-Bulman, Ronnie. *Shattered Assumptions: Towards a New Psychology of Trauma*. New York: Free Press, 1992.

Joseph, Stephen. *What Doesn't Kill Us: The New Psychology of Posttraumatic Growth*. New York: Basic Books, 2011.

Levine, Peter. *Healing Trauma: A Pioneering Program for Restoring the Wisdom of Your Body*. Boulder: Sounds True, 2008.

Levitt, Shelley. "The Science of Post-Traumatic Growth." *Live Happy*, February 2014.

Naparstek, Belleruth. *Invisible Heroes: Survivors of Trauma and How They Heal*. New York: Bantam, 2004.

O'Hanlon, Bill. *Thriving Through Crisis: Turn Tragedy and Trauma into Growth and Change.* New York: Berkeley Publishing, 2004.

Siegel, Daniel J. and Marion Solomon. *Healing Trauma: Attachment, Mind, Body and Brain.* New York: Norton, 2003.

Van Der Kolk, Bessel. *The Body Keeps Score: Brain, Mind, Body in the Healing of Trauma.* New York: Penguin, 2014.

Wolfelt, Alan. *The PTSD Solution: The Truth About Your Symptoms and How to Heal.* Fort Collins, CO: Companion Press, 2015.

TRAUMATIC GRIEF

Armstrong, Courtney. *Transforming Traumatic Grief: Six Steps to Move from Grief to Peace After the Sudden or Violent Death of a Loved One.* Australia: Artemecia Press, 2011.

Green, Bonnie L. "Traumatic Loss: Conceptual and Empirical Links Between Trauma and Bereavement." *Journal of Personal and Interpersonal Loss* 5.1 (2000): 1-17.

Jacobs, Selby, Carolyn Mazure, and Holly Prigerson. "Diagnostic Criteria for Traumatic Grief." *Death Studies* 24.3 (2000): 184-199.

Litz, Brett and Yuval Neria. "Bereavement by Traumatic Means: The Complex Synergy of Trauma and Grief." *Journal of Loss and Trauma* 9.1 (2004): 73-87.

Pearlman, Laurie, Camille B. Wortman, Catherine A. Feuer, Christine H. Farber, and Therese A. Rando. *Treating Traumatic Bereavement: A Practitioner's Guide.* New York: The Guilford Press, 2014.

Prigerson, Holly and Selby Jacobs. "Traumatic Grief as a Distinct Disorder: A Rationale, Consensus Criteria, and a Preliminary Empirical Test." In *New Handbook of Bereavement: Consequences, Coping and Care*, edited by M. S. Stroebe, W. Stroebe, R.O. Hansson, and H. Schut, 613-645. Washington, DC: American Psychological Association, 2001.

Stroebe, Margaret, Henk Schut, and Catrin Finkenauer. "The Traumatization of Grief? A Conceptual Framework for Understanding the Trauma-Bereavement Interface." *Israel Journal of Psychiatry and Related Sciences* 38.3-4 (2001): 185-201.

A – ANIMALS

Beetz, Andrea, Kerstin Uvnas-Moberg, Henri Juliu, and Kurt Kotrschal. "Psychosocial and Psychophysiological Effects of Human-Animal Interactions: The Possible Role of Oxytocin." *Frontiers in Psychology* 3 (2012): 1-15.

Brody, Jane E. "Easing the Way In Therapy With the Aid of an Animal." *New York Times*, March 14, 2011.

Fine, Aubrey H. *Handbook on Animal-assisted Therapy: Theoretical Foundations and Guidelines for Practice*. Amsterdam: Elsevier/Academic, 2006.

B – BREATHWORK

Brown, Richard and Patricia Gerbarg. *The Healing Power of the Breath: Simple Techniques to Reduce Stress and Anxiety, Enhance Concentration and Balance Your Emotions*. Boston: Shambhala, 2012.

Rosenberg, Larry. *Breath by Breath: The Liberating Practice of Insight Meditation*. With David Guy. Boston: Shambhala, 2004.

Sultanoff, B.A. "Breath Work." *Handbook of Complementary and Alternative Therapies in Mental Health*, edited by Scott Shannon, 209-227. Amsterdam: Elsevier/Academic Press, 2001.

C – COUNSELING

Friedman, Howard S. *Encyclopedia of Mental Health*. 2nd ed. New York: Academic Press, 2015.

Friedman, Matthew. *Post Traumatic Stress Disorder: The Latest Assessment and Treatment Strategies*. New York: Compact Clinicals, 2000.

Hayes, Steven. *Get Out of Your Head and Into Your Life: The New Acceptance and Commitment Therapy*. Oakland: New Harbinger, 2005.

Katafiasz, Karen. *Grief Therapy*. St. Meinrad, IN: Abbey, 1993.
Marzillier, John. *The Trauma Therapies*. Oxford: Oxford University Press, 2014

Neimeyer, Robert A. ed. *Techniques of Grief Therapy: Creative Practices for Counseling the Bereaved*. New York: Taylor & Francis. 2012.

Segal, Zindel, Mark Williams, and John Teasdale. *Mindfulness-Based Cognitive Therapy for Depression*. New York: Guilford Press, 2002.
Shapiro, Francine. *Eye Movement Desensitization and Reprocessing: Basic Principles, Protocols and Procedures*. 2nd ed. New York: Guilford Press. 2001.

Worden, J. William. *Grief Counseling and Grief Therapy, Fourth Edition: A Handbook for the Mental Health Practitioner.* 4th ed. New York: Springer Publishing, 2008.

D – DOING YOUR HOMEWORK

Brewster, Liz. "The Reading Remedy: Bibliotherapy in Practice." *Australasian Public Libraries and Information Services* 21.4 (2008): 172-7.

Jack, Sarah and Kevin Ronan. "Bibliotherapy: Practice and Research." *School Psychology International* 29.2 (2008): 161-82.

Jackson, K. "Bibliotherapy: The Healing Power of Words." *Social Work Today* 16.6 (2016): 10.

E – ENERGY THERAPIES

Baldwin, A., A. Vitale, E. Brownell, J. Scicinski, M. Kearns, and W. Rand. "The Touchstone Process: An Ongoing Critical Evaluation of Reiki in the Scientific Literature." *Holistic Nursing Practice* 24.5 (2010): 260-76.

Hover-Kramer, Dorothea and Karilee H. Shames. *Energetic Approaches to Emotional Healing.* Independence, KY: Cengage Learning, 1996.

Oschman, James L. *Energy Medicine: The Scientific Basis.* 2nd ed. London: Churchill Livingstone, 2015.

F – FLOWERS & FRAGRANCE

Buckle, Jane. *Clinical Aromatherapy: Essential Oils in Healthcare.* St. Louis: Elsevier, 2015.

Fiedler, Chrystle and Bridgette Mars. *The Home Reference to Holistic Health and Healing: Easy-to-Use Natural Remedies, Herbs, Flower Essences, Essential Oils, Supplements, and Therapeutic Practices for Health, Happiness, and Well-Being*. Beverly, MA: Fair Winds Press, 2014.

Haviland-Jones, J., H. Rosario, P. Wilson, and T. McGuire. "An Environmental Approach to Positive Emotion: Flowers." *Evolutionary Psychology* 3 (2005): 104-32.

Perkus, Benjamin. *The Aroma Freedom Technique: Using Essential Oils to Transform Your Emotions and Realize Your Heart's Desire*. Sandy, UT: Aroma Freedom International, 2016.

G – GROUP SUPPORT

Corey, Marianne, Cindy Corey, and Gerald. Corey. *Groups: Process and Practice*. Belmont: Brooks/Cole, 2014

James, John W. and Russell Friedman. *The Grief Recovery Handbook, 20th Anniversary Expanded Edition: The Action Program for Moving Beyond Death, Divorce, and Other Losses including Health, Career, and Faith*. New York: HarperCollins, 2017.

Kaunonen, Marja, Marja-Terttu Tarkka, Marita Paunonen, and Pekka Laippala. "Grief and Social Support After the Death of a Spouse." *Journal of Advanced Nursing* 30.6 (2000): 1304-11.

H – HIGHER POWER HELP

Alexander, Eben. *Proof of Heaven: A Neurosurgeon's Journey into the Afterlife*. New York: Simon & Schuster, 2012.

Bidwell Smith, Claire. *After This: When Life Is Over, Where Do We Go?* New York: Avery, 2015.

Chopra, Deepak. *God: A Story of Revelation*. New York: HarperCollins, 2013.

Fiore, Carol. *A Grief Workbook for Skeptics: Surviving Loss without Religion*. Denver: Flying Kea Press, 2014.

Kubler-Ross, Elizabeth. *On Life After Death*. Berkeley: Celestial Arts, 2008.

Kushner, Harold. *When Bad Things Happen to Good People*. New York: Random House, 2004.

Lamott, Anne. *Thanks, Help, Wow: The Three Essential Prayers*. New York: Penguin, 2012.

Newberg, Andrew B. and Mark Robert Waldman. *How God Changes Your Brain: Breakthrough Findings from a Leading Neuroscientist*. New York: Random House, 2009.

Sittser, Jerry. *A Grace Disguised: How the Soul Grows Through Loss*. Grand Rapids, MI: Zondervan, 2004.

I – IMAGERY

Hensley, Barbara. *An EMDR Primer: From Practicum to Practice*. New York: Springer Publishing, 2009.

Naparstek, Belleruth. *Invisible Heroes: Survivors of Trauma and How They Heal*. New York: Bantam, 2004.

Rossman, Martin L. *Guided Imagery for Self-Healing*. Novoto, CA: New World Library, 2000.

J – JOURNALING

Adams, Kathleen. and Deborah Ross. *Your Brain on Ink: A Workbook on Neuroplasticity and the Journal Ladder*. London: Rowman & Littlefield, 2016.

Caughlin, Angela. *Journaling Through Loss to Transformation: A Guided Approach to Understanding Grief*. Houston: Bright Sky, 2009.

Desalvo, Louise. *Writing as a Way of Healing: How Telling Our Stories Transforms Our Lives*. Boston: Beacon Press, 2000.

McCarthy, Mari L. *Journal Through Your Grief: 7 Steps to Healing Your Heart*. Pennsauken, NJ: BookBaby, 2012.

Pennebake, James W. *Writing to Heal: A Guided Journal for Recovering from Trauma & Emotional Upheaval*. Wheat Ridge, CO: Center for Journal Therapy, 2004.

Weinstock, I. J. *Grief Quest: A Workbook and Journal to Heal the Grieving Heart*. Encino, CA: DreaMaster Books, 2012.

K – KNOWING YOUR ENVIRONMENT

Harold, Rena, Lucy Mercier, and L. G. Colarossi. "Eco Maps: A Tool to Bridge the Practice-Research Gap." *Journal of Sociology and Social Welfare* 24.4 (1997): 29-44.

Kingma, Daphne Rose. *The Ten Things to Do When Your Life Falls Apart.* Novato, CA: New World Library, 2010.

Thomlison, Barbara. *Family Assessment Handbook: An Introduction and Practical Guide to Family Assessment.* Belmont: Brooks/Cole, 2010.

Turner, Francis J. and William Rowe. *101 Social Work Clinical Techniques.* New York: Oxford University Press, 2013.

L – LAUGHTER

Dean, Ruth Anne Kinsman and David Gregory. "Humor and Laughter in Palliative Care: An Ethnographic Investigation." *Palliative and Supportive Care* 2.2 (2004), 139-48.

King, Brian. *The Laughing Cure: Emotional and Physical Healing—A Comedian Reveals Why Laughter Really Is the Best Medicine.* New York: Skyhorse Publishing, 2016.

Olver, Ian and Jaklin Eliot. "The Use of Humor and Laughter in Research About End-of-Life Discussions." *Journal of Nursing Education and Practice* 4.10 (2014): 80-7.

M – MEDITATION

Boyce, Barry. *The Mindfulness Revolution: Leading Psychologists, Scientists, Artists and Meditation Teachers on the Power of Mindfulness in Daily Life.* Boston: Shambhala, 2011.

Chodron, Pema. *When Things Fall Apart: Heart Advice for Difficult Times (20th Anniversary Edition).* Boulder, CO: Shambhala, 2016.

Kabat-Zinn, Jon. *Full Catastrophe Living: Using the Wisdom of Your Body and Mind to Face Stress, Pain, and Illness*. 2nd ed. New York: Bantam, 2013.

Kornfield, Jack. *Meditation for Beginners*. Boulder, CO: Sounds True, 2008.

Levine, Stephen and Ondrea Levine. "The Grief Process." Audio Cassette. Sounds True, 2000.

Miller, Richard C. *The IRest Program for Healing PTSD: A Proven-Effective Approach to Using Yoga Nidra Meditation & Deep Relaxation Techniques to Overcome Trauma*. Oakland: New Harbinger Publications, 2015.

Williams, Mark, John Teasdale, Zindel Segal, and Jon Kabat-Zinn. *The Mindful Way Through Depression: Freeing Yourself From Chronic Unhappiness*. New York: Guilford Press, 2007.

N – NUTRITION

Hyman, Mark. *The Blood Sugar Solution: The UltraHealthy Program for Losing Weight, Preventing Disease, and Feeling Great Now!* New York: Little, Brown and Company, 2012.

Johnson, C.S. "Nutritional Considerations for Bereavement and Coping with Grief." *The Journal of Nutrition, Health & Aging* 6.3 (2002): 171-6.

Lee S., E. Cho, F. Grodstein, I. Kawachi, F. B. Hu, and G. A. Colditz. "Effects of marital transitions on changes in dietary and other health behaviors in US women." *International Journal of Epidemiology* 34.1 (2005): 69-78.

Wilcox S. A. Aragaki, C. P. Mouton, K. R. Evenson, S. Wassertheil-Smoller, and B. L. Loevinger. "The Effects of Widowhood on Physical and Mental Health, Health Behaviors, and Health Outcomes: The Women's Health Initiative." *Health Psychology* 22.5 (2003): 513-522.

O – ORGANIZING YOUR SUPPORTS

Bisconti, T.L., C. S. Bergman, and S. M. Boker. "Social support as a predictor in variability: An examination of the adjustment trajectories of recent widows." *Psychology and Aging* 21.3 (2006): 590-9.

Dyregrov, Kari and Atle Dyregrov. *Effective Grief and Bereavement Support: The Role of Family, Friends, Colleagues, School, and Support Professionals.* London: Jessica Kingsley Publishers, 2008.

Hamer, Kim. *100 Acts of Love: The Girlfriend's Guide to Loving Your Friend Through Cancer or Loss.* Printed by author, 2015.

Whitson, Stephanie Grace. *How to Help a Grieving Friend: A Candid Guide for Those Who Care.* Colorado Springs: NavPress, 2005.

P – PEER MENTORS

Bartone, P., M. Bates, D. Brown, K. Kasper, N. Money, M. Moore, and J. Roeder. "Best Practices Identified for Peer Support Programs." *Defense Centers of Excellence for Psychological Health and Traumatic Brain Injury.* 2011.

Brody Fleet, Carole. *Happily Even After: A Guide to Getting Through (and Beyond) the Grief of Widowhood.* Berkley: Cleis Press, 2012.

Carter, Abigail. *The Alchemy of Loss: A Young Widow's Transformation.* Deerfield Beach, FL: Health Communications, 2008.

Saltzman, Nancy. *Radical Survivor: One Woman's Path Through Life, Love, and Uncharted Tragedy.* Colorado Springs: WoWo Press, 2012.

Wolterstorff, Nicholas. *Lament for a Son.* Grand Rapids, MI: Wm. B. Eerdmans Publishing, 1987.

Q – QUOTES THAT INSPIRE HOPE

Cohen, Geoffrey L. and David K. Sherman. "The psychology of change: self-affirmation and social psychological intervention." *Annual Review of Psychology* 65 (2014): 333-71.

Hay, Louise and David Kessler. *You Can Heal Your Heart.* Carlsbad, CA: Hay House, 2014.

Koole, Sander L., Karianne Smeets, Ad van Knippenberg, and Ap Dijksterhuis. "The Cessation of Rumination Through Self-Affirmation." *Journal of Personality and Social Psychology* 77.1 (1999): 111-25.

Robins, Rachel. *Positive Affirmations: Daily Affirmations for Attracting Health, Healing, & Happiness Into Your Life.* CreateSpace, 2014.

R – RIGHT-BRAIN RELEASE

Carey, Lois. *Creative and Expressive Arts Methods for Trauma Survivors.* London: Jessica Kingsley Publishers, 2006.

Edwards, Jane. *Oxford Handbook of Music Therapy.* Oxford: Oxford University Press, 2016.

Malchiodi, Cathy. *Art Therapy Sourcebook.* 2nd ed. New York: McGraw-Hill, 2006.

Marich, Jamie. *Dancing Mindfulness: A Creative Path to Healing and Transformation*. Woodstock, VT: SkyLight Paths, 2015.

Homeyer, Linda and Daniel Sweeney. *Sandtray Therapy: A Practical Manual*. New York: Taylor & Francis Group, 2011.

Thompson, Barbara E. and Robert A. Neimeyer. *Grief and the Expressive Arts: Practices for Creating Meaning*. New York: Routledge, 2014.

S – SLIDING INTO EXERCISE

Craft, L. and F. Perna. "The Benefits of Exercise for the Clinically Depressed." *The Primary Care Companion to The Journal Clinical Psychiatry*. 6.3 (2004): 104–11.

Dixon, Zachary and Kalen Iselt. *Anxiety: Fitness Is the Cure: The Hidden Mental Health Benefits of Exercise & Fitness*. Printed by author, 2015.

Ratey, John J. *Spark: The Revolutionary New Science or Exercise and the Brain*. New York: Little Brown, 2012.

T – TOUCH

Hess, Samantha. *Touch: The Power of Human Connection*. 2nd ed. Portland, OR: Fulcrum Solutions, 2014.

Linden, David J. *Touch: The Science of the Hand, Heart and Mind*. New York: Penguin, 2015.

Field, Tiffany *Touch*. Cambridge, MA: MIT Press, 2001.

U – UTILIZING NATURE

Louv, Richard. *Last Child in the Woods: Saving Our Children From Nature-Deficit Disorder*. 2nd ed. New York: Algonquin Books, 2008.

Louv, Richard. *Vitamin N: The Essential Guide to a Nature-Rich Life*. New York: Algonquin Books, 2016.

Ober, Clinton, Stephen T. Sinatra, and Martin Zucker. *Earthing: The Most Important Health Discovery Ever?* 2nd ed. Laguna Beach, CA: Basic Health Publications, 2014.

Plotkin, Bill. *Soulcraft: Crossing into the Mysteries of Nature and Psyche*. Novoto, CA: New World Library, 2003.

V – VOLUNTEERING

Ahmadi, Homayun. *Volunteering: Personal, Social and Community Benefits*. Bloomington, IN: XLIBRIS, 2013.

Parmley, William. "The Power of Volunteerism." *Journal of the American College of Cardiology* 43.6 (2004): 1101-2.

Steffan, Seana and Alice Fothergill. "9/11 Volunteerism: A Pathway to Personal Healing and Community Engagement." *The Social Science Journal* 46.1 (2009): 26-46.

W – WESTERN & EASTERN MEDICINE

Bui, Eric, Mireya Nadal-Vicens, and Naomi M. Simon. "Pharmacological Approaches to the Treatment of Complicated Grief: Rationale and a Brief Review of the Literature." *Dialogues in Clinical Neuroscience* 14.2 (2012): 149–57.

Cohen, Misha Ruth. *The New Chinese Medicine Handbook: An Innovative*

Guide to Integrating Eastern Wisdom with Western Practice for Modern Healing. Beverly, MA: Fair Winds Press, 2015.

Keown, Daniel. *The Spark in the Machine: How the Science of Acupuncture Explains the Mysteries of Western Medicine*. Philidepha: Singing Dragon, 2014.

Scheinbaum, Sandra. *Stop Panic Attacks in 10 Easy Steps: Using Functional Medicine to Calm Your Mind and Body with Drug-Free Techniques*. Philadelphia: Singing Dragon, 2015.

Shannon, Scott. *Handbook of Complementary and Alternative Therapies in Mental Health*. Amsterdam: Academic Press, 2001.

X – ExAMINING YOUR POSITIVES

Bono, G., and M. E. McCullough. "Positive Responses to Benefit and Harm: Bringing Forgiveness and Gratitude into Cognitive Psychotherapy." *Journal of Cognitive Psychotherapy* 20.2 (2006): 147-58.

Emmons, Robert A. and Michael E. McCullough. "Counting Blessings versus Burdens: An Experimental Investigation of Gratitude and Subjective Well-being in Daily Life." *Journal of Personality and Social Psychology* 84.2 (2003): 377-89.

Hanson, Rick. *Hardwiring Happiness: The New Brain Science of Contentment, Calm and Confidence*. New York: Harmony Books, 2013.

Hanson, Rick and Richard Mendius. *Buddha's Brain: The Practical Neuroscience of Happiness, Love, and Wisdom*. Oakland: New Harbinger Publications, 2009.

Kubler-Ross, Elisabeth and David Kessler. *Life Lessons: How Our Mortality Can Teach Us About Life and Living.* New York: Simon & Schuster, 2001.

Y – YOUR SELF-CARE

Biegel, G., K. Brown, and S. Shapiro. "Teaching Self-Care to Caregivers: Effects of Mindfulness-Based Stress Reduction on the Mental Health of Therapists in Training." *Training and Education in Professional Psychology* 1.2 (2007): 101-15.

Richardson, Cheryl. *The Art of Extreme Self Care.* Carlsbad, CA: Hay House. 2009.

Skye, Alexander. *Self-Care for Life: Find Joy, Peace, Serenity, Vitality, Sensuality, Abundance, and Enlightenment—Each and Every Day.* Avon, MA: Adams Media, 2011.

Z – ZZZZZs

Institute of Medicine (US) Committee on Sleep Medicine and Research. "Extent and Health Consequences of Chronic Sleep Loss and Sleep Disorders." *Sleep Disorders and Sleep Deprivation: An Unmet Public Health Problem*, ed. H. R. Colten and B. M. Altevogt. Washington, D.C.: National Academies Press, 2006.

Meadows, Guy. *The Sleep Book: How to Sleep Well Every Night.* The Sleep School, 2014.

Thompson, Karin Elorriaga and C. Laurel Franklin. *The Post-Traumatic Insomnia Workbook: A Step-by-Step Program for Overcoming Sleep Problems After Trauma.* Workbook ed. Oakland: New Harbinger Publications, 2010.

ACKNOWLEDGMENTS

There are so many incredible people who have lifted, pulled, held, supported, encouraged, listened, boosted, nurtured, strengthened, inspired, motivated, and held my hand on this journey toward healing. Words cannot capture the profound gratitude I have for all of you. You have changed my life for the better—emotionally, physically, socially, and spiritually. It does take a village! An enormous thank you . . .

A: To "Bogey" Scofield, "Cooper" Litrenta, and "Dash" Edwards for licking me back to life and unconditional love while I was finding my way. To Nicole Andrews, dog trainer extraordinaire, for helping me locate and train the perfect animal for our new life.

B: To Hanna Kluner, HHP, for teaching me it was okay to breathe again, then showing me the way. To the biofeedback specialists at Scripps Center for Integrative Medicine, for helping me realize I could actually have some control over my system again.

C: To Deborah Lapidus, PhD; Christie Turner, LCSW; and Sue Ann Edwards, LMFT, for your individual knowledge and dedicated teamwork that moved us from a place of horror and fear to a place of hope and health. To Cathirose Petrone, ND, for altering the new narrative of my life into one I could visualize. To Claire Bidwell Smith, LCPC and Thea Harvey,

MFT, for giving me the Ojai opportunity to express grief within a nurturing community. To the extraordinary Gail Gerbie, LMFT, for your continued empathy, mirroring, and "bag of tricks" that have guided me toward the stable ground on which I now walk.

D: To post-traumatic growth researchers Steven Joseph, PhD; Lawrence Calhoun, PhD; Richard Tedeschi, PhD; and the PTG Research Group at University of North Carolina–Charlotte, for giving me a bright ray of hope to hold on to in the darkness.

E: To Jean Haner, for introducing me to the concept of small, positive energetic shifts. To Reiki Master Teachers Serena Poisson, Shirley Williams, and Chris Chaplin, for your ability to shift, integrate, and balance.

F: To Brent and Jacob MacNab, the remarkable father-son duo who brought scent healing (and a million other good things!) into my life.

G: To Joe Pirrello, LMFT, and the interns at San Diego Hospice, for graciously supporting my first grief group experience. To John James and Russell Friedman of The Grief Recovery Institute, for adding some much-needed structure to my grief experience. To Mary Lee Moser, Ann Gonzales, and Maya Naik, for holding me up with the support, love, and community I so desperately needed. To Chris and Trish Lovato, for giving me your grace, compassion, and friendship when I had nothing to give back. To the San Diego Regional Group of Soaring Spirits International, for becoming supportive family members on this wild journey.

H: To Jerry Sittser, PhD, for being my first life-line to grief, trauma, God, and healing. To the pastors and members of Penasquitos Lutheran Church in 2012, for bringing immediate prayer (and meals) to our shattered life. To the priests and prayer warriors at St. Therese Catholic Church, for providing an inexplicable healing mass. To Reverend Kerry Maloney, for marrying us "till death do us part," then enlisting prayers from Harvard Divinity School when death arrived too soon. To Father Jim Poulson, for inviting God back into the room during discussions on human suffering. To Rabbi Harold Kushner, for helping me understand my suffering experience through the eyes of your suffering experience. To Bob and Vernagene MacNab, for sending bountiful prayers in our direction, even though your own world had crumbled. To Marni Scofield, for consistently scooping me up with compassion, love, and prayer amidst the anger. To Suzanne Rollow, for your intuitive consultations that brought understanding. To Antoinette Spurrier, for your incredible vibrational gift that changed my life forever. To Fleur, for your compassionate and accurate mediumship that has given me peace and understanding. To Pastor Joel Osteen, for providing a daily dose of encouragement, hope, and sunlight through despair. To all of you who silently prayed for us, for keeping the prayers coming even years later.

I: To Belleruth Naparstek, LCSW, for providing simple, safe, stable imagery-based tools I use anywhere and everywhere.

J: To Maureen Levangie, for jumping off that train with me and encouraging me to write it all down.

K: To San Diego State University's School of Social Work, for introducing me to the many tools and resources I needed to heal my own life.

L: To Evelyn Lafferty, for providing endless opportunities for us to laugh through the pain. To Steve Islava, for creating Laffy Laffalot and bringing us back to life. To Jim Gaffigan, Brian Regan, and Sinbad, for comedy sketches so funny I couldn't help but laugh through the tears. To the talented actors from *Seinfeld* and *Big Bang Theory*, for being perfect companions in the dark.

To Justin Heimberg and David Gomberg, for writing the absurdly funny books my son can't seem to put down. To Kelley Lynn, for making young widowhood a comedic journey—who knew?

M: To Jon Kabat-Zinn, Pema Chodron, Brené Brown, and Karen Sothers, for opening my mind and heart to the gentle teachings of compassion, ease, and empathy.

N: To Mom, for being my first "health and wellness" coach, teacher, and nutritionist. To Heather Holter, for consistently mailing restaurant gift cards even when you needed them yourself. To Christine Bearden, for knowing we needed that enormous cooler of Omaha Steaks. To Amy VanLiew and Andrew Jacobs, for reminding me that nutrition is important, food is medicine, and that sometimes it helps to just put down the fork.

O: To Jennifer McCartle, for saying those perfect words as a Stephens Minister and becoming my first true BE-er. To Brian and Denise Fogarty, Steve and Patrick Hannifin, Great Auntie Janie, Honor Hannifin, Marco Alessio, Shannon and Teri Oakley, Christine Youngs, Tom Nishioka, Mike Mathieu, Shannon Cary, Adam Cooke, Bill Dean, Anne Marie Vorbach, Elizabeth Furnari, and Stephanie Allen Knox, for showing up (or waiting patiently on the shelf) for the BE-ing and DO-ing of it all.

P: To Robin Litrenta, Kathy Thompson, Lisa Dean, and Joe Qualls, for suddenly appearing in my life as unofficial peer mentors and then staying by my side as lifelong friends. To Adele Buffington, Lynn Aguilera, Elaine Wilson, and Christina Rasmussen, for reaching out through common ground to show me stable ground. To Michele Neff Hernandez, Kath McCormack, Dianne West, Rachel Kodanaz and the entire inspirational community of Soaring Spirits International, for providing a soft place for me to continuously fall and get back up again.

Q: To Louise Hay, for providing a reason and system to love myself back into wholeness.

R: To Gail Gerbie, LMFT, for providing a plethora of right-brained creative options to help heal my traumatized self.

S: To Tori Brillantes, for training my physical body and emotional mind back into healthy existence. To both "old life" and "new life" girlfriends, for letting me drag you up mountains and across beaches. To Sweathaus Health and Fitness, for giving me a calm space to heal, grow, and rebuild.

T: To Big Gap, for giving me profound breaks from the pain and throwing me back into life. To Kathleen McCabe, for listening, supporting, and massaging out all of my rough and tender edges.

U: To Dad, for being my first camping, hiking, fishing, exploring, and traveling teacher.

V: To Boston College Campus Ministry, Jesuit Volunteer Corps Northwest, Polinsky Children's Center, Casey Family Programs, Build a Miracle, Love on a Leash, Shoal Creek Elementary School, and Miracle League of San Diego for embracing me within the healing world of volunteerism.

W: To Valerie Doyle, for introducing me to acupuncture, wisdom, and wellness. To Dr. David Leopold, for gathering your resources at Scripps Center for Integrative Medicine to weave together a comprehensive plan for my healing. To Dr. Kevin Pansky and the staff at ASIS Physical Therapy, for putting my broken body back together again. To Dr. Doug

Roche, for believing my back would feel better and then continuously making it happen.

X: To Suzan Clausen, for showing me that gratitude can be a powerful place to start, both at the beginning and at the end. To Dr. Rick Hanson and Greater Good Science Center at UC Berkeley, for giving me weekly reasons and research for which to be grateful. To Dr. Brian King and the Institute for Brain Potential, for filling me in on the importance of gratitude. To the Dalai Lama, who is gratitude embodied.

Y: To everyone who encouraged me to take care of myself, for giving me permission to do so.

Z: To Big Brother, for being my first role model and biggest sleep cheerleader.

A2Z APPRECIATION

There is another set of talented people who have believed, appreciated, advised, edited, suggested, explained, promoted, inspired, motivated, and held my hand on the journey toward writing this book. What started out as a desperate attempt for my own individual healing slowly transformed into a passion to help others who would also walk this grief-trauma-healing-road, and I cannot thank you all enough for believing in me. It does take a village! An enormous thank you . . .

To Monika Curlin, for attending my first A2Z workshop and declaring, "You do know this twenty-six-page folder needs to become a book, right?"

To Jack Levangie, for pulling me along every step of the logo-website-graphic way and donating your time, energy, and creativity to driving all things A2Z.

To Robin Litrenta, for coaching me on social media, marketing, photo shoots, and life.

To Brian and Denise Fogarty, for putting us first with your unconditional love, support, and time.

To Honor Hannifin, for acting as my first knowledgeable "A2Z Tech Support Help Desk."

To Margo Hannifin, for loving me into believing I could and would make a difference for others.

To Stacy DenHerder, for funding the printing costs of those first A2Z conference workbooks.

To Kelley Lowery, for helping me work on my life while you are still working on your own.

To Michele Neff Hernandez, for trusting me with hundreds of your conference and workshop attendees.

To Claire Bidwell Smith, for encouraging me to write and publish when I couldn't imagine it for myself.

To Tom Zuba, for attending that Tampa workshop, leading the new way, and being "Hope on a Stick" for us all.

To Nancy Saltzman, for inspiring me to be a radical survivor, especially in times of great doubt.

To Paula Stephens, for insisting this book, my message, and our friendship needed to be out there in the world.

To Suzan Clausen, Mary Lee Moser, Lydia Lombardi, Shannon Cary, and Mike Mathieu, for initial editing, revising, and reviewing of this publication.

To the mothers, fathers, wives, husbands, partners, sisters, brothers, daughters, sons, and friends who donated a piece of their heart by writing a Healing Story for this book, for lighting a pathway through the darkness by showing others your courage, perseverance, and intentional healing.

To Amy Quale, Rhiannon Nelson, Dan Pitts, Patrick Maloney, Roseanne Cheng, and the interns at Wise Ink Creative Publishing, for guiding me through this process, putting the many pieces together, and making this book a reality.

About the Author

Susan is a social worker, educator, and community organizer who has spent her career teaching and leading health and wellness workshops, classes, and support groups for children, youth, and families across the Mainland USA, Hawaii, Canada, and Australia. She holds a master's degree in social work from San Diego State University, a bachelor's degree in education from Boston College, and credentials as a teacher and school social worker.

Susan's life took an unexpected turn into the world of grief and trauma (and ultimate post-traumatic growth and continued healing) after the sudden death of her bagpiper-surfer-professor husband, Dr. Brent MacNab. She is the founder of **A2Z Healing Toolbox®**, an organization that provides powerful tools, resources, and support to accompany and accelerate the healing journey of those living with grief and trauma. With both a personal and professional understanding of what it can take to restore, renew, and rebuild a life after profound loss, Susan assists others in integrating authentic, practical, action-based tools to use while healing with intention. She lives in San Diego with her son, her therapy dog, and an inspirational community of peers, mentors, and supporters.

A2Z Healing Toolbox® offers:

- Workshops, Conferences, and Retreats
- Media Interviews and Keynote Speaking Presentations
- Professional Training and Development
- Guidebooks as Therapeutic Curriculum

Connect with Susan at susan@a2zhealingtoolbox.com

Learn more about A2Z Healing Toolbox® by visiting
www.a2zhealingtoolbox.com

Join the A2Z Healing Community on Facebook at
www.facebook.com/A2ZHealingToolbox